# Women
*in*
# PRISON

BARBARA WARNY

ISBN: 978-1-4669-7513-2 (sc)
ISBN: 978-1-4669-7514-9 (e)

*Trafford rev. 01/16/2013*

 www.trafford.com

**North America & international**
toll-free: 1 888 232 4444 (USA & Canada)
phone: 250 383 6864 ♦ fax: 812 355 4082

# INTRODUCTION

A friend surprised me with two black plastic bags of letters he'd received from a deceased girlfriend more than a decade before. He asked, "please do something nice with these." He was moving out of state and not taking them. Suddenly, I had an obligation to tell her story.

While the events and stories these letters told were probably true, the location and characters are fiction, some added to better explain what Rachel and her friends lived through. If anyone else who has experienced this nightmare can relate to any facet of it, then I have done my job. For any who will think twice and not roll the dice after reading this, I've done my job. If family and friends of the incarcerated have become more patient and understanding, I have done my job. If a C.O. can better assess and deal with their charges, I have done my job.

Thank you, Penny, for your encouragement and brilliance. Thank you, Grace, for all your wonderful input.

Barbara Warny

# BRUCE AND LOLA

It was an early evening in late fall, and nothing had gone entirely right so far, at least for Lola. Bruce didn't care one way or the other. The mild temperatures and earlier rain made the digging easier than it could have been. Both labored, but tears were still sliding down her cheeks. Not tears for the two lives they had just taken, but for the baby girl she wouldn't have.

Earlier that day they'd laid in wait for a very pregnant woman. They didn't care who she was or what she looked like. She just needed to be late into a pregnancy. They didn't know if they would find her today, but as luck would have it, they saw her get out of an older dark blue car. She found an empty cart in the lot and waddled with its support into the supermarket. "There's our mama," Lola said excitedly. Once their target disappeared inside, Bruce pulled their car up close to hers and anxiously awaited her return.

"She looked just perfect," Lola said. "I just get all warm and shivery thinking of holding another baby." They watched her go in. "I'm glad we didn't take that one yesterday. She was too small. This one is really in blossom."

Bruce turned on the radio, switched stations half a dozen times during the next half hour then shut it off. "What's keeping the dumb bitch? What can anyone find so interesting in a store?" Bruce Muley asked his wife as he squirmed restlessly in the seat. He wasn't interested one way or the other about this caper, but it was important to Lola. There was just no peace living with a restless woman. She looked over at him when he stilled and thought him to be snoozing.

Once inside, the lady pushed her cart up and down the rows giving a lot of thought to her choices and what her two children who were in school and her husband who was at work would like to eat for the week. Her doctor said that she was doing well and her weight gain would slow from now on. She still had two months to go and already gained nearly fifty pounds. Thinking about this and the fact that she didn't even need maternity clothes with her first one and not until her third trimester with the second, made her feel ready to explode. She thought of the job ahead—losing all that extra weight, and sighed. What did Scarlett O'Hara say? "I'll worry about that tomorrow."

There were two people in line ahead of her, both with big orders. The cashier was new and had someone with her watching and guiding her. There were two other uniformed employees waiting at the far end of the station. When it was her turn, these two other cashiers stepped forward and took the cash drawer and replaced it with another. The new cashier thought she should leave with them and started to follow, but the "watching cashier" stopped her. "Where are you going? You're not done yet." Good! The pregnant lady sighed. She was really getting uncomfortable standing. "That was just a surprise audit." the experienced cashier explained. "What did you think they were doing?" The new cashier shrugged and started ringing up the food.

Realizing the cashier was new, the customer tried to relax her. "Well, at least they weren't wearing masks."

"Yeah, that would be a problem," she responded.

The experienced cashier said that the other day she was buying gas at the station on the corner and she'd just finished pumping when several plain-clothed police ran over to a car flashing their badges that were on a tether around their necks. Then more police drove up in cars with flashing lights. She said she was scared and didn't know what was going on, but the bad guys didn't give them any trouble and she got into her car and left as fast as she could.

The pregnant lady commented that there was a lot of bad people out there and one couldn't be too careful. She paid her bill with her credit card and wheeled her cart out.

Lola focused on the door, tense and alert, as she watched people come and go. She half worried that the lady would have the baby inside the store, that an ambulance would come rushing up and she'd miss her chance, but nearly an hour later murmured, "Here she comes pushing food for a week."

Bruce jerked up from an almost doze, instantly aware. "You get all that damned food of hers into our back seat." He reached across the car, grabbing her by the throat, forcing her to look at him. He needed her attention. His fingers bit in and that look on his face always scared her but she knew he did it for her and their family. It was a violence kept banked just below the surface. She knew he would never turn it on her. "Do it fast then meet me where I told you." He released his grip. "I'll take care of her." He left the car and seemed to walk away from it. She didn't look, but sat and waited.

As the pregnant lady keyed open her trunk, Bruce Muley slipped up behind her, stooped, lifted her legs and toppled her in. It happened so quickly she didn't even yell. Maybe one squeak as the trunk slammed shut. He snatched out her still dangling keys, got behind the wheel of her car and started it up. "Made to order," he chuckled. "Go," he mouthed as he drove off.

Lola rubbed at her neck and seemed to pay no attention to him as she got out of her car and pulled the now abandoned and loaded grocery cart closer to her car. She couldn't help but notice the variety of foods she was unaccustomed to buying. Once everything was loaded in and the cart returned to the proper bin, she started the car and left the lot.

If anyone saw the abduction, no one called out. If there was banging from inside the trunk, no one noticed. He left the city and it's traffic, passed a field of cows, some huddled under a tree to enjoy some shade, then he came to a wooded area. There he turned onto an access road and drove until he reached the pond he and Lola visited earlier. He'd been there several times before, and so had others, according to the beer cans, broken glass and a nearby burned-out campfire. This place was his today. Anyone that wanted to argue that could have it—permanently.

The woman in the trunk felt the car slow and felt the jolting as he pulled onto an unpaved road then stopped. She screamed when he opened the trunk. He couldn't tolerate that. What if they weren't as alone out there as it seemed? It was just reflex as he used his karate-trained fist to silence her. Tooth chips sprayed to his left as his rumble ring connected. "Stupid cunt!" He rubbed his scratched hand, then wiped it against his pant leg, stretched and looked around. Satisfied no one was around, he got back to work.

Hauling her limp body out of that trunk was harder than tumbling her in, but he got her out and carried her a few feet. He had just laid her on the ground and pulled out his jack knife from his pocket when he heard the crackle of car tires breaking sticks and crunching newly fallen leaves on the dirt road. It pleased him to see Lola's car approaching slowly, having been somewhat worried she wouldn't remember how to get there. She's pretty good for a broad, but he'd never have to depend on her. Squatting next to the woman, he set the knife on the ground next to him and withdrew a pack of cigarettes and the lighter tucked into the cellophane wrap. Within seconds she was at his side, staring anxiously at the woman's tummy. He lit up and spewed a plume of smoke into the air.

Lola saw the woman's bloody face but it didn't concern her. She had just one thing on her mind. "Hurry up and get it out Bruce. I want my baby."

He took another drag, smiled big until his cheeks crinkled, then held up the knife with a confident glint in his eye. Then he slowly cut the woman's clothes from the front of her body, spreading them to the side. "Nice looking bitch," he commented. "Wouldn't mind getting a piece of that before we do it."

"Do what you have to do, but make it quick," she responded. "I just want my baby." Red and gold leaves silently fluttered down from the trees, trying to make the world a peaceful place.

He passed her the cigarette then slowly pulled away the woman's skirt, cut loose her bra and panties. He flipped her over and lifted her over her folded legs. He was somewhat hard and asked Lola to give him a lick to get him started. She smiled at his request, anxious to be needed, and made him instantly ready. He drew up a hawker and spit it onto his hand and rubbed it on the woman as Lola took a hit off his smoke. Ready now, he entered her in one push and a few seconds later he emptied himself and flipped her onto her back.

"Okay," from Lola. "You've got yours, now I want mine."

The woman started to stir and make sobbing noises. "Step on her face and shut her up." Bruce barked as he stood up and pulled up his pants, but his Lola was a gentle soul. He looked at her, thought "inferior" and chuckled as he kicked the woman on the side of her head. Once again, she was quiet and he suspected she'd be quiet for a while.

Bruce picked up his knife from the ground and punctured the woman's abdomen, then sawed a cut cross it as if he were cutting a pie. Blood and other fluid spilled out as he reached in and pulled out the baby. "What the fuck do you do with this green thing and all this shit it's attached to?"

"That's the cord. You have to tie it then cut it loose." She watched as he ripped a piece from the woman's shirt for a tie then made the cut. "I don't know if you did that right, Bruce. It's not what I was thinking," she murmured. "Oh, I think she gurgled. Did you hear that?" Then several seconds of silence.

"Why isn't the thing crying or something? Aren't you supposed to smack it? It looks kind of purple. He chuckled a low rumbling sound. "Here, you take it. Do what you want with it. Give it a smack. I'm going to the water to get this slime off my hands."

Lola swapped the baby for his cigarette, and held out the blanket she'd unfolded and wrapped the baby girl. "It's so still. I don't think it's breathing," she worried as he walked back to her from the pond flinging water from his hands.

"It's okay. Just knows when to keep its mouth shut." He brought two shovels from the car, telling her, "Let's get this hole dug and get out of here." He shook out another cigarette and lit it with the butt of the other.

She gave the still baby a quick hug then set her on the car seat and took a shovel. The digging was easy except for a few tree roots. When he figured the hole was deep enough, Bruce picked up the still bleeding woman and dropped her in with a thud and a grunt, followed by his cigarette butt. "Go check on her little rat and see if it's okay."

Lola did, and returned hunched over and crying. She held out the small bundle and sobbed. "She died, Bruce. She's so dark and isn't breathing."

He took it from her arms and tossed it into the hole like so much garbage and started shoveling in dirt. "Come on, let's get this done and get out of here." Lola didn't move, just stared at the hole and the few leaves drifting into it. "Hopeless!" he thought. "Okay, you go through her stuff. Get credit cards, cell phone, money, you know!"

Lola slowly obeyed red-eyed and zombie-like, sad about not getting her baby. Her four boys were at home and this would have been the girl she'd always wanted. Resentful now that she was talked into getting her tubes tied after her twins, and they weren't babies any more, she craved holding another baby. This would have been her first daughter, she thought as she searched and sorted through the woman's things. She ignored her dripping nose, then dumped the non essentials back in to the woman's car, bagging the keepers.

Once the hole was filled, Bruce tossed hands full of leaves over it, then added some twigs. It was starting to rain again. He was sweating and the light wind and drizzle was cooling. He walked over to a quietly sobbing Lola, kissed away her tears as he gently unsnapped and lowered her pants. He hoisted her onto the still warm hood of their car, spread her legs and entered her as she forgot her loss.

Lola took her bag of keepers, got into their car and drove half a mile back up the road. Bruce backed up the woman's car maybe half way to her, got out and doused the interior and trunk with half a can of gasoline and set it ablaze. With a little luck, the assholes will find the car but not the body until well after the animals. He jogged to his own car and looked back to see the smoke and fire doing its job. "Don't worry, baby, we'll get you another one, next time one already born. No fuss, no muss."

She considered it a wasted day. He liked how his plans unfolded like clockwork. Tough about the baby, but shit happens. It wasn't his fault the thing was too weak to live.

They rode home in silence, he planning his next move, she exhausted but thinking of their four boys, two probably already home from school, the twins to be picked up from "Head Start."

He told her to go out and buy anything she wanted with the bitch's credit cards. "Get the kids some clothes and toys, fill the car with gas, wipe your prints off the cards, then toss them. I'll stay home with the kids tonight."

After today, she knew she wouldn't be able to deal with shopping tonight. That would have to wait until tomorrow, but she didn't say anything. Tonight she had to work to clear her head, and the light rain that was still falling wouldn't slow down business. She had her two boys help bring in the lady's groceries and she put dinner on the table while Bruce picked up the twins, then she dressed for an evening of work. That always straightened out her thinking and lightened her mood. She wanted to be there for her regular customers, but didn't plan to be out late. Lola took a quick shower and looked at herself in the mirror. She wasn't young, beautiful, or even pretty, and admitted she was more than somewhat overweight. She cared little for any of that knowing her body knew how to please a man. She ran her hands over her clothes, smiled, and headed off to work.

Bruce enjoyed playing with the kids after dark and before he put them to bed. His favorite thing was "the fish game." The five of them would crawl/slither around on the floor in the dark pretending to be girl fish – maybe mermaids. There was always a lot of giggling as they bumped into each other. They had to make silly "girl noises" and try to escape from those hunting the fish who would pull their hair and yell, "I got me a girl," and the game would resume with one of the boys sometimes slinking off in a corner. Bruce explained to his boys that girls were inferior, that their mom was necessary but still not as good as a man. When the kids got tired, he'd say in falsetto, "I'm a girl and I need a beat down, and they'd all converge. He couldn't figure out why after all these weeks of playing why his one boy couldn't get into it – soft like his mother. Bruce told him he spoiled the game, then put all the boys to bed.

# BRUCE AND RACHEL

The kids asleep and Lola not home yet, Bruce got on the phone. He always got a kick out of keeping dumb bitches thinking about him. The phone rang twice and a sleepy voice answered.

"Hey, what's up?"

"Who is this?"

"Thought you'd be out with our buddy."

"Where'd you get my number? Why are you calling me?"

"I get everything I want. I can do anything!"

"Gotta go. I have to work tomorrow. Bye." Click.

Bruce chuckled, waited 20 minutes and called back.

"Hey babe. I think we got disconnected or something."

"Leave me alone. I need my sleep. Call someone else."

"I killed a bitch once. Did 7 years for it too. I'll tell you about it."

"Not interested in anything but sleep." Click!

Twenty minutes later he tried to call back but the busy signal indicated she'd taken the receiver off the hook. He wasn't bothered. He was sleepy too, and tomorrow was another day.

# BRUCE AND LOLA

Lola came home and found the house quiet. She left $125 on the table. It was a slow night, but easy and relaxing. She needed that, she thought as she took a bath and joined her sleeping husband. If she knew anything about the "fish game" she never let on, but did notice secret smiles they shared when they knew she was going out to work. Too much testosterone in this house she thought.

Bruce got up early, and said he had to visit another drug house and asked if she wanted to drive again. He needed to make a score and didn't want it to be local. They got the kids to school then drove across town to an apartment building. She didn't know how he knew about these places and didn't really care. This time of day there probably wouldn't be too many people around. She heard some yelling, then he came running out with a bag, jumped into the car and ordered, "go." She was pulling out of the parking lot when they heard shots. Someone was shooting at them, maybe from a window, maybe not, but she just speed up and they got away.

"Bruce, we don't need all the stuff you take such a chance to get. What do you do with it all?"

"What do you think that money is from that you pick up every so often at the police department? That T.I.P program gives us cash flow. We just have to bait the line with this stuff, prime the pump, you know. Besides, we have a good time with it too."

Just two weeks ago, she'd picked up another envelope with $800 from "Turn In a Pusher." She'd done it with a couple of other organizations too. She'd call them and tell them who was a drug dealer and where they lived and told them what Bruce had told her to say. The police would raid. Then a few months later, after the conviction, she'd pick up her money. She didn't even know these people and liked the free money every couple of months.

Every time they did this, Bruce knew he was gaining credibility with the police department, and with every contact with them, his Lola made herself known as well, but she never charged them for her services. Those working vice usually let her know when they were setting up a sting in her neighborhood so she knew not to be around.

Some nights, Bruce went out to "work." Sometimes he was gone a few days. She wasn't sure what he did, only that he carried a gun and whatever it was, it was for their family.

A week or so later, he asked her to come with him to do some driving. They drove across town and parked on the street. She kept the car running while he went inside a house. She heard a lot of shouting and he came running out with a box which he tossed through the open window. Then he turned around to face three men who had chased him from the house. He grabbed the arm of one and slung him into another and they fell tangled to the ground. The third took a kick to the gut and went down. It just took seconds. Bruce hurried to the car and they drove off as someone cussed. He settled calmly into his seat. "We've hit the mother lode this time, baby, the mother lode, and I've got big plans."

# MATTIE

At the neighborhood Head Start pre-school, Mattie one of the teachers, noticed one of the twins in her class behaving strangely, not wanting to participate in class, play with others or even talk. Mattie later talked to the administrator about it, thinking something might be very wrong. She was in an abusive relationship at home and was sensitive to it in others.

Mattie lived in the neighborhood and even though they weren't friends, she knew the twins' mom, Lola, and what she did for a living, but that wasn't her business. Her kids were always well dressed and clean. She didn't know what Bruce did but suspected it wasn't good, seeing him as trouble to avoid. Again, not her business. When she saw Lola on the street, she mentioned to her that the school was concerned about her boy. Lola didn't appear worried, and told her that she hadn't noticed anything different at home, and suggested that maybe he was "coming down with something."

The unusual behavior at school continued for another couple of weeks and the administrator of the school called to have a social worker talk with the boy. Maybe she could get to the bottom of it and solve the mystery.

# BRUCE AND LOLA

Lola was called to the school and invited to watch the interview through a glass in the next room. After a lot of prodding, the boy told her he didn't like playing the "fish game" and explained how it worked. Lola told the administrator that the boy was making it all up and she didn't know why. Then the twin brother was interviewed.

Later that day when the older boys came home from school, the social worker accompanied by the police came to the house and took all four boys. Lola cried. She screamed. She wanted her kids back. She was told they were taking them to the hospital for observation. She wanted them home. The police wanted to talk to Bruce, she wanted to talk with Bruce, but he wasn't home.

Bruce came in later that evening. As soon as he walked in the door, Lola started yelling, beating on his chest, crying trying to find out what was going on and demanding he get the kids back. She explained how they came and took the kids to the hospital. "Don't act the crazy woman. I'll get the kids for you."

He walked over to the hospital a few blocks away, found out where the kids were and strode to their room. They were wearing silly little hospital gowns. He told them to follow him as he carried one in one arm, hoisted another onto his shoulders and ordered the two older boys to stay close and follow him out and "don't let anyone grab you." The shocked nurse, her station by the elevator, asked him where he was going and he simply said, "home." Security met them at the door, but backed away quickly when he drew his gun. No one wanted shooting around the kids. He walked the boys home, got them inside and left, knowing the police would soon be there.

Lola told the police that Bruce came, dropped off the kids and left. They made it clear they were after Bruce and didn't want to further traumatize the kids and would not take them back to the hospital. She told them she had no idea where he was or when he'd be back. She suggested they come by later and check, that she'd make their effort worthwhile.

The police all knew Lola worked the streets. She was easily recognizable with her waist-length red hair, and they didn't hassle her. They even let her know when they were going to set up to bust the johns. What they may not have known was Bruce was frequently nearby to beat up and rob her customers.

Bruce didn't go home that night. He didn't know if there was a warrant out for him but suspected there was and he wasn't ready for that yet. He'd hoped for a quiet evening at home, smoke some weed with Lola or share some lines. Instead, he laid in his motel-room bed and thought long and hard through the night about what caused his problems today, then focused on his nosey neighbor, Mattie. He'll have to show her she has to stay out of his business. A plan came to him. Then he glanced over and saw the phone next to his bed. Might as well call that dumb cunt Rachel.

"Hey babe, what's going on?"

"I'd like to know where you got my number and wish you'd lose it. I don't want to talk to you, especially in the middle of the night."

"Yeah, I know you want me to come to your house and see you in person," he joked. "Nice, house, by the way. You must like flowers."

Suddenly, she was wide awake and on alert. Did he know where she lived too?

"Why you so quiet? Yeah, I was over there earlier. Those your dogs in the yard? Heh, heh!"

She said nothing, just disconnected and left the phone off the hook.

He was still chuckling as he dozed off.

Two days later, he was home. The kids were back in school and no one seemed to be looking for him. Thank you Lola for sharing your favors. He'd spent the past few days mulling over and perfecting his plan.

The next day, he put it into action, briefing his wife as to her part.

# LOLA AND SAM

After dinner Lola called Mattie's home to talk with her husband, Sam, who was an occasional customer. When she made her offer, she was told, "Uhh, I think you want to talk to my dad." Oh, shit! She had to repeat her offer when Mattie's husband came on the line. "Hey, big man. I'm feeling really lonely tonight and I'm so hot, I'm running down my leg," she breathed. "Thought you'd like to meet me in the park and make me smile."

"Be there." and hung up.

"I'm going out for a pack of cigarettes. Be right back," he told his wife as he set the phone back on the table. He briefly met his son's eyes. The boy looked away. He'd never challenge his dad and his mom didn't need more of it. The car door slammed, the engine started up, and he was gone.

The teen-aged boy walked to his mom who was cleaning up the kitchen after dinner and put his arm around her and she felt the unspoken words. "It's okay, honey, sometimes I'd just as soon he be out and how much better it would be for all of us if he kept on going. Life would be easier."

Sam parked in a corner of the park where lines of trees would give a little privacy on two sides. It was dark and the air was crisp. The only light came from the headlights of a car that illuminated a basketball court where half a dozen boys were enjoying the hoops. He could hear their voices but not their words over the thump, thump of the ball on the court.

He saw her jogging toward him, her tits swinging across her chest, and glimpsed her long red braid dancing on her back. Lola wasn't pretty, but wasn't ugly either. She was average height and generously built. He felt himself growing hard in anticipation. She smiled at him as she got into the back seat and rolled the windows down as Bruce had instructed. "Come on Sammy. There's more room back here." Ten seconds later he'd joined her and his pants were down past his knees. He sat next to her as she took him into her mouth, but she pushed him away when he jammed her head down on him to finish. "Not so fast, Sammy. You're not paying for this so I get a turn too." He laughed.

She straddled him and opened her sweater. Those huge melons never ceased to amaze him and the nipples were incredibly long and pale pink. He buried his face between them, then took one into his mouth and tongued and sucked as he kneaded her breasts. She guided him into her and his hips pistoned and she rode.

Neither noticed Bruce push a pillow through the opened window and fire two shots into it and Sam's head.

"Good job, Lola, now get out NOW," He ordered.

She did, coughing and spitting. "Damn! Half his head splashed into my mouth."

"Get out of here. Go home. You're an ugly fucking mess. Good thing it's dark. Don't let anyone see you. Take a shower and a bath and burn those clothes. I'll take care of this. See you in half an hour. We'll finish what you started here once I get home." He chuckled that deep sound that comes from a heavy-chested man.

As she jogged home, kicking through a foot of fallen leaves, she could hear the slap of the basketball on the concrete. For some, life goes on.

Bruce drove the car and its back-seat passenger two blocks and around the corner and parked it on the street in front of the Head Start school. "A good night's work," he thought and his Lola was something else. Sometimes he felt like putting a fist through her face, but tonight she was all right. He carefully wiped down the door handle and the inside of the car in the event she'd touched anything. They weren't connecting this to him.

He strode home in good humor and it reflected on his grinning face. The cops were going to wreak havoc on Mattie's life. It's what she had coming for interfering with his peace—and he couldn't have peace with Lola unhappy. A job well done and a sense of calm settled over him like a warm blanket.

\*     \*     \*

Days later, it was close to midnight and Lola was working a couple blocks away. The kids were asleep and Bruce was rolling dice on a neighbor's porch with a couple of friends and he was encouraging them to let him know what they'd heard about the murder in their neighborhood. The unwelcome flashing lights of a police car caught his eye and the men picked up their money. Two police officers slowly walked over and addressed the men by their names. Then, "Bruce, would you mind taking a ride with us?" It wasn't a question. Bruce knew he had no choice but to say goodnight to his friends and leave.

It was hours later and they didn't drive him home, but he felt that things went well. He'd always done a lot of walking and felt the fresh air kept his brain alive. He planned ahead and was ready when he had to execute. The night sky was beginning to lighten and Lola was asleep when he got home. Once she got rid of the kids for the day, he'd explain the master plan.

"So, I had a visit last night from our friends in blue. All that bullshit about the kids and the gun at the hospital. They wanted the gun because of that stint I did 13 years ago. Told them I sold it on the street because I needed the money. They asked if you weren't making enough to take care of me. I told them that with so many of them getting freebies, you didn't have time to make any money." They both laughed, then he continued to fill her in on the details. "They want me to do time for the hospital thing and said that if convicted, I can't live at the house with the kids.

"But Bruce, we're a family. They can't do that to us."

"Trust me! I have a plan and I need you to understand every step of it." She loved when he had a plan. It made order in her head. "They're talking about the welfare department and counseling for the kids, the prosecutor's office being hot after me and there is little they can do this time. So, I presented to them the possibility that I could solve the murder in the neighborhood the other night. Their eyes got all shifty as they looked at each other. They were hungry to get that conviction. I told them that you and I were out walking in the park because it was such a beautiful night. Told them we heard the shots and saw one man running from the car and the other car drive away. Didn't know anyone got killed until we heard it on the news. Then they asked if I recognized anyone, and I asked them what kind of deal I could get on the kid thing.

We were talking in their locker room, you know, all their sweaty underwear behind those little metal doors. I think there were three of them. Others came and went. You know them all. Anyway, they are going to talk to the prosecutor and see what they can do. Don't want to do no time. They let me go until they come up with something. They may come to the house or meet you on the street and ask you questions about that night, so just tell them we was out, we heard the shots, saw some guy running from the car and the car drove away. You didn't even think that someone got killed. Don't say nothing else."

"Okay! You think they'll forget about the hospital thing when we do this?"

"I'll take care of you, babe. Everything is under control. Trust me. And do exactly as I say."

# COUNTY JAIL

Rachel Williams was half-aware half-asleep when the telephone rang some distance away. The only phone in her house that rang was downstairs because she doesn't like to be jarred awake by the jangle of it. She reached out for the quiet extension on the night stand and woke abruptly as her knuckles slapped a concrete block wall. The memories gushed into reality and the real live nightmare. At least she had her own room now. No more sleeping on a mattress on the floor, watching critters, probably mice, but she didn't know, skittering across the floor and in and out of the drain in the middle of the room. The high-pitched screams of one of a dozen girls still out there on the floor and intimidated by them continued. Last night it was her turn as one woke her as it scampering over her arm.

Life was cold. She felt half-dead living with odd bunch of women, most half her age, tables and chairs bolted to the floor. All were waiting for court cases, sentencing, or transport to the penitentiary if found guilty. Rachel was found guilty of possession of drugs. She tried to convince the jury she was mentally exhausted and too totally frightened of the man who owned the drugs to do anything but what he asked. Truth be told, he didn't appear that scary in court, but then he didn't have his bullet-proof vest or gun, and his beady dark eyes didn't seem so intimidating.

Still trying to wrap her mind around what happened to her, Rachel had to view it from afar or throw up. A really bad movie! They'd been sitting at a casual restaurant when Bruce sat down with and the guy she'd been dating. He said a few words and got up and left. She didn't like the guy but assumed that was the end of it. He was supposedly a friend of Cort, the man she was with and had gone out with a few times. Then the strange phone calls started coming at all times of the night. She told Cort that his friend wouldn't stop bothering her and to please ask him to quit. He repeatedly told her "he's harmless" and denied he gave her phone number to anyone. Cort seemed to be all fun and travel and no substance, and she didn't think she wanted any more than that.

Nothing ever came of the relationship between her and Cort. It was over before it started, but she asked him to meet her, hoping he could help her shake this friend of his. She told Cort about this continual harassment from this scary creep, and he wouldn't take her seriously. She practically begged and said she was on the verge of calling the phone company and see if they could do anything. He only responded by inviting her back to his place to "talk about it." God! How could she have wasted her time with him. But she went, hoping he would see how desperate she was go get the phone calls to stop.

She drove to his place and wasn't surprised to find the door unlocked as usual, and he was high on something. The TV was on and he was staring into it, telling her what a good time he was having, his speech really slow. She tried to talk with him, but wasn't getting through and he soon fell asleep still sitting in his chair. Rachel was upset about the unproductive and wasted evening. How could this idiot be a respected member of the community? She had to let him know how she felt. She went out to her car and brought in a length of clothesline and tied him up. He didn't stir as she bound his hands and feet and secured him to his chair. As she dove into her purse, her imagination went wild. She painted his toenails and fingernails with pink polish and drew targets around his nipples with her lipstick. Then she just left him there. Maybe he'd remember she'd been there, maybe not.

*    *    *

Bruce Muley had called her several nights a week at all hours when she had to get up before dawn for work. He'd ramble on about all kinds of unbelievable crap, like how he killed a woman and dumped her body by the road just off the interstate near the County line, or he robbed a drug house in Riverview for drugs and money. She'd hang up and he'd call right back and tell her he was diddling one of his kids. She'd take the phone off the hook. Where did this freak get her phone number? Then he showed up at her job—not to do anything or say anything—just to let her know he was around and could find her anywhere. She buried herself in her work, trying to deny his existence. It didn't work. One evening he called with a story, detailing how he was messing with a guy and laughed as he described how he'd used his power to "reduced him to dirt." He said he'd first surprised the guy in the American Steel Works parking lot next to his car and forced him to watch him screw a chicken. He told her the chicken died and the guy heaved. He said a week later, he'd followed this guys kids home from school and threatened his wife while she was at work. He demanded money to stop the harassment and threats and the guy took out a loan on his house, then another from his credit union. His wife left him and the bank foreclosed on his house. He bragged that he had this guy, and wasn't going to stop there. A few days later he called to continue the story, said he'd loosened the lug nuts on his car while he was at work and followed him home, waiting for the wheels to fall off. When it didn't happen fast enough to suit him, he shot at the car which caused the guy to swerve. Said he turned the car into a piece of junk and chuckled. A coworker drove this guy to work after that, he told her, so he waited for them after their shift and "scared the piss out of them with his 44 mag." and told them, "we're going to Connecticut." Always more stories!

While doing business at her bank, Rachel met Eric. They went out to dinner a couple of times, and although the relationship had possibilities, neither of them made any move to take it to another level. He seemed like a really nice guy but she was just not good at picking men and knew it.

Rachel was working 12 hour shifts and needed her sleep. The phone sent chills over her whenever it would ring, and it was usually Bruce. She didn't know or care if the stories were fact. She just wanted them to stop. Sometimes she didn't answer and let the phone ring. What if her parents were trying to reach her? What if something was wrong with one of her kids, if they needed help? She'd pick up the phone and hear his "chesty heh heh heh" laugh of satisfaction. Why was he doing this?

Rachel arrived home from work late, dead tired after a 12 hr. shift and who was waiting on her back steps but Bruce Muley. How did he know where she lived? He handed her a medium-sized box. "Just keep this package for me until tomorrow. Don't open it! Just leave it be until I come for it." He had a gun tucked into the waistband of his jeans and made sure she saw it. She was so relieved that he left and didn't try to push his way in, she did as he said; put the package just inside the door and went to bed, hoping for six hours sleep.

It was the middle of the night. Half dozen police crashed through the door, charging into the house screaming. It was like what you see on TV but scarier, because it is real and loud and happening to her. They went right to the package left by the door. They handcuffed and arrested her after finding drugs in it. They quizzed her about where she bought them and she told them the truth, but they didn't believe her, shoved her into the back of a police car and took her to City jail. Her shoulders ached from the restraints. Rachel had never been arrested before, never had any dealings with the police. What the hell was happening?

First thing in the morning Rachel used the jail phone, called work and told them she wouldn't be in that day. In all the years she'd worked there, she'd never called off before. Then later that day, Rachel and one of the hookers from a nearby cell were handcuffed and driven downtown to the Coombs County Criminal Justice Central to be booked and fingerprinted into the City jail. She went through the process in zombie mode.

The cells were like you see in the movies, all bars and lined up on both sides of a long room. Glaring, un-shaded light bulbs hung from the ceiling and tried to light the room, but it was still shadowy, dark and dank. No windows. Each cell had a cot and a toilet and open on three sides. No privacy.

The half a dozen girls already there asked her why she was in. She told them. She was surprised they knew Bruce Muley. Said he was bad news, that his girl, Lola, worked the streets and he robbed her "johns," which gave their business a bad name, that his girl had half a dozen "trick babies" because she was stupid. They were all young hookers, talking their trade. Rachel had never met people like this. Most east-siders bragged they used protection, against what they didn't say. Some south-siders, used protection only when requested by a client and the east-siders thought that was disgusting. Abuse and all the possible risks didn't seem to be a concern. It was just a part of their job description they accepted. Discussing this was a big deal with them. It was their life. One of the younger girls who was very pretty said her father was a vice cop and begged her not to work the streets. She asked that we not look while she took a shit. When she flushed, her cell flooded and she got all kinds of unwanted attention.

Everyone was given a box of dry cereal for breakfast and sandwiches for lunch. The snack truck came by later but Rachel didn't have any money to buy anything. The girls bought her what she wanted. They all had money and were generous with it. A couple hours later, we were each given an orange. Most didn't want theirs, so rolled them across the floor to Rachel. They were wonderful—both the girls and the oranges.

Someone warned her the cot probably had lice, but she wasn't concerned because she didn't expect to be there long enough to use it. One girl was bailed out and was back in about four hours. The girls all left in the morning, but not her. She stood by the bars and extended her hands through them. It was a good feeling. Her body was caged but her hands were on the other side of the bars in the free air. That made no sense, but none of it did. The next night some of the same girls were back and some were different. Same old, same old prattle.

City Jail isn't the best place to sleep, but it was her third night standing after being routed from bed at 3 am when her door was broken in with a sledge hammer. Her hands now gripped the bars to support her weakening legs. The steel mattress-less cot was starting to look as acceptable as anything. She was cold. Her legs were getting wobbly and her mind fuzzy. Leaving on her winter coat, she pulled the hood over her head and laid down on the cot, lice or no lice, and her body gave into sleep. She didn't wake up until she heard cell doors slamming and lots of chatter. A tall thin man was swabbing out the cells with a foul-smelling mop. The stink lingered long after he left or until she got used to it and didn't notice.

After three days of not being able to wash up, comb her hair, change clothes, and in zombie mode from very little sleep, her body which didn't seem to belong to her anymore was handcuffed to a dozen other girls and taken to a courtroom. A lawyer was there for her and pled "not guilty." Bond was set and they were all taken to a little room with a bench. One by one the girls were called out, and didn't return. Then she was told to collect her belongings (her watch) at a nearby window and go home. The policeman behind the window commented that he liked her watch.

"Did they drop the charges" she asked. She wasn't a criminal and was glad that someone finally figured it out.

"Go! Just get out of here," he snarled. "You'll get something in the mail."

The words sounded so good, she didn't want to think beyond them. Her mind wasn't in gear. Every movement brought up three days of body stink up through the neck of her jacket. She wanted to go home, eat some real food, soak in bubbles, wash her hair, brush her teeth and have a bowel movement.

Rachel walked around the Criminal Justice Central building, enjoying the freedom of movement she'd been denied for days, going up and down the steps and escalators, looking for her friends who she'd expected to see at court. It suddenly dawned on her she had no money and couldn't make a phone call or take the bus home. She went back to the property window where she'd picked up her watch and explained her predicament to the officer. He asked her if she wanted to sell her watch. She cried. She only wanted to go home. He reached into his pocket and gave her two quarters. She was so grateful.

Walking toward a phone bank, she saw the lawyer who had represented her in the courtroom an hour or so before. He seemed shocked to see her walking around and asked what she was doing out there. She simply told him they told her to go home, that they were going to send her a letter. "Something is wrong," he muttered. "Let me talk to Brownie over there and check something." He asked her to stand behind a pillar and listen. She heard all this commotion as several police officers were blaming each other for letting someone out of their custody. She heard her name. They were talking about her.

Brownie was a bondsman. He went around a corner and came back scratching his head, telling her, "There's been a mistake, that she couldn't leave. She'd have to go back until someone posted bond."

"No, I won't do that," she cried. "I won't go back." She panicked in near hysteria with the thought of returning to that filth. "I have to go home, take a bath, wash my hair, and burn this coat."

"They're going to put an 'escape' out on you and they will be at your door by the time you get there," the attorney explained. She sat down exhausted, melting onto a bench while the two men conferred with someone a few yards away. When they came back, they asked, "Do you think you could go home, do what you have to do, and be back by 4 pm with the bond money? Then you will be home tonight."

She agreed. She would have promised them anything, but she had to call somebody and get home. Just as she looked up her eyes filled with tears. There were her friends walking toward her to take her home. Brownie and the lawyer explained to them she had to be back before 4pm. As they drove into her driveway, the first thing she saw was the garage door stuck half-up and crooked, the result of it being pulled off the track by the police search.

The bathtub was her first stop. She used extra bubble bath and just soaked in it's comforting warmth. Friends milled around downstairs, talking as she got dressed. She threw the coat out on the back steps, next stop garbage can.

Later that day she made it back downtown with her friends. Brownie was waiting and bond arranged, but it took several hours to get fingerprinted, another mug shot and more questions answered, this time for County. She put her house up as security for her bond and borrowed for the bonding fee. Her ex-husband had a friend who was an attorney and he recommended D.D. Knight as a first-class attorney. Not knowing any other, she hired him. He promised the best defense available.

Maybe she should have slept good that night in her own bed, but she kept waking up, re-living the fear of four nights ago. The next day she viewed the devastation inside her house, towels and clothes all over the floor, cigarette butts in the carpet, ashes on table tops, and drawers tossed and dumped. Her great-grandmother's clock was on the floor broken. Adult paperbacks she'd kept in a locked file drawer were now scattered in every room in the house. It was hard to straighten things up as anytime she looked at the mess, she cried uncontrollably as the ugly memories of that night returned. Sometimes she'd just sit there for hours and stare, realizing she should be cleaning up, but then back the thoughts would come then the tears and she was useless. She could still feel the ache in her shoulders caused by the hours of hands cuffed behind her back. Even a year later, her body reacted almost the same way to thinking about it.

# ERIC AND RACHEL

Rachel hesitated to call Eric. He was a good solid man, and she knew that he'd want nothing to do with her when he found out what happened and where she'd been. He was a bank manager, for Pete's sake. They met when she renewed her CD and was totally surprised when he asked her out. She dreaded the thought of answering the phone, knowing it might be him. She knew he'd dump her but wasn't ready to hear it. When he finally got through to her she couldn't talk about it. They went out to dinner and she was unusually quiet. He kept looking at her strangely. Over a delicious prime-rib dinner she couldn't taste and hardly touched, he asked her what was wrong. She couldn't answer, only shook her head. He reached over and took her hand staring into her face. Her eyes were wet and ready to spill. She couldn't swallow fast enough and thought she was going to throw up. His concern was so evident, she broke out in quiet tears. He came over to sit next to her in the booth and put his arm around her back. She cried even harder knowing that he wouldn't want to touch her if he knew how dirty/soiled she was.

He signaled for the waiter to come over and box up their food and continued to hold her tight. He didn't know what else to do.

Dinner bags in hand, he walked her out to his car and got in. At first he just sat there next to her hoping she'd say something, but she just continued to sob. He started the car and drove back to her house. Then, "I don't think we should see each other anymore." from her. She didn't want to lose him, but knew it was over.

"What's the problem, Rach. Whatever it is, we can work it out."

"Not this, not ever." and she unbuckled her seat belt and started to open the door.

"Whatever it is, it concerns both of us. Talk to me. Please."

The sobs started up again and she just shook her head. I'm not letting you go like this, Rach. Talk to me. Trust me. We can work it out."

She was quiet now but breathing hard. "Come on inside and at least let me hold you. If you don't want to talk about it now, that is okay. I just want to be with you."

"You wouldn't, if you knew." He was glad she finally spoke.

He got out of the car and opened her door for her. She just sat there for a minute, staring blankly ahead. He took her hand and they walked up her front steps, their bagged dinners forgotten.

For several months Rachel continued to work as there was nothing in the paper and no one was aware of her problems. She dutifully turned over every other paycheck to her attorney. Not a day went by that she didn't worry that her arrest would become public and she would go into work, be fired and sent home. Several times she had to take off from work to go to pre-trial things, but her attorney never once showed up where he told her to meet him. Don't know if these "meetings" were postponed or never occurred, but she never once attended a "pre-trial" hearing. She always called his office on these occasions and if he was in he told her to stop by his office to talk while she was downtown. It was just across the street so she went right over. He'd ask a couple questions he'd asked before but didn't seem to remember. Spent maybe five minutes with her, then had to go somewhere. He dodged her questions. She never learned if these pre-trial things ever happened or what they were about. Frequently, the attorney wasn't in his office when she called, so she went back to work or went home.

What was most important to her was that Eric was still with her—every step of the way. After that troubled night at the restaurant, and she told him of the police arresting her, they'd been intimate for the first time. He stayed the night and held her as he promised. He didn't berate her, but just listened. She'd never met a man like him.

Well-meaning friends said the police would be out to confiscate her ten-year old car. She couldn't think of why they would, but knew they do what they want to do, so hid it at her parent's house and took theirs to work, only to wreck it on the way home. Her nerves were shot but Eric was there almost every day, even if for only an hour or so.

The phone calls, from Bruce Muley continued to come most every night. On the advice her attorney, she recorded them on cassette, an apparatus that Eric set up for her, and gave her attorney the tapes. On them, Muley admitted bringing the drugs over to her house, bragging of robbing a drug house to get them, and also said he had a friend named Wallace in Connecticut that "took care of him." He laughed as he said there were places who paid him, crime stopper programs, so he had to do things, but he'd fix everything. Since the tape recorder was on, she asked if Wallace was a first name or last name. He just chuckled. Lola, Bruce's wife, was on the extension and she didn't know it until she spoke up. "You're not going to get Wallace involved, are you?" Then he'd said for her not to fret, that when court time came, he'd do what he had to do and admit the stuff was his and they'd let her go. She wanted to believe him, but the attorney said no, he'd have no reason to admit anything. That made sense. The tapes should help.

Bruce told her that he and his wife had a "special relationship" with the police and they've all been working together for years. He had everything under control. Hours of ramblings on maybe a dozen cassette tapes, and she was confident when she gave the tapes to the attorney that all would be well. She'd even transcribed a couple of them for him.

During the months waiting for trial, she and Eric started to bond. That was a new thing with her and it scared her. One weekend he asked her if she ever fished. No, she hadn't. Fall was approaching and he said he'd like to take her out. He told her that she'd been under a lot of stress and knew this would relax her. He had lots of gear for the trip and she could pack them some food. She wasn't sure she even wanted to go, but it seemed important to him. When he picked her up the next day, she'd stopped at KFC and bought them lunch, a six-pack of water and a bag of snacks. They drove north for a couple of hours and rented a small fishing boat at a dock he seemed familiar with. He bought her a fishing license. The man on duty advised him where he thought he'd have the most luck, and off they went.

He set up her rod and reel and showed her how to use it, then baited her hook with a fat disgusting night crawler and cast it out for her, explaining she had to let the fish nibble and yank the line once she felt he had the whole thing in his mouth. Then he set his own line up using a colorful black and gold lure. Almost immediately, he got a hit but was disappointed when he reeled it in that it was a sheepshead.

Then she felt the little nibbles and yanked gently. The fish was on her line and she started reeling in slowly.

"What are you doing?" he inquired.

"Reeling in," She answered without showing the emotion she felt.

"Why?"

"Because it's time," she stated.

"You mean you've got a fish on there?" he asked. "I can't keep stopping to bait your hook."

She didn't answer. When the fish saw the boat it panicked and tried to get away. He told her to keep the line tight so it wouldn't tangle in the anchor rope. She did and he scooped it out with his net and put it in the cooler. "Nice fish, he commented and congratulated her with a hug and re-baited her hook with a huge ball of night crawler and again cast it out for her. She was having a good time and was so glad she went.

Soon the familiar tugs of a fish excited her and the little pulls became more demanding. She tried to visualize what was going on down below and didn't want to yank the feast away from the fish. Eric saw the rod dipping and said, "Hey, I think you have a bite!"

"I know I do," she laughed.

"Did you set the hook?" he yelled.

She couldn't believe he meant it as seriously as he sounded. "No, not yet. It's not nice to disturb a meal."

"Set the hook, dammit. It'll get away," he insisted.

"It's been on here five minutes now and hasn't gone anywhere," she answered.

"I'll set the damned hook," he threatened harshly. He reeled in his line and started making his way toward her.

With a strong pull she set the hook and only the drag slowed that fish as it took off toward open water.

"I'll take over now," Eric asserted matter-of-factly, trying to take the rod from her hands.

The fish had her attention and she was excited. The other fought but didn't run like this one. It turned and came back toward the boat. She reeled as fast as she could to keep the line taut, yelling at Eric for him to get the anchor rope up, at the same time moving her shoulders to shake him loose from her. Obediently, he did, but only to return.

"Give me my rod," he demanded. "You're going to lose my fish! Let go and run the motor." She didn't know anything about running the motor and his hands were on the rod and he was trying to peel her fingers loose.

"Get away from me," she demanded. "It's my fish." They were standing in the boat wrestling over the rod. The fish had control and Rachel was unsure she could fight both battles. She was stubborn and he determined. Thoughts occurred to her to nudge him out of the boat, but she knew the dangers of that and she couldn't swim. What was the fish worth? His arms were everywhere and in her way. She bit the one that was bending her head.

"Bitch," he screamed. "Let go of this rod. You're going to lose my fish."

"It's my fish," she answered vengefully, smelling the day's sweat oozing through his shirt. "Get away from me."

"It's on my rod so it's my fish," he reasoned, claiming it. "You're only holding it for me."

"Bull shit! I hooked it, it's my fish. Just let me alone. I want to bring it in."

"You can't bring it in. It's too big. You're going to lose it." He was yelling at her like it was a matter of life and death.

She didn't know if she could bring it in or not, but she wanted the opportunity and fun of trying. This was supposed to be fun, not war.

They were still struggling after twenty minutes, so she knew the fish was hooked securely. The struggle was violently rocking the boat. Her arms ached, her hands were scratched and bleeding and the fish seemed to be patiently waiting, perhaps enjoying and even curious about the commotion above.

People were starting to gather at the shoreline and waving their arms. They couldn't hear what they were yelling as their focus was on the fish.

The boat lurched as the fish took off and Rachel lost her balance and they both went crashing backwards against the seat, then into the bottom of the boat, but both held onto the rod. The fish felt it had a chance and took off for more open water and the line started singing through the ratchet. The monster was towing them into rougher water. Waves tossed the boat and water spilled over the sides. Rachel was worn down, bruised, and the probability of her landing the fish was waning. Hurt, disgusted, and weary, the importance of this fish diminished. "Okay, okay!" She eased out her hands that were numbly sandwiched between his and the rod.

Elated, and talking constantly, he played the monster back to the boat. The head and mouth were larger than anything she'd ever seen. He brought in a huge northern pike, it's teeth chewing air. The lure was deep inside the bony mouth and he had trouble extracting it. His little black tackle box scale weighed it at a little over 32 lbs. He put it on a wire stringer attached to a length of nylon rope, and we headed back.

Rachel felt very sad and dejected. Tears rolled silently down her face. The half dozen or so guys waiting by the dock stood there expectantly. "I got it, I got it!" he called repeatedly to them. These strangers seemed genuinely interested in the fish.

"Creepy phony," she thought as Eric headed toward the dock. She watched him proudly lift the stringer and admire that mighty body that was her fish. Her chest got tight and her head was aching. Then, strangely, she saw that giant fish smile and slide gracefully back into the water and disappear, the stringer still in the hand of her bewildered fishing buddy.

"What happened?" asked one of the onlookers. Rachel didn't hear the response because she started to laugh. That laughter drew off all her tensions. Nothing could have made her feel better. She lost the fish to him, he lost it to a carelessly tied knot and the fish won its freedom. She loved it.

It was a long ride home. Rachel didn't have much to say to Eric. They would have eaten their picnic lunch at the tables near the dock, but neither wanted to discuss what the onlookers had seen on the boat or the fish. They drove off.

About half an hour into the ride home, Eric pulled over at a picnic area and he laid out the food she'd bought. They were both hungry.

"I'm sorry," he said quietly. I didn't understand that women could like to fish, just like men do. Most women are content running the motor and cooking. I'll never do that again. I just got all caught up with that humungus fish. I'd never tied into anything like that myself and the excitement just took over. I've learned my lesson, believe me."

She wanted to, but why were men always trying to control her life? Other than having their first major fight, she had a good time and learned she did like to fish.

\*     \*     \*

Eventually, the trial came. One day for jury selection, one for trial. The police testified against her. Bruce Muley testified against her wearing an orange jump suit, so he must have been locked up for something. She was found guilty the next day. GUILTY! Not very much evidence was provided for her defense. Her attorney didn't call her witnesses. Several friends were there to attest to her character. In court, he failed to bring her receipts for the personal property confiscated during the raid, her jewelry. Then there was her mother's wedding ring, silverware that was a wedding gift three decades before and a coin collection belonging to her son. He said the tapes weren't significant. Obviously he'd never taken the time to listen to them or have his secretary transcribe them.

She couldn't believe what just happened. She wasn't prepared for it. She was scared. Eric was at work, not in the courtroom. Her car was in the parking lot outside.

What would happen to it? As the deputy grabbed her arm to lead her off, she tossed her keys to a girlfriend who had accompanied her to court. She was in a seat behind her several feet away. The deputy cussed that she did. Everything was so quick. She was not a criminal, but suddenly a convict.

It was another couple of months before the sentencing and she was taken to Coombs County Jail during this time to kill time. It was run by Corrections Officers and for the most part was comfortable and clean as compared to the City Jail which had space in the same building but was the absolute pits. She phoned her parents and their first thought was to get her out of here, but this time there was no bonding out. She tried to call Eric, but he was at work and his answering machine couldn't accept collect calls. She'd try later but knew this would be the end of their relationship.

# COUNTY JAIL

Morning starts with breakfast
   It's served to us in bed.
We eat what we can stomach
   Brush our teeth and hit the head

We push a little button
   That turns our water on
We push a little button
   That's how we flush the john

Our beds are made up early
   Then they let us out to play
Mostly spades and rummy
   What a way to kill the day

We try to reach our lawyer
   Or friends to make the bond
Only to discover
   We're forgotten, left and conned

We know we have each other
But tension is always high
We think of how we got here
With tears behind each eye

"Chow time" calls the C.O.
And we all get in line
Force ourselves to eat the swill
That's how we do our time.

The thing that's most important
Is when we get our mail
Knowing someone thinks of us
Here at County jail.

Her attorney repeatedly told her, "Not to worry. Everything would be okay." Nothing seemed real—or maybe she just didn't want it to be. It was hard to convince herself she was really here. Her life seemed to be going down those big ugly tubes that served as a sculpture outside the Criminal Justice Central building. She couldn't allow herself to get depressed. Had to eat right, exercise and stay healthy as best she could. She had to stay strong to work though this mess. She had to trust her attorney. He must have a plan. This just couldn't happen.

\* \* \*

Back in jail. The room is 40 ft square, ringed by our rooms. All is clean and well lit, which is good because all the windows are painted black. Rachel figured this was just to confirm to her that there was no world beyond this room. This would be her home for the next two months, unless her attorney could get her out. The acoustics are bad, but the ventilation is good. The corrections officer has a station in the middle of the room and a desk just outside the door. When everyone is locked into their room, sometimes they wheel a TV in which we can watch standing at the window in the doors. Football, wrestling and cartoons were popular but to watch, it was stand and stare. She had to read or write. She had to contact her attorney.

There were three phones available for collect calls to family and friends and a pay phone. No one had any money, so that one didn't do anyone any good. If anyone knew the number, someone could call in, she supposed. She saw thousands of numbers penciled on the wall behind the phones. First she tried to call her attorney to get a grip on her situation, trying to believe what he told her. The lady who answered told her he wasn't in. She needed to talk. She needed more information. She really needed help!

Rachel was surprised when she was called for a visit. It was hard to see the hurt on her parent's faces. They didn't ask her much except how she was doing. There were tears burning behind her eyes and probably theirs as well. What indignities did they have to go through to get to see her. She just couldn't imagine what they were going through. She asked them to call the attorney to find out what he was going to do to get her out. How long will it take?

She needed to go over everything with D.D. Knight, her attorney. She only talked two or three times in his office before the trial and never at any length, but she's not sure now that he was ever listening to anything she said. She'd telephoned him with myriad questions over the months, but his answers were vague. Told her repeatedly that "worry was his job, let him do it." He came to court seemingly totally unaware of her case, not bringing pertinent paperwork, receipts, and was clearly unfamiliar with her situation. When she asked if she should bring character witnesses. He said, "if you want to." She introduced him to her witnesses at trial, and then he seemed to forget they were there.

He might as well have told her that life as she knew it was over and the "system" didn't care. But she wouldn't have believed him. She had to fight to survive, to trust he was working for her and find her justice. But life didn't exist outside these walls. That's what the black paint on the windows was about.

Eric. He was history. She wasn't sure of who he was anyway, after that fishing trip. No man would stick to someone in this situation. What would be the point. Did she even want him to.

Rachel was sitting at a table with three other girls, playing cards. Edna was talking about her family in Nigeria. She learned English in school as early as kindergarten and came to America to further her education. Although sidetracked by the birth of four children, at 32 she hoped to take her C.P.A test next year. Her dreams have been derailed.

Her strong determined face carries her Yoruba tribal markings (horizontal scars on her cheeks beneath her eyes) and her quick wit is accented by expressive eyes and British lilt. She said that her father was a retired civil engineer for the Nigerian railroad and her mother owned a restaurant.

Kathy, a young girl beside her with lines of drug tracks on her arms along with a big hairy mole brightened up at the thought of exotic food. She asked Edna, "Do they serve elephant in African restaurants? Do you eat monkeys?"

Edna looked horrified as she answered, "NO!" and quickly reached over and yanked hairs on Kathy's mole. Kathy was shocked and quickly protected her mole with her hand. "We have the same meats as here, lots of fruits and vegetables." Edna finished as she dropped a couple of the mole hairs on the table.

Edna said she doesn't smoke, drink, or take drugs, a gram of heroin was found in an unused purse in her closet—an offense she would be executed for in her homeland. Rachel admired her perfect teeth and Edna pointed out a missing one. "I pulled it out with a pliers," she said. "The dentist told me to wait until the baby came, but it was too painful."

She was in tears today—no bail! A couple of months ago her brother sent her his wedding invitation and enclosed round-trip tickets for her and her children. At the time of her arrest the police took the tickets and her passport. They told her that she'd go back to Africa if they give her bond. She told them that she would go back for the wedding, but also told them she'd be back because she likes America and wants to make her life here.

She went on to tell us she had a dream of opening a real African dress shop, specializing in dressing weddings for Americans of African descent—authentic African fashion, fabric and accessories. She had the knowledge and desire to succeed and family ties in Nigeria to help her. Good ideas that may never come to fruition. She's waiting for a court date and a decision on deportation.

Another visit. This time a girlfriend and her husband. Why didn't she tell them she was dealing drugs. They could use some extra money. Maybe because she wasn't! No one wanted to hear that. Her crime was possession, not dealing. She asked Rachel what it was like inside. Told her about "strip searches" and "pat downs" all the time and mentioned that she had to file her raggedy fingernails on the tile grout in the shower. In a couple of days Rachel received a magazine in the mail with an emery board fastened in the fold. It sure was appreciated, but she didn't want to get caught with it—contraband. She found a small slit in her plastic mattress and tucked it in. She did share it with her new friends, so it didn't last long. It was really appreciated, but she didn't want any more "contraband" mailed to her.

Rachel tried to call her lawyer again. Still couldn't reach him. She's started to realize that lawyers aren't like Ben Matlock or Perry Mason. They don't investigate their cases and surprise the court with the true villain. Damn! D.D. Knight didn't even call witnesses that have come to court for her. Courtrooms are more about theatrics than attention to detail and justice.

Danny was a friend. When he needed money to pay an attorney to help him get custody of his children, Rachel loaned it to him and took his gun collection as collateral. They were old but never been fired pieces, including an early unfired Browning (made in Belgium) in its original box, two S & W's, a Colt that had been in a bank vault for decades and the original receipt was in its box. Danny had a detailed receipt for this transaction with him and gave it to the attorney. All the pieces had boxes, the Dirty Harry gun in a blue velvet show case box as well as the original box. Well, the police confiscated all of them and the next time Rachel saw them was in court where they were tossed into a grocery cart, the boxes gone and was horrified at the lack of care and respect for them. Rachel was glad that they were photographed when confiscated because some were missing in court. She was sure someone had intentions of putting them in their own collection. The attorney had the police find and return them the next day.

Well, Danny came to court every day to testify about them, but her attorney never called him. She asked why and he said, "trust me, not to worry, I know what I'm doing." She didn't understand, but then she didn't have a law degree. This was her first time dealing with an attorney or court.

She finally caught Eric at home and apologized for all the trouble and distress she'd caused everyone. He said he'd tried to call her and the machine answered. Then he called the Clerk of Courts and found out what had happened to her. "Don't worry, Rach. I'm with you all the way. We can handle this together. I don't know anything about the law, but I'll do what I can. Don't give up on me."

Kathy went into great detail about how to forge prescriptions and do drugs. "Stay at the counter while the pharmacist fills it unless he gets on the phone—then split. Make sure when filling in the DEA #, if it's not printed on the form, the first two letters match the doctors initials." She went on to say, "Script for twenty eight Demerol's cost $12-$20 and sell for $35-$45 per pill. Why work all week when you can make it in an hour. "I don't swallow them, but crush and shoot. Personally, I don't even like Demerol. It makes me sleepy, bitchy, greedy and suspicious, but that's what my man likes. It's not a social drug. You don't do it at parties." What kind of life does this poor girl have? What about holding a job and working for a living?

"Doesn't it hurt when you put the needle in?" Edna asked.

"No, it feels good. There's nothing like it."

Another girl walked over asking, "What you talking about?"

"She's teaching me how to steal and be a junkie." Rachel confessed.

There were a couple of showers in the big room, that are out in the open with no curtain. Most girls shower regularly. Some not. Some just watch. For those who want to use a razor, there is one sitting in a cup of water on the C.O.'s desk for all to share. Russian roulette, anyone? Someone should educate these people about hepatitis and AIDS and ways of becoming infected.

Rachel showers early every morning, before breakfast and before most girls are up. Mortified, she closes her eyes to shut out the "watchers." She knows where everything is so doesn't need to see. She wraps the towel around herself and hurries to her room—to cry.

Charla was slovenly in dress and hygiene. What few teeth she had left were discolored by coffee, nicotine, neglect and scum. She'd become the "jailhouse lawyer" and among the boxes in her room were copies of the Illinois Revised Code. She's been here about four months collecting cases and claimed she hadn't yet seen a judge. Every other week, she's been called to other counties to face more charges. There were ten charges from other counties, mostly Cook and mostly drug related, grand theft, forgery, bad checks and uttering, whatever that is. Charla has spent much of her 33 years locked up, and picked up a college education in the penitentiary, and to her it is a way of life. She'd sit down at the card table in her food-plastered clothes and usually win. She's resigned to being here and feels it is as good a place as any.

Sylvia was on the phone talking a language Rachel couldn't get a grip on. Most of the sounds were rough and seemed to come from down inside her, yet when they came out her mouth, were strangely soft. Later, Rachel asked her what language she'd been talking and she answered, "Gypsy." A letter came in the mail addressed to: Sylvia Mascus, and the entire address phonetically spelled. Amazingly, it found its way from Michigan. She was excited, sung silly phrases loudly and off key, and danced around like a beach ball on sticks. She couldn't read it so Charla read it to her. It was from Barney, her husband in a Michigan jail. Like a couple of others here, Sylvia can't read, but she sure can play cards. She's a thief. Get distracted from your food, Sylvia has it in her mouth.

She spent a lot of time in her room suffering from various maladies—an infected nose which could probably have been cured if she refrained from digital excavation, cramps, chest pains and the like. She avoided the shower and often sat scratching and fluffing a snowstorm from her head.

During the week we were escorted to a dining hall for most meals. On weekends, we got room service.

Edna bought Oreos at commissary. They were in her room, and someone stole them. The next week, she figured she'd find out who did it, so opened up a cookie, stuffed a hairball inside and closed it up again. An hour or so later, Sylvia told her that the cookie was good once she took the hair out. Edna told her she was an empty headed scum bag and told her next time she'd put shit in a candy bar wrapper.

Edna has been trying to get her thyroid medication for some time. She's been taking it for several years and has been without since her arrest a month ago. Her neck is swollen and swallowing is difficult for her. A social worker came by today and told her she could have the thyroid medicine. She's relieved and hopes she gets it soon.

Another girl who had a horrible cold avoided sitting near others. She asked the C.O. (Corrections Officer) to put her on the list for medication and she said she would. Later, when the "med cart" came by she was refused access. "Only the first ten on the list get medication."

After being here three days Rachel's lips got really chapped and she asked the C.O. for Vaseline.

"Fill out a kite," she was told.

"Where are they," she asked.

"We don't have any" she answered. "Maybe when the nurse comes she can help you out."

The nurse told her she didn't have any kites and couldn't dispense Vaseline without a directive, but Rev. Weems can help. Rev. Weems showed up and told her she had to fill out a kite, and no, he didn't have access to any.

We had our medical exam—blood pressure and a series of questions, then was asked, "Any problems?"

She said, "check my lips!" which were bleeding. Whoever she was said she would see what she could do and dismissed her. Rachel went back and borrowed some from another girl. The black girls can sometimes get Vaseline for their hair. The next day Rachel was summoned to the dispensary.

"Are you here for murder too," a big black girl asked her as they waited on a bench together in the small room."

"Might as well be," she responded as she was called to pick up her very own Vaseline.

Kathy lost to the room robbers while she was on the telephone. She's really raising hell while the culprits are playing cards with heads down and smirking. Edna told her to piss in a cup and throw it on their beds.

Sylvia approached Rachel to inform her that she was on the list to be robbed. Do robbers really make a list? She told her she wasn't worried about it. Sylvia said she told them to leave her room alone. All Rachel had to do is give up her Polish sausage next Saturday. "No deal," she told her and Sylvia shuffled off to her room.

The room robbers never bothered Rachel. The victims put hair or staples in the Oreos, shit in candy bars and cleanser in granola bars. Then no one could enjoy them. Seven colored pencils were stolen and soon many girls were sporting eye shadow, eye-liner and blush. Thievery was a game. Even the corrections officers had a problem. Cigarettes and pens went missing and even an ashtray, but they got even. "Shakedown!" Everyone was herded into a small room while all the rooms were searched for contraband—which could be anything from a pack of sugar from the dining room to possession of something someone reported missing or maybe something smuggled in during a visit.

About half the girls got an 8 hour lock-up. Brenda was one of them. She was also suspected of being a room robber. If there's a game to be played, she's in on it. A nice, personable and intelligent girl, she was curious and spent a lot of time trying to figure Rachel out, saying she didn't fit. Rachel took that as a compliment. Brenda made every effort to stay one step ahead of everyone.

Rachel finally got through to the attorney. He told her again, not to worry. That was what he was paid to do, that he'd see her in court for sentencing in a couple of days and answer all her questions. He hung up. Short. Too cold. Her breath started to come in short shallow puffs. Her eyes started to sting. Trust? She suspects she's done too much of that already.

So many people have written letters on Rachel's behalf and she's had at least two visits on each of the three visiting days every week. She's been sent many books, magazines, writing material, stamps and whatever she needed. She felt so lucky that people cared.

Short, stocky, Sharon laughed and gave details of her life as a thief as she talked about the things she stole before she was caught. She'd break into houses, steal jewelry, money and electronics and frequently if the keys were laying around, steal their cars. No mention of drugs. Just stealing. Now she was sick, just had her seventh miscarriage and says she needed a D & C. She's cramping and had a fever. Rachel suggested she call her lawyer and tell him she needed medical help. She said she did—two weeks ago. Then her lawyer called the jail and they told him it was all taken care of. On the phone with her lawyer today, he asked her if her medical issues were resolved and she told him she'd heard nothing from anyone and she hadn't made it to the hospital. He then got a court order to have it done.

Edna looked at her tattoos, snickered and told her she looked like a biker. Sharon's attorney did secure a court order for her to get to the hospital and they kept her a week. While there, she learned that her son was in an automobile accident and was in a coma.

Another visit. More family. These visits were so hard on everyone. No one asked about the case but want to know what they can do to make her comfortable. She told them to keep sending the supermarket rags. She enjoyed the light reading and could share them once they're read. She just hated to see her family so hurt by this. After leaving the visiting room, she cried through the standard search. Life was so out of control and there was absolutely nothing she could do about it. No way to help herself.

A quiet girl, Darlene can usually be found at a card table. She taught Rachel the game of spades and casually asked her if she was interested in women. A negative answer elicited no more conversations on that. She and Darlene played partners quite a bit and she referred to her as partner or sister. Brenda usually played against her and Darlene and entertained with her ever-present sense of humor.

If sex is an issue with anyone here, it is very low-key. No one is ever alone, but loneliness is intense. Some of the girls tap on a pipe, hoping for a response from somewhere in the building, fantasizing it is a man if it happens. Most probably, any response would be from a couple rooms over. On the way back from breakfast one day, a man crossed in front of them and dropped a piece of paper. One of the girls scooped it up quickly, but the C.O. snatched it away before she could tuck it in her bra. Any contact with a man was valuable—something to fantasize about.

Some of the girls were anxious to get to Lotusville, one of the state prison for women, to get involved with the girl-on-girl action. Some say they might do it there where it is acceptable, but would be embarrassed to do it on the street. Rachel found that an interesting concept—they wouldn't admit to being a lesbian or bisexual, but if the setting was right . . . .

It was such a strange culture. Everyone bragged about their crimes and argued about who is the biggest slut—like they're giving out trophies for "whorehood." It really contradicted the stereotype claim that "they all say they're innocent." They certainly didn't mind being here, except for the separation from their men—who for the most part were behind their being here.

Rachel went to court for sentencing and was given 4-15 years. Years! How can that be? She didn't do anything to warrant that! The judge said, "I strongly recommend you appeal this case." Was he trying to tell her something? Did he say that at the end of every case, or did he see something very wrong or was he familiar with her attorney? Her lawyer told her that he'd file an appeal right away, but she'd probably get out on shock probation before that. She had myriad questions but as usual he said he was in a hurry. Told her to stop worrying and left. She saw her parents in the courtroom. Eric was there too. There was no opportunity to say anything to anyone. She was hustled in and hustled out. Cold.

She was brought back from court in a daze. Charla asked her what happened and Rachel told her. She assured Charla that her lawyer was going to file an appeal right away. Charla snorted. "That's just B.S paperwork. Doesn't mean a thing and won't get you anywhere."

"Well, he told me that he'd file for shock probation."

"Who is this guy, anyway? A Prospect Avenue pimp? Your drug charge doesn't allow for any shock probation. You're not eligible for shit! Come here, I'll show it to you in writing." With that, she goes to her room and pulls out a box of papers. "See! Right here!" As she read from the Illinois Revised Code, Rachel's stomach churned.

Charla told her that someone should pick up the clothes she went to court in and replace them with jeans, a sweatshirt and tennies. She explained her clothes would travel with her to wherever she was sent, probably Lotusville and if they weren't acceptable attire there, she'd have to pay to mail them home. Casual clothes would be much appreciated once she got there. She also suggested she have someone put money on her books here so when she gets there she will be able to buy necessities at commissary. Charla, an alumni of Lotusville would know. Rachel called home to see if that could be accomplished. No, not new clothes. Just something from her closet, and take the purse with you. The switch was made at their next visit.

Then she needed to call that attorney. Ask him. Get him to tell her she was reading an expired Illinois Revised Code, that she was eligible for something. Finally a phone was available. He wasn't in. Wasn't expected back that day.

It was a weekend. Another visit. This time, Eric. It was his first and only visit. She asked him what he had to go through to get in.

"Nothing compared to what you are going through," he commented. "I could only get here on the weekend."

No details. She thinks she wants details, to know what her parents were dealing with on their visits. God! What is she doing to everybody?

The visit was short. That was probably good. She wasn't sure what she wanted from him and was still trying to figure out what to make of him after that fishing trip. Who was the real Eric? Wasn't there anyone out there that would just let her be who she was? Guards were always tapping someone on the shoulder to tell them time was up. One girl let out a howl when her boyfriend was tapped on the shoulder. Not Rachel. She was too uptight to know what she felt. Eric told her to "Hang in there," as he left. Don't they know what people go through emotionally and physically to visit? They spend more time seeing animals at the zoo. Is that what she is? An animal?

She wondered if she would ever see him again. Probably not. He seemed to be a good and caring man, but there are limits and she didn't know him that long or that well.

Lily, who at one point let Rachel borrow her emery board, was taken to the psych floor, along with a new girl who tried to hang herself in her room—but only after attending church. This is such a sad place.

Edna asked Rachel to read a long letter to her judge. It was poetry. It was prayer. It was beautiful. She goes to court in three weeks. Rachel hoped to keep in touch with her.

Because she had trouble operating the water in her room, Rachel chose to brush her teeth using water in the mop room sink. She was nearly through when Pat, a huge black snaggle-toothed girl came over with a concerned look and told her that she sure took a long time to brush her teeth. She rinsed her brush and told her that was because she had a few more teeth than she did. Pat walked away laughing, saying "That's a good one!" Later she was told by someone to avoid her, that she was crazy. That evening Pat got into a fight and was escorted out.

She tried to call the attorney again. New day, but he wasn't in. Or was he? It might have been really interesting to find out who else was paying him. No, that only happened in the movies. Feeling despair and frustration, she went to her room and cried.

A quiet girl took Pat's place. She sat studying a bible and kept to herself. Rachel asked Charla if she knew anything about her. She mumbled, "that's Mattie she killed her husband." then bid her cards. WOW! A real murderer amongst the whores, druggies and thieves. She's got to stop judging these girls. None of them judge her and most are good company. She seems to be the alien and will have to adjust her thinking.

Friends mailed Rachel the Globe, Enquirer, Star, and various light reading material. After she read them, she shared them with whoever was interested. Charla was mad at her for doing the crossword puzzle in the Globe. She wanted to do it. Such a simple pleasure coveted! There are so many outdated periodicals thrown out every day in the outside world when so many in here thirst to read.

Rachel took a couple of her scandal rags over to Mattie and asked her if she'd like to read them. She looked up with sad eyes, and thanked her. Mattie didn't socialize with most of the others. Didn't talk about her case. Didn't play cards.

Edna had a C-Section five months ago and never healed right. At the time of her arrest she was being treated for fluid accumulation (draining and antibiotics) When she picked up her thyroid medicine, she told the nurse that she had recurrence of pain and fluid. The nurse told her not to worry. "Something is wrong! I am in pain. I am scared. I don't want to die. I have my kids," she cried. The nurse sent her away, not even looking at her. Jail is no place to find empathy. She called her lawyer who said he'd take care of it right away.

Edna's case was Federal, probably because she's not a citizen, and within forty minutes, the marshals were here accompanied by the local medical staff (who told her she got them in trouble.)

"Good," she responded stoutly as they took her to the hospital.

Rachel never saw Edna again as that night she was woken up at 4 am and hustled off to the penitentiary.

# PRISON

The ride out was uneventful and unexpectedly pleasant. The rising sun turned the spent corn stalks to gold. Light fog sifted through the low-lying areas and over the swift running rivers. It was a beautiful morning to enjoy—aside from the purpose.

We woke at dawn at County
    Washed and ate our fill
The sun was bright, the traffic light
    We rode to Lotusville.

A crow observed us from a wire
    A red squirrel from a tree
From nerves or apprehension
    We felt the need to pee.

On we on rode down the highway
    Gina, April, Deb & me
Faces gawked from passing cars
    Noting we weren't free.

We rode what seemed like hours
    Our hands cuffed in our lap
Big streets, small, and country roads
    The driver had a map.

When we finally reached the gate
    The drivers shed their guns
They turned in all our paperwork,
    Said "get out and shake your buns."

They took us into Warren East
    And told us it was home
The smoke was thick, the faces blank
    'Twas life within the stone.

We swallowed our humiliation
    As we were stripped and sprayed
Our hair and private parts burned like hell
    When double-dosed with Raid.

Washed our hair and sewed name tags
    Then went out to meet the group
Learned the rule to sign the list
    When we had to pee or poop

I sat there in that crowded room
    Roaring noise and smoke and mess
Screaming girls and C.O.s
    Of all, I could care less

For days and weeks I cried and stared
　　My eyes burnt from the smoke
No place to write or walk or hide
　　Just sit there, breathe and choke.


If you want to make a phone call
　　First you send a kite
I wanted to get out of here
　　I wrote attorney, D.D. Knight


All my letters went ignored
　　Like I never sent him mail
That's the way he treats a client
　　Once they've gone to jail.


Rachel walked off the police van still handcuffed, out into the late fall sunshine, down concrete steps to a dark, dank basement. Things went from very bad to worse. It was like Alice tumbling down the rabbit hole into hell. Over 200 girls lived there, underneath an old stone three story building called Warren East. So aptly named. If it wasn't a "warren" 100 years ago, it certainly was one now. It seemed everyone smoked and the C.O. only opened the narrow windows up by the ceiling along one wall two or three times a day. The air was used, foul and thick, like some would imagine a medieval dungeon would be. Rachel was surprised there were no limp figures shackled to a wall. One had to blink twice and stare to make sure.

Four girls from the Riverview area were joined with seven others from towns in Karo County in the southern part of the state. All were stripped naked in the shower room and sprayed with Raid, special attention to the hair, armpits and crotch. They all sat, humiliated, burning from the chemicals while they sewed name tags into their new uniforms that weren't new.

Four plumbers marched in to fix a shower. We were sitting on a bench naked and in they come with tools on their belts. Then we're told they weren't men, but inmates that thought they were. Rachel was not sure what to think and glad she only had sit there, swallow her embarrassment and observe. What kind of place has she been dumped into? This can't be real!

When she figured no deeper humiliation was possible, Rachel, along with the rest, was subjected to a "cavity search" and they were not talking dental exam. Finally they allowed the group to shower and wash their burning scalps and private areas. After getting dressed in their little cotton dresses, everyone reentered the large room they were first paraded through. Rachel saw everything in sepia tones, drab and noisy, with only a few signs of humanity. The roaring noises had to be voices, but her ears couldn't make out the words.

Long rows of heavy wooden tables lined the room, chairs so close no one could get up unless the person behind scooted in. Except for meals everyone just sat there unable to move. Rachel was one of the lucky ones. She was offered a chair at a table. Many skooched over to make room for her. Blank, zombie-like faces sat in chairs that lined the walls. They didn't have a table to lay their head.

Alice, the girl who sat next to Rachael told her that on the way down here from Marley County, she heard truckers talking on their C.B's that the trooper in the van had a "lady of the night." Alice commented to the person driving that if that was the case, she would be home in 24 hours. Rachel was terrified being there. Somehow, sitting next to Alice made her feel safe. She didn't understand how or why.

Alice kept her head down most the time covered by her coat. She had breathing problems and was probably trying to filter out the smoke—also to give herself a little privacy while writing letters or maybe just closing her eyes, trying to reach another life away from here. She was as horrified of being in this environment as Rachel. They listened to the young girls brag of their murder and mayhem as if they were on a lark.

Alice's crime was obstruction of justice. Her boyfriend escaped from jail and the police came to her house to see if he was there. He wasn't and she told them so. They told her to let them know if she'd heard from him. An hour or so after they left the boyfriend called her and said he was out and needed a place to stay. She told him to stay away, that the police had been there looking for him and she hung up. A few minutes later the police were back. They'd been listening in on her phone and she was arrested. An FBI agent said she wasn't just going to jail, that he was going to lift it up and put her under it. He kept his word.

Alice had class. You could just feel it. She was separated from her husband who was a workaholic, never finding physical or emotional time for her or their kids, but he had been a good financial provider. After a decade of loneliness, and when the handsome "bad boy" came on to her, she was vulnerable and took the leap. She knew he had issues, lots of them, growing up in a poor family, he'd always craved money and big flashy cars. While still in his teens he had two arrests for armed robbery and knew his way around the dope world.

They shared comical stories like he putting a case of bottled beer in his cart at Meijers and going to the bottle return and put the entire case of full bottles, one at a time through the slot and collected $2.40 for the bottle return. He had his problems and she gave him emotional support, hoping with her help, he could turn around. Now, with both of them in jail, deprived of each other, their love seemed to grow.

All Rachel's worldly goods, those issued to her after the "painful cleansing" were kept in a paper grocery sack—a cotton gown for sleeping, underwear, toothbrush and paste. It never left her sight. Rumor has it there is vocational training here, but so far all she could see of that is "bag lady." She'd never thought about prison and had never known anyone sent to one. When is her attorney or judge going to get her out of this mad house?

Rachel started to write letters home, but had trouble remembering addresses that were once etched into her mind. She wrote Eric. Didn't expect to ever hear from him again but was driven to write. She had to put onto paper the details of what she was dealing with—whether he was interested or not. He didn't have to read it, but she had to write. She couldn't tell family. They'd worry about her and they didn't need that. Either Eric would try to understand or he wouldn't. She needed to write—it eased what she was dealing with. It was selfish, she knew, but this man who she'd only known since her arrest was going to be her sounding board.

She was asked to fill out papers about her ancestors. People that she knew and spent time in their homes, and the names just wouldn't come. Her mind was muddled, her brain turning to mush. What was happening to her? She's scared for her sanity! She did write letters back to County jail to see how everyone was doing and advised them all not to come here—as if the choice was theirs.

The low roar of a couple hundred women's voices in the room was constant and she fantasized about some quiet place to walk, somewhere to be alone even for a few minutes. Nothing was quiet and there's no place to sit comfortably, never mind walk. When the din became nearly unbearable, the C.O. would shriek, "Quiet," and for a few seconds it will be. Then someone would giggle, and it would start all over. She was grateful for a chair. She was safe next to Alice. The air was bad yet the girls complained of being cold on the rare occasions the windows, which were small and up near the ceiling, were opened.

A new day dawned and the red maple across the courtyard flaunted its colors, but no one noticed that nearly as much as the cooler breezes that threaten to violate their bodies. Rachel was in sort of in a stupor as she walked in a long line from her sleeping quarters in the hospital corridors back to the dungeon called Warren East. She was becoming despondent and was disappointed when awakened each morning and it was confirmed she was still there. This kind of life just can't go on.

Any direction Rachel looked, just beyond every building, just beyond the trees, just out of reach but not out of sight there was coils and coils of treacherous razor wire atop a tall chain-link fence. She knew she had to live in this giant cage because she'd been labeled a danger to society. She cried for her family, her friends back home, and for herself.

On her way to lunch one day one of the girls pointed out to her a girl walking around in a wire box which surrounded a tree and included a bench. "She's on death row," Rachel was told. "Killed her baby and fed it to her husband." Seems he was paying more attention to the baby than her. The story goes that he was half way through his meatloaf and asked where the baby was. She told him, "You're eating it."

"I think he's in a crazy house somewhere" she added. A short time later, they took the cage down. Maybe her sentence was changed. Maybe it was just a story. This place was full of wild stories and the nut cases that lived them.

Every day, a county or two brought more girls. Occasionally they took someone back with them—someone awarded shock probation after serving 30 days or someone returning to county for more charges, or possibly someone who finished their sentence. Every day Rachel was hopeful that someone would discover the truth and she would be free. Was her attorney still working for her? He told her she'd be shocked out. She waited but it didn't happen. She waited and heard nothing from him. There was that sunshine that could brighten our day, that waited dutifully on the other side of that door and just out of reach. All began to rot in the damp dungeon on the wrong side of the door.

An elderly Corrections Officer advised everyone that while in "admissions" everyone should get any problem they might have taken care of because once out into "population," there was usually a long waiting list for medical or dental service. Anyone who had been there before knew what an understatement that was.

One day a dozen or so girls were lined up to get a blood test. Haven't a clue what they were testing for. Rachel walked two-by-two with the group on a sidewalk to the hospital. A tall thin girl a few feet ahead of her stepped on the edge of a man-hole cover in the middle of the sidewalk. It tipped and she all but fell in, barely catching herself with her arms as she went down. Two girls pulled her back up to the concrete, but she was really hurt, screaming and couldn't walk. The C.O. radioed for help and left her lying there wailing as her group continued being processed. The thought occurred to Rachel that we lesser humans, walking obediently in two's might suddenly revert to our wild nature and attack. We had to leave the girl behind and be delivered before we could start trouble.

Several of the girls were there on drug offenses and the "pseudo phlebotomist" with the needle couldn't, after several tries, access one girl's vein. The girl behind her said, "Let me do it. I'm better at it than you." Sure enough she accomplished what she had to do in one stab. One can only hope they weren't re-using needles. No trouble getting Rachel's blood, yet the next day, she had a bruise where the blood was drawn, the size of a half dollar in the crook of her arm. Several girls had the same thing. The girl who fell into the man-hole was gone on our walk back to Warren East and the man-hole cover was set back in place. Everyone gave it a wide berth, but what of the next person walking by?

At 11 pm every night, about 30 girls were escorted over to the "hospital," walking two by two to the sleeping quarters. The walk was long and Rachel, along with everyone else, froze in their cotton A-line dresses. The warden insisted all dress like ladies. None were used to bare legs in this weather. But, nevertheless, any walk became a delight. Any chance to leave crowded Warren East's fetid air was a Godsend, regardless of its purpose. This night, there were a family of skunks, all sizes, prowling just outside the entrance—one so pregnant she could hardly walk. Someone said, "Oh look, they're so cute." All took a wide berth around them. The corridors were double bunked, row after row, and that's where Rachel's group slept. One of the skunks must have sprayed the bushes because the smell permeated the hospital corridors all night long.

The mail brought a "thinking of you" card from Eric with a short note. That was nice.

There was an intense lack of couth here. So many of these girls stood around talking with each other, digging in their crotches. When they were done, they would pull out their bunched up dress and flatten it out and their conversation didn't miss a beat. Everyone was disinfected for bugs. Did they have something else? Was it a habit? Rachel wondered if they do it when they're home too? Or maybe they watch too much baseball on TV.

Everyone slept on stacked up cots in the hospital hallway trying to ignore the sleep sounds of grinding teeth, moans and snoring. In rooms just two feet away there were girls locked up in cells, screaming to get out, howling obscenities, banging on their doors, and pouring foul-smelling something underneath. It was truly the cemetery of the undead. Crazies, she was told. One girl claimed she recognized her aunt. Says family lost track of her. Well, if they weren't crazy when they got here, it wouldn't take long to attain that status. What had they in store for us? Rachel was so tired when she got there, she usually fell right to sleep, ignoring the racket. She was lucky to log in five hour sleep a night because at 5 am, everyone was ushered back half sleep-walking, washed up, and went for breakfast. Several other groups came back from sleeping in other hospital corridors and other building's hallways.

Rachel was excited to see an apple on her tray at breakfast and ate it right away. Brenda Slims from County gave her another one later in the day, probably stolen from the C.O. Brenda's putting herself out to be friends with her, but Rachel's skeptical because she always seems to be involved in things that could result in trouble. In truth, Rachel didn't want to make any friends here. She just wanted to stay healthy and go home.

Everyone has to respond to roll call by standing up and saying "here." There was a very short girl who happened to be sitting on a tall stool. When called, she answered "here" but didn't move. The C.O. reminded her she had to stand to be seen. She slipped off the stool, answered "here" and was now a foot shorter than she was and couldn't be seen. Everyone chuckled.

Rachel learned that to use the bathroom, one put their name on a list, then got in line that was usually 15-20 girls long. There were lots of toilets, but they only allowed in one person in at a time. Ginger, who was obviously retarded, burned and abused, became impatient and used a convenient wastebasket. Most people laughed at her, some screamed she couldn't do that so she dumped the wastebasket into the nearby garbage can. The C.O., drawn to the noise, told her to wash out and disinfect both the wastebasket and garbage can. Ginger hollered out, "What's wrong with you people? I just peed in it, I didn't shit!" Anyway, it caused a lot of commotion and the girl had to wash out both—which held up the line even longer because the C.O. wouldn't let anyone use the toilet until the deed was done.

Meals were served in a building referred to as P.F.S., on well-worn and rarely clean plastic trays that have separations for different foods. Servers, usually girls just out of admissions, slopped the soft food from ladles and food that can be hand held, was. Everyone got the same thing and sharing or trading wasn't permitted but happened constantly. The butter was real, the hamburger wasn't. The chicken was good, the pork chops fake.

Over lunch Rachel listened to Ginger talk. No one sat with Ginger so she was thrilled to have company. She told Rachel about the many men who had raped her. One put her in the trunk of his car for a couple of days, her hands tied behind her back, no food or water, and only opened the lid when "he wanted to get sucked off." He let her out after finding her unconscious and threatened to kill her if she called the police. She didn't. She was a prostitute that entertained in her apartment. Customers would knock on her door and expect service. One evening she was tired and didn't want company and told the person knocking to go away. He kept knocking, so she pulled out her gun and emptied it into the door. She heard a "thunk," the knocking stopped and she was pleased. A neighbor heard the shots and called the police. The man was dead.

She told her she'd spent time in Apple Creek which was a mental facility in another state before they closed it down. Ginger was just pitiful. She said she gave birth to her first daughter there. She was deemed unfit to raise a child so they took the baby and she never saw her again. Her thin body was badly scared from cuts and burns and she said she was medicated with thorazine. She has a slow speech pattern which jumps from subject to subject and decade to decade. Then she was sent to a foster home where she conceived a daughter, now fourteen. Said she'd like to see her someday because she was her mom. She couldn't read or write, but was an incessant, discombobulated thinker.

The C.O. distributed shampoo in little cups to those who wanted to wash their hair. There was some kind of mix up. It turned out to be a strong floor cleaner that burned the scalp. For a couple days girls faces were swollen and skin discolored. Some lost their hair. "Just an oversight."

Rachel put her name on list to use the steam iron to press her dress. Brenda Slims, crept over and asked to borrow it to press her hair. She hunkered down and steam ironed her hair. As a "thank you," Brenda ironed her dress for her. She'd never seen anything like it but was getting an education. This world was so foreign to her.

Big uncoordinated Mary was a sad creature who always plodded around heavy footed grunting and toothless. She didn't talk much. One day, someone nudged Rachel and pointed out to her, a big blotch of blood on the back of Mary's dress. On another day, someone saw her washing out her underwear, blood drooling all over the sink. It seems she was trying to take care of herself but didn't have the tools. So many sad situations.

Most of the girls have been here before so Rachel leaned on them to learn the rules and got a lot of bad and conflicted information. When they don't know, they made something up. She wondered how the visiting worked and tried to find out what is permitted. Who can visit? When? Can they bring treats? Pizza? She knew her family and friends would want to visit but had been given no information about this except that a visiting list will have to be processed at a later date.

Her days were spent quietly observing the girls around her. The average age was about twenty five which astounded her, then more so to hear about their medical problems. Seizures were common, 35% talk of high blood pressure, 10% heart problems, 80% no or few teeth, 20% foot problems, 20% complain of hemorrhoids and nearly half have had hysterectomies. Back problems haunt several, and the scars from accidents or surgeries are many. The older people here appear to be in much better health than the younger. Maybe they just don't talk about their issues.

All the rooms and dorms were full
    The hospital put us up
Along about 11 we trekked on over
    About 5 they woke us up.


We walked in 2's to P.F.S.
    An endless long green line
In rain our coats are on our heads
    With hope the sun will shine


We recognized the hazards
    Safety, fire and health
She put our life in danger
    The warden took in the wealth


After about a month went by
    Some moved into a dorm
Then we got a good night's sleep
    No problem keeping warm.


After about six weeks, Rachel graduated to sleep to a dorm so the nightly treks to the hospital halls ended. It was a big room on the other side of the bathroom in Warren East, double bunked for over a hundred. Some of the bunks had to be accessed by crawling over another one. It was comparatively quiet and no one was smoking. The paper grocery bags were traded in for a metal foot locker next to the bunk that could be locked. Those that had money in their account at County found it transferred here and they were now able to go to the commissary and buy necessities like soap, shampoo, deodorant, toothbrush and paste, envelopes, pens and writing paper. Thank you, Charla for the heads up on this. Some bought snacks. It was almost like being alive again.

When Rachel first located her assigned bed and set the folded bedding on it, the girl in the next bed greeted her with a cold "is that your bed? Are you sure? Well, I guess I'll have to live with it." Rachel figured that if there was a problem, it was hers, and left to take her shower. When Rachel returned, the girl apologized all over the place and offered to help her make the bed and introduced herself and couldn't have been more helpful. Later the "lice lady" who bunked above her explained. "She mistook you for the child molester, but Brenda Slims straightened her out." Brenda was familiar with her case because they were in county together. There must be another girl here that looks similar.

Brenda later asked if she would switch beds with her just for the night. Rachel asked why and she told her to use her imagination. She later found out she had some plans with the lice lady. She told Brenda not to involve her in her silliness. Rachel didn't know where the lice lady's nickname came from but hoped the problem had been solved.

Rachel felt good. Freshly showered she rolled her hair and was in bed for the night and it was only 8:30. Her days of trekking to and sleeping in the hospital were over. She would miss the walk back and forth and of course the "adventures" socializing with these girls, but she was comfortable here for the first time in nearly 2 months. Just the quiet and the fact that no one was smoking was wonderful. Everyone still had to sit all day in that horrid Warren East, but the evenings came early, uninterrupted and peaceful.

There was silliness going on in the bathroom one night and that brought the C.O. running, hoping to catch someone doing something. About a dozen girls, all in their state issue great white gowns ran behind her, hunched and on toes to see who was being caught at what. It looked like a cartoon. They all came running back ahead of the C.O. who didn't catch what she expected so hollered at so many girls being out of bed creeping around. Rachel's bunk was next to the bathroom and she laughed at the sight. She must be adjusting to being here, and that was a scary thought.

One of the girls observed roaches and other vermin scampering around one of the lock boxes. The C.O. learned the box belonged to Big Mary and demanded she open it up. The stench was pretty strong. Mary was asked to empty it out. Blood and urine stained gowns, fouled underwear and used sanitary pads were among the treasure. Most everyone heard the C.O. make the usual comments about Mary's dirty ass, then saw Mary trudging back toward it with a broom and dustpan to scrape up scraps of food and whatever.

Deb, one of the girls who Rachel rode out here with, expected to be home by now, but her shock probation never happened. Her husband called her attorney, D.D. Knight (wouldn't you know it) and learned he was sick and never filed for it. His partner said he'd get right on it. Sure! Rachel decided she'd better write his office to make sure hers is filed and have her family call him as well.

Nearly everyone was told to go to "rec." a couple mornings a week. That was in the gymnasium. It was mandatory. They supposedly used this time to swab the floors and do general cleaning at Warren East. Also, there was a rumor that an inspector of some sort was expected and they didn't want him to find over 200 of us packed into the crowded room with one small exit. Rachel passed on the volleyball but participated in the aerobics and had a good time with it. It felt good to challenge herself and she needed to move around. On the walk back to Warren East, girls waved and cat-called from their dorm, some hollered like horny construction workers. It was hard to keep in mind that this place wasn't co-ed.

Rachel hadn't any chance to walk around this place, but from what she could tell, there was a sidewalk from Warren East to P.F.S., where everyone ate. She passed by what she was told was the laundry building, a school, and what seemed to be a power plant with piles of coal behind it. On the other side of the sidewalk were century old brick buildings with lots of grass and large trees. To continue past P.F.S. there was a newer maybe 1950's style building. Turn left and there were the three new buildings, their construction nearly completed. Turn left again and there was the hospital. A nice oval track was wedged among the trees and lawns, framed by more buildings where girls probably lived. At the far end was the infamous Jefferson Cottage. It was by the road in and the gate and reportedly where girls lived who had long sentences. It's placement seemed odd, but there must be a reason. There were other gray stone buildings where girls lived upstairs, while downstairs was the mailroom, various administrative offices and the visiting hall. There was a place somewhere around here where they sewed flags and ground eyeglasses and the made the clothes they wore, but she hadn't learned where these places were yet and hopefully won't be here long enough to ever know.

Eight girls were called out to a small office by the social worker for various reasons. Four finished quickly and were escorted back. At 4:20 pm the office workers day ended and they left. There was still one girl being processed behind a closed door. Rachel watched the other two of those waiting in the office going through the desks like flies to shit. They claimed legal pads, pencils and pens, combs, emery boards and whatever else they could conceal under their coats and in their pockets—except for a pen with red ink which they agreed would be bad luck to possess. She was shocked to see people steal things, just because it was there and unguarded.

She met up with April in the mail room where they had to go to pick up and open their legal mail. April was denied her shock and was really shook up. Someone there assured her she could file for super shock in six months. It's probably in her best interest not to have gotten it as she had every intention of picking up where she left off once returning home. Maybe the judge knew that. Two other girls got their shock conditional on acceptance in the "Monday Program." That's drug Rehab. Rachel's "legal mail" was political mail telling her who to vote for. What a "downer" when you're looking for something from your attorney. It sure would be nice to be able to close our eyes, click our heels twice and follow the yellow brick road.

Out of the blue Rachel is told she has a visit. That was a real surprise because she was told that there would be no visits while in admissions. It was her parents. They'd found their way here with a birthday cake and other food but couldn't bring any of it in. They were really disappointed for her and she for their effort, but it was nice to see them. Getting here to visit took over two hours. She was sure they were as thoroughly searched as she was to get to the visiting room, but they didn't say anything about it.

She just hated to have them suffer that, then to see her here; hated for them to make that long drive. She'll have to arrange somehow for someone to drive them in the future. The guilt of her being here was smothering. She's thought long and hard about it and knew she should have called the police that night—but God knows how tired she was. She would have if she'd known drugs were in that box. Yes, she was too worn out to do anything but feel the relief of evil retreating when the door clicked shut.

Leaving the visiting room required strip search and squats, legs spread to dislodge any hidden contraband her parents may have smuggled in. They checked ears, fingernails and mouth, picked through hair, checked shoes and socks, bra, then the searching C.O. grabbed hold of her nipples and made her squeak. Pervert! She held her ID tag up to the light, inspected seams in clothing and hemlines. They detailed her jewelry to insure she wore the same stuff out and back. Humiliating! Some C.O's took their job a little more seriously than others, and she hated to give much thought as to where they recruited them.

Didn't know what building she had been assigned to, but spoke with Charla, from County, briefly and noticed she had all her teeth pulled. It was an improvement. She said they were making new ones for her.

There were several ancient three and four story tenement buildings here easily bigger than most apartment buildings where the girls sleep. They called them cottages but no sand and no beach, nice names for ugly places. The person who thought the girls needed to wear thin cotton dresses year round must have also decided that they must sleep in "cottages." Some of them were named after presidents, others just named. Those girls with serious behavior problems lived somewhere in the hospital, but rumor was they were building a special place for them. Lots of construction going on here, so who knew.

During lunch at P.F.S. a big ugly whore, probably mentally ill, grabbed her crotch and announced loudly from a cafeteria railing, "If anyone is hungry, they can eat this." There were a few laughs but no takers. If the warden thought that pink cotton dresses would make ladies out of these women, she should get in touch with reality and take another look.

There was a search on the way out and one girl saw it coming and quickly unbuttoned her dress. When told to open up her coat for the search, she put her humongous watermelons on display for the C.O. "If you're game, I'm game," the C.O. said, and searched the inside of her bra as well. A male C.O. tried to position himself to view, but the girl told him there was nothing there for him. Finding nothing in the search, the C.O. told her "Don't show your ass around here anymore."

The girl responded, "That wasn't my ass, honey," and proudly strutted out.

Rachel thought about her lawyer and hoped he was working on that appeal he promised her. She hadn't heard a thing from him, and was getting frustrated.

During the day, everyone was back in the crowded, smokey room. If someone needed a sanitary pad, they had to ask the C.O. for one. She always wrote the person's name on it with a permanent marker in the event the girl got creative, it could be traced back.

Coombs County rode today and brought three girls. Karo came in two vans bringing ten. A smaller county brought one. A big hunt is on for chairs for them to sit. It is like the Roach Motel, everyone goes in but no one goes out. No chairs and no place for them anyway. By the time they get sprayed and showered, it won't be safe to go to the bathroom. Your chair will be gone. What is happening to Rachel that makes a chair so important?

A bus load of girls were taken off the premises to sleep elsewhere. Someone said they were going to Bedrock, which is a men's penal facility near Springfield. Dozens of girls who have already been classified as "minimum" have been taken there because of the overcrowding here. Anyway, the plan was to return these girls back to Lotusville when the new buildings opened up, that facility returning to a men-only status.

Fred and Barney, in their gray prison garb, drove the bus, along with Dino, their aptly named bloodhound the State used to track runners. Fred was his handler and frequently took him to work with him. You never know . . . . Besides he was good company.

Overheard, one driver talking over the radio. "Yeah, I had this crazy dream last night . . . . No, just listen. Put the cat out at night and it ate a magic mouse. This big orange cat grew huge. An hour later it came back home and put me out."

Laughter on the other end, then talk the girls couldn't understand . . . . then, "No, fool! The cat not my wife." And he clicked off his radio, bored and annoyed.

The girl's spirits were high as the two prison busses followed each other over the roads through farmland for nearly an hour. They were excited to be leaving Lotusville and better yet going to Bedrock, a men's prison. Fantasy's were rampant as the girl's loudly expressed and tried to outdo their companions' desires, and Fred and Barney listened and got fantasy's of their own.

A girl came back from her County in handcuffs and tears one morning. She left to get "shocked out" and was—on one charge—but not the other. Being gone one day, she had to be sprayed again and lost her bed and chair. Quite an emotional roller coaster.

A mouse scurried behind a cabinet. Traps were soon set every 10 feet around the room. The girls snapped them to scare each other. The mice ate from the safely sprung traps as the girls stood on their chairs and screamed. The mice were the brown variety. Rachel personally preferred the little gray ones with a white undersides.

One girl on learning she was getting "shocked out" promised she'd never be back here because she's leaving the state. Says she loved money too much to think she wouldn't caper. Like other states don't have places like this.

It was a cold rainy morning when Rachel was called to the C.O.'s desk. She'd been summoned to the warden's office and a fellow inmate was there to escort her. Good thing because she didn't have a clue as to where it was. She felt really good about it. Whenever she was at work and called to the boss, it was always for praise or something positive. On the walk over she could only think that someone had somehow found the truth and she was to be released. Her attorney had finally done something good for her. They entered an old stone building, down a corridor or two, and the inmate wrapped on the closed door. Rachel entered while the inmate backed out.

"Rachel Williams? The lady behind the desk barked.

"Yes," she responded with an eager smile.

The lady, who never introduced herself, slapped a white packet on the desk. Rachel's eyes were drawn to it and she saw it was her request for an absentee ballot from the Board of Elections.

The lady flew off the handle about it. She screamed, "Don't you know felons can't vote?"

"Well, I don't think of myself as a criminal so I thought it would be all right."

"Yours would be a fraudulent vote. We could bring more charges against you for lying."

"No, I was honest, I just checked the 'out of county' box on the application. It is not a lie that I am out of my county."

"We will return this to the Board of Elections and have them cancel you."

"Well, have them cancel all the 'vote for me' mail I get here every day from the candidates that arrives as 'legal mail' and I get all excited thinking my attorney finally wrote me then get all frustrated when I see all the junk. In fact, I was sure when I was called over here that you had my papers and were going to release me and apologize."

"Get out of this office," she said in a threatening voice.

When Rachel turned and opened the door, her inmate escort was waiting with a smirk on her face. Without a word, they walked back to Warren East.

No jewelry was permitted in admissions. Those girls with pierced ears were afraid the holes in their ears would close up, so they would take a piece from the end of corn broom and put ¼ inch pieces into their ears to keep the holes open. Didn't hear about anyone getting an infection so maybe it worked.

Rumor had it that everyone in admissions were to be moved over to the new buildings in the next couple of days. Rachel had heard that rumor repeatedly since she got here. Everyone lies. She was anxious to leave Warren East behind. She was anxious to leave this whole place. But if she has to stay for now, it would be nice to have only one room mate instead of 200.

A bird flew around the cafeteria at breakfast and everyone said "that's a sign something bad is going to happen." A little over an hour later at church, the minister announced that the C.O. whose job it was to see that everyone delivered their silverware to the right place when they were through had just died of a heart attack.

After breakfast everyone was ushered over to the gym to spend the day. Some girls played volleyball. The girl officiating that game was here for helping her mother cut up and dispose of her father's body. She'd been here a few years and still justified her part in it. He must have been a real nice guy. Her mother was here too, but for the actual murder. Some watched a movie or played cards while there, others wrote letters or laid down on in the stands and slept.

Inspectors were probably back and the girls certainly couldn't be found in Warren East.

Vickie, who carried a breach baby, went home on shock one day. Everyone was happy to see her leave. It is no place to carry or birth an at-risk baby. This was a God-awful place! When someone said "time flies" it caused Rachel's stomach to tighten, forcing acid up into her throat. Every day is a week and each week a month. It is beyond the imagination. Mornings come and there was no desire to open her eyes to see the drab block walls, ceilings and floors. She wondered why they just don't give her a shot—to end the torture. How much can the body and mind take?

Pat, (not as many teeth to brush) and labeled crazy in County was being tortured by a large fly during lunch. She swung wildly and caused those around her to duck and dodge to avoid being hit. Finally, she caught it in her hand and threw it violently into the bug zapper. She pointed angrily at the fly and as it sizzled, and yelled. "You fucked up." One had to tread lightly around Pat as anyone could easily have been that fly.

Sometimes, Pat could be very philosophical. Rachel was waiting outside P.F.S. in the lunch line, waiting to be lead back to Warren East. Several girls were hanging all over each other grabbing feels. Pat commented, "They're looking for a lot of fights when they get in population. Best they can hope for, if that's what they want, is a good roommate, as that's all they'll have a chance to get. Then they'll be fighting over the other bitches they can't have and someone else is getting." All Rachel could think about is that her attorney had better get her out of this zoo before she goes mad.

Rachel had a look at the paperwork she came here with. She spent four miserable days in City and that wasn't included with the County time. She was told to contact her attorney to have it straightened out. When you're here and every day is a nightmare, four days are a long time. She wrote D.D Knight, then a family member and also a friend, hoping that together they would get on him to do something. Life was so out of control.

The weather was turning cold fast and everyone was so "under clothed" some of the girls had cut the bottom out of their socks so they could pull them up to their knees. Then they pulled another pair over the first pair. Those little cotton dresses were so impractical.

Lunch was sausage. The place, the March Hare's picnic. A girl at Rachel's table put nearly the whole eight inch serving into her mouth, withdrew it and proceeded to suck and lick that thing until there couldn't possibly be any flavor left. Back in it went, practically down into her stomach and out again. Another girl said, "if you're not going to eat that thing, give it to me."

To which the girl responded, "I'm going to need it tonight. You can have it tomorrow."

It was a blustery afternoon and we were really cold waiting in the line outside after lunch, plumes of vapor streaming from everyone. Brenda Slims snuggled up behind one of the bigger C.O.'s for a windbreaker. The C.O. stepped aside saying, "You don't know me that well."

"Who knows you better?" Brenda asked kiddingly

"My husband," responded the C.O.

"What's her name?" laughed Brenda.

Tension ran high constantly. The bawdy laughter that usually followed such conversations relieved some, but there were fights every day, yelling, flying fists or a good chase—mostly over really petty stuff. You never knew when it was going to break out, so it was hard to avoid.

At the dinner table, talk was about babies and sizes of families. April said, "I wonder if I can have one. Ever since I started doing it I wondered. I never used anything and I've never been pregnant. I just wonder if I can. Someone told me to go on the pill for awhile, then quit and I'd get pregnant. I don't want a baby until I'm about 30, but I just want to know."

"Give yourself time, you'll have plenty," commented someone.

"What would you do if you did get pregnant?" asked another.

"Get an abortion." April responded sadly.

Then another girl told her that she had a morality issue and said, "God would never give you the gift of a child with that attitude." Then she linked arms with her "girlfriend" for the walk back to Warren East.

One of her friends surprised April for her birthday. She was thrilled with the attention and the opportunity to "wish" for her shock before she blew out the match sticking out of a hole in a cookie.

Mail means a lot when you're in here, but lack of it can mean even more. A pregnant girl wrote her boyfriend a "final" letter last night. She hadn't had a letter from him since she got here three weeks ago. When she was in "county" he visited her all the time and pledged his love. Now, nothing. Her body gets bigger and bigger and only her family writes her. Is it his baby? "Maybe, but I'll know for sure when I get a look and maybe when it grows a little. That's how I did my other one. Being pregnant has nothing to do with me and my man."

Ronnie threw up lunch, along with a lot of blood. She had an ulcer and was supposed to eat in the diet kitchen, where they make up meals for those with special dietary needs. Since she was not on the list to do it and hadn't been given a pass to get there she ate with the rest. A couple hours later, they had her go over to the hospital. There weren't any doctor's over there, so they could only hope they fed her right.

For the second time this fall Rachel woke up to snow, but this time it was heavy on the ground. There was a snowman in the grass to greet us as we headed to breakfast. Thank you somebody. Hundreds of birds lined up on the wires to watch us. Once inside, she contemplated catapulting a butterball at them with her spoon, but since it would only stick to the window, she reconsidered. I'm really losing it, she thought, and it started to really worry her.

Rachel's group had orientation from Captain McMinnion, the safety and security man this afternoon. Big Mary walked around with blood running down her leg into her socks. He paid no attention to her as he told the his audience that the fourth inspection on the new buildings showed it was not ready for occupancy but "be patient." He hoped it would be ready next week. A C.O. said something to Big Mary and they walked out together.

He explained that "the boilers weren't working so no hot water, the sprinkling system was on the fritz and the electronic door locks weren't functioning—but give them a few days." He emphasized he didn't want us to occupy an "unsafe place."

It was scheduled to open six months ago. Many challenged his believe that our present place was safe. 200+ girls in a 40X80 room, one exit, poor ventilation, rodent infested, etc. All were sick with colds. Again he pleaded, "be patient."

Last night, just before they locked the door for the evening count, one girl told the C.O. she had to go to the bathroom and was told to go and sit on her bed and be counted. She could go after count. She refused, saying she had to go. Almost instantly, it started running down her legs, soaking her socks and shoes and turning the concrete dark in a puddle around her feet. The C.O. returned, saw, laughed and told her to clean it up—no soap or disinfectant, just paper towels she casually tossed in the wastebasket.

Clocks must have been moved back last night as it became light early this morning. No one said anything. It's so strange. No access to T.V., newspapers or radio. Is there still a world out there? Little to do here but to exist—and wait for the attorney to get her out.

Two girls that didn't know each other prior to talking at the table and discovered they were both from Chicago's south side. The inevitable questions came up. Do you know . . . . and Pat this and Mike that? "I was married to him for three years," responded one of them totally surprised. Small world. One of the girls was two months pregnant and not getting any mail from home or from her baby's father. She spent a lot of time with her head down on the table during the day. She'd gone to the doctor because of horrible pain and discomfort between her legs, sores that oozed, then stuck to her underwear, and ooh the pain when trying to drop her panties that stuck to the scabs. Sometimes she'd have to urinate through the panties to loosen them up from her. What an embarrassing situation to live with every day. On top of learning she had herpes, something she'd have to live with for the rest of her life, he told her she was also pregnant. Just what she needed to learn after being arrested buying weed for her boyfriend. Her doctor explained that the sores would come and go and sometimes be worse than other times, that he'd give her medication to ease the discomfort. Now, she's pregnant, and in jail, and as far as the medication goes, they said they'd look into it.

Later when she walked to the front of the room to get her "pregnant snack," a nearby girl stood by a mirror with her hands down her pants. A C.O. hollered at her "stop that" then charged off in that direction. "What's the matter with you," she asked the C.O, "it's my stuff." The C.O. must have agreed because she marched away without saying a word. One of the girls watching the C.O. said, "She knows how to move those hips, boom, boom, boom, boom." The observer moved her head and eyes back and forth as if watching a tennis match. The pregnant girl, who rarely smiles walked back with her peanut butter sandwich as a girl commented to her, "You're just miserable because you've got a bump in your tummy and don't have a daddy for it."

Having had enough of the negative chatter, she threatened, "Get out of my way, you bald-headed bitch or it will be ON."

Rachel received a letter from Edna McDaniels today. She goes to court in about three weeks and is afraid she will be deported back to Nigeria. Her attorney advised her to let her four kids go and let them get acquainted with her family there. That doesn't bode well for her attempt to stay here. She didn't say anything about the wedding.

The commissary didn't sell gum, yet most of the C.O.s brought it from home and were constantly chewing it. Rachel saw a C.O. finish chewing her piece, wrap it in paper, and toss it into the wastebasket. Seconds later a girl fished this well-chewed treasure out of the trash. She chewed it for awhile, then stored it behind her ear for the night so she could resume chewing again in the morning.

*     *     *

A week later rumor was that most of the problems with the newly constructed buildings were in Pierce cottage, the medium security building. The sprinkling system hadn't been turned on, the security system still had electrical problems and there is supposed to be a gas leak somewhere.

Three big busses brought girls back from Bedrock, all dressed alike in khaki pants and sweatshirts. Shivering in little cotton dresses, all envied their attire. They moved into Wilson Cottage which was minimum. One of the new buildings was for admissions, one for minimum and one for medium security. Everyone expects to follow suit imminently Once settled in, everyone will have new color-coded clothes. They'll be based on classification, decided by the one who decided we needed pink cotton dresses and on how much time we have to do and in some cases behavior.

Those girls that can't get along with others because of mental/behavior issues are classified "close" and will live at the hospital until another building scheduled to be built especially for them is opened. Those with life sentences will have a "maximum security" label until much of their time is done. Don't know where they draw the line on "medium" but it is probably around three to seven years time left to serve. Those with less than three years left to serve seem to be minimum. As one's time runs down they are reduced in classification, but repeated tickets will increase it. You can't accumulate "good time" with behavior issues. Those living in a building with a minimum classification have more phone call opportunities and can stay up a couple hours later if they choose to.

A few days later, they started moving about thirty girls a day from admissions and more from other buildings over to the new buildings. These three really huge structures haven't all passed inspection yet, but part of it may have. She learned that one of the new buildings is for "admissions," Wilson for minimum security and Pierce for medium.

The new building looked ready to us
    "It's unsafe" says Captain McMinnion
But two days later we were in
    What the heck, we're only women

The fire alarm goes off at will
    The electronic locks don't function
Ceiling tiles are hanging loose.
    Call the priest for holy unction

When Rachel's name was called to leave Warren East, she eagerly walked over to the new building with a half dozen of her acquaintants. She had enough of Warren East and didn't look back. She'd learned that her new roommate, Kenny, had been at Lotusville for a couple of years and was already moved in to their room. She discovered the building held a mix of those from admissions and those that had been here for a while. It was absolutely wonderful to be in a smoke-free above-ground area with windows and space to walk around. She was issued pink tops and khaki pants like everyone else in the building and was rid of those dresses. There were two tiers of rooms along the back and a big common room with tables and chairs, the C.O.'s elevated area nestled between the rooms and the door. At the time she didn't realize how lucky she was to have a room on the first floor.

Yes, there were structural problems in the building, but things were new and clean and the problems would eventually be fixed. The electronic door locks would smoke and burn during the night, which set off the fire alarms at all times. Each room had to be individually locked and unlocked as the main lock at the C.O. desk didn't work. Good thing there's no real emergency because no one was going to manually unlock all our doors if the place was burning down. The C.O.s were usually the first ones out the door when the sirens wailed. No hot water in the building yet. The upstairs shower had water running down the hall and into the rooms. A plumber was called to clear the drain. When tried to use his snake to clear it, he found no drain. There was just concrete under the metal grate. Rachel's room was downstairs, so only heard about it. About half the rooms weren't occupied yet for various reasons like toilets that don't flush and doors that don't lock.

Bessie cried most of the morning. She wanted to go home. displayed snapshots of her kids at her table—teenagers, a boy and a girl. She was good at what would best be described as a "stage mumble," loud enough for anyone nearby to hear, grumbling crazy to herself about killing this person and that junkie when she got out. It seems she fired a gun to chase off a dealer trying to sell drugs in her front yard to her son. She's going to quit one church and join another because one didn't support her during her trial, and they aren't looking in on her kids now. She wrote her daughter, 19, a letter of abusive language because she hasn't gotten her out of here. Her daughter hasn't come to visit often enough or brought the younger boy and no one writes often enough. She wrote her boyfriend of 14 years a similar letter for not hiring a lawyer competent enough to keep her out of here and for not visiting and sending money. She says she'll kill herself before coming back here again. Says she had two lawyers working independently of each other and one of them was dismissed. She cried, she can't work, can't eat, can't walk, ordered a big food package from home and wants someone to pick it up for her because she has high blood pressure. She doesn't take medication for it and can't wait to get out of here to check into a hospital for a rest. Yet, she's the first ones out the door (after the C.O.) once the siren's start. She'll do three years for the gun, then start the court-ordered sentence.

The Pierce building rules were new to those from admissions, where everyone did things pretty much at the same time and there was little moving around, and the C.O.s were disorganized which caused screaming headaches and confusion. In Pierce there were rules for everything and the C.O's didn't baby-sit every move.

Bessie's roommate, Skyla, woke early to discover she needed sanitary pads. Being fresh out of admissions, neither had any. As she descended the stairway in her housecoat to get one at the C.O.'s desk, the C.O. called a warning.

"Get back to your room, no housecoats permitted down here."

"I need a sanitary," she pleaded in her naturally loud voice.

"Get back to your room," the C.O. demanded.

"I'll get my dress on," Skyla conceded.

"You do and you're in trouble," the C.O. responded. The night before, Skyla had signed to leave her room at 10:45 am and it was only a little after seven. Lots of girls were milling around downstairs that had signed to leave their rooms early—most likely to go to their jobs or attend a class. No one was allowed to give Skyla a pad under penalty of a ticket. Nevertheless, Skyla started down the steps again after about fifteen minutes, where she was again confronted by the sharp voiced C.O. telling her to get back.

"I said I need a sanitary," she repeated.

"You're not getting one and you're looking for trouble." threatened the C.O.

"I'm supposed to bleed all over myself?" she questioned.

"Yes!" was the answer.

"As she turned away, she said more quietly but loud enough to be heard around the room, "you bitch."

The C.O. got on the phone and called in the reinforcements and she was taken out in handcuffs. Don't know if she ever got that pad. She spent the next week in discipline control where there is no flush toilet and where she was stripped of all clothing except her gown and not permitted to wash her hair or shower while there.

It was still early in the morning and we thought the excitement was over for a while, but one of the electrical devices in a door shorted out and started belching smoke. The girls inside beat on the door to get someone's attention. The C.O. tried to open it from the desk panel. That didn't work. In a panic, she walked over to the door and used her key.

Everyone was assigned a menial job. Most girls fresh out of admissions worked in the main kitchen while the more infirm did housekeeping in the building. Rachel was assigned to diet kitchen in the basement of the hospital. Big Bessie was assigned there as well. When they first went down those steps and smelled the heavy odor of gas Rachel mentioned it to the C.O. She was very nice and easy-going and didn't have the military demeanor of the others. She admitted she also smelled the gas but said, "oh don't worry about it. There's a little leak somewhere that's been here a long time." And she smiled saying it! During the course of Rachel's shift, she kept sniffing for the gas leak because she considered it a definite hazard.

She and Bessie sprayed and wiped out the dirty ovens, cleaned what must have been months of grease off the floor around them, then mopped. Others cleaned out the refrigerator, snacking on whatever they thought they could get away with while some organized the storeroom, complaining about but getting rid of rotting potatoes and a variety of bugs and rodent droppings. Various surfaces and windows were polished.

Crawling around Rachel traced the gas leak to a flexible pipe connection behind a gas grill on wheels. Apparently someone pulled the grill out to far or knocked into it and loosened it up. She told the C.O. and showed her. The next time she came in the smell was gone so someone did something about it.

These jobs are temporary, while the C.O's assess one's work ethic for other jobs. Rachel checked around and learned she could take college classes while here and that was her intention. At the present time, diet kitchen worked for her. She's one of a dozen assigned to the early shift. They put together meals for inmates with specialized dietary needs, like diabetes, those that need low-salt/fat food, are pregnant, or lived in the hospital upstairs. The C.O. was very pleasant, and easy going.

Brenda Slims joined the crew. She was loud, a lot of fun and worked hard cleaning up at the end of shift. She complained one day about the stinky gray mop and no bleach. It reminded Rachel of the mop the jailer dragged across the floor in City Jail, and that just wouldn't do. She found a can of Comet and dumped some in the wash bucket after Brenda was done for the day. After it soaked overnight, the mop whitened up and she rinsed out the Comet. Rachel liked working with Brenda, but she, like most of the young girls there acted so much like the kids they were. Being there was just a daily inconvenience, not something that would affect the rest of their lives.

When it came time to fill the trays for people to eat, Rachel wasn't sure what the rules were, what food to put with each diet. She wasn't told and nothing was written down, so she asked the cook. She was told, "baked chicken for everyone, no waxed beans for the low salts because they come from a can, no milk or dessert for the diabetics. They get sweet and low and peaches and a little extra fried chicken.

Blands don't get gravy. Some girls try to keep it straight, some don't care." There were no special diets to accommodate religious dictates.

Rachel tried to portion and distribute the food correctly. Then the dieters say, "I want a breast" or "give me a leg."

The cook says, "fuck that and give them whatever you want. If you like them, give them more. If they're nasty, give them a double helping of prunes."

Alice was assigned to another building so Rachel didn't see much of her any more except at diet kitchen. She didn't eat there but she stopped by now and again to pick up some medications. They had a "carry out" window just outside diet kitchen where the girls would line up to get their medications. She only had a brief chance to say hello, but it was nice seeing her each time.

After an easy day at work, Rachel returned to the Pierce building as usual and went to take her shower. She gathered up her soap, shampoo and conditioner with every intention of spending some time shedding the kitchen stink. A girl that was leaving as she went in commented that she'd be lucky to get through before the fire alarms went off, as the building had been "booming" all morning. The girl was referring to the dampers in the chimneys that clang shut automatically when there's some malfunction so not to allow a draft to encourage fire. She'd just rinsed out the shampoo and it started—that loud pulsating siren. "Fuck it," she thought. "I'm finishing." She applied conditioner, rinsed, then dried her hide. She wrapped the towel around her hair, put on her big fluffy terry robe, gathered up her toiletries and left the shower room. The air was filled with the acrid smell of hot steel and no one was around.

Oops! She set her stuff down on a table, grabbed a coat off the rack and joined the crowd of terrified girls huddling outside the door in the snow. One girl had her coat over her head crying to Allah. Another screamer was sure she was going to die right then. "They're going to cause me to have a heart attack. I was going to take a shit but this scared it back up." She continued to wail.

Just then a workman pushed his way through the door. "The fire is out," he told the C.O. "but no one goes back in until you get clearance."

"So, there was a fire," an inmate commented. He'll probably get days off for admitting it in our presence," she chuckled.

After we went back inside, the unit manager told us everything was fine, that a motor had burned up. Someone asked to see papers that the building had passed inspection. Those girls from Warren East were anxious to get over here, while others who were transferred from other buildings wanted no part of it. One girl asked the unit manager if he'd sleep in the building locked in a room and be comfortable with electronic locks on the doors that didn't work. As soon as he reasserted that the building was safe, the alarm went off again and stayed on for 10-15 minutes. The burning stink returned.

The fire alarm went off again at about 8:45 that evening and they refused to let anyone out the door after dark. That was okay with many. They didn't want to go out in the snow and cold. Others cried about never being able to see their kids again, they knew this was the end.

The workmen wandered back in scratching their chins. The ventilator fan came on unusually loud for 10-15 seconds then shut off immediately, followed by the alarm. A few girls ran for the door but were called back. Those who had gone to bed early joined with those who stayed up. The loud pulsating fire alarm had frightened girls into being afraid to return to their rooms to be locked in. Everyone just sat at the tables in the rec. area, defiantly refusing to leave for bed. The C.O. on duty stood up with the girls against the administration and a deal was made over the phone. At eleven o'clock the girls returned to their rooms and their doors stayed wide open for the night and everyone was satisfied.

When that fire alarm goes off, the C.O. is usually the first one out the door. No one checks to see if someone is sleeping or locked in their room—or taking a shower, as Rachel happened to have been. She's supposed to be able to turn a key and electronically unlock the doors, but that system didn't work, at least not yet.

The wristwatch has been dropping off Rachel's arm because the clip on the band was loose. She tried to bite it tight, but that didn't work. Then Rachel saw a workman sauntering by with a belt of tools. She stopped him and asked if he had any needle-nose pliers. He smiled and said he did. When she showed him where her watch band needed tightening, he held them out to her. Fixed, and thank you.

Deb's family made dozens of calls to the penitentiary and also to Central Office. They worried about their daughter's safety at the hands of the ugly C.O. the girls nicknamed Uncle Festus who offered to trade her gum for sex. Rumor had it, he was married with seven daughters. A "white shirt" came by to find out from her what she'd been telling them that had them calling here all the time. As she started to talk about not feeling safe around Uncle Festus as well as the structural problems in the building, another girl walked over with her own list of complaints. Deb let them take over the conversation, afraid if Uncle Festus got word she was reporting him, he would come after her. The white shirt asked, "what's happening here in Pierce. All of a sudden there's six C.O's that have requested they not be assigned here."

Deb spoke up, "Maybe they are afraid, just like us, because the fire alarms have been disconnected and the automatic sprinklers are shut off, and certain C.O's are creeping us out." She was afraid if she mentioned Uncle Festus by name and gave examples she would not be able to sleep at night for fear of him.

Rumor was that more building inspectors came by on a scheduled visit. Great strides were made cleaning up after the workmen but he cited them for loosened wooden chairs, ripped seats, broken tables, falling ceiling tiles, loose floor tiles, dripping water pipes, gas leaks, broken windows, torn screens and other maintenance problems. Someone commented that they'd have to give him three virgins for him to agree to keep quiet, and he won't find them here.

\* \* \*

Cute as any on a card, there's a little white kitten that huddles next to the closed window in diet kitchen for warmth. The cook fed it when she thought no one was looking. There are a lot of cats walking around everywhere. The problem is, the many cats are all on the outside and the inside of these old buildings is teeming with rodents.

Because going to "rec." was a good thing in "admissions," Rachel thought she'd give it a try now that she was in "population." Bad idea! She understood that there is a certain percentage of girls that like girls. In "admissions" there was a lot of talk about girl-on girl stuff and she heard the rumors, but "rec." seemed to be the place for everyone to flaunt their wants and desires, slinking off under the grandstands or spending a lot of time doubled up in the showers. So many of the young girls (mothers for the most part) figured that was the acceptable thing to do while locked up and made no secret of their indulgences. The C.O.s supervising the "rec." seemed to turn a blind eye. After the one time, Rachel didn't sign up for it again.

*     *     *

Some of the buildings, Warren East for example, didn't have small rooms to sleep, but big dorms supervised at night by a C.O. Rachel's roommate came from one of these and was full of stories about what lengths they'll go to be together when they are assigned beds on opposite sides of the room. One girl, nicknamed Elvis, poofed up her blanket into a human form under her bedspread and slithered off her upper bunk. Across the floor and under others bunks she crawled, rearranging shoes in her path. Bumping into bunks she alerted would be sleepers to what was going on. Later, on her return trip, she was abruptly stopped as her hair became ensnared in someone's bunk springs. Try as she might, Elvis couldn't get free. Those quietly trying to help her only tangled it more and all were aware that the ensuing whispers might alert the C.O to their plight. About half an hour of sweat, pain and attempted silence elapsed before someone passed her a razor to cut herself free. For some time, she was a modified Elvis, but it didn't modify her nocturnal adventures.

Ginger started working at diet kitchen. She was so frail people worried about her. Actually she was quite useless, but she did try. She could load the dishwasher if given enough time and she talked all the time whether or not anyone was listening. They kept her there for about two months and during that time she sure changed. Her face and arms filled out and she looked about six months pregnant. Her state jumper split at the sides and under the arms. The girl could really eat and now seemed less drugged and more social.

Ham was on the menu one night and it was delicious. Before eating Rachel spotted some plums leftover from lunch. She couldn't resist temptation and plucked out and ate a dozen of them. She'd better watch herself or need her state clothes replaced too.

New rule: For those who wanted a shower, they must take them right after dinner. This was the rule for all three new buildings. The problem was there wasn't enough water pressure to accommodate this plan. But it was convenient for the C.O.'s. It would make sense to let the girls shower at a convenient time for them, depending on work and school schedules, but being practical isn't a part of this place.

At Pierce it became obvious to Rachel that lots of girls were coupled up and there was fierce jealousy over choices. She thought back at what crazy Pat told her when they were in admissions. We weren't a bunch of newcomers any more like in admissions, but a mix of the total population. Many of the young girls temporarily switched their sexual preferences because of the convenience and the desire to do something now. They were playing at sex, playing at not being caught and felt some kind of prestige at "owning someone." Yes, they claimed ownership and fought, to keep it.

Bessie decided that diet kitchen wasn't for her so applied for the job as washer-dryer person in our building. After the C.O. broke up an argument complete with vile threats and throat grabbing, she told Bessie that it was a probably a better fit for her. Something was always brewing with Bessie. Once in a while, she had to return to diet kitchen to fill in for someone who was ill or needed to be replaced.

State clothes are supposed to go to the main laundry, while the casual weekend and evening clothes are done in the building. Most of the girls wash out their underwear in the sink. No bleach is available so if panties got a stain, they'd wash them as best they could, then set them on the windowsill and hope the sunshine would finish the job. Usually it did. Sometimes in the winter, someone would set a can of Pepsi between the window and the screen to get it cold. It frequently froze and burst and created a mess that more often than not didn't get cleaned up. Soon there was a new rule where no one was permitted to put anything on the windowsill, so if noticed by a C.O. from inside the doorway or one prowling the perimeter outside one would get a ticket.

With Bessie, the attitude never quit. While she was doing laundry in a little room near the stairway, two girls came in, and said nothing to Bessie. One sat on the table, spread her legs to her friend who pulled up a chair in front of her. The girl on the table tossed her dress over her friend's head and they proceeded to make intimate noises. Bessie was offended. She told them to get the hell out of "her" room, then left and told the C.O. loud and clear that "there's two girls eating each other out and I can't work." The C.O. not wanting to get involved in a "lay down" ticket called the girls out of the room from just outside the doorway. Had she actually seen anything, she would have had to write tickets and have them cuffed and hauled away. That meant paperwork.

Bessie just couldn't deal with it and didn't like the way the situation was handled. She announced loudly that she wasn't putting the "bull-dykers" clothes in the machine unless the crusty-crotched underwear was rinsed out. Cowboy, (nicknamed here because of her strut and because she's always singing country and western songs) a very young but very bold girl and took exception to Bessie's public announcement and having her panties returned unwashed with a note attached as to why. Bessie told her, "Said the pimp to the whore, get your own machine because I ain't doing it no more."

A few minutes later, Bessie got into it again when Kim, a tiny blond girl beat her to the clothes dryer. "No ugly white bitch is going to do that to me . . . . No! Let that word nigger part your lips and I'll go to max for parting your head with this." She held up Miss Raines cane.

"Lick it!" Spat Kim.

"Stop it now," called the C.O. who was tired of all the bickering.

"Slippery roach," uttered Bessie.

*    *    *

Rachel's roommate, Kenny, (most dominant lesbians assume masculine names) who had a job in the main laundry, was in the mood to talk. "My father has always been in and out of my life but he and my mother were never married. In my wildest imagination I can't dream of how he got her into bed to conceive me and she's certainly been celibate since. There were never any men around the house, just my mother and grandmother. Mother said of sex, 'I don't understand the big deal of having someone sweating on me.'

Dad is from Jamaica and spends most of his time between there and Florida. I don't know how he makes his living but I expect he's a criminal. His roots are in a very backward and primitive community in Jamaica where women are the educated leaders and sex between the sexes is only for procreation. Homosexuality is common.

I visited my father in Florida when I was in my mid-teens and was able to talk with him as I never could my mother. I confessed my fears of being different from my friends in that I had more of a sexual magnetism to girls than boys. He told me to follow my instincts and avoid men. He said they were all dogs and can never be trusted, which I thought strange coming from a man, but he repeated it several times over the summer. Having always been an observer of human nature, I noticed that although he had women friends, he also had an attraction to young boys.

My daughter is the product of a five minute one-time fling with an old friend after some heavy partying. He said he couldn't stomach the thought of having sex with a woman, but wanted very much to have a child. We spent long hours discussing and sharing our feelings about the attitudes of society about homosexual relationships. He had Polynesian ancestry. About a month later he died in an accident and it bothered me for a long time he never had the pleasure of knowing he fathered a child. My father was openly disgusted on learning of my pregnancy.

I've been married twice and wasn't enough in love, I guess. After a few weeks I just had enough of it. I often wondered if my mother understood the truth about me. She's never said anything but it doesn't seem possible she hasn't figured it out.

I wasn't 'turned out' here and don't chase girls. In the four years I've been here I've had three girlfriends and the first two went home and I was happy for them. For me, relationships develop slowly and I have a good one now."

Rachel's eye was drawn to a hand-drawn card on the desk of two girls behind bars, the caption "Love is Jailin' Together." The lifers and those with incorrigible behavior live in their own building and wear orange clothes, but they all mix for evening "rec." Her girlfriend was there because of an escape attempt that didn't pan out. She says a male C.O. caught them once and told her the only reason she was "gay" was she'd never had a real man. She told him she hadn't seen any real men around here.

Kenny was a thief and from time to time Rachel noticed little things missing from her drawer. She didn't say anything until she went looking for her long underwear. Of course Kenny denied knowing anything about it and Rachel continued to rant. Finally Kenny got up and walked out of the room. After that only minor things like tampons were missing.

There was a fight in Pierce and Rachel was called as a witness to testify to what she saw. They asked if she saw one girl slap the other. She told them, "No." They asked if she saw one of the girls raise a chair off the floor. She told them "No." They asked what she did see. "After hearing a commotion, I looked over to see one girl's startled face. She was backing away from the table, dragging her chair and facing the other. There was lots of noise from a gathering crowd. I don't know what was said or what it was about. I was 20-25 feet away." She had to sign a paper that she witnessed no physical contact between the two. Later, she heard it was about smoking.

\*   \*   \*

Once or twice a year, usually on a holiday, fried pork chops were served and everyone went to get them They were excellent and a real treat. Rachel trimmed the meat from the fat and bone. Eager fingers snatched up the discards. "The fat is the best part," commented one girl. "I can suck on the bone for hours," said another. They all laughed. They always cooked up plenty for everyone, and always ran short at the end of the day. Thievery in the kitchen was rampant and real pork chops were a commodity to trade.

Two or three times a month, pork chops were on the menu, but a very different version was served. Somewhere in Indiana, old boar and sow were ground up like hamburger and shaped into triangles to resemble pork chops and sold to the penitentiaries in Illinois, Ohio and most likely elsewhere. By the smell of them cooking you knew that most of the meat was dead long before it was slaughtered. The stench permeated the air and hung low so everyone knew what was being served that evening. It was only palatable when drenched in a thick hickory flavored barbeque sauce. Some foods are not meant for human consumption, and Illinois law prevents the sale of this in Illinois but they can buy it legally in Indiana and bring it back. This was just another reminder convicts didn't qualify for human hood. Rumor is that Central Office pays retail for the old pork but the full amount never reaches Indiana, the difference finding someone's pocket.

\*　　\*　　\*

Rachel received an answer to a kite she sent about her unsuccessful search for a cardboard box to store her clothes under the bed. It is permitted in <u>A</u>dministration <u>R</u>ules 20 and 23 which is on the C.O.'s desk for all to peruse in Pierce. She was told that because the rooms were so small, a box would not be permitted. She wrote back, "since all beds on the premises are the same size and boxes must be stored under the bed, what difference does the size of the room make. Also, since the rooms are small, it only makes sense to utilize the area under the bed for storage." She assumed no one would answer, so kited a different "white-shirt" about it. She knew it only a matter of time before she got a food or clothes box from home that she could use, but she just figured on rattling a cage because she could and it was her way of letting the administration know their thinkers weren't working.

No Kotex in Pierce for several days and it started to create a minor panic as personal supplies were depleted. A C.O. found an abundance in admissions and sent a girl over to get some. A few feet from the admissions door, she slipped on ice and couldn't get up to reach the buzzer. She banged and yelled but wasn't heard. Then she called to a C.O. walking by but wasn't heard, so crawled back to Pierce where she was heard banging on the door. About an hour later, a nurse who'd been summoned came to the conclusion that the girl couldn't walk and requested a stretcher for the first leg of her journey to I.S.U. for X-Rays and treatment. It was later determined she'd broken her ankle. The outside bone had two breaks and now had six pins. The inside bone now had a screw and a plate. She said that she got excellent care at I.S.U. because her husband's insurance policy covered it. After six days, at I.S.U. the warden insisted she be brought back, as that was "far too much hospitalization for a broken ankle." She was brought back to hobble around on crutches.

As for the Kotex, Bessie passed Rachel walking away from the C.O's desk, mumbling, "what kind of place is this? Now we have to share Kotex!"

Bessie was just grumbling to herself, but Rachel had to ask, "Do you get firsts or seconds?"

"What?" She asked, a disgusted look passing over her face.

"You wash them out when you're done?"

With that, she smiled. "No, we just have to share a twelve-pack."

Kenny just had her basket (book carryall) confiscated by a white shirt while she was at work in the laundry. She says she had enough contraband in it to send her to "max." Rachel believed that as she got sugar and a plastic knife from her. With all the thieves here, whatever gets stolen/confiscated can be stolen/confiscated back. She recovered her basket stashed in the sheet room, apparently unsearched. She has it but hasn't brought it back to her room yet. A friend is holding it for her to see if they come looking.

Everyone had trouble getting clothes back from the main laundry. Rachel sent kites every week to everyone from the laundry, to the storeroom to the social worker about the problem. Some of the items were missing over a month and if she hadn't been sneaking the last of them into her personal laundry for Bessie to wash, she would have long since run out of clean state clothes which she is required to wear Monday through Friday. After learning that the social worker was leaving to work in a men's facility, and she saw her in the building, Rachel confronted her directly. The next day there was a load of laundry hanging on her door.

There's a girl in admissions with an ill-fitting artificial leg. She was told, "any more complaining and we'll take it away."

Rachel flushed the toilet shortly before midnight and it kept on flushing. There sure have been a lot of broken toilets here. It was flushing loudly three feet from her bunk and she tried to convince herself she was in a tent camping near a waterfall and a mountain brook. About an hour later, when she was getting used to it, the brook dried up.

An older lady sat at a table by herself wanting to go to bed, but the lock on her door was stripped and the key wouldn't open it. A maintenance man worked for about an hour and couldn't fix it. She can be glad that she isn't on the other side of that door with the fire alarms are going off. She had to sleep elsewhere but it took awhile for the white shirts to make a decision as to where.

There's usually a long line of robed girls waiting their turn outside the shower. Cowboy was a teenage girl who had probably taken her sex wherever the most convenient partner was and her hands were all over the girls around her.

"Keep your hands to yourself, Cowboy," the C.O. called.

Cowboy giggled an acknowledgment but playfully pushed off the shoulder of a nearby friend.

The C.O. warned her again, but Cowboy giggled again. "You laugh at the wrong times young lady," the C.O. threatened.

"You going to give me a ticket for laughing" Cowboy challenged as the C.O. turned her attention to other horseplay inside the shower.

Kenny popped her head out of a nearby room. "Cowboy, you've got some nerve fooling around with all the girls you do in this place."

"Me?" questioned Cowboy feigning innocence. "Who am I fooling with?"

"There's at least three here in this building, plus whoever you can get your hands on."

"Like who?" Cowboy smugly invited information as a dozen pair of eager ears strained for this information.

She tossed out three names and Cowboy just laughed saying she was ONLY right on one of the names, but didn't elaborate on which one.

Kenny laid into her. "There's no ONLY with you, Cowboy. It's "ducks in a row." I saw you holding hands with one girl while rubbing another's leg at the table. Then the electrician came in and you slammed your friends hand onto the table and went over to him. It's a wonder you didn't slide on the juices running down your leg and onto the floor as you lusted after that man.

Cowboy's face reddened and her frozen smile remained but Kenny continued. "It's people like you who give homosexuality a bad name," she accused. "There's more to relationships than how many people you can put your hands on. How would you feel if one of them started their own ten-minute rodeo?"

"I wouldn't like it." Cowboy's voice was deceptively low.

One of these days someone else isn't going to like it either, and you'll both end up in MAX for brawling," she stated and walked away. She might have thought that she'd gotten through to Cowboy, but Cowboy thrives on defiance.

Toward evening Rachel decided to go to bed early. At 8 pm the C.O. peeked her head in to check her presence and left. At the next room she backed up quickly, and Rachel listened to her voice.

"I'm sure I'm not seeing what I think I'm seeing. I'm sure there's no one in this room who isn't supposed to be. I'm sure I don't see Cowboy with her clothes off."

"You're not going to give us a ticket," wheedled Cowboy.

"Get dressed," the C.O. snapped as she marched over to her desk and picked up the telephone.

Shortly after, the escorts came and cuffed the two and off they went singing, *"That's What Love is For."*

Cheryl came here maybe 15 years ago as a rebellious sixteen-year-old. For the first two years she lived in "A.I." the adjustment unit for girls with serious behavior problems who can't live with others. Whenever she'd get into a disagreement, instead of arguing, she'd slip away, then unexpectedly return to catch her adversary on fire or catch her bed on fire. She's not here for arson, though, but for tossing a baby over a bridge. As a young newlywed, she was babysitting for a friend and had trouble handling her charge. Rachel asked her why throw a baby over a bridge? "Who knows," she replied, tossing her hands in the air as if reliving it.

The girl that fell when the man-hole cover flipped has been assigned to another building, but several girls did see her walking all bent over, almost at a right angle. Someone said she'd been in the hospital for a while but is now in population. This place is full of rumors and one of them is that she's faking trying to get early release. Don't know what her case is or how long she has to be here. But it has been months and who could imagine anyone walking around with her torso parallel to the ground all this time if she could walk any other way.

\*     \*     \*

A couple of years ago, a pregnant inmate delivered a baby and filed papers so her mother could come pick it up. The male social worker handling the paperwork was careless. When the grandmother came to get the baby, she was told it wasn't at the hospital, that the County Children's Services had it. There she was told it was sent to Cook County to be adopted. The frantic Grandmother demanded the baby be found and threatened to sue. The baby was found two days later in the home of a family hoping to adopt.

That same social worker soon became a C.O. at Lotusville. Within a few months nearly ten girls testified he had sex with them. In all probability, all these girls wanted and probably initiated the sexual contact but since it wasn't permitted, he was ushered off the premises and charged with rape. Rachel investigated further, mostly by keeping her ears open, and learned that one of the girls intentionally got into trouble once in a while so she could go to Max and have some privacy with him. Since returning to population, she has become a celebrity. He'd been known to tomcat around a lot. He entertained a girl who worked with Kenny in the laundry. He also had a drug case pending, buying cocaine in

Springfield, most likely to share with his lady friends here. He didn't last long.

Well meaning friends sent Rachel books, strips of stamps and envelops, none of which she could keep. In county yes, but not here. They had to be returned. She did appreciate knowing that someone was thinking of her comfort—but the attorney wasn't one of them. Maybe he's dead.

*　　*　　*

Commotion again at diet kitchen. Brenda Slims was almost sent to "max" today for trying to scald a girl with a pitcher of hot tea. Don't know what that was about. The C.O. on duty was a very grandmotherly type who let a lot slide.

Lots of excitement today. One of the C.O's was drunk on the job and another got caught stealing meat. Then one of the kitchen workers sneaked a patient some cigarettes and matches while delivering a food tray and she caught her room on fire. Another kitchen worker was "semi-caught" smuggling a bundle of goodies to a friend doing time in MAX. She wasn't apprehended at the time so claims they can't prove it was her. Until someone admitted to being the culprit, though, the C.O. on duty wrote everyone tickets, probably after being instructed to do so by a white shirt. Rachel wasn't about to accept a ticket so told the C.O. that she'd take it to the R.I.B. (white shirts sitting in judgment of the tickets) and would call that C.O. as a witness that she had never left the basement. She said she'd be glad to be a witness for her, but never heard any more about it.

One of the ladies at the card table kept getting up to go to her room, saying she didn't feel good, stomach cramps and diarrhea. She commented she messed up her bed earlier. Upon hearing that, her roommate asked her if she changed the sheets. She shook her head no, then said "not yet, anyway," and continued to play her hand.

There was a girl here who had written lots of bad checks and had been sentenced to serve seventeen years. The judge shocked her out after 30 days. Then she failed to notify her parole officer that she got married. When he found out, he had her sent back to do the seventeen—YEARS. There are several girls here that had highly publicized cases that Rachel recognized from the papers. She doesn't usually put it together, though, until she hears their stories.

Kenny showed Rachel boxes of her books. In the building she was in prior to coming to Pierce, she had a room to herself and could keep several boxes. At Pierce she was permitted only one box—according to the A.R. There just wasn't room for all her stuff. But she brought over at least a half a dozen boxes and stashed them out of sight under her bed. She told Rachel that about a year before, she was asked to help clean out an attic in another building so they could move in cots, and she came across a load of old magazines. When she asked if she could keep a few of them, was told to "take what you want, the rest will be tossed out." One was dated Dec. 1941 "*Spot*," and carried a story on Lotusville. Rachel read the story. There were lots of pictures of the prison in it. The story said there was one building for whites and one for blacks, the pay was $9 a month. It's $12 now. She considered the magazine a real collector's item and glad she was able to save it. She said that the girls here used to be able to have pets in their rooms and the cats we see roaming around are probably descendents of those cats.

One thing Rachel found hard to adjust to here was the fact that the light in all the rooms was on all night long. One night, though, there was a storm and all the lights went out everywhere. Girls started screaming. Rachel thought the darkness was wonderful—until a generator somewhere flickered the lights back on.

Most everyone played cards pretty much constantly. Fortunately Rachel had some crossword puzzles to do and lots of mail to read and answer. Eric was writing most every day and sometimes sent nice cards. She answered everyone of his letters and detailed her days. He talked of his job and how much he missed her. He'd spoken with her parents and said they were doing well. The mail was slow getting to its recipients, sometimes taking over a month to pass through the mailroom. Maybe that is partially because two thousand women get mail and right now that there's a lot of women shifting around to different buildings. It would make too much sense to temporarily assign an additional girl or two to the mail room.

\*     \*     \*

Big Bessie was sitting alone at a table when a girl meandered over to show her a picture of her baby. While Bessie looked at the picture, the girl noticed white spots floating in the Bessie's coffee cup and bent over it for a closer look. Bessie resented someone inspecting her coffee and let loose. "How did you get such a nice looking baby when you're so fucked up?" Before she had time to respond, Bessie continued. "I'm sorry but I tell it like I see it, and you're an ugly mother-fucking gorilla and you curdled the cream in my coffee just looking at it."

She was in a bad mood because a money order to be put on her account for her commissary was denied at the mailroom and returned to her family. Her daughter stopped at a drug store to buy it and gave it to her grandmother to put in a letter to her. Because the money order didn't have the same name as the letter, it was rejected in the mailroom. That didn't seem right so Rachel asked to see the A.R., the rule book that they are supposed to use to run this place. It said that anyone on the visiting list can send a money order. Both her mother and daughter were on the list. She told Bessie, but instead of doing something about it, she just groused.

Rachel was becoming familiar with the A.R. Last week she had time and wanted to clean her room and was told that Saturday is cleaning day. She asked to see the AR which said "any day the inmate isn't working they can clean their room." She showed it to the C.O. who grudgingly gave her soap and disinfectant. "I can't do much about my roommate leaving her dirty clothes everywhere," she told a girl standing outside her door watching her clean, "but I do want a clean sink and I got up as many dust bunnies as I could."

Tension was constantly high among the girls that can't conform or adjust to the "prison lifestyle." When Rachel received a particularly nice card in the mail she shared it with some girls that didn't get any mail. These girls were on the verge of tears all the time and it was very contagious. When they saw the card several let loose with tears, howling, "I want to go home." Mail from the outside world and visits did a lot toward keeping Rachel in touch with family and the real world. So many girls here with long sentences do lose touch with their family and life on the outside. People have their own lives and they do get tired of having to make contact when they only get the usual requests for money in return. Frequently families think, "you were convicted, so you must be guilty. So, it's your problem you're there. Don't put it on us."

Everyone around Rachel was just sitting around waiting . . . . waiting for word from their attorney, an appeal, a board date, even mail. Frequently, someone got lucky. Funny, though, others were comfortable and seemed to like being there. No family duties or responsibilities but to do as you're told, food prepared for you, laundry done and sex when you can sneak it in. There are so many lost souls, many crazies and the C.O.s, too, have their own agenda. She tried to get along with all—listening without hearing for the most part. She's depending on D.D. Knight to get her out of here and hopefully soon, but she's not banking on it, if that makes any sense. She'll do what she has to, to make the most of her stay here, however long it may be, and maybe something positive will come of it.

For some reason, thoughts of her ex husband came to mind—and how he laughed at her when they discussed their marriage. She asked him what he was thinking when he made the marriage vows. "That is what is said in church to please the old people sitting there. No one is stupid enough to believe any of that." Then she asked him to explain "love" to her and he thought for a moment and said, "being able to tolerate someone." And as to why people got married? "To have a steady piece of ass." She doesn't think she'll ever be able to trust anyone again.

There's been a female white shirt sitting in the middle of the rec. area all day "hearing" tickets and dishing out punishments.

A dozen girls not involved are hanging around taking it all in. That is something that should be done in the privacy of an office. Here, it's open court. She even runs the sentences "consecutively or concurrently." Next she'll wear a robe.

When Rachel received a box from home she discovered it was full of clothes from her closet, sweatshirts and jeans, shoes that fit and underwear. It was so wonderful. She could only wear them evenings, weekends and for visits—but talk about a happy person. She even had her own box now to store things under the bed.

Bessie's family sent her a food box. She'd given her family a list of what she wanted and they did their best to accommodate her. It arrived weighing 62 lbs. There are restrictions on the size and weight of the box and it has to arrive between certain dates. The box was retuned. Max weight for a food box is 25 lbs. The family repackaged the box and resent it. This time it weighed 26 lbs and again it was rejected. The last date for receiving a box was nearing and Bessie was not happy.

Working in diet kitchen, Rachel heard lots of stories about who was "upstairs" and for what. She understood that Cowboy was somewhere in the building. Anyway, rumor had it that one of the girls in Jefferson smuggled a cat into her room and encouraged it to perform a sex act with the aid of tuna fish she'd bought at commissary. A few days later the girl developed a horrible rash and had to visit the hospital. Just a rumor, but this was prison.

Rae was a fast and efficient good cook in diet kitchen. She had confidence in her abilities. She always put food out for the cats. On one particular morning, she asked Connie, a girl from Karo, to help her carry a heavy bucket of just cooked oatmeal. She did. As they were setting it down, Rae "went off" for no apparent reason. The C.O. came running at the commotion and Rae screamed "she was going to dump the whole bucket of hot oatmeal on me." Passive Connie looked up surprised and the C.O shrugged her shoulders and walked away. For the rest of the shift, everyone acted like everything was okay. Rae was here for killing her husband three and a half years ago. She says he'd be alive today if her in laws had kept "that thing on the front of their face" (their nose) out of their business and hadn't "praised the Lord" so much. Maybe there was something to that, but Rae did have a problem. Similar things have happened several times in the few weeks Rachel has worked over there.

The latch on the refrigerator door was broken and it was propped shut with a chair. Brenda made a silly $450 bet with the C.O. that the bottom of the fridge wouldn't fill up with water overnight. In the morning it was seeping onto the floor, Brenda losing the bet.

"Put up or shut up," the C.O. joked with Brenda.

"But I don't have any money, Miss Tolis," whined Brenda from across the room. She stood about two feet from Rachel who always observed but rarely participated.

"Maybe she'll take trade," Rachel whispered to Brenda.

Brenda's eyes got big, and she doubled up laughing. She called "Miss Tolis, I'll be glad to pay because I don't welsh on my word, but you'll have to take trade."

"Brenda," the C.O. gasped. "You certainly don't have anything I want, so don't worry about paying. I wouldn't have paid you anyway if I'd lost."

"You mean you'd welsh?" Brenda asked. "I'm going to bring you a bible and may God bless you."

Some of the girls thrived on rumors and more often than not, started them. An older lady that spent time in the hospital told Rachel that the room with the girl who had hepatitis was not washed down after she left—she knew because she was right across the hall. Later, Rachel had occasion to talk with the girl who was assigned to wash it down and she said she did. Anyway, this girl with hepatitis ate off disposable dishes with disposable plastic flatware. Rachel fixed her food. Her laundry was packed in paper bags designed to dissolve in hot water and washed separately with special soap. Her roommate did that. So much for that rumor. Whenever Rachel saw that lady walking towards her with a glint in her eye, she knew to walk the other way as not to hear the next story.

There are many mental patients here who need specialized care, and they don't get anything but a locked door and a pill. We were never promised life to be fair. Rachel heard that there were a couple of girls here with AIDS that are in population. Since AIDS is mainly transmitted through sex, maybe they felt she won't pass it because no one is supposed to have sex with each other. A man in a nearby prison (again a rumor) passed it by spitting in an inmate's food. Since then, they take all AIDS-infected men to a place called Gastone which is probably a medical facility better able to deal with it.

A bad cold has kept Rachel from smelling it, but several girls complained for three days about the smell of gas while in their rooms at night. Said it was making them sick. Most woke up with headaches and watery eyes. Rachel felt that way every morning when she opened her eyes and realized where she was. No one wanted to hear the complaints. The smell is most intense in the rooms and is hardly noticeable in the rec. area. The next morning a dozen excited men were running through this place trying to fix a gas leak. When the heater fans came on, they said the smell got pretty intense. Within hours Rachel figured out how they fixed it. They turned off the gas and it got pretty cold. Construction workers were all over the place, scrambling up their ladders and picking up ceiling tiles and peeking underneath. They'd scratch their chins, make their "man noises" and move on. Someone had to make a lot of money on this project as unqualified workers cobbled this complex together and got away with it.

A young female C.O. caught Brenda on the toilet twice in fifteen seconds. Brenda got mad and told her to stop peeking at her. She told Brenda to button her blouse and Brenda asked why she was so concerned about her titties. After Brenda went to work, the C.O. called over to diet kitchen to verify if Brenda arrived with her blouse buttoned. Over there, the C.O. wanted to know what it was about, and Brenda was Brenda. "She's always peeking in my room, but especially when I'm on the toilet. I can tell when she's out there because the door gets hot."

Big fight in admissions next door. Must have been a good one as they took one girl out in handcuffs and the other on a stretcher. Most fights here are kid stuff, they tangle a bit and it's over with a few scratches. An hour or so later rumor spread that it wasn't a fight after all. A guard beat up a girl they claimed was trying to escape and they took her friend away. Admissions is isolated from the general population, so no one here knows the details.

Commissary sold loose tobacco and rolling papers much cheaper than packaged generic cigarettes. There was one rolling device in each building and those needing it shared. Then it went missing. There was a big search of all the rooms which turned up lots of contraband. Everyone was upset at Big Mary when it was discovered in her room. Bessie lost some food she'd sneaked from P.F.S. and let Mary know how she felt. She dropped her pants from her big butt and said, "Eat my hemorrhoid!"

Kenny got a letter and money order from her mother today that was postmarked two and a half months ago. It was accompanied by an apology from the mail room. They said they held it up because her mother wasn't on her visiting list so the money order was not acceptable. Standard procedure for that situation would be to explain the problem to the inmate, then return the money order to the sender. Her mother, however, had been on her visiting list for nearly five years. Obviously the letter and money order were lost and recently found in the mailroom.

Everyone could shop at the commissary once a week unless lack of funds or bad behavior restricted it. The state paid most inmates $12 a month and they had to buy their own soap, tampons, (if they prefer them over the frequently unavailable state pads) deodorant, tooth paste and brush, lotion, as well as pens, stamps and writing paper. Some food and snacks were available for those who had the money. The rules allow each person to possess only two combs at a time and to give, sell, lend or trade things is a ticketable offense. Yet, the commissary only sells combs by the six pack. The men's facilities had ice cream and gum and a lot of things, for some reason, forbidden to the women. One would go nuts trying to figure out the reasoning.

After about a month in this building there was finally warm water in the showers. The gauges on the boilers didn't register right and were replaced and that supposedly corrected the problem. A C.O. standing just outside the door supervising the showers was flirting with the naked girls. When a girl that had been here before saw what was happening, she told the C.O. to turn her head while she undressed. "What?" the surprised C.O. asked.

"I saw what you were doing and I get money for tricks. You don't watch me for free."

*   *   *

The first long winter gave way to spring. Warmer weather was an opportunity to spend more time outside and expand her life beyond Pierce. Rachel went to breakfast with an elderly Riverview lady, Miss Raines who usually spent her time at one card table or another. Rachel remembered seeing her in admissions in Warren East and only noticed her because of her age and ever-present cane. Dawn was breaking as they passed through the light fog that blanked this evil place. Had the fog been dense, breakfast would have been postponed until it lifted. Miss Raines walked slowly with her cane and Rachel helped her with doors and her tray. She told her she'd get her something from commissary in exchange for her help. Rachel told her she only needed her smile and thought it's a shame, but this woman probably paid for a lot of simple courtesies.

Her husband kept money on her books. The first time he visited her, he didn't have his marriage license with him so couldn't prove their relationship and they turned him away at the door. Rachel assumed he's well into his seventies as she is, and his drive was two hours. On the day she heard he was around, she went outside to see if she could spot his car. When she saw him she started waving her cane. He saw her and stopped the car, got out and waved back. She was thrilled and giggled about it hours later, even though they didn't accomplish the visit. Later she found out that Social Security learned she was incarcerated and discontinued her checks until after her release.

Many women wait months for word from their attorney about their appeals. One of them got a letter from hers, and it told her to be patient, that these things can take years. Woof! That was enough to take one's breath away. Well, at least he wrote. Rachel's doesn't write at all. "I don't have a clue what is going on with mine," she confided. "If my friends and family, who I nagged constantly to get in touch with him to find out what is going on, ever had any news they never say." She is constantly frustrated thinking about it and wonders if they know something and are not telling her. No, she doesn't let herself dwell on that possibility.

Bogus paperwork circulated that declared that everyone locked up is eligible for SSI when they leave here. Asking around Rachel discovered that anyone that was eligible for it when they got here will probably be able to get it when they leave. Eligibility is dependent on one's ability to work and their financial status. If you could hold a job before you got here, it is assumed you can work when released. Of course, there's always the very real possibility of losing one's sanity while here. Holding on is an uphill battle.

Most of the door locks functioned now—except Rachel's. She loved it. It doesn't lock—ever. She wished Kenny would stop sneaking out to get ice from the machine at night. During the day too many people constantly got ice and the machine couldn't keep up. Then someone from another building that didn't have an ice machine would come over and fill up their ice chest. There was never enough ice during the day. At night, the ice would collect. If Kenny was caught out of the room they'd fix the lock. Rachel liked the idea that in a true emergency, she could get out and maybe help others.

It's over 100—the humidity high
    The sun's on a tear—
Burned the clouds from the sky
    We need ICE

The heat in the air sears life from our skin
    The plants die back
The insects come in
    And bring lice

Gold is not riches to dried grass and fields
    Helpless and hopeless
Squeezing life from God's yields
    We feed mice

Four months without rain, just dust in the drain
    And the golden egg is sterile
Cut a deal for a drop of rain
    Roll the dice

Some days were really warm. The new buildings had no landscaping—no trees to block the heat and no flowers for mental comfort. The older buildings had huge trees, and the walk/jog track was well shaded. Some girls make the most of the sunshine, spreading a towel out to enjoy the rays. The short sleeved shirts we must wear left a "penitentiary tan." Most found the sun relaxing. Those that allowed themselves to get burned got tickets. There's no sun screen here.

Rachel tried to do some reading in the big room, but the flies were thick and buzzing, landing and biting. For some reason no one was around. They must have gone to an event at the ball field. Rachel needed the time to herself and not locked in her room in the unforgiving heat. She asked the C.O. if she knew where she could get a fly swatter. She reached behind her desk and gave it to her. Then for then for the next hour or so she committed mass murder.

Thousands and thousands of dead flies, tiny ones to those the size of butterflies littered the table tops and floor. The crowd started drifting in when she was still on her search and kill mission. Most found the sight truly disgusting—and loudly complained they couldn't walk or sit anywhere without touching the carcasses. No one made any attempt to sweep up the mess or clean the tables. They just stood, bitched and stared in horror.

Rachel thought she'd done a good job, and sacrificed her personal time to do it. She was proud of her accomplishment and it wasn't appreciated. It seems they'd prefer to have the flies alive and buzzing and biting them. Rachel didn't want any appreciation. She didn't do it for them, but for herself. She was happy. The C.O. asked everyone to clean off their tables and grudgingly they did, grousing they didn't make the mess. Three others on housekeeping detail swept the floor.

The air was thick with the hottest summer on record. The rooms were so hot and muggy the girls slept on the cooler concrete floor risking a ticket from an unsympathetic C.O. for not being in bed. The air didn't circulate even with the windows open from the top and bottom mostly because the door was closed. The only fans were out by the C.O.'s.

Kenny asked Rachel to check the back side of her ear. She'd scratched her recent surgery and it was bleeding and wondered if it was healing okay. She checked it and took the stitches out for her and assured her she had a healthy scab and no infection. She seemed to trust her judgment.

Rachel took a shower and an hour later felt like she needed another one. The fat people sweat all the time, rivers of water running down their faces, necks and into their blouses. Strangely enough no one had the body odor problems of many on the street. The black girls were very clean and were forever talking about how bad white people smell. One young black girl said she'd dated a couple of white guys, but no more—they smelled bad. Then she looked at Rachel and said, "sorry, but that's the way it is.

There was an ice machine right outside the room door. Kenny and Rachel listened to the fresh ice dropping into the bin every half hour or so. No one was around to take any because they were all locked in for the night. Wonderful cool ice just sitting there.

> We're supposed to wait till 11 am
>     To get our cup of ice
> But working hard and dripping sweat
>     We raid the stash like mice

Some of us go off to work
    And plan a lunchtime pop
We get our buckets, tubs & baskets
    And fill them to the top.

"So what we're put on ice restriction
    As long as I got mine
    I don't care about the others
I refuse to toe the line."

Mr. Wooden watches us
    Ms Follest hears the lid
We boost all the ice we want
    Just like a selfish kid

We don't share with each other
    PIERCE can go to hell
As long as I am keeping cool
    I am all—and all is well

We're here because we're greedy
    We need more than our share.
We cheat and lie and cheat and steal
    Until the cupboard's bare

We're dirty little rodents
    Scampering untamed.
It never has occurred to us
    That we should be ashamed

Kenny watched out the window in the door. She waited until the C.O. went to the bathroom, then quietly slinked out the unlocked door and filled her cup. During the day the machine is mostly empty. Too many girls and not enough time for the ice to form. She wasn't figuring on a white shirt coming in the door. Kenny got caught sneaking out of the room. It was just a matter of time. Rachel pretended to be asleep. The C.O. asked her how she got out and she just gave her some mumbo-jumbo. The C.O. had them move to a vacant room upstairs. It was vacant because the toilet didn't flush. When Rachel discovered that, she banged on the door and caught the C.O.'s attention and she came upstairs bristling. Her roommate didn't care one way or the other, but she told the C.O. we needed a bucket to flush the toilet and a can to fill it from the sink. She obliged, then said she'd just put in a work order for the lock on our door as well as this toilet.

It was so hot in that upper bunk in the upstairs, Rachel couldn't breathe. It was at least 10 degrees hotter up there. She moved her mattress down onto the floor and wet herself down as best she could. It was miserable and nearly impossible to sleep. Kenny was very sloppy and Rachel was surprised she bucket-flushed in the morning before leaving for work. Three days later, during a commotion, they snuck back down to their old room. No one noticed or said anything—even at count. Guess they just assumed it was fixed and they had permission to be there.

Then a new C.O. came on duty just as Bessie said, "What are you doing down here? They haven't fixed the lock on your door yet." Rachel didn't respond. The C.O. turned around but didn't know who said what to whom and didn't ask. Bessie had just learned that her daughter was expecting twins. She broke down and cried that she wanted to be with her family. Then hearing nearby women discuss the sound difference in wet and dry kissing, Bessie announced loudly, "the women here are all like puppies, they'll lick anything."

Two girls in a long-time "couple" relationship got into a heated argument. The night ended but the feelings continued and erupted when they saw each other the next morning. One of them took the lid from a tin can and cut the throat of her friend. Kenny said, "They're probably going to give us some kind of can-opener restriction now—maybe go around and collect all our can openers—or stop selling canned food at commissary."

Rachel's name came up for a phone call so called her parents. They didn't seem to have much to say and even hesitated about accepting the charges. Then her mom says, "We think that is a good place for you." She was so shocked and hurt and tears came to her eyes, but then thought, look what she has done to disrupt their lives—just being here. It just proves that those on the outside have bad days too. The guilt flowed through her. She knew they loved her and would do anything for her.

There were workmen all over, but none attempted to fix the door. The problem wasn't electrical. The door was hung slightly out of plumb so the deadbolt wouldn't go in the hole, but caught slightly. Nothing a file wouldn't fix. From the outside it looked locked and it registered closed on the C.O.'s desk panel. A young C.O. knocked on the door when Rachel was inside by choice. She asked her to turn the knob and try to get out. She didn't want to get moved back upstairs and she didn't want to be reprimanded for moving back downstairs without permission and she didn't want the door fixed. She smiled brightly at the C.O. and made an issue of turning the knob, then quietly let it slip back into place and yanked the door. The lock held. She pulled several times to make a point. The C.O. was satisfied and left. She felt bad deceiving someone who trusted her, but you've got to do what you've got to do.

Workman were still testing the alarm system and everyone had to leave the building while they set off smoke bombs to see if they worked. Yes, only too well. Rachel took the opportunity to walk on the track for an hour trying to clear her head.

Couldn't expect any help from the overworked D.D., the attorney who was apparently working night and day on her appeal so decided she'd try to file for Executive Clemency from the governor on her own. Had to do something. Lists for library use were long and time there limited. She'd hoped to find some kind of pattern to follow, maybe find out what points they were looking for. She was not sure where to look or what to look for. Maybe she should try to get to a social worker for advice if nothing else. The library was about the size of a small bedroom. There's no one there to advise her.

The C.O. at diet kitchen asked Rachel if she would consider working nights at diet kitchen. She hadn't a clue as to what happened there at night, but she said there would be no C.O. there to supervise. She went on to say that the job required a minimum classification. Rachel told her she was a medium and she said she would see what she could do about having that changed. That would be great, with more phone calls there would be more opportunity to badger the attorney.

After work, she kited the unit manager and told him that she'd like to accept that job at diet kitchen, but her classification prevented it. A couple of days later, he called her into to his office and told her she was borderline medium 3 and medium 2 and he couldn't see how it was possible to get that job. Time is the factor that reduces the classification while tickets boost it up. She'd never had a ticket and couldn't do anything about the time. She was a lot more interested in the reclassification than the job. A week or so later a girl working in the kitchen told her that she was being reclassified. She'd probably overheard someone talking, but Rachel knew it wasn't true.

Getting into school interested Rachel more than anything. She applied to one school but they said there wasn't any more grant money. She signed all the papers for grants for Cooper Technical Institute, a school offering classes here, and was still waiting for confirmation. It seems that the hold-up is the fact that she had over $30,000 income in the six months before getting locked up last year and that alone would disqualify her from grants. She won't be making that kind of money this year so she needed a "special circumstance" form which seemed to be an unusual happenstance here. Others have their grants okay, but hers is still lagging. She's written them four letters of inquiry and they have been ignored. One of her friends said they are probably mad at her for writing them. Finally, a family member came up with the right form and mailed it to her. They were surprised to see it at the school. Rachel was not looking forward to being at Lotusville for the time it will take to get a degree, but she would be doing something worthwhile with her time—and her state pay would go from $12 a month to $22. Finally she got a note from the school that she did qualify to attend, but they were still waiting for the grant money.

*　　*　　*

Rachel worked most every day with Autumn, a very young and pretty girl whose drug habits got her into serious problems that still gripped her. She's here for robbing a drug store to support her habit, but was caught when she fell flat on her face as she tripped going out the door. She's playful as a six year old and always lived on the surface of life. She had no apparent interest in dealing with reality or its consequences.

More food was walking out of diet kitchen than was getting eaten. With all the new C.O.'s working, the thievery was rampant. Autumn pulled up her dress as she walked up the steps to show Rachel half a barbecued chicken she had chucked in her panties. As she flattened her dress in front, she asked Rachel if it was obvious. Autumn is a very slim girl and she told her the truth. "You'd better go straight to your room when you get to Pierce because half the place will try to get a jump when they see you."

"Walk in front of me," she pleaded. The funny thing was, Autumn was a vegetarian and didn't even have a home for the chicken. She stole it because everyone else was stealing. Who she gave this pussy-flavored barbecue to, who knows, but she later complained the sauce burned her snatch. "If you ever want any chicken, I'll be glad to get it out for you," she offered. Knowing how it traveled, Rachel declined. She ate all she wanted while she was working and did not find a need for carry out.

Others were not as successful. Rae stored stolen food from diet kitchen by the garbage dumpster just outside the hospital with the hope of picking it up after her shift. On one particular day, she stashed an entire picnic, loaves of bread, jelly, salad, a pound of butter and lots of meat in the little bundles. She carried out her treasure with the pretense of taking out the trash. There was a guard watching the dumpster with binoculars and she may soon be working in the laundry instead of cooking when she gets out of max.

A new C.O. was just ushered out. He was giving one stick of gum for head—unlike Uncle Festus who had to give a whole pack. The girls don't do it for gum. They don't do it for sex. They just had a continuing need to break the law, a need to defy authority.

Danita had a big crowd around her and they were all discussing their cases. Rachel had to stroll over there to see what was going on. Danita had a deck of cards spread out on the table acting like a fortune teller, and advising them how much more time they will have to spend here. The girl was always talking nonsense and loved attention so this didn't surprise her.

While a girl laid on the floor convulsing in the heat, a male voice seemed to come from the girl's mouth, speaking of possession of her soul. Everyone stared at the poor girl, fascinated. Brenda Slims lurked nearby and it wouldn't have surprised anyone who knows her that the voice came from her. All attention was on the convulsing girl, not Brenda. She's such a kid! The C.O. tried to clear the area explaining it as a seizure and asked that no one consider any other thoughts or foolishness. Lots of superstition and voodoo thinking. Of course everyone stared and preferred thinking she was devil possessed. A bible thumper said that the Lord punished her for her sex habits. Then the C.O. watching the seizure keeled over. Someone said she had a heart attack.

A lot of seizures happened here. Rachel saw it a couple times a day and suspected that the cause was the medication. Everyone, regardless of the prescription they used on the street, got the same generic medications. That just didn't work for everyone.

Miss Raines grabbed Rachel's arm saying, "Let's have a card game." They walked over to where big Bessie was sitting by herself reading her bible. Danita talked constantly about nothing and was always ready for a card game solely to have an audience for her chatter. "Danita," Miss Raines ordered. "Sit down here for some spades."

"Girrrl, stop!" Danita sang delightedly in her falsetto voice.

Miss Raines split the deck in two then spliced them together, but not in the neat fashion of most dealers. They fell in two loose casual piles with the corners barely mingling. "Cut them thin so I can win," she offered the deck to Danita.

"Miss Raines, you ain't got nothin' comin'. Danita laughed and cut.

The cards were dealt and bid. Bessie lead and he came out with three consecutive aces.

"I'm scaaaared of you," sang Danita with the same high pitch. Danita is close to six feet and well over 300 lbs. Her eyes are pushed shut by her full cheeks.

"I thought you knew." replied Bessie confidently, then noted her roommate walking by. Bessie can watch everything in the room as well as her hand. "Look at Skyla swishing like she was on the 'ho stroll. Hey Skyla, you get you some business!"

"Someone is going to find you out behind a building one of these days, tramp," she chuckled. "Stinking!" she added over her shoulder, not missing a step.

"Helloo" gushed Danita.

Bessie led a king but Miss Raines trumped it. "You ain't for the right thing," she pouted.

"Shuuuut up," sang Danita, dragging her vowels gleefully.

"Someone stole a letter out of my bag the other day," Miss Raines said seriously. "If I would have seen who it was messing with my stuff, I would have gone over to the coffee pot, filled up a glass with hot water and throw'd it in her face." She then led out a king which Rachel trumped.

"Oooh, I've got no understanding," squealed Danita. "I don't have nair a spade."

Miss Raines trumped my next lead. "You kill my cat, I kill our dog," she chuckled.

"That'll work," squeaked Danita. Her murder charge was recently reduced to voluntary man slaughter.

Bessie led her two jokers after regaining the lead. "That's the way it's laying." she said, then threw out the six of spades.

"Just look at the nice hair on my legs." Danita picked up her leg and stretched it out displaying and pressing down on the hairs with her hands. "I brush them every night," she offered smiling.

Miss Raines had the deuce that took the book, but Bessie reached for it. "That's my two" claimed Bessie.

"I didn't come here deaf, dumb and lead by a German shepherd dog. Get your hands off those cards. They'll bite you," warned Miss Raines.

"Ooo giirrrl, you're tripping out," sang Danita.

"Don't treat me like I've got a tail between my legs," Bessie grouched. "Because I don't."

"You're 14 carat crazy," Miss Raines commented rather matter of factly. "You're not here for shooting a gun either—more like welfare fraud," Miss Raines insulted. She rose slowly, painfully from her chair with the help of her cane. "That's it and that's all! Period! Dot," and limped off with arrogance and pride.

Bessie called out "I'm not the one," but declined further agitation out of respect. Then under her breath hissed. "I thought you knew!"

*   *   *

A girl here who molested her two kids and, broke the pelvis on one of them sidled over to the table where Bessie and crew had been playing cards. She was such a thief no one wanted her around. Her former roommate said she'd squeezed all her toothpaste into a plastic bag and left her an empty tube. Now she complained of chest pains and, light headedness. Said the room was swimming. Bessie told the C.O. and she said she'd have to be patient, that she was busy. An hour later, they took the girl out on a gurney. Three days later rumor was they flew her by helicopter to I.S.U. hospital with a heart attack. Lots of serious illness here—mental and physical and most are very young. Rachel wasn't aware of her past history, but learned that she'd had a hysterectomy a few months back at I.S.U. hospital. Once returned to population, her stitches repeatedly popped and left her tummy gaping. She had to go back and be re-stitched each time. Later, she was caught removing her own stitches and prying herself apart. Guess she had a need for attention.

The fire alarm went off after supper. Most grabbed coats and walked outside. The C.O's panicked and got on the phone so it most likely wasn't a scheduled alarm. She left the building, leaving several girls banging on their door, still locked in their rooms.

Kimalee spent the day crying. She'd just received notice that her R.N. license was being revoked. This was her second conviction resulting from a morphine addiction. "Didn't they receive my letter asking them to suspend my license rather than pull it?" she sobbed. She didn't seem to understand that using the morphine prescribed for her patients was truly immoral, that being a drug addict RN put all her patients at risk. To her, it's all about Kim, and nothing to do with her selfish behavior. Her 3 ½ year old visited her and asked why she wasn't home. She told the baby, "When children are bad, they get spanked. Bad adults go to jail." With her first offense, she did her time in a drug rehab-hospital and her license was only suspended. She wasn't so lucky this time. Rachel has to stop judging these girls, but she's getting really tired of it.

Kim worked with Rachel in diet kitchen and became quite attached to the cats that hung around for a handout. She kited the superintendent, asking if her family could pick up the blue-eyed white one and take it home on their next visit. The request was never answered, but the C.O. who worked the kitchen told her that the cats were state property and the humane society routinely comes out and gathers up as many as they can and puts them up for adoption.

The girlfriend of Rachel's roommate, was "flopped" by the board and was told they'd review her in six months. The reason, she was told, was because of her "drug problems." Being here for robbery and never having a drug problem, she protested but was ignored. She had an inmate friend who worked in the records office and had her check her file. Sure enough there was a drug problem on it with details. She contacted her lawyer who had her original records verified by county officials and had the administration at Lotusville clean up the records so she did expect to leave here in a few months. She suspected that the additions were made to her file after she was involved in a "sit in" a couple years ago when a male officer beat up an inmate.

Girls were decorating this place for Christmas, but the C.O. told them they were wasting their time, that Santa wasn't coming because they'd been bad. They kept decorating, and Santa was born at a nearby table, courtesy of scraps of paper and a lot of creative talent. It made everyone feel good to watch it happen. A couple of the girls received Christmas plants from home and they set them out for all to enjoy. Give them credit for trying to make this a cheerful place.

Many girls observe Ramadan which means they aren't supposed to eat during the day. There are no accommodations for them to eat in the evening so these girls have to buy commissary so they can eat after dark. At P.F.S. all year round, everyone is given the same food. Those inmates that don't eat pork products are still served it and it is up to them whether or not they consume it. Most sneak it off to an eager friend, hoping they don't get caught "passing contraband."

A girl left here today that's been here over a decade. She'd lost track of the state clothes that were issued her years ago and they told her to "come up with them now or stay here until you do." She finally agreed to pay them for anything that was missing. She left. They have to show they are the boss right to the end. Rachel could never wear the shoes issued her so decided to turn them in right then and there.

There had been rumor for some time that this whole place was under investigation by the Feds, that many heads would roll this year along with that of the warden. Also, the woman who ran the commissary was under scrutiny for theft. She did it as a part-time job as she was a policewoman in a nearby town. A couple weeks later Rachel heard that the warden retired amid rumors of embezzlement and scandal. Friends and family sent her newspaper clippings from their local newspaper about it. Looks like she cut a deal from what was in the paper. Haven't a clue what is true. So many stories. Heard one about one of the wardens here years ago that took a "chosen few" lifers into Springfield on weekends and pimped them out, after they had hysterectomies. These stories came from inmates that knew the girls involved. Rachel didn't know what came out of the hearings about the scandal here because being an inmate, Rachel had only newspaper clippings that were mailed to her, and is fair to assume that some of them were probably stopped in the mailroom. They censored all the incoming mail.

Big Mary was on her period again, having stained four dresses and a new chair. She knew to bring a towel with her to sit on, then wear it over the back of her dress after it was stained but somehow forgot the pad. Mary didn't have any friends or relatives on the outside that cared enough about her comfort to send her a box of casual clothes. She was always in State issue. The C.O. told Mary to take a shower and minutes later, she came to the door naked and wet announcing to us all that she didn't like a dirty shower, that the floor was so funky her feet were sticking to it. No one else had a problem so, it must have been her feet.

Now that Mary was cleaned up, she got into her roommate's things and came out of her room flipping earrings and sporting makeup. She said she was going to rec. and get herself a. Rachel told her she needed a license for that. "For what?" she challenged.

"Duck hunting," she told her. Duck is kind of a slang term for a girlfriend's girl—a temporary soul mate.

There was a cat that hung out near diet kitchen that looked a lot like Mary. They had the same tortoise-shell hair color and she was just as disheveled and matted. When the cat's hind leg scratched itself, the toes filled up with a wad of fur. Haven't checked Mary's feet.

Kenny came back from the Board with a long face, them telling her she hasn't done enough time yet. "Come back in another year." Eighteen months ago she was "flopped" for the first time. Since then she was involved in a "sit-in" at the ball field when a guard beat a girl and put her in the hospital. She suspected that was the reason the board didn't approve her release but they didn't say. Someone took pictures of everyone sitting there. When Rachel realized they can keep her here 15 years if they want to, her stomach contents rose up into her mouth.

A lady she'd never seen before came in after supper to quell fears of problems and imminent disasters in the building predicted by Jean Dixon. She explained that Lotusville switches its water supply every winter from creek water to well water. That accounts for the difference in taste and smell. As for the gas leaks, a major gas problem was found and the offending line was turned off, the yard is trenched up, the line will be rerouted and be back in service in about a week. She explained that the reason there is no hot water in the showers is because the gauges on the boilers weren't registering the temperatures correctly. Meanwhile, the cooks have no gas to heat to heat and prepare food, so everyone was served a lot of sandwiches. Good thing Rachel worked in the kitchen and could select her own food.

Alone in her room she had the privacy to express herself in writing letters without someone coming over to talk, play cards or having to listen to the sad stories. Out there she had a shell around her and kept everything to herself. She had to. Whenever she thought of being away like she was with no control over her life and no idea when she would be back with those she loved, she just cried at the hopelessness of it all. She needed the time to relax her mind and feel human—not the robot she had to be out there.

A young nine-week pregnant girl was taken to the hospital in pain, diagnosed with a cyst on her ovary and returned. After dinner she threw up and became dizzy in the bathroom. She just laid on the floor crying that she didn't want to lose her baby. They took her back to the hospital.

The C.O. at diet kitchen insisted everyone wear a slip and had everyone called to her desk one at a time to check. The girls in the kitchen furiously borrowed slips from those already checked. It was funny to watch. The C.O. must have known what was going on because she announced she's checking for bras tomorrow. That would be even funnier but it never happened.

Overnight what was a minor water drip from the ceiling at diet kitchen for a couple of weeks, became a major flood. The cooks had been complaining about it dripping into the food for some time, but were told not to worry about it. It seems a waste water pipe from upstairs in the hospital rotted through and everyone's been eating it in their food.

A different girl moved in next door in Pierce. She was supposedly gay and a friend of Rachel's roommate. She was here for biting off her son's dick. Girls talked about it as if discussing a sporting event.

One of the male C.O's that was suspended for messing with the girls came back and everyone seemed glad to see him. They all crowded around him, dogs after his bone. He sat around talking with a half dozen of them for some time. Ginger, the retarded prostitute, who shot a client through the door, wore her heart on her sleeve for this man and was really upset because she wasn't included in the conversation. Becoming more and more impatient with him, she demanded loudly within earshot of other C.O.s "Why do you let these other girls suck you off for gum and you can't even say 'hello' to me?" If there was any possible way this black man could have blushed, he would have glowed.

But Ginger didn't let it go. She paced around and around telling everyone his purpose in coming back to work was to distribute gum in the hospital. All were surprised someone didn't shut her up and lock her down. Maybe she was looking forward to being carted off to some private time with him there. Anyway, she was probably just spouting the truth.

One of the new boilers in the building blew up, but the alarms were shut off at the time so there was no panic. The big problem from our point of view was that once again we didn't have any hot water for showers.

Letters from home were so important. Rachel was fortunate that family and friends wrote. She really appreciated all the attention from Eric but was afraid to fantasize about anything further. She was just glad that he wasn't totally turned off by her letters that detailed her days. They all sent a lot of newspaper clippings that she found interesting and it was one way to keep in touch with the outside world. She went to pick up her mail the other morning and the C.O. was reading a People Magazine someone sent her. Hmm! Was she reading about movie stars? No! The crossword puzzle? No! She was perusing the last page of "personals" titled "buy a friend." You'd think she got enough of freaks here.

One night when Rachel went to her room, Kenny was sitting on the edge of her bed with a grouchy face. Said she didn't feel good. The next day at count she didn't report back to her room. "She's at the hospital," the C.O. told her. "They took her there from work." She was back at dinner time, diagnosed by Dr. Ovens as suffering from malnutrition. He told her to start eating or he'd put her in the hospital and make sure she ate. She's thin but a long way from emaciated. She wouldn't be surprised if his diagnosis is wrong. This all started after she went to the board and they gave her another year. She still hasn't told her mother she's not coming home. She may be getting an ulcer.

Rachel took shorthand in high school. Her in-laws thought it would be a good time for her to brush up on her skills. They mailed her two or three pages out of a Gregg book every week. That obligated her to practice and she spent hours on it. Something constructive to put her mind to. Whatever use it could ever be was a mystery, but it was just another thing she could learn. She was out at a table practicing when a girl she'd never met leaned over her shoulder and was reading her work as if it was a regular book. She told Rachel she took a class in it here and would lend her advanced book when she thought she was ready for it. She seemed like a nice girl. After she walked away, another girl came over and told Rachel that the girl was there because she knifed and killed a "john" for wanting to "go twice" when he'd only paid for "a once." She had the same sentence as Rachel but does not have actual time. That means the Judge can bring her home any time he wants, not that he will.

Rachel got into a spades game with a new partner, transferred in from another building, who was about 20-25 years old and from Riverview. She asked to get together on the walk/jog, that she'd like to talk with her. She said she would. It seems she heard of a girl named Bethany in Harding who also knew Bruce Muley. She said she'd have Bethany meet them on the walk-jog.

Bessie had been having a rough time. She didn't receive much news from home and those close to her suspected her teenage boy got into some trouble. She worried about her 20 year old daughter who was responsible for him and was now expecting. Bessie was always crying out to someone, saying, "I've got to go home to my kids," she moaned. Someone who'd had enough of the bellyaching responded, "You don't have to do anything but stay black and die." She'd been flying off the handle at the least little thing, and if she didn't watch herself she would end up at the hospital. She talked about hoo doo, voo doo, evil spirits, had her cards, palms, and her head bumps read by Danita. Life was all about Bessie and had nothing to do with anything else. Every time she saw the Coombs County van drive up—about twice a week—she was sure they were coming for her. For the most part they just dropped off more girls for admissions.

A girl from a town in Karo County was assigned to loading dishes into the washer at diet kitchen. It wasn't long before she started throwing them around. The C.O. asked her what was wrong and she cried that she hated the dishes. The C.O. promised, with a friendly smile, to put her on pots and pans the next day. That's real work so she quickly begged off on that. So many of the Karo girls are screwy. You see the silly antics and you ask, "Are you from Karo?" They answer "yes, how did you know?"

One girl was crying to another that she wanted to get out of a lesbian relationship. "I know it's against God and it's the Devil pulling me. I certainly wouldn't continue this lifestyle on the street. I'd be embarrassed. What I really want from her is friendship, but we have what she wants. I don't know how to get out of it without both of us getting hurt."

One night we had "steak" for dinner. It was a skinny three inch square of "something." Rachel was at diet kitchen and asked the C.O. about it. She said "They didn't send enough meat." Earlier in the week the menu read "roast beef." There were two paper-thin slices—hardly a taste. Again, the response, "They didn't send enough meat." A lot of the food that is donated to this facility never reaches inmates plates. Most would bet that the C.O.s had plenty on the table at the C.O. dining hall and at home. Rachel took a separate plate and loaded it 4" high with salad. A male C.O. stopped her and asked if she ate there or worked there. "Both" she responded and took a seat.

Then he questioned her C.O. and she told him she did more than her share. "Of which," he asked her.

"Both," she told him. He wanted to write her a ticket for eating too much salad. Is that stealing state property?

Bessie came back from diet kitchen toting a bag of tuna salad. She was gloating over getting it out but at the same time bitching, "I had three big jars of salad, bags of dill pickles, slices of pork and crackers. When I went back to get it, it was gone. Those bitches want me to pack it up, then they steal it. I do all the work and they do the gettin' down." She did make use of the days she worked there.

On the rare occasions there were real pork chops the girls stole all they could get. On those days here was always a search for contraband before they left. In the dressing room, the girls were packing their baggies full and tucking them down their pants and laughed, sure their panties wouldn't be searched. They play, humping each other with the new bulges at their crotch. Pockets are searched and depending on the C.O. sometimes a bra. One girl made herself some French toast to smuggle out, but the syrup got loose and gummed up her bra and slip. That day, all the food walked out.

Bessie sat around, complained and expected someone to tell her she could go home. Rachel asked a young girl who was always bouncing around singing and was in the church choir, to push Bessie into becoming part of it. She made an effort and it seemed to be working. Bessie felt so good when she came back from church, it was obvious she got a lot from singing for the Lord on Sunday and also the two practices a week. She truly had a beautiful voice. Rachel told her the Lord sent her here to inspire someone with her voice and he wasn't going to let her leave until she had.

Rachel went out of her way to cover up the few illegal things she did so as to not to get a ticket. A ticket is the administration's way of controlling behaviors. She didn't want them taking her privileges away, especially commissary restrictions or her 10 minute collect monthly phone call. It could include early beds even for minor violations like stepping on the grass or doing laundry at an unapproved time. Major violations like speaking disrespectfully to a C.O, running, touching another inmate, or threatening or fighting which can result in being caged without sanitary facilities for a number of weeks. As tickets accumulate you not only lose privileges, but classifications change and girls are moved to different housing.

One morning before dawn the C.O. woke up Rachel and Kenny to tell them to get dressed and go to the hearing office for tickets. Rachel had no knowledge of a ticket. About twenty girls were there, including Big Mary who had five tickets, mostly for her hygiene habits. Kenny had two tickets, one for having an empty pill container. Once pills were used up, one must throw the bottle away. She didn't. Her other ticket was for all the boxes of books and clothing she'd accumulated over the years. Rachel's turn. She's charged with aiding and abetting. She told them that she neither helped nor encouraged her to have all that stuff, that it frequently got in her way when she was trying to clean the room. They told her she wasn't being charged with helping and encouraging, but aiding and abetting. She politely asked if they had a dictionary that would help her understand the charge against her. Someone found one and she was relieved to find the words were pretty much interchangeable. She was found not guilty. Kenny, however, had her old magazines confiscated and was told she'd get another ticket for stealing them. She had to send a lot of her stuff home.

A few days later, Kenny seeked out and found the C.O. that was on duty to supervise the cleanup of the attic in Garfield Cottage several years ago, where she got hold of the *Spot* Magazine she'd shown her. The C.O. told her, "Yes, I remember that magazine. There were three of them. We were cleaning out the attic of Garfield Cottage and they were to be thrown out. The inmate girls helping with the project asked to keep the magazines and I told them yes." Kenny told the C.O. that they were confiscated during a recent search and she was given a ticket for theft and contraband. "They are neither stolen or contraband. I will be your witness if you need one. Captain James was there too. I hope you get them back."

The mail brought an unexpected letter. Rachel didn't realize who it was from until she had read it a couple of times. Mattie from County, convicted of killing her husband was now in admissions. No one was allowed to talk to anyone from another building, but Rachel felt she had to talk with her. Mattie detailed her case in the letter, and it was Bruce Muley who testified he eye-witnessed her brother and another guy kill her husband, which she claimed never happened. She said that in befriending her he laughed as he told her about a girl he'd set up by robbing a drug house, taking the drugs to her house, then got a reward from a group (maybe TIP—but there are several of them) for turning in a drug dealer or any kind of criminal. In County, she didn't know Rachel was that person but her name was mentioned in her trial. She admitted in the letter that her husband was no good and beat her a lot and she was glad he was dead but didn't have her brother do it. She said that she thinks her attitude went a long way toward her conviction. She told them that it was about time someone gave him his due.

Here Rachel was, trying to write a clemency to the governor, being totally ignored by her attorney with the appeal, and now she had this information from Mattie that someone should find useful in getting her out of here. New evidence? She wanted to talk with Mattie, and after waiting on a list for the social worker for over a week, she was finally called. The social worker said that there was no way she could talk with Mattie, that she should write to her attorney and let him do the talking. Rachel asked her if she could talk to Mattie and write down what she said. She told Rachel that she had lots of evidence in the letter, that she couldn't talk to anyone in admissions, that they were isolated. Rachel wrote D.D. Knight again and explained the letter she got from Mattie, copying it verbatim hoping he could find something in it to help her case. She didn't want to send him the letter because he'd lose it, like so much of the other things pertinent to her case. She asked him to come down here or send someone to talk with Mattie. Then she sent the letter to a family member to have it Xeroxed and a copy sent to D.D. Knight.

She wrote Mattie back and told her we had to talk, but until she was out of admissions that wouldn't be possible and made arrangements to walk the track most every day in hopes that once she was assigned to her new building she could find Rachel out there. With the two thousand plus girls here, what was the chance that Mattie and Rachel were the only two put here by Bruce Muley? What about this Bethany person in Harding? We had to work together, ask around and find out.

Deb (they shared lawyer D.D. Knight) from admissions stopped by to talk. Said her boyfriend just hired another one for her, and "this one doesn't have dog dick breath."

*     *     *

The diet kitchen C.O. dropped her keys in front of Rachel. "You're going home," she said. "You're going home," she repeated. "That's what it means when you drop your keys in front of someone like that." Rachel won't count on it but it did bring a smile to her face. So much silly superstition here. But the thought was a good one.

After the special dieters left, Rachel walked into the dining room to wipe down the tables. There was an elderly lady still there, sitting by herself and having quite a conversation. She's been known to wander off on a nice day. Rachel didn't know where she belonged. She said something about watching someone sell their body to a space boy. "One of these days, they're going to come back over and get her." About that time, a social worker came to get her.

"Come on, Gracie, we're moving you upstairs to the hospital." Rachel found out later that when she was convicted her son shot the judge and her daughter shot the lawyer, so funny things might run in her family. Couldn't find out if she was crazy before she got here or if this place did her in.

Diet kitchen was in the basement of the "hospital" and the word was used very loosely. There's a dentist office directly above. Whenever anyone were to run water or flushed a toilet upstairs, the pipes would vibrate and all this white dust would drift down over everything. It is a constant mess to clean. Looking closely, Rachel saw a fine powder full of little straight white fibers which she suspected was asbestos. One day Rachel jumped up on a table and broke a tiny sample off a pipe and put it in her pocket. If she were searched leaving, it could pass as lint. Then she mailed it to someone she knew could have it analyzed. A week later, she sent another sample, just in case the first one didn't get through.

Everyone was usually searched leaving diet kitchen after their shift. With some C.O's it's more thorough than others. There was a tall chubby, loud-mouthed, know-everything young C.O. that worked occasionally in admissions but mostly upstairs in the hospital. His chief duty seemed to be playing cards and whatever with inmates who are locked in all day. At the end of shift, this new male C.O. voluntarily came down to assist with the searches. He must have been intrigued at stories of Miss Tolis' daily searches of her employees, patting them down and having them drop their panties. He had started doing searches of admissions girls who were hospital sleep-ins and was getting away with it. Then he tried it in diet kitchen and Miss Tolis was surprised to see him show up. He acted with such authority she just sat at her desk and let him have at it. The girls refused to let him touch them using a variety of reasons. They stood en masse cussing him with rare and entertaining phrases. He threatened to lock everyone up for disrespect, which encouraged the girls further. Miss Tolis supported neither side, just sat at her desk afraid to side with the girls, while knowing he was wrong. There will be many kite complaints on both of them within a half hour, but would the girls' take on what happened be believed over the C.O.s? Several of the girls went back to their buildings and filled out kites of complaint. Two others told their C.O., Miss Hunter, about what happened. She's a loud and opinionated elderly woman who had the girls detail their "adventure" on paper. Then she filed all this in a complaint. He hasn't been back to diet kitchen since.

\*     \*     \*

I saw your big titties in the shower last night," Bessie informed a girl new to Pierce, "and your nipples were this long." Bessie held a couple inches between thumb and forefinger.

"What you looking at me for?" The girl questioned, laughing.

"Because I'm going to be your pimp." Bessie was matter of fact.

"I've never had a pimp," the girl said.

"Well, you got one now!" Bessie rolled around in her seat as only a big flexible woman can do.

A little later, Bessie had a fall. She was shuffling across the floor in her house slippers and hit a wet spot. Her feet stopped abruptly while her 300 lbs kept going. When she yelled, Danita commented that it was the sound of the devil laughing. Miss Raines said she hoped she wasn't hurt but wouldn't know for a month because it was like landing on an innerspring mattress. Such sympathy!

\*     \*     \*

Rachel watched a pickup truck cruising around and saw two male C.O.s get out and out, walk around. One of them had a long stick with something hanging on the end, but they were too far away for her to see much. She watched as she walked toward them and discovered they were catching cats. There was a noose at the end of their stick. They'd catch a cat, swing it around and slap it to the ground a few times, then toss the carcass into the back of the truck. The next day at diet kitchen she noticed a trap outside the window. One of the cooks went out the window and sprung the trap. She did this for several days, until we were learned that an excursion out the window would bring an "escape charge" that would add two years to a sentence.

The guards continued to wage war against cats. One of the goofier ones pounded on the window at diet kitchen demanding fish to bait their trap. "Go to hell," called the cook. "You're only going to kill them."

"So what," he answered with a leer. Bang, bang on the window again. He caught Rachel's eye and demanded a couple pieces of fish. "We're told no food leaves the kitchen," she called back.

Pissed, he hopped out of the window well and walked around and in the door. Tramping over to the cook, he demanded fish pieces she was cooking up. "You're not getting anything here," she snapped.

"She won't give me any fish for the trap," he whined to the C.O. sitting at her desk in the kitchen. "I have to catch those cats."

With her C.O. leaning over her shoulder, the cook grudgingly gave him a piece of fish.

The next morning, there was a cat in the trap when Rachel got to work at 7am. Lisha was in a panic as she needed two more inches of arm to release the door with the broom handle. Sarah refused to help as did Brenda. Lisha hated cats, but loved to defy authority. She sneaked out the back window and around to open the door. The frightened cat "grew" in the cage as it stretched up on its legs and hissed but wouldn't come out. Lisha backed off and came back inside and had just settled her 80 lb. frame into a chair as the C.O. came in. She glanced up at the open window and smiled." Obviously, the C.O. didn't want to come into the room until she knew she wouldn't see anything she shouldn't. And these girls think they are so slick. Let's get to work, Lisha," she suggested.

"I just sat down for a cigarette," Lisha replied casually.

Breakfast out of the way, Lisha was still tormented thinking about the caged cat and tried to encourage it to get out. No luck. Then when we were all out of the room eating lunch, Lisha tossed a glass of water at it and the cat dashed out. We were surprised no guard had shown up by then, but it was a weekend.

It was only a short time later when the guard did show up to check the trap. "Damned cat's smart," he mumbled as he dropped poison into the water dish. "It gets the food out of the trap without springing it."

Sadly it wasn't long before there were very few cats. This place was overrun with skunks, and they set out to kill the cats. Rachel could only think of the police arresting her because she was easier than catching the real villain.

The men were still on their cat hunt, gathering up the rest of them. "We're taking them to the vet to check them for rabies," he lied, then we're going to bring them back."

"You're just killing them, aren't you." Brenda accused. The story circulated that a C.O. or a nurse, depending on who told the story, was bitten by a cat. If they didn't find the cat, a pregnant calico, in three days, the person was going to have to have a series of painful shots. Probably more lies to cover the killings.

*    *    *

Workers come and go at diet kitchen. Brenda and Rachel stay. There are worse jobs. They had a big "to do" upstairs. They had to clear corridors to move a very large and violent woman from one place to another. Rachel learned that there are bed-ridden women up there with cancer, some have hepatitis and three dying of AIDS and several that are having problems with their pregnancies. One of them told her not to leave her Ensure on the tray because someone would steal it before she could get to it. She's right. The girls fight over those cans that are only rationed to those confined and on special diets.

Rachael finally met up with Bethany in Harding. She was a little girl, maybe in her twenties. She said she thought she was friends with Lola, Bruce Muley's girlfriend, but she turned on her and she ended up here. Rachel asked her what her case was and she got nervous, maybe embarrassed talking to her about it. She didn't detail anything, only said that "they were a bad duo." Rachel mentioned that they did her wrong and also her friend Mattie, who was here on a separate case. Actually, Rachel hadn't met up with Mattie since their days in County, but figured she might be more open to talking if she thought others here would understand her situation. She told her that they planned to put their cases right back on him once they were out and would she want to join them? She looked at Rachel like she was nuts. "Don't you know how dangerous they are? You must be crazy. I get out in six months and never want to see them or this place again. No, you leave me out of whatever crazy thing you do. You know he'll kill you if he finds out. I have kids! No! Forget me! Forget you know me." She ranted on for another few minutes then stalked off. Rachel never saw her again.

# LOLA AND BRUCE

Back in Riverview, Lola has a wannabe john that wants unusual play and has no cash, only a credit card. He's been bothering her as well as a couple of her "street friends" for a while now. At first he was a moment of entertainment, something the girls could giggle over, but they were out there to make money and after a few times, they realized he was only wasting their time. Bruce told her he'd take care of it, that he'd be hanging close tonight.

It was a nice breezy evening and Lola satisfied four clients, three of them regulars the first hour she was out there. She hadn't seen Bruce, but assumed he was nearby. Things were quiet for a while, then she saw the old car cruising and slowing. "Jesus, Bruce, where are you."

Lola walked over to the car and opened the door. "Hi Stan, what's up?"

"Same as before. $200 for you and I spring for the room. Two hours of your time and it's my equipment."

"My husband says I shouldn't do it without him. Do you have the cash?"

"Okay, I'll do you both. Let's go get him," he said with a gap-toothed smile.

"I think he just wants to watch, not to be part of it." She backed away from the car and saw movement to the side. Bruce was here and loping toward them. "He's right here, and you can save money on the room. We live right around the corner. You have the $200?"

"I've got a credit card. You do take MasterCard?"

"Stan, you know I do a cash business. We've talked about it. Go up to the bank machine and get cash."

Bruce caught the last bit of conversation and spoke up quickly. "Sure, we take MasterCard." He slipped into the front seat of Stan's car. "We can go to our house now and set things up. Lola still has some work to do. Stan looked a little surprised to find himself sitting next to Bruce.

Lola spotted a customer and slowly walked to his car. A little conversation and she got in and they drove off.

Bruce gave Stan directions to his house and in less than five minutes they were walking into the front room. "Have a seat, Stan, Lola will be here in an hour or so. Have to keep her working, you know."

Stan chuckled nervously. He was anxious to get on with his own work. He wasn't sure about this husband stuff, but the guy seemed nice enough.

"Turn on the TV, get comfortable. Wanna beer?" Stan picked up the remote and set it down. He didn't want TV. Bruce plucked two long necks from the fridge and handed one to Stan. then picked up the remote and turned on a news show, but made a point of keeping the volume low. "Got kids sleeping upstairs," he offered.

Lola opened the door less than an hour later. Stan greeted her with a brilliant goofy smile, like she was a goddess. "I'm going up and take a bath." She disappeared.

"Well, Stan, looks like it's time to get your party going. What say we go downstairs and set things up. It will be more private down there in case the kids wake up. He got up and Stan followed him through the door and down the steps. When Bruce flipped on the light, Stan stopped. It was an old cluttered, dirty basement. It just wouldn't do. "Not here . . ." he started, but his voice was silenced by a karate chop to the side of his head. Bruce caught him as he staggered and kicked out his knee. This time he let him fall. Stan's ribs cracked as he jumped on his chest. A whoosh of air shot from him along with a strange wet noise. A quick twist of his head and Bruce heard the neck crack. Bruce got a rope, then propped and tied him to a support post. The arm bones had to be broken to tie him tight enough to keep him upright. Bruce kicked his torso and chest repeatedly. "Got to stay in shape" he told himself. Stan's eyes were staring lifelessly and it was giving Bruce the creeps, so reared back with a mighty thrust and put two fingers directly into his eye sockets.

Lola came downstairs, looked around and shrugged as Bruce landed two bare knuckle punches to Stan's jaw. "Looks like you had a good time."

"Oh yeah! I take MasterCard, but don't think he'll be paying it." Bruce laughed. "Get me some trash bags. I'll get his wallet and keys and get him out of here. You clean up the mess."

Lola returned with the bags and filled a bucket with water. She didn't seem to think it was an unusual way to spend an evening. She didn't question Bruce, but watched as he folded Stan into a heavy-duty black bag with a brown lining. Once in, he secured Stan's belt around the bag and hauled it up the steps on his back. She felt a cool draft when he opened the door and heard the trunk of Stan's car slam shut. She bagged the bloody ropes and washed the post and floor, tossing the rags into her washing machine.

"Well, honey, I took out the garbage," Bruce teased in falsetto.

Lola was tired and she supposed Bruce was as well. It'd been a long day. The kids were still asleep and there'd be a couple more hours before she'd' have to get them up for school. The two of them would get a little rest before then.

Lola woke before Bruce. She fed the kids and got them off to school, then took the twins to Head Start. Bruce was still asleep when she got home so she quietly cleaned up the kitchen. She was still dragging and would have liked a couple more hours of sleep but it wasn't to be.

Bruce appeared in the doorway, energized. He bent over and touched his toes. "Got lots of stuff to take care of today so let's get an early start. Pack us a lunch and we'll have a picnic."

No, she wasn't going to ask. Just do.

"We'll hit the road early. I have the credit cards and keys. The garbage has to go before it stinks. Walk around the house. Make sure we have everything. Nothing in the basement either. Scatter things around so it doesn't look freshly cleaned." She was going to do that last night but everything was still wet. It'd be dry now.

Within an hour they were on I-90 heading east. Lola was sleepy and nodded off. Just inside the Pennsylvania line, Bruce pulled off at a rest stop. It was a chilly morning, but they had their picnic. Lola was bagging their waste when

Bruce commented he thought they'd driven just about far enough. Lola just nodded. Bruce always had a good plan. So far, though, she'd rather be home in bed. Soon they were off the highway again.

Bruce drove off an exit and onto a woodsy side road, then turned again onto an unpaved road. A half mile or so later, he stopped the car and looked around. He listened. Everything was quiet. They were in the middle of a deep woods. Perfect! He got out, stretched, did a few calisthenics, took a leak, looked around again and opened the trunk. Lola watched as he quickly hiked the big bag onto his shoulder and disappeared into an opening in the trees. She rolled down the window and listened to all the birds and bugs singing from the trees, then got out and walked around. It felt so good to stretch her legs, but she was so tired she soon got back inside. Twenty minutes later Bruce returned with a light coating of sweat on his face and his shirt drenched.

"Everything okay, Bruce?" she greeted his return.

"Baby, get out here. Now! I'm burning for you." He pulled her to him, his manhood already free and took her standing up as she wrapped her legs around his waist."

On the drive back, Bruce's energy flagged and he asked Lola to drive so he could nap. She was tired, too, but slid behind the wheel and drove for about an hour. They were only twenty minutes from home, now. She got off the highway, preferring the side streets. She was driving west, into the sun. Her eyes were burning and heavy. She looked at the clock on the dash. They'd be home soon. Suddenly it was 4th of July, lights flashing in her face, reflected from the mirror. Cops! She nudged Bruce as she pulled to the side of the road. "Cops, Bruce."

"I'll take care of it. Just look stupid and don't say much."
They knew the cop was running the plate. It never occurred
to him that Stan might have been driving foolish, expired
plates or even a warrant. Bruce gently caressed the S.& W.
he'd tucked between the seats. Then they saw him get out of
the police cruiser and walk to them.

She rolled down the window as the officer asked for her
license and proof of insurance. She handed them to him.
Then he asked for Bruce's ID, which he had.

"Whose car you driving?" asked the officer.

"My friend, Stan loaned it to me to get her to the
doctor," Bruce explained. They were near Riverview Clinic.

"You went through a red light back there," the cop said.
"I have to write you a citation." He did and handed the pink
sheet to Lola through the window. "Drive carefully and have
a nice day, he said before returning to his cruiser.

"What you going through a red light for anyway. Why
did you get off the highway. Go! Drive! Before he comes
back. Get out of here."

"Don't yell at me, Bruce. I'm going. Lola was aware of
the dark violence brewing inside Bruce, but she didn't fear it.
She knew he'd never turn it on her. They were a family.

They got home in time for the kids. "Get the twins,
Bruce, I'm going to bed.

\*       \*       \*

One breast cancer patient Rachel took a food tray to
refused it. The next day she couldn't get her breath and told
the staff she was dying and she wanted to see her sister who
was in Wilson. They told her they were taking her to I.S.U.

165

hospital. Her sister was summoned and they visited for about fifteen minutes while awaiting transport. The sister asked to ride in the ambulance with her, but they told her "no, say your goodbyes now." Rachel heard she died a few hours later.

Back downstairs, Brenda got into a heated discussion with a new girl. Brenda settled the matter by throwing some plastic trays from a distance into the dishwasher which splashed water and got the girl all wet. The girl complained to the C.O. who told Brenda to "be nice." Brenda laughed and said to Rachel, "beats scalding her."

Uncle Festus, who trades gum for sex, came down into diet kitchen and plodded straight over to the cook. She did a stint for murder years ago and was now here for arson. She yelled, "Get out of my kitchen!" Defiantly, he lifted the lid off some cooling pork roast, reached in and helped himself to a generous chunk of meat. The cook grabbed a frying pan and chased him out the door hollering something about his booger-caked fingers.

Later that night, Uncle Festus went into the hospital and got into an argument with an inmate. She spit on him and that's all he needed to beat her up. This girl was here for robbery and after doing her minimum the board gave her more time. This, when added to custody problems with her kids, gave her escape ideas. She left and made it home, only to be beat up by her boyfriend who called the police. She's been locked up in the hospital ever since.

Diet kitchen, compared to the general kitchen may be cleaner but it was crawling with roaches. At least the rat found under the dishwasher was dead. Rachel always felt the food was carefully prepared and handled. Nothing is perfect and this is the last place to look for perfection. Bessie got into it with two girls preparing food in P.F.S. for the general population, saying they weren't going to handle her food and make what she ate taste like where their unwashed hands had been. She always groused about something, mostly with cause.

There was another case of hepatitis in the hospital. Rachel did not know the details of it. The girl was and had been in isolation, and had been fed on reusable plastic trays—until today. No one knew as no one said anything. Then the directive changed and she was fed on paper plates. Some kind of oversight. The cook who went to visit her said she looked bad with "a sick complexion and sunk in cheeks." The girl told her the only medical attention she gets is Motrin and Tylenol.

An unconventional fight in diet kitchen. Brenda found some old Jello in the refrigerator and started lobbing handfuls 40 feet away at the cook. Some of it went awry and splattered bystanders who picked up the thick rubbery stuff and flung it back in the direction it came, regardless of the target. Splotches covered everyone's clothes and hair. All the commotion brought the C.O.s running and they were lucky not to fall on the slippery pieces scattered about the floor. It was all in fun and taken as such and was cleaned up in no time. They had pretty good C. O.'s down there.

Brenda Slims felt confident she could get away with anything. She took an instant dislike to for a new girl working in diet kitchen and had picked at her all morning. She glanced at the clock, then around the large room. Everyone was preparing their own lunch. No one watched Rhoda slip a sharp knife into her deep uniform pocket next to the newspaper clipping someone had mailed her. Her apron concealed the protruding handle.

The women who worked there all wore cotton dresses, worn by many and washed thin over the years. They filed out of the kitchen and into a room off a short corridor carrying their lunch on a tray. There were half a dozen mixed-vintage mostly wooden tables and many unmatched chairs in the otherwise barren room. In less than an hour it would be filled with women needing special diets. But for now, it belonged to those who prepared and served their food. Sunbeams on the curtain-less glass accent fingerprints. Someone tucked two pieces of wrapped fried chicken into the wastebasket. A friend who will eat here later will sneak it out—perhaps to trade for a dental appointment or sinus pills. Just goes to show how getting such everyday commodities can turn a piece of chicken into the goose's golden egg.

The air was soon laden with smoke, flies, and gossip, but today it would be the scene of a tense encounter. The last to come in was Brenda, who hollered out before quietly shutting the door, "Is everybody in that's going to be eating?" After another girl wandered in, Brenda purposefully approached the newest girl in the group, the one she'd been taunting all morning. No one knew her name or cared. The closed door drew everyone's attention. It was always left open.

"So you like snatching kids off the street for sex—you and this guy." The girl kept eating and ignored the question. Brenda waved a newspaper clipping in the air. (Our friends at home frequently send us stuff from the newspaper, of trials and people on their way here.) "Isn't this you in the picture?" The girl shook her head in denial, but convinced no one. "You gave these kids syphilis and gonorrhea and who knows what else," she accused. "How could they let a dirty scumbag like you work in the kitchen? You belong upstairs in the hospital—or better yet dead." Brenda violently clapped the paper to the table with the flat of her hand.

Everyone in the room hushed—first out of curiosity, then shock, as they saw her slowly, yet dramatically draw a bread knife from beneath her apron. There was silence except for the buzzing of flies playing tag on the table. All eyes flit from Brenda to the menacing knife. The gleam of the large shiny blade foreshadowed treacherous possibilities. She slashed the knife through the air, then into the table with a firm crack.

"You answer me when I talk to you, bitch!" Brenda was staring into her face with an unbelievable intensity. "Says here you lived in dumpsters with your man and waited for kids to come along. Is that true? Don't you live in a house?"

"I'm not here for that," she said in a high-pitched strained voice. "My case is over a nickel bag of weed."

"Bullshit!" challenged Brenda. "I have a newspaper clipping about you—with your picture. Isn't this you? Isn't this your name? She reached out and held the girl's ID tag. It says here you abduct boys 11-14 for sex. Do you have kids?"

"Yes, she answered, "But that isn't my case. I'm here for weed."

"Do you fuck your kids? Do you want others to do it? We know the social workers tell the child molesters to say they're here on drug cases."

The short greasy-haired girl about eighteen didn't look up. She sat inches from where Brenda stood, her head bowed and motionless except for her eyes which darted around the room as if looking for someone to save her.

"Can't you just imagine this glob of used lard living in a dumpster," Brenda called to her co-workers. "Smells like a dumpster, too. The judge gave her 2-10," Brenda reads.

"With good time she could be back out there in 18 months." *Out there with her son who she isn't home to protect.* Brenda bent forward slightly to ease a growing cramp. Nerves?

Water turned on upstairs which caused pipes to vibrate overhead—pipes wrapped years ago probably in asbestos. Neglect and plumbing repairs opened their seals and tiny but deadly fibers float almost unnoticed through the air. It added to the eeriness of the room, and Brenda took advantage of it.

Brenda brandished the knife close enough to the girl's face to make her blink. "Go ahead and eat," Brenda offered. Then her voice became strong. "It's probably going to be your last meal. I'm supposed to go home after 11 years—murder—next month, but I don't think I'd mind a bit doing eleven more if it was to get rid of the likes of you." Brenda screamed her lie, eyeball to eyeball with the knife poised in the air.

She slipped quickly behind the girl and yanked her head back as she grabbed her hair. "I could make a cut like this," Brenda continued as she slid the knife to an angle from the girl's ear to her throat in the manner of a beautician discussing hairstyles with a client. Her fingers gripped the girl's hair and further raised her head so all can see the position of the knife as well as the stark terror on her face. "Or like this," she added, shifting the knife with apparent pleasure. Then she stunned everyone, as she drew the sharp steel blade straight across, pressing the knife deep into her neck.

The girl's eyes became strangely blank at the touch of the cold metal, as though accepting death. Her mouth emitted an almost inaudible gasp, Her face paled. Her open palm hesitatingly rose to her throat. Her eyes bulged and mouth opened as if to suck in a final breath. She cautiously withdrew her hand, looked for blood but saw none.

"I used the back side of the knife—this time," Brenda announced loudly. A born actress she loved to control her audience and knew she had them spellbound.

"Don't let me keep you from eating. I'll respect your last meal," Brenda reassured her with a theatrical flourish. "I'm doing 17 to life," she lied, her body now paced anxiously. (Brenda probably had two years to do, most probably on some scam, but because she is constantly getting tickets will probably have to do every day of that.) "Maybe you'd bleed less if I scalded you first," Brenda pondered, emphasized *bleed* and *scald* and spoke slowly.

A roach scampered across the table. Crack! Brenda slammed the blade into the table, wood chips flying, the knife embedded. The brown runner had made its last run. The girl jumped inches in the air.

The door suddenly burst open and an inmate cook, Lisha, broke the spell. She scanned the room with instant comprehension. "I don't even want to know what's going on." The cook did some time a few years ago for something her husband put her up to. She swore that when she got home she'd kill him—and she did just that. Smiling, with her lips strained tight over her prison dentures, she confidently walked into Brenda's space and moved her toward the center of the room. "Stop being a fool and put down the knife," Lisha demanded with her hands on her hips, shoulders back and staring into a pair of challenging eyes just a stride away.

Brenda fended her off, with the blade between them. This is not the way she planned it to end.

With her frozen smile still intact over pursed lips and glaring eyes, Lisha strode into the knife, which forced Brenda to pull back to avoid cutting her.

"I was just funning with her," laughed Brenda sarcastically. She then stepped back to imitate and ridicule Lisha's posture. Lisha took the knife and left. The incident won't be reported.

\*　　\*　　\*

The white kitten acquired a gray friend. They both appeared well fed as they watched from the window. The mice jumped from can to can in the pantry. Rachel thinks the cats are on the wrong side of the glass.

One girl got a letter from her attorney, dunning her for $400. Rachel thinks for the first time that maybe it is a good thing she doesn't hear from hers.

A girl at diet kitchen just returned from getting a new Federal case. On her ride to court, another girl in the van asked her if she knew Rachel Williams from Riverview. She told her "She was my best friend in County jail." It was Edna McDaniels, the girl from Nigeria. Said she was sentenced a month before to two years in the Federal Penitentiary in Lexington and then would be transported to Texas where she will do one month, then be released. Her husband was sent to Minnesota. Never heard from her again and suspect she was deported.

\*　　\*　　\*

Another new girl arrived in for Rachel to train. This girl opened up the huge refrigerator in diet kitchen and saw a can of grapefruit/orange juice combination. That was a first as none of us had seen anything like it in diet kitchen. Special treats are always kept under lock and key and usually consumed by C.O.'s. "Who is this for" she questioned the cook.

"Us," she laughed. We split it three ways.

About a week ago, one of the girls Rachel arrived with in admissions asked her if she'd help her with a letter to her judge. There seemed to be a sad story behind every face. This girl had received a very disturbing letter from her younger brother which indicated he had lost his ability to cope with the situation at home and was joining the army. Her other brother was left to care for their 46 year-old mother suffering from chronic alcoholism and weighed 76 lbs. Because Rachel didn't jump right to it this girl asked someone else to write it. Good! That effort died, or so she thought. She came back to Rachel one evening during a card game. Rachel told her she'd get to it. In the past months this girl had told her much of her case and family life. She read the letter from her brother and past letters to her judge. After sleeping on it, Rachel woke and wrote her letter and tucked it under her door. When she came back from "count" the girl took the letter to her room to read. Count over, Rachel was sitting at her table and was approached by a big tear-eyed smiling face. Her arms went around her in a big hug. "You were inspired by Allah," she cried. "Thank you."

Autumn sat two tables over, flirting with Uncle Festus. He sat with her at a table talking inches from her face. Her head cocked, her chin in her palm, long-lashed blue eyes blinking into his. As her tongue, displayed its possibilities, their legs rubbed together under the table. Either she missed her roommate terribly or she's really into gum. Such a waste of a beautiful girl. Drugs will do that.

Brenda Slims came over to Pierce to live. She's gotten too many tickets to stay in Wilson. She spent most of the day with Autumn which is good because Autumn really needed a friend.

Every day Rachel walked about 10 laps around the track, hoping Mattie would see her and come out. It was cold so she had to push herself to do it. Didn't know if she was out of admissions yet, but figured she would probably be assigned to Jefferson where the other lifers live and their time on the track is limited. It was right next to the track, so it was possible she could spot her and make it out. Rachel wasn't sure she'd recognize her, though. As she walked, she observed thieves coming from the storeroom with carefully concealed packages between their legs and under their skirts—5lb hams, restaurant-sized cans of juice, or frozen treats like gallons of ice cream or Sarah Lee pies.

\*     \*     \*

An interim boss was named. Rachel didn't know his name but recognized him as a short, white-haired man who seemed sensible, taking down all the silly threatening signs, telling guards the girls aren't "out of bounds" unless they're over the fence, and had them stop writing tickets for stepping on the grass. He found them serving cold coffee at breakfast, he had them dump it out. At commissary, he asked why generic cigarettes were sold when his understanding was they were supposed to be free and he didn't like the idea of girls with tickets not being able to use the telephones to stay in touch with family. He made too much sense to be here long. He found this place in such a mess that Central Office decided not to name a new warden until things were fixed.

Rachel had breakfast with a girl who was sort of new to her. She was very talkative, didn't have much time to do and didn't have any family support or clothes other than what the State issued her. On the way in to P.F.S. for breakfast she commented about seeing a litter of kittens underneath a hollowed out concrete slab walkway. On her way out, this girl risked a ticket as she bent down and tossed the cats a handful of her scrambled eggs she'd smuggled out. "They need to eat too, don't they?"

Bessie was all excited that her daughter visited and was delighted her pregnancy is going well. Her sons didn't come and she was upset about that. She told them to keep the money coming.

Three of Rachel's new acquaintances are in the hospital recovering from broken legs, the result of slipping on the ice. She was on her way to work at diet kitchen when one of them called to her from the second floor window that she's doing fine, but said she needed some candy and cigarettes. She would try to get something together for her and have someone deliver it. If it were a smaller order like cigarettes or sugar, Rachel could write a letter to someone here that doesn't exist. Then enclose the contraband and use her friend in the hospital's own name and number for a return address. Then the mailroom would return it to the sender—for insufficient postage because of the bulk and being unable to find the intended recipient, the girl would get the stuff. She didn't want to get involved in making up packages to have someone deliver it, risking a ticket for these non-essential needs. That is a lot to ask of someone, but she'd see what she could do.

> Baby flies are maggots
>> That feed off our waste
> They give the food we eat
>> That special prison taste.

Rachel had lunch at P.F.S. because she didn't work at diet kitchen that day. They had dried hamburger the size of a silver dollar and a scoop of mashed potatoes. The server behind the counter picked up a tray for the girl in front of her and just as she dropped on the potatoes, a roach scampered from the bottom and over the lip. Smack! Buried. She supposed she'd eaten a lot of filth since she's been here. It's one way to get rid of the creepy critters.

Brenda Slims watched a friend share a cigarette with another and warned her. "Watch who you let hit your cigarette or use your cup." There's some kid of mouth fungus going around. You never know where that mouth has been."

"What? Like herpes or cold sores?"

"All I know is that it's a mouth fungus," she repeated.

She'd just gotten out of "lock up" for one of her pranks and as usual came back with a story. There were two other girls in her room, all clothed only in their state gown and all three had to share a potty chair. One of the girls was a very outgoing bull-dyker. Brenda had played at it but had never gotten seriously involved with anyone. She listened to these girls discuss in detail their experiences and techniques and her face must have reflected the awe she was feeling because one of the girls asked her if she was all right. Not wanting to show her naivete, she said she was feeling sad. The girl leaped down from her bunk and told her to spread her legs, she wouldn't be sad any more. Ronda pushed away her greedy head and assured her she was feeling better already. Persistent, the girl told her she loved her in a special way and wouldn't expect reciprocation. She laughed as she told the story. Then she said, "They don't have enough linens in the hospital, so when someone has to go there, they have to strip their cots and take the bedding with them."

Thanksgiving came and we all looked forward to turkey. All the ovens were going for days and nights cooking up the birds. There must have been hundreds of them. Come Thanksgiving Day, half of them were missing. Lots of someones had a nice dinner and most of the girls ate tuna-fish sandwiches.

The boiler alarm went off at 5:30 am. Then the fire alarms went off. No one could evacuate because the doors were locked. Rachel knew hers wasn't, but wasn't going to disclose that unless she knew it was an emergency. Men were running around everywhere hollering. The girls all banged on their doors and screamed to be let out. They shut the water off so the toilets didn't flush. After an hour or so, they did flush. Knowing the water was on, Rachel decided to wash up for the day in her room. Then the C.O. banged on her door telling her not to use any water until they had the pressure adjusted.

One of the ladies who broke her leg and was now back in her room, complained loudly she has been ten weeks in a cast and she wanted it off. Rachel half serious, offered to do it just to shut her up, but she refused the offer. Two weeks later she went to the hospital and had it removed. Now, she's in pain and afraid to walk on it. Said she needed therapy. Everyone told her she was on her own for that and she'd better start stretching, massaging and walking if she ever wanted that leg normal.

Rachel was still very interested in going to school and spent a couple of days in a computer classroom where girls were doing a lot of word processing, but she decided she needed something more challenging. She'd signed up for college classes. She'd filled out lots of forms, applications for school and grants, and much more. She was pushing to do something more with her time than work in diet kitchen. Everything seemed to be on hold now and there didn't seem to be any more she could do. Classes would start soon and she wanted to be in them.

In the event school doesn't happen for her, Rachel signed a sheet to be considered for a clerical job in a white shirt's office. White shirts have a higher rank than the gray-shirted C.O.s who have to answer to them. She thought she would find it interesting to see what she could learn about this place. She was pretty sure they would not select her because of her continual use of kites. She had kited all them all a dozen times and she thinks they might consider her a troublemaker, even though they were always legitimate complaints.

Diet kitchen served its purpose and she hoped she left it a better place than what it was. After six months, logic had her pretty much given up on the attorney helping her to get out of here. She knew now he was grossly incompetent and she could do little about that—but she wasn't ready to let her mind give it up. Why couldn't her family and friends see this? She had begun to suspect that in the event she was released early he wouldn't have had anything to do with it. She refused to let herself ever be reduced to the level of those here and that included both inmates and C.O.s so she kept stroking through the muck towards the surface. There were a few good people here, but most of them were low-life's.

The day Rachel was notified that she was accepted for school was an emotional turning point. She didn't look forward to being here long enough to complete the courses, but with no control over what she'd been able to do so far, here was a choice, hope on the horizon, this was her rainbow and it glowed fiercely against a darkened sky.

Her last day at diet kitchen was kind of fun. She was trying to find dishes clean enough to use. She called one of the dish girls over to show her the problem—not enough water in the machine. While they were talking, Brenda Slims sneaked up behind the girl and pulled up her dress saying, "I've just got to see your stuff." The girl let out a little scream. Brenda backed away quickly, laughed and said "Oh, I'm sorry. I didn't know you were wearing a pad."

Autumn wanted to move into Rachel's job at diet kitchen, but the girl was usually so strung out on something she just didn't function. Whatever she was on may be prescribed to her here or maybe a C.O. or visitor is brought her something, but she was always a mess. She tried to be diligent and do right but it didn't always pay off. Rachel came into work that last day and there were thousands of eggs stacked in her work area, three dozen in a box. Moving them into the commercial size refrigerator was a simple project. Autumn came over to help. She always wanted to help. The work was nearly done, so Rachel gave her the nod. She picked up two boxes and dropped them on her way to the refrigerator. There was a big juicy mess on the floor and Autumn apologized all over the place. Then the C.O. assigned a new girl to Rachel's job and told Autumn she could help her because she knew the routine. She got all upset and cried because she didn't get the job. It all paid the same—$12 a month.

A girl fresh out of admissions, sentenced to one year, tried to escape one night. She cut herself up really bad trying to get over the razor wire. They took her to I.S.U. hospital, transfused, stitched her up and returned here the next day. Friends told Rachel they saw her strapped spread-eagle on a cot in the "death row" section of the hospital saying she was a danger to herself and others.

\*      \*      \*

Just before classes were to start, Rachel was called over to the school to pick up her supplies. The two people running the school were young, probably just out of college. They were very welcoming and put themselves out to be kind and helpful. They were a rare find here. Books, paper, pens, notebooks, pencils and a pocket calculator, everything laid out and waiting. Math, English, Finance, Computers, Intro. to Business. She took a look inside the books once back in her room and found it scary. What did she get herself into? Worried she won't be able to handle it being too long out of school, she spent about an hour in the math book. She worked all the problems in the first two chapters to see if she could come up with the answers in the back of the book. She had to make this work for her.

The first night of class relieved some tension and anxiety. Some classes were early in the morning. She hoped her apprehension about school eased off. She kept to her room studying, not wanting to get involved with the endless issues out by the tables.

There was definitely a different class of girls that attended school, compared to the general population. Rachel didn't know any of them and didn't put herself out to know anyone. Everyone seemed to be in the same position—not knowing anyone and hesitant to become acquainted. As the weeks went by, Rachel got to know a couple of girls. She's not here for that. She must be a successful student. She didn't see much chance to get to know anyone well, though, because they only see each other in class.

Then she got mail from the school cashiers office in Springfield, telling her that one of her grants never came through. She asked at the school and showed them the letter. They tried to put her at ease and told her not to worry about it, that all was okay, but where had she heard that before? The frustration weighed heavy enough to crush her. Were they feeding her empty words like her attorney? She'd lost her ability to trust but she continued to go to class and planned to do so until they refused to accept her.

Rachel locked herself in her room and reviewed algebraic equations, studied budgets, income and expense statements and spreadsheets. She found this very challenging since it was a long time ago she had this kind of math—high school decades ago—and much of it was totally new to her. She felt good when she figured out how to solve the problems. She buried herself in the books to absorb as much she could before they confiscated them from her.

Then another notice from the cashiers office in Springfield saying she was being withdrawn from classes because the grant money didn't come in. She went back to talk with those running the school and they told her all the grant money was in, so they let her continue to go to class. She'd spent the evening studying the Computer Lit. book. Please don't take this opportunity away. She was always on edge about one thing or another. Couldn't relax.

To be eligible to take college classes, one had to be within a couple years of a board date. Most of the girls in the class have been there for quite a while, all of which were from other buildings so it was her first time to talk to them. Some she got to know, others never, with no regrets. Rachel really got into this change of pace. She found herself in another element in school and discovered that just because they had her body, her mind didn't have to be locked up. Some of the subjects really challenged her but she cut through each class as though her life depended on it. Maybe it did.

She did talk at length with Bonnie, one of the girls in her classes when they had an opportunity to meet on the walk/jog. Bonnie arrived here more than a year ahead of Rachel and only spent a month in Warren East admissions. The overcrowding was just getting underway. She went directly to Adams Cottage, which is a very old building, and was given a single room. Living right next door was a young and playful girl nicknamed Slurp. Both girls had a great sense of humor and clicked immediately. At one point they tied a string from window to window on the outside and passed notes—not that they couldn't have conversed, but the note idea was more fun.

About a year and a half later, somebody that Bonnie knew told her of a girl that would be arriving there shortly and asked that she get to know her and look after her if she could. This isn't often possible, but in this case things worked out when a tall slender Ellie happened to be assigned to Adams Cottage. She, Bonnie and Slurp became good friends and all started college classes together.

During the winter, Bonnie's room became very cold at night and she frequently woke to a pile of snow inside on the sill. Bonnie described those first months in prison as living in a walking coma, convinced that she wasn't there, that it was all a nightmare she couldn't wake from. She did a short stint working in diet kitchen, then signed up for computer classes. Her time inside the nightmare became more believable to her as the months went by, but her brain was never able to totally accept it.

A few months before Bonnie went to trial, she met the love of her life. He'd had a massive heart attack months before and was on the mend and was back to work. They dated, partied, traveled and life was glorious. When the time arrived for her trial he sat in the courtroom, listened and observed. One evening she woke up to find him packing suitcases. She asked what he was doing.

"We're getting out of here," he told her. "Things aren't going well for you in that courtroom. We've got to split."

"No, no, no. We can't just pick up and leave. I've got responsibilities here. My mom needs me. My son . . . ."

"You don't understand," he stage-whispered so not to wake up the whole household. "They're going to find you guilty and they're going to send you to jail—for years."

"I can't believe that. I'm not going anywhere. Sit down and let's talk about this." Bonnie watched a lot of movies and couldn't visualize herself being a fugitive. She loved this man, but taking off with him in the middle of the night, abandoning her family and job seemed crazy.

They talked into the night. He rationalized his decision by saying that his doctor didn't give him much more time before his heart gave out. Yes, they wanted their time together, but she was sure they would have it. Yes, she shot up a cheating boyfriend's car, but he wasn't in it and no one was hurt. How serious is that? He told her he didn't like the way things were going in court and he knew he was going to lose her. She assured him that she had confidence in her lawyer and all would be okay. Grudgingly, he acquiesced to her wishes.

His premonition became truth and she was found guilty and sentenced. Because she fired the gun in the City, three years mandatory time was attached to the beginning of her sentence. She had to do every day of that before starting the years the judge assigned her.

Bonnie completed her computer classes, secretarial classes and every other class she was eligible for, and it gave her confidence to sign up for college classes.

Once she was somewhat settled, she petitioned the penitentiary for permission to get married. This became an obsession with her. She got all kinds of mixed answers about it depending who she asked, but at the end of the day she was denied. She heard about other people getting married while locked up, but she couldn't convince anyone at Lotusville. They told her that there would be no consummating the marriage while here, so it wouldn't be a real marriage anyway. She told them that they had already consummated it—many times over so it could be grandfathered in. They didn't buy it.

His visits were something she looked forward to, and he never missed the once a month opportunity. He told her she was the other half of his soul. He wrote constantly and sent colorful and happy cards to cheer her. They made plans for a life together once she was free, but it wasn't to be. Within months she received notification that he had his final heart attack. She was devastated and wanted to die with him. Someone told her that burning Styrofoam created a poison. She gathered up as many Styrofoam cups as she could find and burned them in the sink, breathing in as much as she could. Fortunately, it didn't work. It took years for her to resign herself to his passing.

*     *     *

Trying to study in her tiny airless room was difficult for Rachel. The common area outside her room had its issues. Interruptions were constant and made it difficult to focus. The girl that fed the eggs to the kittens wasn't in school but helped her a lot with some classes. The math seemed to come naturally to her. She put everything in order and made it easier to absorb. Rachel found her really bright.

One afternoon, she ventured out to a table and was trying to understand a concept that had been eluding her when out of the blue a girl she didn't know sat down next at her table to say she had a fear of vampires. Her fears were quelled when Rachel assured her, in all seriousness, not to worry, that AIDS would eradicate them. It just didn't stop.

Rachel received a letter from Alice, her friend from admissions. Her sentence was one year and was offered shock after a few weeks but turned it down. Sounds crazy but she wanted to return home and not be entailed by paperwork for the rest of her sentence. She said that after she was released she moved out of state to be near family and found a job. When she filled out the job application, it asked if she'd ever been convicted of a felony. That question was on all job applications she filled out. She answered "no" figuring if she told them she did time here she wouldn't have been hired. She needed the job and it was hers. She loved it. Later she learned that in most cases, an employer will run a credit check, not a background check. That was good to know. Then more recently heard that they not only do a background check but also require a pee test. Rachel was always happy to hear from her.

She graduated college and got married—all while Rachel was still behind the barbed wire fence. Married life wasn't all what she'd expected. Her husband was from where big cars and money were goals in life. Maybe she figured that signing a legal paper would assure her husband she was making a real commitment and hoped he'd understand and feel the same. "But life with him became a series of being together and then apart, either because he was locked up or he moved in with some woman to sell drugs from her house. It always ended the same way. He'd beat her up, go to jail, and I'd stupidly let him come back."

The child molester that broke her child's pelvis got a letter from home that her husband was in a coma from an auto accident. She cried until a couple of women got tired of hearing it. One told her he was a bum, that he visited her only once in the two years she's been here and was drunk when he did. Another reminded her that he's never sent her any money to buy necessities at the commissary and he has never written her. A week later she was told he was out of the coma and doing well. Her roommate wasn't so sympathetic, telling her that if she didn't take a shower she was going to wake up in a plastic bag.

Most all Rachel's days were spent studying and she found it a refreshing change from diet kitchen, but she did miss the food. It was a serious group of girls attending school. For the most part, their life was centered there, not in the foolish fights and squabbles back in the buildings where they lived. At least they didn't bring it into the classroom. It was a challenge to ace the tests and Rachel frequently accomplished that, being really proud when a classmate told the instructor that Rachel's test paper was the answer key.

Some classes were at night and as the weather warmed up it was beautiful to walk outside in the dark. Well, there were lights everywhere, but the sky was dark beyond the lights so she appreciated what she could get. Rachel carried 18-22 credit hours each quarter so her time was all studying. The young couple that administrated the school really cared about the students and were not employed by the penitentiary. They met in college and recently graduated. They seemed to be a happy couple and everyone was happy for them. The teachers were a mixed batch, most of them doing their best to educate.

It was hard to focus in math class. The instructor paced up and down in front of us lecturing, sweating heavily underneath his shirt. When we first got to class there was a tiny wet triangle at the waistband in the back of his pants. Then, shortly, the front of his shirt just below his boobs. Most disgusting were his profusely sweating armpits which were coloring his white shirt an intense yellow, indicating he must have been on a medication causing this. The wet triangle on his pants got much bigger. His cologne or deodorant or whatever he was wearing made the air heavy as a wet fungus. It was a long three-hour class. Then he told us that he deducts 10% off the grade for a missed class. We can't miss class except for visits or serious illness. He didn't seem to understand that this wasn't the real world.

She thought she'd aced a test in Financial Management, but soon learned she'd missed a question on inflation. Learning the material is more important than the grade anyway. The correct answers measured what she had learned, the wrong ones taught her to understand why.

The English teacher gave tests that really had everyone thinking. Like "what on earth did she have on her mind when she wrote this question?"

Another teacher was so interesting because he always related his teachings to real life. He was the deep voice on a Subaru commercial.

One assigned a lot of written homework in every class and always returned it with a check at the top. Rachel doubted he even read any of it which insulted her because she always spent a lot of time on it. Midway into the second paragraph of one assignment, she told a short joke. Several paragraphs down, she put in the punch line. Received it back with the usual check on the top. On the way out the door, she asked him the joke. He didn't know the punch line.

Most of Rachel's days were spent locked up in her stuffy room preparing for tests and that was pretty much her choice. She had a handle on most of the classes by now and sort of figured she knew what the teachers were looking for. It was much more interesting than hearing who left in handcuffs for being caught in whose bed.

Lots of noise outside. Male prisoners from a nearby facility were putting up a second row of razor wire. There's a racket of tractors and other heavy equipment. The evil curls gleam in the sunshine. Girls here wave and call from their windows to the men, but there's too much equipment noise for anyone to hear.

During one of her classes Rachel was called out for a phone interview. It seems someone read one of her letters complaining about her attorney and his ineptness. She was totally unprepared for this, and was frustrated because her mind wasn't ready. Since school started, she'd pushed thoughts of D.D. Knight out of her mind. The person on the phone asked lots of questions about her trial and case. She tried to give answers but so many things just didn't come. Her time on the phone was very limited and she was nervous because a C.O. a few feet away, watched the clock and tapped her wristwatch. She wished he would have showed up in person and she could have been prepared to explain her attorney's inexcusable negligence or she could have done it in writing where she could have thought about and formed her answers, but it wasn't to be. She left the phone feeling everything was totally unfinished and never heard any more about it.

In one of the business classes she enjoyed putting the homework to rhyme just to have fun with it.

> All the world's car industry
>   Was in a state of dread
> Toyota and General Motors
>   Had announced their plans to wed
>
> Would they smother their competition?
>   Could they stay within the law?
> Dwarfed by all their power
>   The other's stood in awe

We'll borrow their technique mystique
    Or quotas are no bars
Two heads are, therefore, better than one
    To build a better car

Well, that never came about.
Then, there was this decision:

    Utah Pies of Salt Lake City
        Made a good and cheaper pie
    Pet Milk, their competition
        Went to war and sent a spy

    Continental and Carnation
        Sold things at less than cost
    Utah took the three to court
        To hear them told they'd lost

    The Court of Appeals reversed this
        "No evidence," they claim
    But when taken one step higher
        The Supreme Court did lay blame.

    "You caused Utah financial woe
        With your predatory way
    Now pay your bill with interest
        Tomorrow's another day."

It was never dark in the building. Well, when a light actually burned out it flashed/strobed all night long for several days or until someone fixed it, which really couldn't be called "half light." Some girls unscrewed the distraction or hung a towel over it, but to Rachel, it wasn't worth risking a ticket.

A very young girl sidled up to Rachel one afternoon. Pam said that she applied for a job making flags and would have to pass a test to get it. She showed her some of the things that she would be expected to know. One of them was how to read a ruler. We'd worked for a while on it, but she couldn't stay focused. She just wanted to talk.

"I was thirteen when I met Mike and fourteen when I left home with him." She said she was born into poverty in rural Kentucky. She remembers three or four step dads. "They were all really nice. I sure liked men, anyways." She gave me a sly smile. "I'm tired of all these women. There were a slew of kids at home. My sister left two of hers while she worked in town. We was always getting in mom's way. Mom'd grab an arm, shirt tail, or head, or whatever she reached and slam us out the door or into a wall or wop us with a pan if we wasn't too quick to be caught."

"It was hard on her when I left. She wanted me home to help with the babies. T' weren't 'till I had one of my own she signed for our wedding. Mike made me real happy and I didn't get slammed around anymore."

Rachel looked at Pam's pretty face, covered with scars. Small ones on her forehead and cheekbones and a long one running down the side of her nose. They looked healed, but she knew they were still festering deep and unseen. Her right eyebrow had a knot the size of an olive under it. Her hair was waist-length, wavy and thick as a rug. We went back to the ruler for a while but without a basic understanding of fractions, it seemed fruitless and she was getting frustrated, so Rachel asked her, "how are your kids?"

Her face lit up to think of them. "Just had a visit with Mike and three of the kids. They're all fine, but he couldn't bring the other one. He's still in foster care." Her eyes fell sadly to the ruler. Mike told her during the visit that he had to get rid of the cats. They were all white with blue eyes and one or another was always having a liter. He told her it was just too much for him to deal with, and that saddened her.

She was pregnant when she came here and two weeks later she told her C.O. in admissions that she was in labor. The C.O. told her she wasn't and to sit down and be quiet. She broke out of the line on the way to dinner that night and made a B-line to the prison hospital. Once there, they locked her up for being where she didn't belong. They put her in solitary where she had the baby—by herself on the concrete floor a few hours later. "He's doing fine now and is home with Mike."

"The boy I got locked up over is in school now. He's the only one in foster care. Mike can visit him there but he can't take him home or bring him here. What happened was me and Joyce, my neighbor, was talking in the kitchen, and the kids were crying and whining—hers and mine. Then mine starts driving a car up my leg and I couldn't stand it no more, so I picks him up and whips him toward the door. Next thing I know, he's bleeding all over his self. Joyce drove us to the hospital where all he needed was stitching up. I told them what happened and they called the police."

"Ma used to do us kids a lot worse and no one never took her kids or locked her up. I've been here four years now and done a lot of thinking about it. Mom was wrong and I was wrong. I was mothering all wrong. Mom's still in Kentucky. Haven't seen her since my wedding day. I was all dressed up real nice and she comes into the room, knocks me down and starts kicking all over me. Mike came running in and pulled her off. One reason we moved here was to get away from her."

When I first got here, I sent her a birthday card and a Mother's Day card, just like I would have if I were home. Then I started thinking and blaming her for bringing me up the way she did. Pretty soon I was saying it was her fault I was apart from Mike and the kids. When I cooled off some I remembered how I hated being beat and of living scared of her all the time. I keep changing how I feel. I love my kids. I don't want them scared of me." Tears rolled down Pam's cheeks as she talked. I want to go home and hug everybody."

Rachel thought of her life as a kid, with parents far from perfect, but she didn't live a twisted nightmare like this.

She talked more about when she gets out she's going to get a lawyer and get her son out of foster care and home so he can know his brothers.

She doesn't play cards or go to school so Rachel doesn't see much of her, but tonight she wanted to talk. She tried to convince her to go back to school and get her GED, that education was the key to happiness. Rumor has it they give one month off a person's time for every grade they achieve—an incentive. It would be nice if that was fact.

Then her eyes dropped to the table as she said she couldn't go back to her room because her roommate, Cowboy, was in there with a "friend." Not supposed happen. No one is supposed to go into a room unless it is theirs, but it's a constant thing. Her main beef is that they are using her lower bunk, it being more convenient than her roommate's upper one. She says their sex play has to do with food and they mess up her sheets.

So many of the girls were losing or lost their families because they were locked up. When family members couldn't take in and care for the kids, they went to foster homes mostly because the fathers went on with their lives without them. Bessie put custody of her teenage boy with her pregnant twenty-year-old daughter and it didn't work out. Now there's to be a custody hearing and Bessie says she will go back to Riverview for it. Says she anxious to see her family and to wear out the phone. Maybe they will invite her to this hearing but doubt they will let her have much say in it.

*     *     *

Lots of commotion. Big strange looking trucks made a lot of noise, dozens of men over at the hospital and several other buildings. Some of the men wore "moon suits tethered to a truck." More walked around hollering to each other. Rachel heard earlier that the sample she'd smuggled out contained asbestos and that inspectors made an unannounced visit and found dozens of infractions. This was the result.

Inspectors gave administration a list of things to be fixed immediately and another list of things which were given a date to be fixed. There was a huge noisy truck parked outside the hospital for several days and a "pure air generator" ran all the time, making sure the men in the moon suits were breathing good air. Those people working in offices upstairs and other places in the hospital found the noise too distracting to work. Construction men filled several trucks with debris and they were hauled away every night. A piece of equipment they brought inside was too heavy for the rotted floor and it fell through into an ancient cesspool of muck and fungus.

The report wasn't sent to Rachel because she would have gotten in trouble had it become known she was responsible for the clean-up. These workers were here to help make this a safe place to live. It was so good to see that something positive was being done.

She later found out that Friable asbestos was found in several buildings the girls were living in as well as tunnels in the powerhouse, around boilers and of course, the diet kitchen complex of rooms. They were getting rid of this problem and hauling it away in big tank trucks.

In the hospital, where contagious diseases were evident, the administration was told that employees (which must include inmate workers) be notified when a health hazard existed. Signs had to be posted. All personnel working in admissions were to be notified of possible contagious diseases. It ordered that employee, including inmates, working with the contagious were supplied with masks, gloves, and whatever else they needed. At present there was none.

Several areas where corrosive materials were used had no facility for emergency washing. They were told to immediately make suitable facilities available for quick drenching or flushing of the eyes and body in both the maintenance building and yard crew storage shed. In the laundry area it was noted that no personal protective equipment such as gloves was available to anyone handling dry bleach.

Inspectors found food and beverages stored in toilet rooms. Also, the food storage area in P.F.S. also contained cleaning supplies and insecticides. They found electrical cover plates missing from junction boxes even in the new building complex. In the back of the hospital in the Disciplinary

Control area where most everyone smokes, they found unsecured oxygen cylinders.

There were falling tiles in Adams Cottage. Water soaked plaster ceilings in Garfield Cottage was threatening to fall. The ceiling in the 2$^{nd}$ quarter bathroom was also coming down, and the Sally Port area of Jefferson had falling tiles.

There was also myriad problems in the new three new buildings, but since it was new, they only sent one inspectors over to it for a quick walk-through. At least they tried to shape things up in the old section.

They found leaky pipes in "Taft" dorm which created an unsanitary accident hazard. Harding Cottage had wet bathrooms and laundry room floors and Jefferson had 1$^{st}$ and 2$^{nd}$ quarter shower rooms with wet floors and hallways.

These violations had to be corrected by certain dates, none longer than six months and many immediately. Further inspections should have noted that very few of the corrections were ever accomplished. More than a year later, when Rachel was moved to Jefferson, the water flowed out of the shower room, through the hall and into her room whenever the showers were in use. So much for follow-up, scheduled inspections.

Within a couple of weeks they may have finished taking the asbestos out of the hospital—at least they took out all their elaborate equipment. They do not let inmates near the place, so who knows what is going on down there. The hospital, along with the older "Cottages" should have been demolished. This was not a healthy place to be, but maybe some things became a little safer. No one has heard any rumors about who might have instigated this inspection or that anyone made any effort to discover, out who did it, and

Rachel has long tentacles into the rumor mill. She had only confided in Bonnie and that was after she learned that the inspectors had been out.

*   *   *

Bessie only knew that Pam was here for felonious assault and she'd heard the story of her giving birth in the hospital by herself. (She threw her son into a door jamb and the incident was reported to the police when he had to go to the hospital for stitches.)

She and Pam spent an hour or so talking over a table about their families and they commiserated about missing their kids. When Pam stood up and left, another girl sidled down next to Bessie. "What are you talking to a child molester for." She asked her.

"She's no child molester. She's here for felonius assault, just like I am."

"Yeah, on her own kids."

I went right over there and gave Pam a piece of my mind," Bessie told Rachel. "She cried. Girl, I was so hurt that she hadn't talked with me before about her case. I didn't know how to respond when I heard that. I didn't want to hear it from someone like that. Next time I see that nosey bitch, telling stories like that when she doesn't know what she's talking about, I'll smack some sense into her."

*   *   *

One night they wheeled in a VCR to show the movie, *Purple Rain*. Some girl watched, while others ducked in and out of each other's rooms. While Rachel has been here she'd noticed that many of the long-timers have steady relationships. Everyone knew who "belonged" to who yet they kept it very low key and it was usually overlooked by the C.O.'s. The younger/newer girls who flaunted their behaviors, doing what they seemed to think is expected of them were continually in trouble. Each conquest was a "duck" and the more you get the "badder" you are. Ducks were usually lonely or confused young girls willing to pay for sex with commissary. They were the kind of women that if on the street would do everyone, male, female, on two legs or four.

Ellie was in the same classes as Bonnie and Slurp and they resided in the same building. To Ellie, sex was a commodity. Before her arrest she traded sex for money and drugs, telling stories about partying with entire professional football or basketball teams. Once into population, she was befriended by a lifer. The lifer's "girlfriend" was released a few months later and Ellie showed an interest in taking her place. There was some open affection for some time, but was later told by the other girl they could be friends, but once she left for home she knew Ellie would lead a straight life and that is what she wanted for her. A "love" relationship with her inside would never work for either of them. But Ellie needed a sexual companion and couldn't distinguish that from love.

Another fight in diet kitchen. The girl Brenda Slims gave a hard time to earlier really took a bad beating this time but Ronda didn't have anything to do with it. Two girls waited in line after lunch to be searched. The girl cut in front of them and they had words. One of them grabbed the girl by the throat and she was thrown against the wall. Her head got whacked bad and her body was pummeled by fists and feet before the skirmish was broken up. Some people's crimes just aren't as respected as others in this strange world.

There was a drug bust in Wilson—smoking pot. Stupid! They lived in such a confined area and that stuff had such a distinctive odor. Those caught implicated another eight. They were all escorted over to the hospital for blood and urine tests. Drugs come in through visiting hall. Everyone was always searched going in and coming out, but Rachel knew a girl that smuggled gum in her snatch regularly and once brought in a half pound of shrimp. Since this was possible, there's little doubt that drugs come in the same way. Also, visitors can hide a package in the "visitor's" john. The visiting room has two washrooms, one for visitors and one for inmates. Once visiting was over, the inmates that clean the johns know to pick up the package, get it to the owner and collect their reward. Of course C.O.'s brought in drugs too.

Rachel was thankful that she was able to view life at Lotusville as opposed to being part of it. She tried to keep her thoughts on home and family. So many girls formed new families here. They called the buildings they live in home. They lost interest in their children who were being brought up by others and frequently had no interest in regaining custody once they were released. She wrote Eric daily. One morning her pen stopped working so sucked on the end and that fixed it. She had to let Eric know this.

Rachel's parents were back to visit and this time brought her two kids. It was so hard to see the hurt on their faces. Hot tears just welled as her little daughter stared at her. She didn't know what she'd been told or what she understood.

She didn't talk. Just stared. Her son just looked so pale. She thought he was going to throw up. He made a mad dash to the bathroom. Maybe he did. Minutes later when he returned, his face was all pink and his eyes were swollen. Oh, what shame she has put everyone through—and she's never discussed any of it with them. No one ever asked her for the details. Maybe they talked with the attorney, and who knows what he might have said—even if he remembered the case.

One girl lost all her kids once arrested. Not that it was her idea. The kids wanted nothing to do with her; no phone calls, no letters, no visits during her two year imprisonment. Once out she moved to Texas. Suddenly and without being pregnant had a baby daughter of Mexican descent, who had apparently replaced her own kids, and was soon scamming businesses and people out there. She found a seemingly nice guy and married him. They drove truck together. Now, she's "home-schooling" the girl because she doesn't have any paperwork for her and her mother is probably in a shallow grave in the desert somewhere. She is in and out of jail, the husband taking the responsibility of the girl.

\*     \*     \*

Uncle Festus keyed open the door of a room that was supposed to be vacant. There was Cowboy and a girlfriend chewing on each other. He just stood in the doorway laughing loud enough that it caught everyone's attention. Several girls ran to the doorway to check out the scene. He told them to get out, and didn't write a ticket. That story traveled fast. There was a lot of resentment about his lack of action and several kites were written to his superiors.

Supposedly Cowboy was doing straight time and she will leave here in a few months so she has a "don't give a damn" attitude about all authority here. One of her latest girlfriends, who worked as an aide at the school, was caught making unauthorized phone calls from her job, was dismissed and locked up.

Another night at an N.A. meeting a girl was searched and caught with drugs and taken out. The next morning a set of silverware went missing from P.F.S. The spoon was found hidden in a Kotex. No sign of the knife and fork. There was a rumor of a war brewing between two buildings. Rachel heard rumors constantly and after thinking about it decided there's more of a chance that the silverware was taken to get the snitch that turned in the girl with the drugs. She really didn't care one way or the other—until she went to eat and was only issued a plastic spoon. There was a lot of finger eating at P.F.S. and gnashing of teeth. Those without teeth were limited to eating soft food. Nothing more was ever heard about the incident.

Deb, who was in county with Rachel was using the toilet after being locked in her room for the night. She heard the click of keys in her door and in walks Uncle Festus. He offered her gum for "head." She was outraged and told him to leave and felt fortunate he didn't press, just left. The next day she kited her chaplain and a couple days later, he called her over to his office and said he'd like to work with her to make some changes. Never heard any more about that, but later that week, Uncle Festus entered another room and woke the girl in the top bunk, asking her to "go for a walk" with him. The girl in the lower bunk woke up when he came in, and seeing his arousal, grabbed it as hard as she could and twisted. He howled a cuss and left the room quickly.

A few days later an inmate who wanted to be "friendly" with him asked him, "Well, how did you like getting your balls grabbed the other night?"

"That dumb cunt didn't know what she was doing." he bragged. "Anyone grabbing me has to use both hands to get any kind of grip."

She smiled and explained that she didn't know that but would like to check it out if it could be arranged.

Shortly thereafter, he walked in on Pam who was in her room using the toilet and she was infuriated. Rachel suggested she send a kite to a white shirt, but Pam was afraid he'd come back to her and get even. About that time, the unit manager came in and she went to him. He told her he didn't want to get involved. A few minutes later, the unit manager talked with Uncle Festus and told him he'd been reported for bothering girls on the toilet. Because he "bothered" several girls every night, Uncle Festus wasn't sure who turned him in and started raging at several girls trying to find out who ratted on him. No one spoke up, so he wrote tickets on half a dozen girls for (1) lying, (2) disrespect, and (3) not displaying an ID. The story is, he runs a cleaning service in Springfield and hires girls after they get out. Exactly what was on their job description, who knows. She couldn't imagine who in their right mind would want to work for him, but they did.

Finally, a "white shirt" came and pulled several girls into a conference. Seems that there have been a lot of complaints about a certain C.O. chasing after sex and making unwarranted visits into their rooms. Good. Maybe those kites do work after a while. The major problem is so many of the girls like the attention and gum, while others are horrified by it. A lot of girls have been coming to Rachel with their issues with the personnel here and they sit and try to work them out. They get impatient, but eventually things do get taken care of. Rachel has become a pseudo mom.

Deb's tiptoed around for a couple of days waiting to be sent to MAX over her recent confrontation with Uncle Festus. It scared her so much she telephoned her family and her attorney about it. When she saw a "white shirt" coming in, she approached him with her worry, wanting to get it over with. He sat down with her and told her that there had been dozens of complaints about that C.O. from inmates who admitted accepting a variety of gifts for sex. The stories brought the problem to a head when it got out that while some girls that accepted gum those in Jefferson got reefer for the same service. They searched the room of the girl in Jefferson and found gum, whiskey, jewelry, and rolls of quarters. Anyway, the "white shirt" told her that Uncle Festus was on his way out so she could stop worrying about him bothering her. She could stop worrying her family and please tell them to stop calling down there. Time will tell.

Rachel was glad they've stopped seeing Deb as a troublemaker but just a girl that was very vocal with her opinions and had little respect for assholes—even when they were wearing a badge.

Rachel mentioned this to Kenny, her roommate. She said, "for someone to slobber on someone to get what they want is one thing—to talk about it is stupid. For anyone to say they did it to him for any amount of money is beyond my understanding. He is absolutely the most disgusting specimen that claims to be alive." She just shook her head.

She said that once she was sitting at a table with a glass of Kool Aid and he sat down next to her. He hovered over her glass of Kool Aid as he talked. "Get away from me and stop leaning over my cup."

"What's the matter with you," he inquired.

"With all your picking, scratching and digging, I don't know what's going to fall out," she answered.

"He must see a lot of action, though," Kenny commented "I saw a young girl flirting with him. Later she told me that that's the way she gets perfume. He walked around like a king, that belly hanging over his belt. He needed a throne with a hole in the seat."

Uncle Festus hasn't been back in the building in a while, so kite's may work when there was enough of them on the same subject. Also, the young enthusiastic male C.O. who strip-searched the girls at diet kitchen hasn't been seen lately, either. Rumor had it he was transferred to the new Riverview pre-release.

Rachel heard there was loud screaming from the shower in a distant building. She didn't hear it, but the grapevine was always full of juicy grapes. The C.O. on duty supposedly ignored it as horseplay, but a passing C.O. rushed to the defense of the girl who was being raped by another girl, a convicted rapist. The weapon was a broom handle. This girl had a history of violence and was here previously for killing a gay man in a bar outside Springfield when there was controversy over a twenty-five-cent bet on a pool game. This inmate victim was in the I.S.U hospital for over a week.

Rachel tried to get a shower. All four showers were busy. No one came in or out for at least ten minutes, but the foggy air was full of voices. She went in to find two girls in each of the four shower stalls—everybody having a good time. She decided to return later for her shower.

One evening her roommate, who chose a later bed time, sneaked in their electrically locked, dead-bolted door, grabbed her towel, soap and shampoo and slinked out to join her friends in the shower. She got away with it that night and she got back in unseen. It's only a matter of time before they discover they never fixed the door lock. At least she's a good sneak. She lurked, watched the C.O's movements, then made a dash. Because she always kept a low profile, they don't watch her too closely.

Coombs County came for Bessie for the custody hearing for her son. Her daughter can't handle him and he choose not to go to school. The thought of her going back to her home town (even for a week) settled her down.

Having a really bad day. Rachel knew her dad should not be behind the wheel of a car. He fell asleep and almost went into a ditch on their way home after the last visit. She didn't want her parents driving down here at all. They insisted. Friends and family come with them but he always insisted on doing the driving. No one seemed to have a personality strong enough to move him out of the driver's seat. What was she supposed to do? Refuse to see them when they get here? Tell them she doesn't want to see them anymore? Can't hurt them like that. Can't smile and say everything was okay any more. No one knew the horrors of this place. She knew it was no one's fault but her own that she was here. That didn't make it easier on any of them. She felt she was becoming an emotional cripple and her world was circling the drain.

There was a girl that has been in the hospital in isolation for some time with hepatitis. Now, they say she has syphilis too. Rachel spoke briefly with the girl that had to scrub down the room when it was discovered how infectious she was. What a nasty job she has.

She learned that the boiler alarm goes off when the water pressure isn't high enough to keep it filled. At first they said "go easy on the water." Then they eliminated clothes washing. When that didn't do it, they eliminated showers which resulted in 200 girls smelling like Hulk Hogan's armpit. Then they shut off the toilets. She hoped this wasn't their idea of a permanent fix.

The flies were really devious and worked in tandem when the girls were at dinner. "Group A" flies went under the table to bite their legs. The girls put down their silverware to bat them away and "group B" attacked their meal. They are accompanied by a million gnats that hover in the air. If one knocks one of these delicate things into the food, they just stick there and they are so tiny you can't possibly spot them on dark food like meat, unless their wings reflected light and twitch. Rachel's grandmother told her that she had to eat a bushel of dirt before she died. The basket was filling up.

Cowboy got a new roommate every time she was caught having sex with the present one. They send her to MAX each time, but that doesn't change her. She knows her out date so doesn't care. Now, they've put Cowboy in with a young girl. Bessie hollered to her, "You're walking like your thing got chewed on." The girl was offended and embarrassed.

The morning C.O. forgot to take the mail when she was going off duty.

"Hey, stop! You forgot the mail again." yelled Bessie as the C.O. was ready to go out the door. "I'm going to have to start writing some tickets," she chided.

The C.O. who is quite a prune, had to come up with a little humor as her temporary relief was a white shirt. "So you're giving tickets?" the C.O. chuckled. "What's my punishment? Early beds?"

"No!" answered Bessie, "you'll be washing out the showers."

"Do you think you'll get her to do that?" the smiling white shirt spoke up.

"If she won't, her mammy will." Bessie offered. Prison humor!

School was lending some purpose to Rachel's being here and she appreciated and enjoyed every minute of it, but still felt she's half crazy most of the time. Her spring is wound too tight. One really neat thing happened at the school. The two people running the school went to a football game over the weekend. The guy hired a plane to fly over the field at half time trailing a banner asking her to marry him. She said yes, and he gave her a ring. It felt so good to hear this nice story. He walked around all puffed up and proud, she glowed as much as her ring. Happiness was so rare here.

Rachel had some pretty heavy tests back to back and she let herself get backlogged with studying. She owed everybody letters. She wrote a lot of letters to release frustrations and never failed to write Eric daily. Being able to tell him all the ugly helped her relax. This was going to be a tough week scholastically, but nothing could have been worse than last week.

The teacher in the business class commented that the two biggest labor unions in the U.S. are the Teamsters and Teachers—neither of which belong to the AFL-CIO. She said the Teamsters were rejected because of corruption high in their ranks. She asked if that wasn't the pot calling the kettle black. The teacher laughingly agreed.

> It only takes one little spore
>     To make a fungus grow.
> It only takes one lazy man
>     To make production slow
>
> If he's allowed to justify
>     And ride that easy path
> Than who's to blame for heartache
>     When all must take the bath
>
> Subsidizing laziness
>     Is the union way of late
> No guilt for "grand theft hours"
>     —A semi-welfare state—
>
> Job security can be obtained
>     By clearing minds of murk
> Lets control the greed within
>     Through hard consistent work

The heat was incredible at night. No air in the rooms even with the windows open. The male night C.O. who looked like a leprechaun, spent a lot of time peeking in the rooms, not just for count but all night long. Everyone was told to "sleep decent" which just excited many to sleep naked. He probably had to stand on his toes to see in the window, then use his flashlight.

The light bulb in Rachel's room finally stopped flickering and died. It is blessedly dark. She can fantasize that the light bulb changers are busy elsewhere and won't be back here for a day or two. Nothing is ever perfect, though. Because of the dark, the C.O. woke her up at 5 am for count. She had to see her face. After she left, Rachel got up because her alarm clock was due to ring anyway.

The food had been getting increasingly bad and many girls have been buying what they can from the commissary to avoid going to P.F.S. Big Bessie walked past a group of girls playing cards. She carried a sardine can to the trash. One of the girls hollered, "take a douche." The world of nasty continued.

The phones do not work and that was blamed on the heat. They brought a fan into the building but the C.O. wouldn't turn it on. Bessie called her an "earth disturbin' big teeth dog." The C.O. that was scheduled today refused to work in Pierce, saying she was afraid of the inmates. This building had a lot of issues that created a lot of tension. There's close to two hundred girls in this building, but only one that's unstable and half a dozen with quick tempers. Nothing different than you would find anywhere but we're living in close quarters.

The building was crawling with mice and Rachel was sure the problem isn't unique to Pierce. Danita came out of her room today with her earphones in half a dozen pieces. Several girls have been badgering the C.O. for mousetraps for several days. Some have given up and some will continue to do so until they get one. The crazy thing was, many of these women would rather live with the critters than hear the snap of the trap. Then they argue with each other about what they are going to do with the dead thing. There are garbage cans and toilets everywhere and with the history some of these girls have, there shouldn't be a problem disposing of the body. Rachel found it similar to the time she killed all the flies.

Vi was a quiet girl. Very sweet. She came here as a teenager on an aggravated murder charge, killing her boyfriend for having sex with a street girl in front of her kids while she was at work. Rachel had known her for over a year and had never seen her mad at anyone, never known her to get a ticket. She had frequent visits from her family who drove up from Karo. Figured she was just enraged when she found out as anyone would be. The problem was, she didn't just pack up her kids and leave or tell the guy to go. When the word got out that Rachel was moving to Wilson soon, she started to cry. She said she was just getting ready to ask her to help her learn to read. Why hasn't she been taking GED classes? Why wasn't that encouraged? Why weren't any of these girls encouraged to further their education?

Rachel's roommate asked her to read her English essay—ten pages on how to iron a shirt. It was comical and she told her it was a riot. Then she handed her a whole page of corrections and suggestions. Hope she didn't mind too much, after all, she complimented her first.

As rumor of her imminent move spread, all the misfits Rachel had befriended had been stopping by her door, letting her know how much she would be missed when she leaves. Little Ginger just left her threshold. They all acted like she was going out the gate instead of next door.

The fire alarm wailed a few minutes before lunch. The C.O. screamed "evacuate" and everyone grudgingly went outside. The alarm shut off, emergency over. A captain showed up and demanded roll call outside, and alphabetically when a name was called one would go inside. One of the last girls in went to her room to find her watch missing. She bitched and hollered and demanded an immediate search, but the C.O. made an announcement that the snake who snatched it should give it up. That'll work! Then all were sent to lunch—a perfect opportunity to pass it on. That's not the only stolen watch she'd heard about. This time the victim was a known thief and rumor was it was someone getting even.

Then, just after returning from lunch, the watch was dropped into Clovis's pocket. "Just hold it for a little while," a voice whispered from behind her. Rachel hated the rampant thievery and suspected she saw the exchange, and to see a major thief become a victim didn't bother her that much. Part of the "jading" process, she guessed. She didn't want to get involved but couldn't resist later asking Clovis if she saw what she thought she saw. Clovis said she took the watch to her room, put it in a plastic bag and sunk it to the bottom of a jar of moisturizer. Meanwhile, the thief furiously knit an animal she stuffed with filling from her pillow, put the watch inside and mailed it home to her sister.

In the back of the building the rooms were stacked two stories high and from there a slanted ceiling down to the common room. The roof has quite a pitch and a skylight. The ceiling tiles were already water stained and every rain has them dripping. That could be what shorts out the alarm all the time, or maybe the girls sneak a cigarette in their rooms from time to time. The administration denies both possibilities and insisted it is because the girls shower with the door closed so now we have to shower with the door open. Maybe we need a vent fan in the shower room.

The parole board met for the month and gave about 20 girls their freedom. Then Coombs and Cook both rode and brought twenty four new girls in one day. This place was overbooked before it opened.

As Rachel's board date neared she was moved to Wilson, minimum security, and her pink jacket was replaced by green. The unit manager told her that in a year's time she would be eligible for a weekend furlough. "Only six girls in this whole place are eligible for this." he told her, in an awed tone used to present this valuable gift. She told him she didn't expect to be here a year from now. Yikes, another year!

Before being moved, the unit manager asked Rachel who over there she'd like to room with. "Give me somebody that's killed someone. I'm so tired of thieves," she answered kiddingly, not expecting anything but the same old same old. The buildings were identical. The lights stayed on all night and drew bugs through the screen. In the morning, the sink was full of the tiny things. It's been a year since she's been in the dark, except briefly when the bulb burned out, and her body craved the dark.

Rachel started walking with Bonnie, the girl from school who lived in another building. Round and round the track, getting exercise, but always hoping to meet Mattie. One bright sunny day they saw this extremely handsome, tall, well built man cutting across the walk/jog. Men were rare here except for C.O.s and to their minds, they hardly qualified. Maybe they were males, but they were hardly men. They sped up to catch up with him and talk. He introduced himself and was surprisingly friendly.

It turned out he was headed to the hospital where he had an office and did some psych stuff for the girls. Well, Bonnie referred to him as Dr. Bob and decided she had to make an immediate appointment with him. She did have psyche issues and Rachel was glad that he might be able to help her work through them. Also, her hair was coming out in quarter sized chunks. Bald spots! What a horrible thing to do to a girl's self-esteem. He brought her vitamins and her hair grew back. He was a really nice guy who cared. Shortly after that, they started selling multi-vitamins at the commissary. Bonnie suspects he was behind that because prior to Bonnie's problems, they didn't sell them.

After he started working there a lady who worked as a secretary in the hospital took a leave-of-absence for hemorrhoid surgery and her co-workers asked Rachel for a "welcome back to work" verse. This is what they got.

In her little office tucked away
    Amid the systems hells
Where a zillion filthy roaches
    Breed like cancer cells

Where people, like in zoos, are caged
    Are tended washed and fed
The staff that rules by shirt and badge
    Should be on special med

Patti's back to work now
    She's left her home and cats
Trading all that's dear to her
    For fungus, slime and rats

The groundhogs feed on apples
　　Squirrels play tag in trees
Cows hump in the pasture
　　Patti works the Swintec keys

We're glad to see her back to work
　　And feeling up to par
Be prepared, however,
　　To let us see your scar

Swintec was the brand of electric typewriter she used.

For some reason, Slurp kept a diary of her conquests and during a random search of her room it was confiscated. She was asked at the time of her parole hearing if she did all the C.O.s and she pondered that for a minute before saying in her quiet, soft innocent voice, "No," then added thoughtfully, "not all of them." She was given another year, After her release she picked up a DWI but wasn't violated because rumor had it that she was taking good care of her parole officer.

Brenda Slims was in Wilson again and welcomed Rachel as she brought in her stuff. She warned her about all the thieves, that nothing was safe. Said she wanted to catch someone trying to steal something from her. Rachel got a long piece of thread from the sewing machine and attached it to a pen. Then she set the pen on a nearby table and waited. Sure enough someone slithered over to it and made a grab. But the pen jumped just out of her reach. When she reached again, the pen leaped to the floor. Brenda went over to her and said, "That pen doesn't seem to like you. It must not be yours." Later, a girl who thought she was a man was strutting around. Brenda said to her, "If you were a man, you wouldn't be here. Don't you bleed?" This place hasn't changed Brenda.

Rachel's new roommate in Wilson didn't want her there. Molly had a room to herself for some time because of her medical issues and liked it that way. When she found Rachel had moved in while she was at work, she spent the next few hours complaining about the situation to the administration. Yes, Molly had killed someone—vehicular homicide—and she was very gracious once she understood that neither of them had any choice and nothing was going to change. Rachel's request for a roommate that had killed someone had been answered. It wasn't long before they became good friends. Rachel heard a rumor that Molly had "shocked out" a couple of years before, then was caught driving without a license so had to come back and finish a ten-year sentence. She had a mass of physical problems, some of them the result of the automobile accident that put her here, some from a recent hysterectomy done here that didn't heal right. She showed Rachel a canoe shaped scar across her entire stomach that still had drains. Her job had her making flags with people from other buildings and she was acquainted with Mattie. Rachel was then able to communicate more often with Mattie and to discuss their situations as regularly as possible.

They talked about their cases and the similarities and both vowed to do their best to make things right. She told Rachel that she had been working in a head-start program where two of Bruce Muley's kids were enrolled. One of the kids was behaving strangely and it was discovered he was being sexually abused, probably by his dad. The police wanted to talk with him at the time but couldn't find him.

They had his girlfriend call him and say she was in the hospital and wanted to see him. When he showed up to see her, he caused a ruckus when the police nabbed him. "They were in cahoots with the police and somehow he got out of that one after a few months." Rachel told her that there was a story in the newspaper about him threatening someone with a gun at a nearby Denny's Restaurant and was arrested for having it under disability because he'd done a stint for murder some time before. That caper was on his record, as well as in the newspaper. Again, Mattie affirmed "they are all in cahoots." She went on to talk about her case.

"One evening after dinner when I was doing the dishes, the phone rang and one of my sons answered it. He said something then handed the phone to his dad. It was Bruce Muley's wife Lola asking to talk to his dad. Sam got on the phone for a minute, then told me he had to go out for cigarettes and he never came home that night. Sam was shot two times in the head and I found his car the next morning when I walked to work. It was parked right out front and I knew I would be blamed when the police showed up." She explained that they had troubles for years so had motive.

"During my trial, Bruce Muley and his long-time girlfriend/wife, Lola, told the police they saw her brother and another guy commit the murder. They were just trying to protect themselves and possibly getting vengeance against us, thinking I turned him in for the gross sexual imposition discovered at the head-start program. Neither me or my brother ever met the other guy until the pre-trial and didn't know what he'd done to offend and get on Muley's bad side. I was in county for eight months, had fifteen pre-trials. Jury picking lasted two weeks. In court, Bruce Muley testified/lied for two days and his character was torn down, but we were all found guilty. The three of us were all given life sentences. In a murder case the judge said we had the right to be tried separately, but somehow that had been denied us. Hopefully, an appeal will work and Bruce Muley will get this case back."

"Our (Mattie's, her brother, and another guy she didn't know) case was written in the paper three times and on the news daily until it was over. They made sure they filmed the fool, Muley, during his testimony and he tried to hide his face." She said she thinks he is through sending people to jail now as everybody on the streets knows what he is and why a lot of people he knew went to jail over the years. Rachel's case was mentioned in her transcript as another victim of him, but the newspapers never mentioned a connection.

"He had been tried, found guilty and incarcerated for several months for gross sexual imposition with his kids and was sent to prison, but found that a few of his other 'victims' there were out for revenge. He requested protective custody and was returned to the Criminal Justice Central building for your trial and mine. Was he wearing an orange jump suit when he testified against you?" Rachel nodded. "Mine, too. He filed an appeal on his own case and was immediately denied."

"Myself and two co-dependents each had two lawyers and a private investigator and I have to admit we had a good defense team. They all worked hard, but it just wasn't good enough. Bruce Muley is a very smart and hateful person."

She went on to say that she had started to write letters to people she thinks will help with the appeal—like battered women's organizations. "I don't have all the addresses that I need yet, but I've kited the social workers for them. I'm a mother of six and a grandmother of three. I deserve to be home with them."

The unit manager at Jefferson, the building where she was housed, decided to raise money for something and sold popcorn to accomplish this. Those with money in their accounts could buy tickets to make purchases. The pop corn was really good, but the opportunity was short-lived. Mattie told Rachel that if she could get the popping oil, she'd make her all she wanted. She couldn't get the oil, but a friend stole a whole pound of butter from the big kitchen where she worked. Just tucked it into her bra and away she went. Rachel got it over to Mattie, and the next day word got back to her it was done and she should take a walk on the track and pick it up.

WOW! She had two huge black garbage bags of it waiting for her. Inside each and stuffed full were at least two dozen bread loaf wrappers housing the individual servings. How was she going to sneak this a quarter of a mile to the other side of the compound? Boldly, she figured, so she set off like a wealthy bag lady. The smell of the freshly popped corn attracted many begging followers as she walked across the compound. Guards watching with binoculars couldn't smell it. If she stopped to give some out, she'd surely be caught. She felt like the Pied Piper. Confident she wouldn't be followed into Wilson, she went straight to her building, straight past the C.O's desk, and straight to her room. And waited . . . . waited. No one questioned her except other hungry inmates who hovered just outside her door. She had no problem with sharing. She couldn't possibly have eaten it all herself. But you just can't have everyone out there eating popcorn we had no business having. When the C.O. wasn't paying much attention or was otherwise occupied, Rachel took it out a few bags at a time in her school bag and distributed it. Most everyone that was interested enjoyed it the three days it lasted. One girl commented that it smelled like dirty socks.

*     *     *

Rachel still badgered her family and friends constantly to try to reach D.D. Knight. What was happening on her appeal? Did he get the copy of the letter from Mattie? Since she was mentioned in her transcript with a list of others "he put in jail with his testimony" would this help? Would he follow this up, bother to read Mattie's transcript? Finally she got a letter from a family member that got through to him.

He told her brother he was keeping in good contact with her (what a liar!) and he's getting ready to file the appeal. Seems he's been ill and unable to do it sooner. He told him he was going to send Rachel a copy of the brief he was filing and wanted her to make changes and additions. Sure enough, she got it a week later. All excited that something was finally happening, she detailed several things that weren't right at the trial. The problem was, most of what was wrong was his ineptness, like not presenting her receipts, not calling her witnesses to corroborate her claims. These were things that would make him look bad and wasn't about to use. At least she knew he was still alive, but didn't know if that was good or bad. A couple weeks later, she heard from a family member he had filed the appeal and had lost on two points but won on another. Strange he notified her. She had no clue as to what points he won and what he didn't. Others here wait weeks/months for the results of their appeal. She never heard anything from the attorney, only through family. This wasn't enough information for someone starving for it. What was the next step?

Rachel felt quite alone and abandoned. It was so depressing to be in a situation where she had nothing to say. No one told her anything. Maybe they heard from the attorney and they're just not telling her. She cried too much, got headaches from it, yet nothing changed. Will she ever get out of this madhouse?

Her son wrote that she was supposed to be called as a witness in an automobile accident incident, but the attorney forgot to subpoena her. The hearing was postponed. Those attorneys are all a bunch of lazy, incompetent and inconsiderate bastards. There were several times she had taken off from work and went down to Criminal Justice Central for a pre-trial or hearings and the things had been cancelled and she wasn't notified by her attorney, D.D. Knight, and several times she had an appointment with him and he wasn't even in his office.

Brenda and Deb were scheduled to leave for pre-release in Riverview next week and were anxious to leave. They won't be able to go home but it will be one step closer. Phone calls and visits will be easier, but it is still going from one jail to another. Since getting the news, Brenda has worn more makeup and tied fancier turbans. There's more bounce to her walk and if possible, she's more animated. Deb hasn't changed a bit.

Rachel went out to the mailbox to drop in a letter and Brenda came over and gave her a hug good-bye. That was really sweet. Of course, the C.O. screamed "no physical contact." What a joke.

Early in the morning Brenda and Deb were both told to pack their things, that they were leaving. An hour later they were both told they weren't going anywhere. Deb didn't take it hard, but Brenda was ready to "perform." Since they were both from Coombs County, they suspected the problem was at the pre-release or maybe a transportation issue. Talk about confusion. A mother came here to pick up her daughter and they told her they weren't letting her go for another year. It is harder on our families when we're here than on us.

Alice wrote again, another of those very long prison-style letters. Opening each one, Rachel hoped things would be looking up for this very deserving lady, but it wasn't to be. She cried for her. Her new husband stole her personal belongings, jewelry and things that belonged to her mother—all to support his drug habit and entertain his friends. He was jealous of the men in his fantasies he thought she was with and became enraged if he saw a bruise a man must have put there. She wrote that she could deal with the weed, but not the heroin and crack that made him violent. A subsequent letter told of beatings she ran from, of escaping from him, bleeding and clothes torn, seeking refuge from a passing taxi, only to have to escape from the taxi driver. What kind of nightmare had she gotten into? She wrote, "There were people who don't understand how anyone would stay with an abuser. I guess the answer is the woman has to make the choice of not wanting that in her life."

A C.O. Rachel wasn't familiar with decided it was too much work for her to deal with her charges during the day so told everyone to go to their rooms and she locked everyone in. It gave Rachel time to study, but it was hard for her to stretch her legs when after two steps in any direction she had to turn around. Those girls who enjoyed playing cards couldn't. If one wanted to go outside and walk around the track, that was out. This was every day that that particular C.O. was on duty. Rachel wasn't hurting as much as some, but knew this wasn't right so once let out to go to dinner, she grabbed a couple of kites, wrote them up and sent them off.

A few days later, the C.O. called "Rachel Williams" loudly and said, "They want you at the inspector's office."

"Where is it?" she questioned.

"I don't know," she answered. "Just a minute!" She got on the phone, found out and told her.

No problem. She found to the properly labeled door and knocked. "You summoned me?" She asked a good-looking well built man sitting behind a desk.

"Take off your coat and hat and shut the door." he said off-handedly. He put a tape recorder on the table and asked if she had a problem if he recorded the conversation. "Of course not, let's get this all on record. I do not lie, cheat, steal or deceive." Her natural voice is soft and low and she doubted the tape recorder would pick up much of it, but she didn't care one way of the other. At first she thought this was about the cardboard box she'd been seeking to store her clothes under the bed. A quick scan of the room showed no box awaiting her. She'd made a big issue of the ridiculous situation and she doubted they wanted to tape record any talk about it.

He held up one of her letters and asked her if she was familiar with it. She told him she'd written a lot of letters to a lot of people, but none to him but she had frequently and repeatedly sent him kites. She had to question him as to what that particular one was about. As he started to read it, she recognized it as one she'd sent to the Bureau of Rehabilitations and Corrections in Springfield in regard to the unsafe conditions and procedures here. She'd also sent a similar note to the Director of Prisons and she suspected one of them was intercepted. There was nothing in either letter that she hadn't already kited this inspector and others about. Yet he seemed surprised and shocked at what Rachel mentioned in the letter about what was going on in Wilson Cottage and asked her what anyone had done that the C.O. had locked everyone up all day. She shrugged and told him "nothing that I'm aware of, but it wasn't just one day. It is every day and all day that particular C.O. worked Wilson." Kenny told her earlier that nothing had changed in that regard with that particular C.O. since she got here five years ago. She always locked everyone in during her shift.

He gave Rachel a strange look, then asked, "if I were to go over there in the middle of the day tomorrow, I'd find everyone locked in?"

"If she's on duty, you sure would."

He said that if what Rachel was saying was true, he'd put a stop to it immediately, that he'd already conferenced with the unit manager and the warden who, he assured her, were both unaware. By the time Rachel walked back to Wilson, he'd already called over there and left the message that she put their conversation in writing. She could only assume that his tape recorder had not picked up her voice and also that he had no business with her letter.

The next day Rachel watched out the window in her door. The C.O was on duty and everyone was locked in. Sure enough he came strolling in. The C.O. smiled at him. "Where is everybody," he asked?

She responded with a grin, "Oh, they're all in their rooms where they belong." He sat down and talked with her quietly for a few minutes, then left as she unlocked everyone's door and let everyone out that chose to come out.

Bonnie went to be reclassified today and she was afraid that if she became a minimum she would lose her single room, which was a rarity here, and she would be moved to a dorm where she couldn't keep her typewriter safe. If she left it unattended, it would be tucked under someone's coat or between their legs and end up in another building. Rachel was amazed at the huge heavy parcels these girls managed to walk with but they weren't always successful. One day as she walked behind a heavy girl she watched hot dogs and bananas drop from her skirt.

Bonnie was re-classed to minimum and requested to move to Wilson Cottage. At first they told her it was impossible if she felt she needed a lower bunk, that there was space in Warren North for her. That's a dorm where 50 girls share a room and no one's personal belongings are safe. A little while later, they told her that a lower bunk became available in Wilson and she was happy with that. Rachel and Bonnie will be able to study together more often. Once there, Bonnie told her she is pleased with the cleanliness of the building, the quietness, and the nice clean showers. The next day she learned they double bunked her single room.

A few months went by since Bonnie started making regular appointments with the psych man, her Dr. Bob, but problems started when Bonnie told several of her friends about this handsome man and that he ended all the counseling sessions with a hug—and they all made appointments and told their friends. Well, one of Bonnie's friends, Slurp, who happened to be "doing" most all the male C.O.s and some of the females decided she'd add him to her collection. Two or three other girls decided to make their play as well. He didn't buy any of it. These girls got really upset at being turned down and made a fuss—and eventually he lost his job.

*   *   *

Bonnie's been "in residence" quite a while and knew a lot of people. One of them worked in laundry and when delivering clothes to one building learned the C.O.'s dining room had lots of various flavored ice cream in their freezer—a donation most certainly meant for the inmates but ice cream is only a fantasy for inmates. Pushing the laundry cart, she relieved them of several boxes, stashing them under the clothes. Bonnie was a recipient of one box and several of us dined lavishly that evening on Borden's Heavenly Hash.

No further word about the grant money problem and Rachel still felt she was not an accepted student, but she never stopped attending classes and had aced most of the tests. They told her at the school not to worry about it, but school was her oasis and she didn't want to get kicked out.

One girl told another that she didn't mind being locked up for bad checks because she'd done a lot worse. She said she was tired of a boyfriend that kept coming around so she shot him as he slept. Then she called a family member who worked in a junkyard. He came over, took the body and stashed it in a car that was ready for the crusher. She got out shortly after telling that story and caught a theft case and last I heard she was on the run.

Rachel's sentence was 4-15 years but those with a drug case could meet a board at 2 years 2 months and 12 days. She watched the board list go up and her name wasn't on it. She asked the C.O. who she should ask about it. She just told her she'd look into it and probably forgot two minutes later. Rachel then kited the social worker. A week or so later the social worker got back to her and said she'd look into it. So she wrote a letter to the Parole Board in Springfield to ask the "horse's mouth" when she should expect to see her name on the board list. No response from anyone.

Another letter from Alice. Rachel loved to hear from her and always hoped the news would be good. This one said she was relieved her husband was arrested again and sent to prison.

Looking back, she understood that their cultural differences made their relationship doomed from the start. He was the middle one of thirteen children, the product of alcoholism and violence, but was now the eldest. Overdoses, beatings, gunshots, and medical issues reduced what's left of his family to turmoil, stealing and using each other and now he's the oldest. A brother is in prison as is a niece.

Her letters indicated she was giving up on the marriage but her behaviors said she was still totally enthralled. She visited him in prison and smuggled in some reefer—taking a chance of ending up locked up again. He told her that his young teen-age son was having problems. His mom was living a destructive lifestyle and the boy needed her help. She agreed to look into it and perhaps have him come live with her.

The boy was angry all the time and getting into all kinds of mischief. When she came home from work, he always had a number of friends at the house, drinking or smoking weed. They'd leave when she got home, but the house was always in disarray and smelled of dope. The arrangement wasn't working out so she told her husband that he'd have to leave, but there was no place for him to go. She soon realized she had a street gang meeting at her house and it scared her to death. She told the boy he'd have to find himself another place and he told her that she was the one that would have to go.

She just left and moved in temporarily with a woman she worked with, not telling anyone she was going or where she was. Not even her husband. Any property of value was long gone so she just picked up what she could carry and left. Said she felt much like the person she was in admissions, living out of a paper bag.

There's a young girl from Cook who met with the board this morning. She's always bouncing around, dancing and singing "*You Sexy Thing.*" She didn't seem to know the rest of the song, but that phrase was always on her lips. When she met the board they asked her if she would do some work to get out of here. She told them she'd do anything they asked. They told her to find out the rest of the words to that song and sing it to them when they called her back later in the day. She didn't have a clue and was in a panic asking everyone if they knew it. She must have picked up enough of it to fake or at least they enjoyed her rendition because they gave her an out date. Later Rachel learned that she was working at an all-night restaurant as a cook and she was hoping she could stop by and visit with her once she got out. But who knew when that would be or where the girl would be by then.

Rachel just got another letter from the cashiers office in Springfield. They are making noises about kicking her out of school again. She just goes back each day and attends class, not knowing if she'll be allowed back the next. It drains her emotionally.

An inmate that worked at the substance abuse center said they needed someone to do clerical work over there and would she be interested if she couldn't attend school. Rachel told her "yes" but she hated the thought of not going to school. The girl said she'd put her name in for it.

Rachel was called over to the school a few days later and worried all the way over that they were going to dump her, but they were just distributing new baskets to carry books to class. She asked about the grant problem and was told that the school was checking with some place in Omaha.

There were two groups of girls taking the same classes but at different times. Most everyone in Rachel's group were new to her. She knew several in the other class, but was glad she was where she was. The girls were friendlier, more real.

All her days were spent studying for one test or another and she had been rewarded by good grades. Some of the girls in the class resented her grades because some teachers grade on a curve. She was just doing what she had to do for herself. Studying for these tests was the one thing in life that she has control over and she was fixated. She just got 37 out of 40 on a math test and didn't give a second thought about what the others did.

She walked the track with Autumn who was all riled up. Said she'd come out of her room after 11 am count and a white shirt asked her if her shirt came in her box "that way." She had altered it for a sexy look. She was told to change it NOW! When she came out she was defiantly sporting a pair of levi cut offs—not permitted.

The white shirt told her to take the pants off and bring them to her. Autumn took off the pants and threw them at her. "You just got yourself a lay down ticket." (MAX)

With that, Autumn thrust her middle finger into the white shirt's face and said, "make it two." Autumn generally isn't like this. She went on to tell Rachel that her ex-husband, who hadn't seen her kids or paid any support for years, was trying to get custody of them and take them out of state. Her mom had them now. Everyone here had a lot on their mind. Meanwhile, she's out on the track, waiting for a couple of uniforms to come after her with a pair of cuffs.

Rachel had an "A" going in every class except Personal Finance and the final in that one was coming up. She felt she has some serious studying to do. She needs the pressure like someone not breathing needs resuscitation.

They were starting two apprenticeship programs at Lotusville. Boiler Operator and Stationery Engineer. One was a one year program, the other three. A sixth grade reading level is the prerequisite. 144 hours of classroom time per year and the rest was on-the-job training. Rachel wasn't interested but that would pay these girls a good wage once out. Here, everything was scheduled and given. On the outside, one has to go after and compete for a job. Most here haven't a clue how to accomplish that.

Mid August and no water for showering or flushing toilets and they said it would probably be sometime next week before there was any. It was so hot and muggy the dirt from the air stuck to their bodies and the only way to wash it off was sweat so Rachel walked two miles on the track. The laundry was shut down. Have to go eat, or at least fight the flies and gnats for a taste. No enthusiasm or appetite for food, but she had to stay healthy. This was no place to be sick. Over at the hospital half a dozen girls to a cell and they share a potty chair which is dumped once each shift. Whether they are puking or shitting, they all use the same one, and no facility to wash their hands. Where is the Health Department?

A girl that just got back from the hospital in Springfield was talking to guards from other prisons and a building contractor that bid on putting up these buildings. She told them about some of the problems. They told her that the contractor that got the job agreed to kick back to the warden and he'd read about it in the newspaper. The warden agreed to early retirement and the state dropped the charges, but the Federal Government picked them up so if found guilty she won't have to come here.

Rachel started walking regularly with Bonnie. She picked up a bird feather, then Rachel picked up another. Before long they both had a handful. As they approached a young maple tree full of low branches, they decided to weave the feathers through the leaves. Every day after that they added more feathers to the tree, and within a month, their "feather tree" was blossoming. In another two months it was hard to find an unadorned leaf and most had two or three. It looked like some kind of American Indian altar. Then the little tree became a stump. Rachel asked someone from "yard crew" what happened to the tree, and was told they had to cut it down because it was "diseased." Maybe from a distance it had that appearance, but to make that decision without a closer look was just ignorance. Perhaps they thought it was incubating birds and that would encourage cats.

Another letter from Alice. She'd stopped by her vacated residence to pick up mail. It was early Saturday morning and there was no sign of life so she went in. The place had become the gang clubhouse, or whatever it would be called. There was no order and if there was mail she couldn't find it. Then she heard a noise in another room and decided it was time to leave.

Reading further down the letter, it made Rachel sick to hear her tell of wearing a full skirted dress and open-crotch panties to visit her husband in the prison. They had sex in a chair in the visiting hall among his friends. She'd planned it, she dressed for it, and claimed it was the least she could do for her husband. Said she didn't get that much from it but he did. How degrading for her.

Someone got through admissions with a bad case of head lice and had infected several girls in Wilson. C.O.s have been told to watch for head scratchers. Just to get attention, several girls scratch frequently.

Rachel's English teacher liked her essay and wrote on the top "Dynamite" and his verbal praise embarrassed her in front of the class. She's glad he liked it, though.

Talked with an ex-prostitute inmate who did some of the billing for Lotusville and admitted she's been selling the wrong thing. She learned that government cheese and butter come in 40 lb cases with only a handling charge of $1 a case. She'd send a bill to Central Office for $80 a case and they pay it back here. All food that is donated is the same. Clothes, make-up, toiletries and the like that are donated to the inmates are sold at commissary after they get their payment from Central Office. She sends Central Office a bill for the retail value, and they send a check back in that amount. Talk about a double dip. It would be nice if once out of here she'd turn them in. Our warden's cronies would look really good in little pink dresses. Those crooks are on the wrong side of the bars. When Levi jeans were donated years ago, they were put in storage as the warden didn't think women should dress like men. It was close to a decade before she could be convinced that it was proper attire for the yard crew and by then there was a lot of dry rot.

Rachel looked forward to roast pork for dinner one night, but learned from the girls working in the kitchen that all of it was crawling with maggots. It's happened before and they just washed them off. This time someone in authority was there and had them throw out the meat for two thousand meals. Good!

That night Rachel sat at the dinner table with a girl from Riverview who was about her own age and ate a peanut butter sandwich. She told her the first time she was here she did an eight year stint for murder. The second time, she was out in twelve years—another killing. In a couple more years she hopes to be back in Riverview looking for another contract. Says she doesn't mind being here, that she's well taken care of.

Another guard picked up a rape case and probably more. He's tall and well built and shaved his head for summer. He was utilizing one of the classrooms for his personal recreation and one of the recipients of his affections became pregnant. The guard told her not to worry, that he'd get her something to get rid of the baby. The pregnancy was discovered and when questioned she admitted who "daddy" was. They arrested him on the job and he left in handcuffs. A search of his home turned up cyanide. It looked like he had more in mind than to get rid of the baby. She was taken to I.S.U. for an abortion.

Two girls who came here together on the same case went to the board last week. One girl was as near a model prisoner as you'd find and had been the five years of her stay. They gave her another year. Her co-defendant had to be taken out of lockup to face the board. She put a lock in a sock and beat a girl's face in. She's been continually in "Discipline Control" since her arrival. They let her go home.

Rachel heard it cost well over a million dollars to clear this place of asbestos. Hopefully they had no idea who reported it. The "routinely incarcerated" just go with the flow and do not expect anything more. After all, they live for immediate gratification, and asbestos clean-up doesn't qualify. As for the C.O.s that spent a lot of time down there, breathing that hazardous drift of asbestos, she wondered if they coveted their jobs their over their health.

\*        \*        \*

Autumn went berserk one afternoon, beating her face into the carpet. She kicked and screamed and fought off anyone trying to help her. She was subdued with cuffs and shackles and carried out. Unbeknownst to anyone here, her ex-husband took custody of her kids away from her mother and moved out of state.

They scheduled a "dance" the last day of class. These crazy broads got all decked out to impress each other. "Aren't you going to the dance?" one girl asked Rachel over her shoulder as she was one of the last to leave the classroom.

"What for?" she asked. "There aren't any men."

"Oh yes they is," she assured her. "If you don't look too close."

"I haven't been locked up that long," she told her. A teacher who had been lurking nearby laughed. Rachel figured it was an opportunity for the girls to burn off energy and have a good time. The "dance" was promoted to have refreshments, but that turned out to be ice water. There was plenty of disappointment with that.

It was the end of the semester at school and Rachel had taken all her tests. There was two weeks off now and she was assigned to a painting crew along with some other students until school resumed. Some students did paperwork inside the school. Report cards came in the morning's mail and everyone was bitching. One girl complained about a "C" in math that kept her off the dean's list. Another told her to "be thankful because he flunked me." They were all talking about "taking the teachers on" over their grades. Rachel kept a low profile, not telling anyone she got all "A's" They were so concerned about themselves, no one asked. No word, either, about the grants. One might think she'd find it unsettling, after all the time and effort she'd spent studying and it could come to naught, but that wasn't the case. She wasn't attending school so much for the credits, but to emotionally get away from prison life.

Everyone picked up their new set of books for the next quarter and they didn't look very interesting. Marketing, Economics, Management and English. Classes started up again the following week. Meanwhile, it was back to painting rooms—and trust me these playful children in adult bodies don't know the difference between work and a food fight. One girl sunk her brush into the bucket and laughed as she dipped her arm in to retrieve it. There was paint all over their faces and hair and clothes. A problem became apparent when they went to wash their brushes in the sink. It was oil-base paint and no chemicals available for cleaning up. What a mess!

An inmate plumber came to clear a shower drain upstairs and discovered someone shit in a nearby stall. Then they finger-painted with the same substance on the walls. She complained to the C.O. who took one look and walked away. The "artwork" stayed up for two days. Then someone went over her head and kited the Sgt. She said she didn't have the heart to ask anyone to clean it, so she got a bucket and did it herself. Bessie had a lot to say about catching the culprit, but tired of the subject, someone suggested she go to aerobics and lose some fat.

"I can move better than any of you bony mother fuckers" she truthfully shouted, "and I'm not going over there to watch the cunt bumping." When someone suggested she couldn't find hers to bump, she showed them all she had to do was lift her stomach. Everyone laughed, but she didn't like anyone talking about her fat but her, and she was hurt.

The light in Rachel's room was flashing and snapping again, like thousands of flashbulbs going off. It was only mildly distracting when the other lights in the room were on or light came in through the window. Trying to sleep with the flashing was difficult so she asked if she could put a cloth over it or loosen up the bulb and was told "no." The girl two doors down said it was a sure sign that someone was going home from that room. She told her it was only a sure sign they were going to replace the bulb.

School started again and it didn't come soon enough. There were a lot of ugly and disgusting happenings all around her, but Rachel's turned a blind eye to it. She could only take so much of the idiocy and had to focus on something positive. School was a lifesaver, a sanity keeper. It was the only place not under an evil hand.

The kitchen has some kind of super Kool-Aid that stains everything it touches and it is hard to wash out and the tables were stained by it. The girls who work kitchen stole it and put it in their hair. Lots of purple and orange haired girls walking around.

A new batch of classes and teachers with different personalities. What she first suspected were boring classes turned out to be interesting. Getting into the books to study became a driving force. The grant issues of last quarter seem to have resolved themselves or at least haven't reared their ugly head. What a relief.

Another visit from her parents. They had someone drive them now and everyone seemed to be more relaxed with the situation. It was still hard on everyone, but it wasn't as horrible as it had been. Eric offered to drive them but he is only free on weekends and that didn't suit them. As they were getting up to leave, Autumn slithered into one of their chairs to chat as her visit was ending too. Her parents got a kick out of that. She was really a cute kid but so messed up.

Classes were scheduled two and three times a week, morning and evening. Rachel enjoyed the walk at night, but it wasn't dark except beyond the lights. This place was lit up like daylight all the time. Her walking on the track was up to four or five miles a day now, but this school schedule would cut into that. She does need that walk time to clear her head.

Vi met her on the walk/jog and went into detail about her case. Said she didn't mean he should die, just be punished.

He moved in with her, ate her food and stole money from her. Rachel told her to write down the details that drove her to do what she did—make a list on paper of all the things he did to her and all the emotional things she was feeling. She was definitely an abused woman. She said she wasn't good at putting things on paper so Rachel suggested she get a social worker to help, then send it to her lawyer. She said that her public defender seemed offended by her crime and wasn't on her side. Understood. It was a heinous crime. Maybe that particular public defender isn't assigned to her case anymore. Trying is better than doing nothing, but Rachel doubted she'd do anything.

There was a rumor that the governor was considering allowing "battered women" as a defense and she may be able to get some benefit from that, maybe a reduced sentence—if someone would bring her case to his attention. Maybe if Rachel had more time with her, got her to talk about her feelings and how this guy reacted to her dissatisfaction with him. Maybe she could write a letter for her. But she is in Pierce and Rachel is in Wilson and the opportunity to talk with her is limited to the walk/jog. God! If only she'd take GED classes and maybe do something to help herself. About an hour of walking, the dark clouds obscured the sun and strong winds ripped the trees nearly bare. To avoid being caught in a storm, she said bye to Vi and headed back.

Macroeconomics tonight and since there was no test, she supposed she was prepared. She'd read the chapter and then reviewed it. She was tired. The fire alarm blared last night at midnight for half an hour and she was up at 5 am for count, breakfast, then Management. The sky was getting fierce again and the wind was whipping the fallen leaves in circles.

There was a C.O. shortage, so they've moved some people together during the day. The male guards were pulled in from outside duty to baby-sit us and what rock they found them under is anyone's guess. The one assigned to Wilson Cottage this afternoon looked as though she had scales instead of skin. Last night's "champion of justice" came into all the rooms to take attendance in the middle of the night. Most just peek through the window. The racket of slamming doors woke up everybody and there was plenty of complaining.

The marketing instructor came to class late announcing, "Boy there was a lot of moving and shaking going on out there," referring to an earthquake earlier in the week. He talked about the expansion of Proctor and Gamble in Cincinnati, Ohio and their new building, calling it the Dolly Parton Towers. Haven't seen a picture of that. He called the little emergency medical centers which have sprung up recently as "Doc. In a Box", then joked about selling tennis shoes to Nicaraguans so they could run from bullets. He's off the wall.

Another teacher talked about the deterioration of society, and said if there was a Pearl Harbor situation now, how many young men would stand in line to enlist. Rachel asked him, "how many classrooms have flags," and he had to admit that schools have failed to teach patriotism and that's where the root of today's problems were. He went on to say "Boys haven't changed. They'd fight anybody anywhere just to win." Two wars now and we weren't allowed to win.

Wilson emptied out for a talent show in the afternoon. Rachel looked forward to the peace and quiet it created. There was so much studying to do she didn't know where to start. Kenny, her former roommate just stopped by to tell her to stop writing and get her face in a book. She no sooner left when the Social Worker from Pierce came over to tell her she had been being reclassified from a medium to a minimum. Rachel told her that it already happened and that was why she was moved over to Wilson. The social worker gave her a dumb smile and showed her how it looked on paper. She was behind in her duties and was doing some catching up.

The unit manager in Wilson Cottage was about Rachel's size and weight. He had a tiny head, glasses and was in no way memorable. Molly told her she was talking with some guards from a men's institution (while on a hospital visit) who told her he was a martial arts expert. He sure looks wimpy so that was a pretty good rumor to have out there. She also heard he doesn't date either men or women, but lives happily with his mother. That part was believable. At least he found her a decent roommate, and as for the rest, who cared.

The thought of dealing with another winter here was mortifying, but school helped her through it. Rachel had to wear jeans, sweatshirt and coat when out walking now. She only did 1.2 miles on a particularly bad weather day and was the only person out there.

There was a beautiful, very feminine woman here nicknamed Gun because of her crime and is sort of the "local color" in Wilson. She kept very much to herself. Her short white wavy hair and sky blue eyes were striking. Both her breasts were recently removed because of cancer and she swaggered around proudly showing off her flat manly chest. She kept a low profile, and in Rachel's conversations with her she knew she had a sharp mind. For visits and weekends, she wore a man's suit. For some reason she never got any chemo for her cancer, at least not the kind that takes out your hair. Maybe that wasn't an option for inmates. Her girlfriend, diagnosed with lupus, was in the hospital with a heart attack.

Rachel went to dinner with Molly and ran into friends from Pierce. They hugged her and told her they missed her. As they walked back to their room, Molly told Rachel she can't believe their reaction, that she knew she has to treat her right. Molly is a perfect roommate—except she does like to talk. Who did she talk with when she had the room to herself? Rachel heard all about who raped whose niece and who shot Virgil in the kitchen. Not everyone can roll their own tampons, as she does, and swear by them. She's real clean in the room, washes down everything every day because she's scared of bugs. There were some pretty wicked spiders lurking.

\*     \*     \*

Rae, the former cook from diet kitchen, now worked in plumbing. Rachel met her on the walk/jog a few times and mentioned that during her move from Pierce to Wilson her TV antenna had come loose from the set and she didn't have any tools to put it back on. Rae said she'd see what she could do. A couple of days later, two girls she worked with came over with a screwdriver and fixed it.

Rachel studied all day and didn't walk at all. Class was relatively boring and very cold. No heat in the school yet so everyone wore their coat. The teacher was excellent but who can get excited over market mechanism, bracket creep and fiscal year. Tomorrow was Marketing and she's fortunate to have another good teacher there. Classes are at 8 am and

2 pm most every day so most of her time was taken up studying. Very little socializing now and the weekends mean studying. She never imagined she'd be so focused on school. She's driven!

They took Gun to Springfield this morning to get her chest checked out. Her friend got out of the hospital today too. She's sure they are anxious to see each other. Rachel heard that Gun had a really good article published in a Springfield newspaper. She didn't get to see it, though, so doesn't know what it was about. Gun did let her read several of her stories and the one that stuck in her mind the most was very descriptive of her first-hand account of her experience in a tornado.

Toward evening Rachel overheard two girls talking. One had just returned from Springfield to have her breast lump biopsied. She'd been in a room with Gun, had heard about her breast issues, and said she'd like a gay woman's prospective on what she'd gone through. Gun had no interest in talking with this girl and told her that she wasn't gay and wasn't a woman, but a man trapped in a woman's body. She refused to elaborate further.

She tried to study, but there was a woman outside her door who carried on both ends of a conversation with the man she killed, punctuating her sentences with laughter. She rolled herself a cigarette and reprimanded him for not having the courtesy to light it for her. Rachel watched her smoke it, inhaling with every breath and it was completely gone in less than a minute. She then talked and laughed with the late Jack Meters again while she rolled another.

In Pierce her room was down at the end near the boiler and most of the noise from the common room didn't reach her. Here in Wilson she was in the middle and there's no getting away from the din.

Bessie saw Rachel heading for class one evening and started "cat-calling" her. Don't know why. There were 20 girls reclassified the day and she was moved to Wilson as a minimum. Bessie is still in Pierce because she's still doing time for the gun and hasn't started the time the judge assigned her. There were a lot of upset girls that didn't make it or did and tickets brought them back. Rachel never did hear about how the custody hearing turned out and who was taking care of her son. Maybe Bessie was just trying to get her attention so they could talk and catch up. She expected that her daughter has had the twins by now, and hoped all was well, but is not going out of her way to find out.

Out on the "walk/jog" a girl she knew from her days in diet kitchen stopped Rachel and said, "Guess what! I'm leaving tomorrow!" She is a very devious person who gets several tickets a week and lives in a building where she's not permitted on the "walk/jog" except between 1-2 pm when no one else is, so she could have gotten another ticket for being out there. Most of her tickets were for stealing, lying, and blatant sex acts. "Does anyone here know you're leaving?" She asked her, half humorously, half seriously. Her black eyes just stared into Rachel's for a few seconds, then she laughed.

"Yes! It's my out date." If that's the truth, she'll be back. If not, who cares. Never saw her again.

It is always nice to see girls leave. The girl who gave her scrambled eggs to the kittens and helped her with her math concepts was told she was leaving. This girl had no support system on the outside, no one to send her a box of clothes. She came here half naked, no shoes, dirty, and was taken to the hospital instead of admissions. She lived in state issued clothes. While she was in Lotusville, her mother was killed in a train/car accident. There was no money on her books to pay for transportation for herself and a guard, so she couldn't go to the funeral. She had no street clothes to go home in and because she was about the same size as Rachel so she gave her the blue sweatshirt her parents brought to her when she was at County. No holes and no stains. She figured she could wear it home. Someone else gave her a pair of jeans. We said our good byes' and they stopped her from leaving, telling her that she'd stolen the sweatshirt from the yard crew. She argued and I guess the labels didn't match yard crew property and after some delay they let her leave with it. She had become a friend and many would miss her and all were glad she was out.

Little Ginger found Rachel out on the track. She was on her third mile. Ginger said she just finished ten days "max time" for calling the C.O. a bitch. She plead guilty to the ticket because she said it, and assured them she was telling them the truth. Now she has twenty hours work duty. That's kind of a stiff sentence since she was on mellaril a psych medicine to calm her down and the hospital had failed to give it to her for the two weeks prior to the incident.

\*     \*     \*

The English teacher is an ex-priest whose marriage didn't work out. During class, Bonnie, a classmate handed Rachel a picture of a naked man that a nurse friend had smuggled in to her. Her class had been assigned to write an essay. She supposed the picture was to warm her up, but it was just too cold in the classroom to get her thinker going. Her coat was on but her hands and feet were so cold. The teacher probably saw the vapor coming from the students breathing and told them to leave and finish the essays for homework. Rachel was writing about the gift of time, explaining how a gift from the wallet can be replaced, but the gift of time can never be recaptured or re-spent. She thinks he will like it.

She heard they moved Cowboy out of Pam's room. Pam is bunking with Charla now, who was in County with Rachel. Pam's happy! Charla is very bright and maybe she can influence Pam to get her GED.

Rachel's Macroeconomics teacher had all kinds of degrees, one of which was a doctorate. He's an assistant warden somewhere and has the build, tan and looks of a rancher. She expected his tests to be complex, but they turned out to be mostly multiple choice which she can usually ace. Well, so much for degrees. Thermometers have them too, and you know where they are often shoved! He seemed quite perturbed when she aced two out of three, missing one question on the last test saying, "no one has ever done that on my tests."

The Marketing teacher seemed to have some physical disability which she could not pinpoint. He acted pretty silly sometimes to compensate. There's a lot of reading and memorizing to do, and that's time consuming. Rachel suggested several ideas on various projects he must have liked because two years after she was home, she saw them in commercials. Good for him if he was able to use them. The administrator of the school came into class one day and asked us to evaluate our instructor and were issued a form with questions. She filled hers out, then added in the comment area, "Your tests are a crap shoot and I'm not talking dice."

The papers were handed up and passed across, so he didn't know who wrote what. He perused them, then started uncontrollable laughter. Bonnie started making funny noises and he asked her if she did it. She said "No, but that person in the pink sweatshirt looks guilty." Then she asked him, "What did she write?" He looked over at Rachel and started laughing again. He got up from his seat, left the room, and laughed all the way down the hall. When he left, Bonnie said to Rachel, "You go for the throat." Rachel doesn't know for sure that it was her comment that had him laughing as she didn't think it was that funny. Ellie, one of the girls in the class, had her eye on him and frequently stayed after class to make her play. We all suspected something was going on between them but if it was, it was short lived—he didn't teach the next quarter. We hope he found himself a good job.

When a teacher really knows his stuff
    When he has his class inspired
Administrators do their thing
    And tell the man he's fired

He's an animated teacher
    That inflames our want to learn
And just because we're felons
    He shows us more concern

A dynamic colorful rebel
    J.D. was born to teach
But an administrative move
    Has placed him out of reach

We've all been touched by J.D.'s wit
    He's taught with heart and soul
He will go on to other things
    He'll seek and find his goal

We're told we know not right from wrong
    That's why we're where we're at
But one can't help but wonder
    Who really skinned whose cat.

As all the weeks and months go by
    And reason comes to rule
All will know what we now know
    The admin was the fool

No one promised life was fair
    We're hurt and feel short changed
A good man's been insulted
    His lie's been rearranged

Few men are as qualified
    Of dedication, there's no doubt
But administration wrote the note
    That told the man he's out

J.D. has earned our respect
    We now salute the man
In our hearts we know the truth
    The wrong man got the "can."

There certainly wasn't much action in Wilson Cottage. It's easy to understand why the C.O.s when given a choice avoided Pierce and some refused to be assigned there. Rachel turned down a card game because she needed the time to study. She heard there was a fight at P.F.S. between girls from admissions and the kitchen help. Drama she has no interest in.

No news on the progress of Rachel's case. No one writes her about it even though she's badgered everyone she writes to find out what's happening. Call D.D. Knight! She wrote him weekly but never got any response.

Studying had become an obsession. She looked forward to the classes and it had once again paid off with a row of A's.

Rachel was in Wilson a few months when Francie arrived. She wasn't new to this prison. In fact she'd been there several years and worked her security status to minimum. She was quite plain, quiet, and kept to herself, and rumor was that she'd lived in almost every "cottage" there. Rachel had seen her at school, but never spent any time with her. Now that they were living in the same building, they gravitated to studying together, and with that talk of a personal nature.

It is hard to avoid the card games, but Rachel had found an empty table away from that action and Francie sidled up to her and asked if she was busy. She had a need to talk. Francie sat and told Rachel that she was divorced now but at the time she caught her case had a not-yet school-aged son. Her husband frequented the bars most nights after work. He worked second shift loading boxcars and told her stories of he and his fellow workers grossing each other out passing gas while working in the unventilated areas. She suspected he also participated in all kinds of bad behaviors, which led to girls calling the house, and sometimes finding lipstick in his sticky underwear. He accused her of "being insecure" to think he'd go outside his marriage. Whenever she questioned or complained she risked being beat black and blue. "I was afraid to leave, afraid to stay, but felt there was no choice but to exist."

"Sometimes he climbed on to the roof from his truck and would come in through a window instead of using his key." she continued. She said she was usually startled awake at the sounds of his arrival, always thinking that one of these days it would be a real break-in, instead of her husband, and she had a child to protect. Rachel nodded to let her know she understood.

"One day he came home with a friend. He frequently picked up 'friends' at the bars and sometimes hitchhikers. Sometimes he invited them to spend the night and that made me really nervous and we had a baby in the house. This time they must have used the door because I didn't hear them come in. I woke up to a horrible stink permeating throughout the house and my husband passed out in the bed next to me. I got up and discovered a stranger sleeping in the basement. His smell was being drawn up through the vents when the heat came on. I assumed he was a street person. Really disgusted, I made a scene, caused a ruckus and insisted he go elsewhere—to no avail. Can't reason with a drunk. My husband woke up. Can't reason with two drunks. Soon it was daylight and they had a rifle. Haven't a clue where that came from. I overheard them laughing about shooting birds and turning them into drifting feathers."

Rachel put aside her schoolwork and continued to listen. Francie went on to explain that any affection she ever had for her husband was long gone, that it wasn't unusual for him to be gone several days in a row. Her house wasn't her own and she felt penned into it, trapped. Days would go by and he didn't call and she didn't care. Everything was good for her and her son when he was away, until the baby found the rifle.

"How dare that useless piece of shit put their baby at risk!" She stewed and steamed, explaining she wasn't in a marriage any more, why did he even want to live there? He was a deficit she didn't need and could no longer afford.

"A few nights later I heard him on the roof. He was back. I waited for him to jiggle the screen and I grabbed the rifle, aimed and fired. I didn't hit him but hoped to scare the shit out of him. I didn't know it but the bullet went into a neighboring house. He continued through the window, stepping in with a goofy grin on his face and a six-pack in his hand. The neighbor called the police and week or so later they came and got me. No one was hurt, but they did frown on me firing the gun."

Bonnie, Bessie and several other of Rachel's friends all fell into that category. They had to do three years for the gun before starting the sentence the judge levied on them.

Then she found herself going from marriage to prison, just another form of incarceration. She was looking forward to getting out now and had a strong pull to find her son, now nearly into his teens. She hadn't heard from him or her husband since she left home and has had no visits or mail from anyone. At least she will probably leave here with a degree.

*   *   *

Cowboy accumulated thirty tickets in a year's time so they moved her to another building. There were two buildings that were very old and said to be "condemned" but they existed and were fully populated and she went to one of them. They had recently been moving girls out of their various attics because there were no fire escapes from the fourth floor so they will probably revert back to storage areas.

Rae happened on Rachel again on the walk/jog and she gave her some perfume. She must be on the "outs" with her girlfriend again. As they walked, they spotted Bonnie across the way with her hands shading her eyes, looking up towards the top of one of the buildings. Someone must have hollered something to her, which is a ticketable offense for both parties. Rachel and Rae watched as a C.O. walked up behind her, told her she had a ticket, and asked who she was talking to. "God" she replied, and he walked away not saying any more. No ticket was issued. They caught up with Bonnie and they all laughed about it. Bonnie looked up at the sky at the cloud formations. They formed a ring around an empty center. "Can you see it? This place is a void. Can you feel it? There's a darkness that has nothing to do with lack of light. This place is empty of love."

Sgt. Fenders oversees the C.O's and gave no quarter to the inmates. She's a big stocky woman whose word is final and no one dares argue with this battleship, whose undertaker must do her daily makeup. More like her are needed.

Sharon was in her mid forties with a husband and teen-aged kids. Her family visited regularly, well once a month because of the overcrowding. She kept pretty much to herself, never played cards and she didn't go to school. Maybe she was new, or most likely just not noticed. She carried a suburban aloofness, but for some reason settled down next to Rachel and talked about bad laws that got her in trouble. According to her she did nothing wrong and the cops were all out to screw up her family.

"It was the 4th of July and the kids wanted a pool party. About twenty of their friends showed up, girls and boys. Some brought their own bottles and we had a pony keg in the garage. They splashed in the pool until dark then lit off some firecrackers. There was no problem," she said. We were sitting at a table sharing a bag of pretzels as she continued.

Rachel had been putting a paper together for school, but she needed a break because it wasn't working.

"Earlier, any kid that drove had to give me their car keys. I called each of their parents to tell them there wouldn't be anyone driving home after the party because they had beer there. I don't know what the kids brought but we had the keg. Anyway, after midnight I started herding the kids into the living room and basement—anywhere inside because I wanted them safe and didn't want them bothering the neighbors or sleeping in the grass.

One of the boys told me a boy was passed out and they couldn't get him up. I tried with no luck and called my husband. He shook his head and said he'd never seen anything like it.

The boy seemed unconscious so we called his parents, then called 911 and the medics took him to the hospital. They said it was alcohol poisoning. Who would poison the alcohol? We were relieved to hear he would be all right. Come morning, the police were out to the house. There were kids everywhere. Whether they had a car or walked, I think everyone stayed and all wanted to hear how the boy was.

The police wanted to know if the kids brought their own alcohol or did we supply it. I told them a little of both, that my sons and I bought the pony keg at the beverage store a couple days before, the kids may have brought something too. Drugs? Of course not, these were good kids. I explained about how I kept the kids from driving home and called their parents so they wouldn't be worried.

I told them everything. I'd done everything right and had nothing to hide. I asked how the boy in the hospital was doing and learned he would probably be released to his parents later that day. He was only fourteen and came with his older brother. Then out of the blue, the cops stood up as if to leave. I did also to show them out. Then they said to put my hands behind my back and they handcuffed me. I was outraged—still am. Went to court and given one year. Several counts of serving alcohol to a minor and endangering kids. They even cited me for fireworks—on the 4th of July. Can you imagine? I just wanted the kids to have a nice party and I kept them safe. Sorry about the boy who drank too much, but I don't deserve to be here with the dregs of the world. My husband was found guilty too, but he got probation. He said I shouldn't have talked to the judge as I did, but he just didn't understand. Isn't that a kick? He's home with the kids."

She rattled on for a while longer, still letting off steam about the cops pretending to agree with her and the judge who didn't understand, that put her life in danger sending her here with all the crazy rift-raft. After all that she still didn't realize she'd broken the law. Rachel didn't care about any of it. She didn't like the woman who would be home with her family soon while she moldered with the dregs.

\*     \*     \*

Someone was making a documentary about vocational rehabilitation in prison and the girls being trained in the building trades. The girls were sent to a nearby prison to display their talents. And they did! Camera's caught them having sex with the men prisoners on the roof of a building. That ended that for that crew. It wasn't the first time and it won't be the last.

Rachel went out on the crowded walk/jog and was about half a mile into it when the girl in front of her started having a seizure. She fell to the ground, her body convulsing, her legs kicking and vibrating. A crowd of inmates gathered. Someone took off her coat and put it under her head which was banging into the blacktop. Such a common occurrence here, but one you would rarely see back home.

Rachel got her test results back in management and was very disappointed with an 82%. The teacher teaches a lot of facts, and tests on concept. She's got to get a better grip on that. He does grade on a curve, and since only Rachel and another girl tied with that high score, she's still okay grade-wise, but has to improve on that 82%.

Danita spotted Rachel at dinner and told her she just had to get out of Pierce, that there's just too much going on over there. She lived to gossip and said she'd gone into the shower and heard voices in the next stall. She stepped out to see and saw two girls doing their "thing" in full view of her eyes. "I'd never seen anything like it and just had to watch. Now I can write my man about it and I know my sister will want to know too." Then she went into detail about their "amazing" antics. She said she just stood there and watched and made no move to conceal her presence. They didn't care. Rachel was sure to be the center of attention for some time, as she tells the story over and over.

Just as count cleared, the damper dropped with a boom, the fire alarm that should have gone off didn't because they had it shut off. The electricity shut down over the entire facility and the emergency generators started up, choking everyone with fumes. Fortunately it was a pleasant sunny morning and no one minded being herded out into the yard until they discovered the problem. The girls in Taft Dorm had to evacuate because their living quarters flooded. Many of the girls slept in the basement of the building along with a lot of equipment. Because the flood shorted out everything there was no electric, heat or water. The bunked beds were moved upstairs into hallways. Until they fixed all of it, no one could shower or flush toilets or have lights but they had to continue to live there.

Went out on the walk/jog with a girl who is a fount of information, but a slow walker. They saw three girls, hands cuffed behind them, being led to Max. Rachel was glad that when the girl ran out of gossip, she quit walking.

It would be nice to be able to shower sometime today, but the chance of that was next to nothing. Two girls saw the C.O.'s back was turned and tried to sneak into the shower, but found the door locked and they had to sneak back to their rooms.

A crazy lady was caught smoking in her room during count. The C.O. didn't want to complicate her life, so just told her not to light up another one. Within an hour, a white shirt came to her room and told her to clean "that rat's nest you're living in." She started screaming back that it was Jack's

(Meters) mess and she wasn't about to clean up after him. (She killed him several years ago.) "All he and his friends ever did was rape my face, she insisted loudly. Not knowing what to say, the white shirt walked away.

The results of that last Macro test will be out in the morning. After that Management test, she needed a bit of good news.

Rachel's parents showed up for a visit. She just hates that they drove up here by themselves and she still doesn't know how to discourage it. She thought they did have someone to drive them, but that seemed to be a sometimes thing. Once there, they kept them waiting in the visiting hall for two hours because they couldn't find her. She was in her room studying and they never thought to look for her there. After she was found and they were all together, they met her roommate, her daughter and granddaughter who were seated at the next table. There was less than an hour left to visit before everyone was shooed out. Then she worried the rest of the day that they got back safely. She has to get out of here and end this nightmare.

Later that day, Rachel's roommate, Molly, showed her pictures taken at the visit, and asked her why her daughter wasn't in any of them—just her and the baby. She said "I don't want a picture of her pregnant. I hate the thought of someone touching her. I can't stand to see her pregnant and don't want a picture that will remind me.

At dinner a girl started choking and couldn't catch her breath. A really big inmate ran over to her, grabbed her from behind and did the Heimlich and a big chunk of food flew out of her mouth. With the jolt she gave her anything would have come up. Good she didn't break her ribs. The girl continued to cough to get her breath after that, but all was well.

Another day and still no showers permitted. Toilets will flush so the water is on. Several girls sneaked into the shower. There was a young male C.O. on duty spotted them going in but didn't feel comfortable pulling them out so called for help. A female white shirt showed up and did the deed. Uncle Festus isn't with us anymore. He would have gotten a kick out of doing it. Later that day, several girls put the make on the young C.O. He wanted nothing to do with them and he got upset with their persistence, suggesting they go to their tables or to their rooms. They ignored him, being explicit about what they were good at and what he was missing. Insulted by being ignored, they planned retaliation as he wrote tickets.

Then Jack Meter's murderer was taken out in cuffs. Guess she didn't clean up after him again. The room becomes very quiet every time someone gets taken out in cuffs, whoever it is or whatever the reason.

Rachel got her Marketing case study back and was surprised to get 24 out of 25. She had to market to the public an 80 lb 12' X 38" fiberglass kayak type fishing boat for two with a 24 lb thrust Shakespeare motor for $500. The teacher liked it and wrote "excellent" over the points she made.

Showers were back on and it was really wonderful to be able to wash off the scum.

She should spend more time studying, but when the mood wasn't there, she had to force herself. Lots of reading and she had to remember what she read. She had to make sense of it to be able to recall. Sometimes she got too serious with a crossword puzzle and then hated herself for wasting the time that way.

No response to her most recent nasty letter to D.D. Knight. Guess it wasn't nasty enough. Maybe he doesn't remember who she is.

A couple of months ago, Danita bought an engagement ring from a girl that would be leaving shortly in exchange for $25 worth of commissary. When the girl was being inventoried out they asked her where it was—and she told them. Dealing is not permitted, and since Danita was wearing the ring, it was confiscated and returned to the girl. Danita said she'd never had an engagement ring and she liked the looks of it on her finger.

Two white shirts came in and apologized for the raw meat served at dinner, saying there wasn't anything they could do about it now, but the superintendent would hear about it in the morning.

Rachel did some walking with Mattie today. She sure was a nice girl and doing a life sentence for someone else's dirty work. She's anxious for Rachel to get out to get started on getting evidence against Bruce Muley, and she's confident that is exactly what she will do. Mattie had a visit from family and it upset her to find out that Bruce was back in the neighborhood and hanging out around her kids. She said, "How dare he flaunt himself around them after what he did to their father." Think about what he did to you and your brother, Mattie.

Rumor has it that they are going to build housing outside the gate for minimums and try to encourage businesses in town to hire the inmates. One wonders how much of the earnings would go to the inmates and how much the penitentiary would keep. The girls would jump at the opportunity just to get away from this facility if only for a few hours and would be thrilled to be able to make $.25 an hour. So far, it's just rumor, but they positioned several more "red heads" (porta-potties) outside the gate indicating there may be construction slated. If I were a red head, I'd take offense to that name.

Bonnie went to choir practice and Rachel had a fellow soprano deliver her a gift. As she passed by a garbage can she spotted a dismantled Halloween display and a very suggestively shaped gourd. She slipped it into the sleeve of her coat and headed for the walk/jog. She happened to run into the child-molester she was mistaken for while in admissions. She was on her way to choir practice so Rachel gave it to her and asked her to give it to Bonnie "to help her hit the high notes." She did, and right in front of the priest. Bonnie later told Rachel she was so embarrassed she couldn't sing, and was still hysterical with laughter as she told the story. In return, she gave Rachel a stick of gum. Not being a chewer, she gave it to a lady having a lonely birthday. This lady was expecting a visit, but no one showed. Her face really lit up and she appreciated the gum. Later, when Bonnie asked Rachel how she enjoyed the gum, she was surprised when she said she'd given it away. Rachel asked her what she did with the gourd. "I rented it out," she answered. Everyone was happy and we do need a laugh when here.

There was a very difficult essay test in Marketing coming up and Rachel prepared for it for several days. Yet she went into the test knowing she didn't have a handle on it. It turned out to be tough.

She watched the yard crew working like the Chinese. Over a hundred of them with rakes, brooms and bags, clearing the leaves like locusts clear a field, just moving along and getting the job done. Suddenly three ceiling tiles crashed down on tables. No one was hit, but it was close. Two more just dangled. What a mess. Someone hollered "lawsuit."

Two girls took their blankets to "rec." the other night. Sneaked them under their coats. They slipped outside and under the first fence where tire prints had depressed the ground. The second fence had to be climbed and the blankets were no match for the razor wire. After scaling the fence, one of the girls was cut so severely they decided to come back. One story going around was that they had someone waiting on the road and another was that they had $900 cash in their pockets. Probably not true. They returned to "rec." as soon as they could and some say that they weren't even missed. Nevertheless, the cuts were serious and the one girl had to be stitched up at I.S.U. Then the discovery of the tell-tale blankets found in shreds over the fence made the case and they were taken to the County jail to face escape charges.

The next night a man was spotted lurking around just outside the fence. Then he got in his car and drove away. Seems someone got their wires crossed. A guard told a girl that no men have challenged the razor wire since it was put up, but the women keep at it. The yard crew has been working outside all day shoveling dirt in the low spots at the base of the fence.

Busy week with tests in every class The studying was a challenge and kept Rachel in her room. The staff was really sensitive about the escape attempt and seemed to be on high alert. Best to avoid them. If the two girls got that close to escaping, it might encourage others and the next try could be successful.

Rachel felt buried in schoolwork with no light at the end. Her English teacher lent her a book he got from the Springfield library on plays for her to read. She had to read through it quickly so he can get it back and she didn't want it confiscated by a C.O as unauthorized reading material and get a ticket. She'd never read a play before and was anxious to read another one. Maybe she could do one. He told her that the money right now was in screenwriting and she should consider it.

She finished her case study on Eastern State College in PA today and didn't put a whole lot of effort in it but it's done. Rachel felt she did a lot of half-ass work this year and is uncomfortable with that. There wasn't enough time to do it right.

Tests were over this afternoon and Rachel thought she killed her chances of getting all "A's" again. She did get a "B" on the last Management test and suspected another one on this one. She studied really hard for it too! Oh well! Once again she's sure she aced Macroeconomics. If she missed anything, she will be disappointed in herself. Before the last case study she had a solid "A" in English. The instructor seems afraid to correct her.

She went out on the walk/jog to pick up some sweet-gum tree balls to decorate the Christmas tree. Yes, her second Christmas here. Bonnie asked to accompany her on the walk-jog so she could "negotiate" something. They walked for a while, and came upon a guard looking for the back of his tie pin that had fallen to the ground. Rachel stopped to help him find it and did. He asked who was working WILSON and she told him Belton. "What do you think of him," he asked. She told him she didn't like the way he handled himself, so she stayed out of his way, mostly in her room studying. Here, Rachel's pockets were bulging with contraband (sweet-gum tree balls) and Bonnie was making some kind of deal less than fifty feet away and she's talking with a guard.

Bonnie got a food box which had a lot of tootsie pops. She gave a few to her friends. The word got out she had them and it wasn't long before she caught a girl sneaking into her room to steal them. She threatened "sticky fingers" would lose an arm if she caught her near her room and the girl walked away.

Three young girls doing life decided to "run." One of them secured a ladder from her maintenance job earlier in the day and stashed it. Ladders were usually counted and chained up at the end of the day. The three girls lived in maximum security housing. The first part of their plan was going to "rec." Three guards were assigned to walk to and from. Once there and the guards distracted, they wandered inconspicuously to their ladder and off they went.

One of them had a change of heart and came back. She was in school with Rachel. She'd told her earlier in the year that she and her sister spent their childhood being raped and beaten by their step-father. The two girls waited until he was asleep and burned the house down with him in it. Well, she didn't go with her friends on the escape, but was part of the original plan. She was pulled from school and will spend the next two years in solitary—two years added to her sentence for not going!

They had a graduation ceremony for those a year ahead of Rachel's class. It was nice to see the girls in their cap and gowns getting their diploma, but only the graduates and their families could stay for the food.

The two girls who escaped were caught in a couple of days. As it turned out, they were aided by a recently fired female C.O. and at least half a dozen others, mostly former inmates. One of the girls' coats got tangled in the razor wire and it had names and phone numbers in the pocket. That's how they tracked them.

During a moment of frustration, Rachel decided to use her one monthly phone call to try to reach her attorney, D.D. Knight. Letters just didn't seem to cut it. They accepted the charges and the lady who answered the phone said she wasn't his secretary, but said that Knight was seriously ill in the hospital, and the secretary would write her about what was happening with her case when she came in. It never happened.

Rumor was that a guard left the gate open overnight. Rachel was surprised that it wasn't electronic and the breach didn't show up on a panel somewhere. Can you imagine the opportunity to just walk out the gate instead of challenging the razor wire? Anyway, no one took advantage of it.

One of the guards that liked the girls here too much was just sentenced to 3-15 years, another, a C.O., 7-25.

A lady died here last night. Thirty three years old. She'd been losing her eyesight and they said she might be diabetic and it might be cataracts. She complained of chest pains but was told she was okay, just go to sleep. She did and never woke up. She was somebody's child and probably somebody's mom. All anyone knew was she was another body taken out.

Rachel's English teacher has been encouraging her to write a teleplay. She wouldn't know where to begin. He says that's where the big market was right now. That would take studying and time she didn't have—at least right now.

For Marketing, Rachel decided to devise a way to easily replace erasers on the back of pencils. All the erasers wear down long before the pencil does and she thinks it would be a good item. The metal piece could screw down the pencil to expose more eraser.

Several of the "bull-dykers" that went to the board were flopped, being told to change their behavior. It seems they are trying to change the impression people have about this place, that it was a machine that turns out lesbians. What a crock.

The woman next door was having trouble with her younger roommate. The girl, in her twenties, has odor problems because she doesn't wash. There was a stack of dirty underwear that stunk and when she told her to do something about it, the girl defended herself. "That's not my panties you smell, it's my socks."

The roommate replied, "I've been gay for eleven years and that's long enough to know the difference between crotch and feet." Great comeback, but doubt it did any good.

All counties were on hold because there were no beds available. Those in admissions were again sleeping in the hospital corridors and in any building with space for mattresses on the floor. They sent about 20 girls to Riverview pre-release one day and more to Springfield and Karo pre-releases the next. The three new buildings that opened shortly after Rachel got here that have 200+ beds each just wasn't enough. No doubt about it now, this place being over-booked the day it opened. There were so many girls here that were not a threat to anyone and there was no reason they should have to stay—except the penitentiary gets paid by the head count.

Bonnie got more packages "delivered" mysteriously. Today she was delivered five pounds of delicious corned beef, lots of mozzarella and plenty of mayo. Rachel feasted with her for two days. When Bonnie returned from school her roommate told her there was something under her bed. She found a half gallon of Borden's Heavenly Hash ice cream in a bucket of ice.

Bonnie took an empty shampoo bottle to school and filled it with floor wax so she could wax her concrete floor. The little bit she left for Rachel didn't make much of a shine. Molly liked the look of the wax on the concrete and got more wax from a friend of hers to finish the job. The C.O. noticed the wax on Bonnie's floor and asked her where she got it. She didn't say. She's expecting to get a ticket over it. Sealing the bare concrete with it was good. It reduced stains and made it so much easier to keep clean and should be made available for that purpose.

One girl got even with another by plugging her toilet with towels and flushing it. As water streamed into the hallway, she yelled "flood." The C.O. on duty told her not to call him because he can't swim. She invited him to skinny dip. The stupidity of this place is really getting to Rachel and she wished she knew when she was leaving.

Rachel's brother sent her a box of fresh fruit for Christmas. She sent it on to her mother. No fruit, fresh or canned permitted because people make "hooch" from it. Odd, though, because at Christmastime, a charitable organization gave everyone a basket of fruit, topped with a bag of cookies. That fruit must not have been "hoochable."

One of the elderly ladies here is rumored to be a relative of Chicago's former mayor. She's known for her violent streak and attacked a young female C.O. with a broom. She wasn't hurt because three other inmates jumped in quickly and separated them. This C.O. wasn't a favorite because she was so "by the book" but Rachel liked her. She was a real sucker for someone that showed her some respect, and a please or thank you really put a smile on her face.

Girls have continued to go to other penitentiaries and job sites to work on various rehab projects. There was a story on TV about it. The bus that took the girls to and from the jobs was hit by a semi. Hit and run. The C.O. that was driving got the license number and radioed it in as it hurtled down the road. It forced another car off the road and into a building. State troopers pulled the semi over outside Joliet and said he was "dirty." No one was seriously injured.

The end of another quarter and lots of tests. Rachel was told that Bonnie, Ellie and herself would be working at the school during the break. Someone Bonnie knew swiped a box of chocolate-chip ice cream and we all dined. That was a real treat. Bonnie sure had a lot of connections.

Another quarter was over and now Rachel thought she did okay. Some lingering doubts about Management, but she did put more time and energy into that class. She can't imagine anyone doing more or better.

The work at the school consisted of watching the Terminator, Golden Child, Raiders of the Lost Ark, and an Eddie Murphy comedy. They took a break to shop at commissary, then went back for a couple more movies. She got so tired of sitting there, but the nice people that run the school go out of their way to do them a favor by showing the movies, she felt obligated to watch, enjoy, and thank them.

A book buyer came out here and bought back the used books. Rachel got $33 added to her commissary account. While over there, she heard some very sad and disturbing news. The couple running the school broke up. It seems that the girl became attracted to one of the girls in the other class. She was such a pretty girl, and her new lover looked like an old bag. Can't imagine anything coming of that but a lot of hurt. This place poisons everything it touches.

Some time ago, Rachel requested an "inter-library loan" which those working in the little library here said they could accomplish. There were some books she'd like to read, but she hadn't heard anything more about that and really didn't expect to.

Went back to "work" and saw American Gigolo, Soul Search and Lethal Weapon. The guy in this one made Rambo look like a wimp. What they don't understand at the school is that Rachel wouldn't mind physical labor.

Bonnie came knocking at her door with a big package of corned beef—again. We ate it all day. They had liver and onions for dinner so it was good we had the food. That girl can come up with anything but the key out of here.

Rachel wrapped a couple of Christmas presents for girls here. One of the girls in Pierce gave her a box of chocolate-covered cherries which really didn't interest her. She owed the big lezzy next door something for a series of favors. She does her laundry and saw to it she got brand new sheets when six sets came in, so she gave them to her. Rachel knows she wanted something else, but she settled for the candy.

There's a new plan rumored to be implemented after the first of the year. All girls with serious drug abuse problems would be going to be housed together in Warren East. They would be given intensive help with their addiction. They've taken out most of the tables and chairs that were once there. Since Rachel was there for admissions, she knew it was a huge dorm and all these girls are expert thieves. Nothing would be safe. Maybe they would learn respect for other's things. Someone commented that it was a good idea to lock them all up together.

Rachel woke up this morning to a letter from the prison legal services telling her she should have filed for 30-day shock a year ago but her attorney failed to do so. The legal services here told her to get on her attorney's back and make him work on filing for her "super shock." She's been beating her head against the walls trying to get him in gear. The person paid to defend her is ignoring his duties. It was so frustrating for her not to have any control over her life.

Grades came today. Rachel felt she got really lucky to have achieved all "A's" again. Bonnie got two "A's" and two "B's." The two of them were the best students there. Ellie was a close third.

Rachel's ex-roommate lent her a book she stole from the library before they closed it. Yes, they closed our library. Good story and she wanted to get it read and returned to her before there's another search, but she had to go watch an Indiana Jones movie today. School started the next week and she was anxious to get into the new books. She read two chapters in Sociology and made an attempt into the accounting.

Bonnie hasn't heard anything more about the "wax" incident and she' s still very much on edge about it.

The unit manager of McKinley Cottage tried to make a C.O. look bad by rolling up a "rug dummy" and putting it in a vacant cot so her count would be off. They are supposed to count faces, not bodies.

*     *     *

Molly asked Rachel if she ever ate chitlins. She told her "no" and she wasn't interested, that she heard they are made from hogs intestines or something like that. Then she asked if she ever ate hogs balls and she had a big eager grin on her face. Was she trying to gross Rachel out? She went on to say that after they're skinned and boiled, sliced, breaded and fried, they're delicious. Molly had grossed Rachel out and told her so. She laughed at Rachel and told her that she is just too white. Rachel wonders what goes through a person's mind when they bite into these morsels and why they wouldn't choose to eat something else.

Molly said she was looking for a white man for herself because black men "aren't about nothing." Her first husband was nearly white. Her daughter had two children by two different black men. She said she's trying to get her to get a white man. Molly told Rachel she's glad she's white because she doesn't want a black roommate. She always seemed worried that Rachel would move into Bonnie's room.

Rachel heard that the superintendent, Mr. Chorris, had a heart attack. Hope it wasn't a serious one, because good things were getting done. He cared.

C.O. Belton, who used to work in Wilson claimed the girls in Grant Cottage attacked him while he was working. He said they grabbed his dick. It's Rachel's personal opinion he had it out waving it at them. When he was here, he constantly teased and backed off, teased and backed off. You don't tease dogs with raw meat and not expect an attack.

A friend of Bonnie's who was there because she shot her cop husband while he slept, was sent on several errands, carrying boxes to various buildings. When she returned exhausted and panting, and told Belton everything was delivered and she was tired out, he assured her, "you always have my face to sit on." How does a girl respond to something like that without getting a "disrespect ticket" or locked up for assaulting an officer. They finally moved him because so many complaints came in about his behavior.

One of the girls who was recently caught having sex on the roof of a building her crew had been rehabbing now claimed to be pregnant. She said if the baby was white, it's Belton's. If black, one of the guys on the roof. Her pregnancy test came back negative, but she still insisted she's pregnant.

An English teacher at the school had a PhD in journalism. Rachel really liked this class, but she's only a week into it. He sure dished out the homework but she had no problem with that. Accounting did not come naturally to her and she spent hours trying to figure things out. Bonnie had a knack for it and had helped her a lot. For Sociology, it was hard to find magazine ads required for discussion. No access to them and she had to invent, but so did everyone else.

The showers got washed down today but no one re-hung the shower curtains. Molly tried to take a quick shower, but a couple girls went in to watch and she gave up. Bonnie said she needed a shower and would hang the curtains herself, but no one seemed to know where they were.

A C.O. who has been a constant "adventure" around here has done it again. He was the one who was supposed to be in charge of the girls during the recent escape. His step-mother is an inmate here. One of the girls in Jefferson Cottage tested pregnant and claims he's the father. He resigned just before they slapped the cuffs on him. The state troopers intercepted him before he got home, searched him before they took him to lock up and found cocaine.

The schoolwork was burying Rachel. She spent whole days working on it and never got it done. The accounting took her two full ten-hour days out of every week so there was hardly time to work on the rest of the courses. Rachel was having a lot of trouble trying to get a handle on the accounting but had no choice but to keep plugging away at it. There was a timed test Wednesday and that bothered her. She muddled through it but had to give each step a lot of thought.

*   *   *

Rachel talked with a C.O. who told her of an escape from Lucasville, a maximum security men's facility in Ohio. A very athletic man pole vaulted over the fence and wire. He had an audience too. The C.O. told her if someone wanted to get over the fence without getting cut up, all they'd have to do is pull a tire over it which would pull the razor wire down with it. Interesting, but where does an inmate get the tire? She guessed they'd need outside help with muscle.

Back to the books. A little sociology and a touch of management, then back to accounting. She heard that the guy who was running the school just gave a ring to a C.O. with a passel of kids. She's really cute but he's so young for that kind of responsibility. He must still be messed up after his girl jilted him for a woman.

Nothing but cold sandwiches and salads have been served for a month now. Things went downhill since the superintendent had his heart attack.

Eric had been leaning on Knight and thought he'd made some progress. He told him that there would probably be a property hearing the following week and that she would return to Criminal Justice Central for it. No news about the shock. Her parents tried to call him to confirm a date for the hearing, but he wasn't in. Phone calls from Lotusville were very limited and each one was valuable. She wrote him another letter explaining she'd heard that her property hearing was coming up and wanted to make sure he brought the receipts for her jewelry, and the guns she was holding for Danny, that her parents would be there to testify that her silverware came from wedding gifts decades before, a coin collection belonging to her son, and much miscellaneous confiscated that night.

At 8:30 a.m. the next day she was told to pack up, turn in all her stuff, that she was going home. This wasn't true and she knew it and explained that it was a property hearing and she expected to be back within a week. They argued and told her to turn in her state clothes to inventory and box up all her belongings which included her schoolbooks. She had no choice but to comply. She didn't get to County until 4 pm as the deputies had to cruise the small towns for sales on bullets and holsters. The three inmates in the van sat cuffed in the cold watching the snow fall. The guards shopped.

Entering the Criminal Justice Central building, there were calls of "fresh meat" from screaming crazies trying to intimidate. Rachel just ignored them and went about her business. Someone asked if she just got there, and when she responded, "Yeah, from Lotusville." Anyone within earshot turned three shades lighter. Big Time! Then the other two she rode in with came in. The "Lotusville Mafia" in their quiet way took control.

This place was more insane than Rachel remembered it. Mostly young screaming ill-mannered girls, one threatened suicide. Dinner was hamburger and the treat for Rachel was a slice of real tomato. It had been months since she'd had a hamburger with a slice of tomato. She brought her schoolwork in with her to study but it was difficult with all the noise.

Sue, one of the girls who rode out with her and was briefly one of Bonnie's roommates was scheduled to have her shock hearing, but she heard there was a bad snowstorm going on outside and the judges elected to go home early and postponed all afternoon hearings. The windows were all painted black so no one could see out, and no one mentioned anything about the weather. Sue's family drove in through the snow from Joliet to pick her up. Now they have to do it again tomorrow. She's upset for them. There's supposed to be a blizzard out there and since her hearing was only a formality, why don't they just let her go home with them.

Rachel asked her parents not to visit. She didn't want them dealing with the weather and she explained that she's on a different floor than she was before and the rules were different. They would have only ten minutes talking through a phone and through plexiglass. That's hard on everyone and a full day of no gratification. Also, she'd be wearing a jumpsuit that says "prisoner" on it and she didn't want them to see her that way even though it wasn't a secret. Visits were very hard emotionally, the drive down here in the snow had to be treacherous, finding parking, then the wait in line once here, then being searched. She didn't want to put them through it. She called her parents and explained she'd see them at the hearing and she'd call every day. They were unable to find anything out because they couldn't reach D.D. Knight.

She talked with her mother at length on the phone and caught up on some of the family gossip. She thought she convinced her that telephone conversations make more sense than coming all the way down here especially if the weather was bad, going through the process, then being able to visit for 10 minutes, then reversing the process to get home. Hours invested for only a few minutes—and even then there is no privacy.

Earlier, a young nearly 400lb girl whose shape was best described as a bunch of balloons in no particular order took a shower. The room was noisy when the C.O. called her name. And although the girl hollered, "whatever it is will have to wait because I'm in the shower," the C.O. didn't hear her and called her again. This time angrily. The girl responded by coming out of the shower and walking across the floor, all parts of her body flipping in different directions. Stark naked and dripping she was a sight that upset the C.O. who in turn swatted her back in the direction from which she came. Everyone was laughing until the girl slipped and fell in her own water tracks. Tits, feet, dimples, ass, all hit the floor with a splat.

"Are you all right?" the C.O. asked.

"I think I broke de flo." she laughed. She had to have gotten hurt, but didn't complain.

There was a "weekender" here that claimed to write romance novels. She's here on the first of four weekends she'll have to serve for writing bad checks. Her books must not be selling. She's claustrophobic so is happy to sleep on the floor. If she ever saw the critters that scamper in and out of the floor drains at night, she might have changed her mind. The TV was always on—cartoons, wrestling and videos mostly. Everyone sat around it and played cards. They have to yell to be heard, then someone turns the TV up louder, and the cycle continues.

Rachel had been trying to keep up with her studies but the lighting was poor and the noise deafening. She's on the 4th floor where the girls come and go all the time. The 7th floor where she was before would have been much more conducive to studying.

Had spaghetti for lunch and had to eat it with a plastic spoon. Try that sometime! There was fair access to wheat bread, but the food was generally lousy. The spaghetti had a kerosene taste and someone's applesauce had a piece of wire in it. One girl's tray didn't have a spoon so she had to wait until someone finished so she could use theirs.

It must be really cold outside because the rooms were uncomfortably cold. Last night she had two blankets and a towel over her and slept in a T-shirt, sweatshirt, sweat pants and socks and woke up shivering. Her legs cramped from cold several times during the night. Everyone had the same problem to different degrees and some tried to talk a weekender out of her blankets. The weekenders left at noon. They had to check out with what they checked in, so it was a "no go."

The toilet in Rachel's room was stainless steel with no seat. She washed down the room herself and was the only one in the room, so she knew it was clean, but that toilet sure was cold to sit on. Even when it seemed she'd spend most of the day sitting on it, it just stayed cold. The suction was so powerful she was sure if she sat on it while it was flushing, she'd end up hollow.

I didn't go for breakfast
    And then I missed my lunch
So I was mighty hungry
    When I finally got to munch

The chicken tasted good to me.
    The broccoli's been around
I chewed the stuff forever
    it scratched as it went down.

Sue got lucky—She went home
    I'm here against my will.
She's eating steak and lobster
    I'm tossing down more swill

Breakfast milk is warm and sour
    Eggs and sausage cold
No chance to catch a virus, though
    The bread is green with mold.

There is no light from windows
    I'm getting wan and pale
Like other guests of judges
    In beloved county jail.

Rachel finally reached D.D. Knight on the phone and he said he will be over here before the end of the week to decide who we will need to call as witnesses. By Friday 10 pm and still no D.D. He was so undependable and inept the situation keeps her too riled up to study. She's glad that her parents are keeping in touch with the witnesses.

The property hearing was scheduled for 2/17 and everyone showed up in the courtroom. Her witnesses waited patiently. Then the bailiff came in and they were told it was postponed because of the weather. It was rescheduled again for 2/22 and again the witnesses sat in the courtroom for an hour before being notified that the date was a mistake, that it would be the next day. Again, all showed up, but again it was postponed. People took off from work which most could ill afford to do. Another flew in from out of state. Rachel's parents made the two-hour treks on the bus through weather bad enough to close the courts. Danny Willsen, who also lived two hours away became discouraged after three attempts and did not show up again.

When Rachel finally got to talk with D.D. Knight in the courtroom, he actually yelled at her. Told her that any receipts she thought he had were a figment of her imagination. He'd lost her receipts! Fortunately, her parents showed up with copies of some of them.

Bonnie sent Rachel a big packet of homework to work on. She needed it because the frustration of dealing with the attorney was driving her mad. Those at the school were told by Lotusville, that Rachel was being "shocked out" and going home and to withdraw her from classes. Bonnie talked with the instructors at school and those administrating and told them she only left for a hearing and should be back soon.

They agreed to let Rachel finish classes if she returned within two weeks of when classes were over and took the finals before the next quarter began. She wrote that they even moved someone else into her room in Wilson. She's so glad that her friends were doing the best they could for her and stayed in touch.

She sure wished someone would call the Board of Health on whoever is in charge of this place and educate the people running it. They still expected and encouraged the girls to share the razor that sat in a cup of water on the C.O.'s desk. Many of these girls are IV drug users, and who knows what they have. The C.O.'s should know the dangers of contracting AIDS, Hepatitis C and who knew what else. Maybe they just don't care.

A shortage of toilet paper was announced and Rachel knew for sure this food they served didn't stick to her ribs. Panic!

There was a little blonde girl about 20 years old and 80 lbs with a heavy southern accent who called herself "Little Bit." All day long she begged, going from one person to another." Do you have any Kool Aid? Can I have a cigarette? I need something sweet." She knocked on Rachel's door, peeked in and says "Hi, how are you?" and all the while, her eyes scouted the place looking for food. She's here for stealing. If Little Bit" makes it to Lotusville, she'll have plenty of commissary, but her face will have to work for it.

No pillows here. Rachel found an abandoned crossword puzzle book two inches thick and put it under the pad that served as a mattress. Her bed was a two-inch thick a pad over a concrete shelf to sleep on. The light stayed on all night long and some of the girls snored and snorted all night long.

She thought she was the only one that washed her hair in the three weeks she's been here, but might be wrong. The black girls just seem to add grease to theirs. One of them asked to borrow her comb and was insulted when told "No!"

The property hearing was scheduled again today, but was again postponed. All the witnesses had to leave to come back another day. Rachel asked Knight to please take depositions from those witnesses from out of town so they wouldn't have to come back again next week. He snapped back at her, "Let me run this thing."

In desperation, Rachel wrote a letter the local Bar Association. She didn't really know what their function was but decided they needed a letter. In addition to telling them how he didn't seem to be handling her case, she told them that D.D. Knight should have a "case for grand theft, fee, and also if they performed such services, to put a grenade in his pants. There should be some protection offered the public against attorneys that do not perform as they are paid so well to do.

Little Bit parked her carcass in Rachel's doorway last night and talked and talked. She was really messed up. She said she shared her bed and body with her mother until she was fifteen, then left home to work for a carnival. There she hooked up with another woman. "I can't stand to have a man touch me." She shivered as she talked on in her W. VA accent. "This woman was into more pills than I could afford so I stole prescription blanks from a doctor's office for her." The "friend" was caught using them and when asked, told how and where she got them." Who knew what the rest of the story might have been. Who cares.

Bonnie wrote a very depressing letter. Rachel's on the verge of tears every minute of the day anyway and her letter tore her up. Her mother was sick, her brother was in intensive care with a heart attack. He had extensive damage to his heart tissue. He's only 50. It has to be a horrible thing for Bonnie to deal with when she doesn't have the power to deal. Bonnie has done so much for her and now she can't be there for Bonnie when she was needed.

Some juveniles on the other side of the fourth floor flushed sheets and blankets down their toilets and caused a flood. Everyone was locked up all day and now there'll be no change of clothes. The electricity was off for a while.

The property hearing finally came off. About half Rachel's witnesses showed up. The prosecutor was tough. Her attorney was so careless and uncaring. Don't know the outcome. Guess she'll hear the decision later. Went back to Lotusville on the next shuttle, tired, disorganized, frantic and depressed. People back in Lotusville referred to her month away as a "vacation"—which it wasn't.

Rachel had a tooth that needed attention. A chunk cracked off. She put her name on the list but knows she'll have to take some firmer action soon like maybe enlisting the help of a C.O. The inside of her mouth was getting shredded and had to put a wad of paper between her tooth and cheek.

Bonnie received her food box. Her mom bought a regular bottle of catsup in a plastic bottle. Only plastic bottles are acceptable. She took the catsup out, washed out the bottle, took it to a local Seafood store and had them fill it with shrimp sauce. Then she sealed it up to look normal. There was lots of canned shrimp in the box to go with it. She shared her stuff for supper. They put another girl in with Molly while Rachel was away and they gave Rachel a room with a crazy woman for a roommate. She'd killed one husband, did her time, remarried, and then killed the next one. She's somewhat senile and has a collection of can lids and plastic knives in the room. The unit manager warned Rachel that she had threatened to cut the throat of three previous roommates. Thanks! On the first night this crazy woman made a point of letting her know she "would not cut her throat while she slept." Wonderful!

There really wasn't any big problems with her—serious problems—other than it was obvious that the woman didn't want a roommate and did her best to get rid of every one assigned to her room. She was a big, tall, and strong woman that Rachel didn't want any problems with. She'd never know why, but about half the time when she went to get out of bed—between 5:00 and 530 a.m. the ladder to her upper bunk was always missing and the crazy woman was never around, At first, she just laughed. Rachel had no problem climbing down off the top bunk, but wondered what was on this woman's mind to take the ladder in the night. Trying to talk to the roommate about it was useless because she'd just grunt and walk away.

Rachel repeatedly talked to the unit manager about it and was continually told the situation was "only temporary." Well, so was life, so she made quite a nuisance of herself until she was told she could have her old bed back, that it was just a matter of paperwork. Be patient.

Then when she went to shop at commissary was told that her money did not come back from County with her. They sent part of it a couple days ago. She had to get on them heavy about that. County tried to say they sent it with her, but this place never received it. Until they got it straightened out, she couldn't buy any stamped envelopes or writing materials. Couldn't buy any commissary at all.

Meanwhile she was inundated with studies she had to make up. School was over for everyone but Rachel Williams. She still had an essay to write and a journal to complete for English. Maybe she should tell the adventures of returning to County. Lots of accounting to do, homework to make up, and two tests to study for. Without Bonnie's help and encouragement, she'd have chucked this semester.

Last night Bonnie had a lady in a wheelchair smuggle in a huge bag of popcorn under her lap blanket. This poor lady was in her mid thirties and totally confined to a wheelchair, the result of an aggressive cancer she's not getting any treatment for. She was doing one year for shoplifting three jars of baby food. Hardly something to do time for in the penitentiary, but it was a third shoplifting offense so according to the law, a felony.

Rachel and Bonnie just heard through the school's grapevine that last semester's English teacher was hospitalized with a heart attack. It seemed that bad things come to all who have anything to do with this place. She had so much catching up to do with the schoolwork and had to complete it this week because new classes were starting. Those at the school have been so patient. She could care less what happened to her grades at this point. She just wanted it over with. She turned in her English essay and the journal. Still two tests to make up in accounting. She will need some help from Bonnie studying for them and she's so grateful she finds the time for her.

Rachel was still bunking with the crazy woman and was desperately tired of the run-around from the unit manager. Somehow the weld broke that supported the top bunk. Books make wonderful levers. That meant they had to move her out. Where there's a will there's a way. Now things were okay and she's back where she was in Molly's room and comfortable.

Rachel spent every hour of every day trying to get the accounting straight. She's tried to lean on Bonnie for this, but Bonnie was rarely out of her room. It's not that it's difficult or hard to understand—there's just so much to remember. She kept going over and over it and tried to remember where the numbers go and why. Repetition! There wasn't enough time for her to read through the book. Maybe, though, she won't have any trouble justifying her checkbook once she gets home—if she ever gets there.

Bonnie has been real sick and unable to get any medical care. She had what appeared to be an upper respiratory infection which caused her trouble breathing. Ten minutes on the track and she's out of breath. Her skin broke out in itchy water blisters and patches of her hair fell out again. She's been trying to see a doctor for months with no luck—but she's on the list. Her mother called Central Office and was polite, telling them about her daughters problem. They promised to look into it. Nothing. Then her mother called the Superintendent here and bitched up a storm. They promised her she'd see a doctor by next week. She's hoping.

It rained all morning and the building leaked onto the tables and floor. The skylight is the culprit, even though the water dripped down several feet from it.

Once the rain stopped and the floors dried, the C.O. sent several girls outside to clean the yard, but refused to give them a plastic bag, so they were coming in and out with hands full of twigs and leaves, and discarded papers. The garbage can was stuffed with lots of crud, while mud and other debris had been tracked across the floor.

Molly had a visit from her daughter and two grandbabies and was excited about it. Problem was she seemed to have the same upper respiratory distress Bonnie had. She sent a kite to see a nurse and has so far been ignored.

Rachel got called to the mailroom early this morning, sure it was a decision on the property hearing. No, it was a response from the County Bar Association to her letter of complaint about D.D. Knight while in County. Because of a conflict they referred it as a grievance to some other bar association. The conflict was—his partner was president of it.

There was a drug bust at visiting hall last weekend. A girl in this building became very agitated when her husband didn't show up for a promised visit. She asked a girl who knew a girl who worked over at visiting hall to see if he had signed in. She learned that the C.O. at the entrance building found some marijuana in his jacket pocket, tightly packed to fit so the girl could wear it inside undetected. They called the highway patrol who noted his identification and released him when he promised to appear in local court. He was refused the visit and told he can't come again. Unknown to him, his hometown police were notified and were waiting for him when he arrived home. They found more there and arrested him again. The girl was all upset, not about her husband being arrested, but frantic about who was going to send her commissary money.

The fire alarm went off again. Everyone tried to ignore it—even those in wheelchairs. It sure was annoying. No one seemed to be around on weekends that knows how to shut it off. The C.O. got on the phone. "What should I do?" At least it was not the middle of the night and we always had the option to go out walking.

Rachel finished up with the accounting class and took the tests. She beat the deadline. It was a while before she heard how bad her grades were for this quarter. New classes started up. Speech that morning then Business Communications tonight.

Bonnie asked Rachel to get up and go to breakfast with her, then never got up herself. She did that one day last week. Breakfast was the best meal of the day. Bonnie was still quite sick, no better than she was, and she moved slowly. Again they promised her family she'd get some medical attention right away. Molly still has it too as well as several others.

The Sociology teacher gave Rachel a "B" last quarter and said he didn't know how she did it because she missed half the quarter. She guesses she's not social enough. Other grades haven't come in yet.

Sent another kite to see the dentist. Rachel thinks it was her third. The tooth is sharp and slices her tongue. She can't put paper-wads everywhere and she has to chew and swallow her food.

She received another clothes box from her family. They sent the wrong size shoes which she can't wear. She'll find someone who can. Bubble Bath? Yes, at home, it is wonderful, but can't have it here. Once they get her money back on her books she will send it home and maybe the shoes too.

Went to Financial Management class today, kind of a combination of Economics and Accounting she figured after reading the first two chapters, but after one day of class she can't make heads or tails of it. The teacher knows his stuff, but teaches over her head. She'll have to sit taller to absorb. She was so thankful she finished up last quarter with two "A's" and two "B's" and that semester was all behind her now. It's flushed from her mind and she's ready to start fresh.

Both Bonnie and Molly were really suffering and couldn't get in to see a nurse or get any help for their medical and dental issues. Rachel's last kite to the dentist was returned with a note telling her to stop sending kites. That may turn out to be their mistake. She sent another kite telling them she'd stop sending kites when they took the time to see her. She kept their note to her for possible evidence if they didn't get to her in a few days. Meanwhile, she'd try to get hold of the social worker or seek help from a C.O.

Bonnie was still very sick and seemed to have a bitter attitude about life. Her hair was falling out in chunks again and leaving bald patches. She's had an abscessed tooth for several months, and her chest congestion still hasn't been checked out and that bothered her. It has to be all tied together. Rachel's parents were in touch with her mom, letting her know what is going on and her mom continues to bombard Springfield Central Office and the penitentiary begging for medical/dental help for her daughter.

A girl approached the table where Bonnie and Rachel were studying. Crying, she told them her mother just had a stroke and was in bad shape. She had talked with her father who was in poor health. Bonnie looked up at her and said, "shit happens." The girl stared in disbelief and walked away. Sometimes there is only so much one can deal with.

There was a finance test and law class to study for and a speech Rachel had already written to practice. No one was thrilled to go to speech class, but it was a requirement and everyone had to attend and give one speech. Everyone in the class dissected everyone's practice speeches and those that wanted had theirs videoed got a closer look. Everyone was uncomfortable in this class, so rather than study, most everyone ignored it and focused on other things like going to a Bingo game at rec. and were drawn in that direction. Rachel jokingly warned them they would end up in Capt. James Hotel (Max) but they just laughed at her.

*    *    *

On the walk over to school, Bonnie started to cry. She was on the verge of a nervous breakdown. She couldn't cope during class and just walked out. She fell apart. She missed class in the morning also and Rachel found her locked in her room, blanket over the window, towel over the light and in total darkness, TV off, laying on her bed with a wig on, just crying. She wouldn't/couldn't come out.

Another day and Bonnie had totally flipped out. The C.O got scared and put her in the hospital—mostly to absolve herself of responsibility. There's no medical staff there. No help. No friends. No running water or flush toilet. Being locked up over there was a punishment and not what she needed. Bonnie wasn't in touch with reality—except for short periods of time. "Everyone is talking about me—even the TV. Everyone is making fun of me. Everything is a plot."

She couldn't read anything, much less do homework, or concentrate on a card game without getting anxiety attacks and panic. She said she received a handwritten message from God.

She trusted Rachel and several others, so several of her friends demanded they let her out of the hospital—where all she did was have delusions and cry. The C.O. must have gotten an okay from a white shirt and Bonnie was returned to Wilson. They took her roommate out of the room so she could have it to herself Then in a really surprising move they let her friends spend time in her room with her. She had the TV on—news—and heard a story of a young, missing presumed kidnapped girl. "See, they're talking about me," she accuses.

"Did you kidnap her?" Rachel asked "Where is she now?"

She wrinkled up her face, tears came from her blood shot eyes and she says, "They aren't talking about me, are they? Why am I so paranoid?" Then 30 seconds later, it's the same thing all over.

Rachel was truly scared for her and knew what time the office personnel left work and caught the psych person, that had been working with Bonnie for months, on his way out to the parking lot that evening. He was on his way home from work and out of politeness he asked about Bonnie. He wasn't aware she'd been in the hospital and didn't know how serious her problems were. Rachel listened to what he had to say, then she told him he was all wrong about her and told him what she had observed and he was stunned. He immediately turned around and went over to Wilson to talk with her.

The next day he ordered psych tests for her—look at the picture and tell me what you see, read the paragraph and tell me what it says, and stuff like that. Then he got her physical needs taken care of and had her put on antibiotics and vitamins. He made sure she saw the dentist and had her tooth pulled. He said she was walking a thin line and she could go either way. Rachel told him her mother was very concerned and has been getting lies and false promises from the administration for weeks and asked if it was okay if they called him to talk. He said he'd call her family.

He went on to say that at this point she needs assurance that everyone cared—even if she can't continue school, even if she had to switch from "contacts" to glasses—even if she was overweight (she's put on 70 lbs)—even if she was practically bald. She needs to know that none of these things meant a damn thing.

Rachel and others explained to her that all the things she perceived as problems weren't real, that she should relax and let the real Bonnie return. When they told her this she asked, "Are you sure?" Then, "Why am I so messed up? How long is this going to last? What's causing it? When will I be better?" Almost immediately after the antibiotics started clearing up her respiratory infection and the poisons from her tooth no longer threatened her health, the real Bonnie started to return.

No word from the attorney about the results of Rachel's property hearing!

This place was insane and the administration did what they could to perpetuate that. The screwball C.O. woke Rachel shortly after 4 am to tell her she is not permitted to sleep facing the wall, that she needs to see faces when she does the count—like she has some control over how she moves in her sleep. She woke up Molly for sleeping with a scarf covering her hair. She woke Bonnie up also for facing the wall. She woke up another girl who screamed in terror. She had a dream she was being snuck up on and it turned to reality.

Bonnie was now about 80% back most of the time, in and out of reality but improving. She had a lot of very bitter feelings, which she was entitled to. For the most part she was her same bubbly self. There were still times she thought people plotted against her or did things to test her ability to cope, but Rachel felt these were everyday occurrences that she took personally and told her so. Many understood what Bonnie was going through because they knew that they were only a step from that same abyss themselves.

Bonnie returned to school and her friends helped her catch up on the schoolwork. That was good because they could explain it in words she understood and she didn't have to read the book.

Pam went to the board and they nixed her, saying she didn't do enough time. Don't know what to say. She was a really sweet girl and Rachel thought she had things sorted out. Maybe a visit to psyche services could figure out where the board's decision was coming from, what they want. Maybe give her the MMPI test again. (That test was supposed to determine in what areas one's thinking was skewed.) and compared it to the one she took when she got here, and perhaps write a letter to the parole board for her. Just talking to the girl, Rachel can see the positive changes she had made in her thinking. All she could do was suggest, the rest was up to her. She didn't pass the test to make flags so now worked in the storeroom, and was thinking of taking GED classes. There were educational opportunities available at all levels here, but no one was encouraged to take advantage of them. One had to be motivated and seek them out.

Rachel went to school, did her homework, played a little pinochle or spades and listened to these girls sad stories, watched a little TV and tried to get enough sleep. Bonnie was back in school and doing well. All could be worse and we all know that. Bonnie was there and helped Rachel through her crisis, and she did what she could for Bonnie during hers, but she has had enough. She needs a dark quiet place to settle into. She feels stretched out and ready to snap closed.

Bonnie was totally out of touch a month ago, but had come back pretty good but the least little thing threw her off course. One morning someone miscounted their minions and everyone was locked in their room and required to sit on their beds for a long while or until they figured it out. There was no using the toilet, no grooming or getting dressed. No laying down or slouching just sit up straight like a statue until told otherwise.

Bonnie was expecting a visit from her family and had no opportunity to do her hair, face and get into some decent clothes for her first visit since she had become ill. The half hour of sitting and waiting must have seemed like hours to her. She started to lose it again, crying, insisting she had no choice but to refuse the visit. Then she panicked and started complaining about being overloaded with schoolwork and had to study. Her eyes reddened and filled with tears. Then suddenly the C.O. unlocked all our doors and there was plenty of time for her to get ready for her visit.

Vi, who was doing life and was recently reclassified as a minimum, had been here five years, studied her Bible constantly yet never found the time to get her GED. She seemed to enjoy talking with Rachel and now she had a problem the Bible didn't give her an answer to—or at least she couldn't find what she wanted to read. She was tempted to get into a sexual relationship with another woman, but couldn't find the justification in the Bible. She was really wrestling with herself.

There were tiny ants on the room floor coming up through the crumbled concrete next to the wall. Rachel asked for bug spray and Molly asked for some from a different C.O. but none yet, so they each stole a bag of pepper at dinner. They pushed the grains into all the cracks and crevasses around the room. Maybe that would discourage the little critters. Last night the popcorn fairy delivered four bags to her door. Rachel and Molly shared a couple of bags and put the rest away for later, being very careful not to drop any pieces.

Rachel got up the next morning and studied her spelling words for class, wrote two complaints on procedure, then settled down to listen to the gossip—grapes—fruit of the grapevine.

A girl was caught naked at rec. lying on the floor with her friend feasting on her. The C.O. that found them (a big young, loudmouthed guy who was upset anyway because one of the pregnant girls here said he was the daddy) made them lie there in that position for several minutes while he invited several others, staff and inmates, come over to gawk, insisting he needed witnesses. Then he handcuffed them, paraded them across the grounds and took them to Max, not letting them get dressed.

The next day he wandered into Wilson. It was Sunday and Mother's Day, and he threatened to send a girl to Max who was going home Monday. "My mother is picking me up at 10am," the girl told him.

"She can wait until a minute before midnight." he told her.

Rachel sauntered by and wished him a Happy Mother's Day and kept on walking. He had the nerve to quickly snap back, "I'm not a mother!" The girls broke into loud laughter and wouldn't let him argue out of that one. By that time he was looking around for the person who said it, but she had faded into the crowd. He didn't take the girl to max after all.

We had a nice C.O. the next morning. He was usually good natured and easy going. This morning he was been a bit of a grouch. When Rachel went for her mail, he noticed on her ID tag that her birthday was the same as his. He commented about it and said he'd been married 31 years when his wife had her cancerous breasts removed. Now two years later she was sick again and he had to rush her to the hospital last night. That explained his grouchiness, but he's never grouched at Rachel.

Bonnie, Rachel and Ellie spent most of the day studying for their Organizational Behavior class and for a mid-term in Business Finance. Sometimes it helped to work in a group, sometimes not. Sooner or later, the subject turned to their personal issues and the studying ended.

Cook rode seventeen in yesterday and there were no beds—no place for them. They brought out cots to the Wilson Cottage day room so the new admissions girls had a place to be and everyone who resided in Wilson had to stay locked in their room all day so the admissions girls could be kept segregated. Coombs and Karo counties rode also. Rachel heard that Lotusville was in a state of emergency because of the over population. Last month their answer to the problem was to release a few girls a week early. It wasn't enough. All the extra girls created rationing not only in space but on available food and the few freedoms they had, and it limited the available bathroom/shower facilities. It was not the girl's fault so everyone tried to accommodate quietly. The parole board should be letting more girls go home, taking into account that many are not violent and a threat to society. Recidivism is so high because they let those go they are sure will be right back. The prison got paid by the number of inmates they house.

Rachel went over to the school to type a report on their electric typewriter, then took a wheelchair-bound lady for a walk around the walk/jog before lunch.

There was a little excitement in Business Finance class. It was hot, some girls smoked, and the windows were open and there were no screens. A little hornet flew in and was quite a distraction until a girl took off her shoe, climbed from her desk to the radiator and killed it. Most watched in amusement. Slurp, a self admitted nymphomaniac took advantage of the distraction and was sucking on another girl's neck. The other girl saw Rachel watching and pushed Slurp away. Everywhere she looked, someone was licking and lapping at someone. Slurp said she did everyone on the street, male or female, but said her preference then was men. Now, she's saying the men she had here were "jiffy jobs" that don't give her much pleasure.

The ice machine ran out of ice because everyone took what they could to go to the ballgame. The C.O. put a sign on it "No ice until 8 pm" to give it a chance to fill up. At 7 pm girls from another building came over to fill their ice chest and the C.O. let them have all they wanted. Those here who waited for their 8 pm ice got jealous and ripped the sign off and helped themselves to what little was left. The C.O. got upset and said, "No ice for the rest of the night."

Bonnie fed the birds and squirrels every day. She took a bag of something—even if it was crackers. She took a galvanized garbage can lid and filled it with water for the birds, but it heated up too fast because there wasn't any shade and she couldn't always get ice for it. All the critters seemed to wait for her. She's done really well on her self-imposed diet, the weight melted off her and she now wore clothes she hasn't been able to get into for several months.

There was a huge black lady who thought it cute to refer to Rachel as "her duck." Hearing it was her birthday, Rachel sent her a candy bar with a note saying "Your duck needs a pair of small pants." She's making khaki pants on her job and answered she knew how to get them out. One thing for sure, she won't be wearing them until they're washed.

Got a letter from the County Bar Association. They said they were investigating the situation with her attorney.

Rachel's resume was finished and her speech outline was nearly done. Her English report was in the works and there was only one test to study for in each subject. Bonnie had caught up on what she missed while she was sick and was feeling so much better. Things were on schedule and looking up.

Rachel was reclassified to a "super minimum" so was to turn in her green jacket for a blue. It didn't happen in a timely fashion, so she asked Pam who was working in the storeroom afternoons while she attended GED classes (Yeah Pam!) in the morning if she could expedite things. Later that day, she was called to the storeroom for the exchange, but couldn't go because she was in class. Between English and Speech, she picked up her blue (honors) shirts.

Between Bonnie's mom and an attorney she hired to get medical help when she needed it, Bonnie had become somewhat of a celebrity. Newspaper reporters have been to their house trying to get more information and want to do an interview with her. Her mom and the attorney might have rattled some cages here, but it was the man from psych services that got her the help she needed. There's rumor of law suit. The more they might have this place riled, the better the chance of her doing more time for it. That's Lotusville's prerogative when one had an open-ended sentence. Bonnie's mom had imposed on the judge and the parole board to get her released in August, but she doesn't have a board date for another four years. Maybe it will work, but Rachel doesn't know how.

Helicopters flew all around this place all day, and girls went out on the walk/jog to holler at them to lower a ladder. Another girl was walking around with a hair piece hooked to the front of her pants. It was said that one might see everything in Times Square, but it had nothing on this place.

Bonnie had been feeling better emotionally, so they gave her a new roommate. Physically? Some of her bald spots had started to fill in, but there were new sheddings on the back of her shirt. The new roommate was a character. She and her boyfriend had traveled all over the country stealing. They both were doing a year for their last caper. They assigned her to work on the dock and she stole everything she could get her hands on. One evening she brought Bonnie a half dozen cans of chicken, a dozen apples and mayonnaise. Someone brought over some nuts and before long she concocted a Waldorf salad. The next night, however, she tried to smuggle out an onion in her pants. Being a skinny girl, the bulge was distorting her shape and when she tried to wear it more snug, she laughed and a C.O. heard her say something about wishing it were a man. When questioned, she produced the onion and it created a hilarious event—so much so, she didn't get a ticket.

She got a letter from her boyfriend. He told her his roommate found a baby chipmunk and they keep it in their room. Says it sleeps in his chest hair at night.

Rachel gave her speech in class and it resulted in a standing ovation. It was on the subject of medical and dental treatment not afforded us in a timely fashion, something they could all relate to. The instructor asked if she'd give it again to another class. What was really sad was one of the girls in the class refused to give any speech. She insisted she just can't get up in front of the class and talk. She was terrified. She was told that if she didn't give a speech, she would fail the class and not graduate. Several of her friends worked with her, encouraged her, did everything they could, but her fear was so great, it wasn't enough.

Rachel thought she had another day to study for the final in Finance, but the teacher sprung the test a day early. Then on the day they were supposed to take the test, he brought a movie and ordered Domino's Pizza. She couldn't describe the pleasure everyone had, the aroma, the hot greasy juice on their hands the moment before eating it. Someone brought a bag of popcorn for everyone and others brought cookies. Rachel supplied ice. It was a truly wonderful two hours and for a while they forgot where they were. The other finals were the following week. A project due next Monday morning, a speech due Monday night, a law test Wednesday afternoon and Organizational Behavior on Thursday afternoon. Then there will be a break for two weeks."

No decision yet on her property hearing, at least none that she's heard of. She did hear that the Black/Knight law firm was involved in some criminal activity. Have asked friends and family to scan the papers and send her any clippings about it.

The weather had been scorching hot. Molly was a riot when in all seriousness she told Rachel about the drought affecting the farmers, "and the nerve of the bastards, whose ancestors stole the land from the Indians. They called in the Indians—Indians whose ancestors were run off that very land. They run them off, kill them, steal their land, then expect them to be on call to dance for more rain when they needed it. If I were an Indian, I wouldn't go."

Rachel had seen the rain dancing Indians on TV. Molly asked her, "If you were an Indian would you do that for those people?

"Sure! She told her. "I think the rain dance is a scam and if the farmers wanted to pay me for a rain dance, I'd do it." Molly got a real serious look and said, "I never thought of that."

School was out again and Rachel had little to do other than see how much popcorn she could score. Ten bags the other night and four the next. She walked past several white shirts like she had license, and no one questioned her, and let's face it, the fragrance of popcorn can't be keep a secret.

Pam took up smoking and her friends seem to be offended by it. She's such a clean-cut girl and the rumor was she's looking for a duck.

Two weeks of no school went fast. Rachel went over and picked up her new set of books. Some of them looked serious, but she knew that in a few weeks, they would all be old friends.

Rachel thought she had a good chance to get out of here later this year. The judge could do it or the parole board. She hadn't heard anything from the attorney about either of those possibilities or any decision on the appeal.

Bonnie's all excited about the possibility of being released after her three year gun specification (she shot up a car, no one was in it) is up. Her family had been to see the parole board, the judge, and prosecutor and they haven't made any promises but the clerk or bailiff or someone told her family the judge planned to bring her back this year, that she'd never have to do her 4-15 which didn't start until after the gun spec.

The new quarter of school was underway and Rachel was once again buried in schoolwork. She tried to keep up with it, but was so hot. Her mind was everywhere else. She hadn't been walking, either, because her foot had really been bothering her. She couldn't find a pair of comfortable shoes. Her mom bought her an expensive pair of Nike's but couldn't wear them and had to send them back. She came here with a $5 pair of Flites that were just perfect, but no one could find more of them. They were old when her family exchanged them for the shoes she wore in court in County and they were really falling apart now.

Rachel got up and out really early one morning and sneak-washed her clothes. She figured the laundry workers would still be sleeping so did her own.

Pinochle playing had been very limited as schoolwork had to be a priority. One of her fellow students was copying her accounting homework. Rachel spent a long time on it and did it over and over to remember the process and why. Did this girl think she'd learn it by copying? She had a lot of reading to do and there was a serious chapter for Law class.

The first day of Accounting class, the teacher said, "I thought you went home."

"I'm back," she told him. When he looked at her strangely Rachel added, "I love this place." Then he looked at her as if she were contagious. He probably thought she'd caught another case. As long as he understood that she needed an "A" from his course, was all that he needed to understand. Rachel would rather be fishing. She often thought of her fishing trip with Eric. The hurt had faded and she was once more looking forward to another fishing trip with him.

Rachel met Danita, who was still in Pierce, at lunch and as usual she was full of stories to tell. "Two girls were caught naked in a room. The C.O. told them she was giving them each a ticket. The next day they were caught again in the same room, doing the same thing. This time they were handcuffed and taken to max." Then she says that C.O. disappeared into another inmates room, and after fifteen minutes, according to Danita who says she was timing it, two white shirts came in (because no one was at the desk to answer the phone) and they broke up a 69. Both were taken out handcuffed, the girl went to "max" and the C.O. was taken to jail. The C.O. was female so may come back as an inmate, charged with rape.

Danita continued. "Then this girl came out of her room all bruised and scratched and stumbling around. She said she fell out of bed but nobody believed her. The C.O. called in white shirts and they all asked her what happened. After a lot of questioning she finally admitted being raped in the shower by a broom handle." Danita smiled as she explained that she moved over to a table close to them so she could hear what was going on. "Two girls held her down while another did the deed. She was really crying and said she was too scared to tell at first because they said they'd mess her up if she did. They walked her over to the hospital. Then they came and got the other girls and put handcuffs on them. I guess they went to jail for more charges." Danita went into a sweat as she told the story, as if she was really living it.

The student's softball team was falling victim to injuries. The shortstop sprained her knee, an outfielder broke her wrist in three places two others got hit in the face with a ball, and another one sprained her ankle. Not much of a playing team left. This is no place to get hurt, but these girls just took it in stride.

Rachel's homework kept her busy and she found that the courses were very interrelated which helped in understanding concepts. Even the dreaded accounting was starting to make sense.

Another hot and humid day. The air was stagnant and heavy with the smell of human waste from the nearby giant septic system's leach bed. Hard to study, can't think, and nearly impossible to sleep. Law test in a couple of days but the two days of studying recently didn't stick. Had to go over to the school to try again. Maybe a different atmosphere would help. Studied for a couple hours there, then came back and did a load of clothes (illegally) stole a bucket of ice, enjoyed a lunch with Bonnie, showered, then started to sweat all over again.

We watched through the window as the sky darkened with heavy approaching gray clouds. The flies bit, girls giggled and took off their shoes anticipating play in the puddles, that never formed. The dark sky was all around and we saw lightning, but the sky directly overhead was blue and cloudless. The Bermuda Triangle had nothing on this place. No rain for nearly three months.

No one seemed to be studying for or looking forward to the Microeconomics class scheduled for that night, and Rachel wasn't looking forward to it either. Now, she doesn't know if she'll even get there tonight. Lockdown and searches. Razor blades went missing from maintenance and they tore this place up. Guess they found a lot of contraband, but not necessarily what they were looking for. Two at a time, girls were handcuffed and paraded across the compound from various buildings to max. They did find some razor blades cleverly implanted into the handles of plastic combs (gently melted to accommodate.) Rumor of a rumble between blacks and whites was still on. Stupid talk.

Danita was said to have had a heart attack. She hugged herself into a little ball at work and claimed she could not breathe. Her face was twisted in pain and they took her to the Hospital, verified it was a heart attack and brought her back to Pierce the same day. She needed to lose some weight but the food we are served isn't conducive to that. Her cheeks are getting so big they've turned her eyes to slits.

Lots of heart attacks and cancer here and these girls were young. Gun's breast cancer came back even though both her breasts were gone. There's a girl about twenty in the hospital who had another year added on to her sentence at her last board, but didn't live to go home. They took her to a nearby hospital twice a day for morphine. An older redheaded lady had a cancerous tumor on her arm. She's very fair so it was probably a melanoma. Bad news! They kept cutting away at it a little at a time every few weeks. She's scheduled for another surgery and was still in a sling from the last one. Her crime was trying to flush the devil out of her grandson holding the garden hose in his mouth. She'll never leave here.

One of the young white shirts had a husband doing life in a nearby penal facility and he escaped. It was on the TV news. Police spotted him at Riverview's new shopping center during a fracas. They chased him through two suburbs then trapped him in a nearby city where he shot himself.

Our unit manager threatened a serious search. Most white shirts avoid that extra work, but he seemed to like dumping drawers and boxes and tearing up a room. A few years ago he called a girl a slut because she had a "girlfriend." The girl took offense and hung a hawker from the side of his head. He broke her jaw and arm—and was promoted from gray shirt to white.

Rachel got an "A" on the Business Law test but not a perfect score. She had to work on that. Three more mid-terms this week and studying was bringing limited success. Three classmates at the table were trying to figure things out.

It's so hot and the air was thick with flies. Rachel and Bonnie took it upon themselves to take the garbage out, instead of waiting for those assigned to do it—just so the things don't breed inside. They're amazed that so many girls could sit and let the disgusting things crawl over them. The laziness was unbelievable.

There was a girl in Pierce incarcerated for robbing two pharmacies with a gun. The "gun spec." was dropped! She came here to Jefferson and after six months the judge shocked her out. Her probation officer found her to have three consecutive "dirty urines" before he violated her. He was supposed to report her after one, but again she was given another chance. Back here she came. At visiting hall she was observed "doing lines" on the table, snorting coke—she and her visitor. They took her to the hospital, took a urine sample and it proved dirty, so they took both her and the guy to Mason County jail to face felony charges.

Bonnie and Rachel studied constantly for their mid terms, quizzing each other daily and were confident they had a grip. When they went to take the first of them, the material looked only vaguely familiar. Bonnie locked herself away in her room for a couple of days, saying she needed to be alone. Rachel studied alone and outlined the chapters. When Bonnie emerged they went through the quizzing process again.

Flies were really bad. Big, thick and miserable. The ants were here year round, but the pepper Molly and Rachel put on the perimeter of their room floor seemed to discourage them from crossing that line. No roaches and it has been way to dry for mosquitoes. Then a hornet, she could swear was three inches long, came flying through the day room and straight into Rachel's room. Molly was sitting there reading and didn't notice when it flew about two feet from her face, and stayed on the window. Rachel came in and asked her to look up. She screamed and ran from the room. The C.O. an elderly former navy man sauntered over to investigate the problem. Rachel grabbed Bonnie's fly swatter which they kept at their table and held it out to him. He said "I've been stung by those things, and never again." and backed away resuming his seat at his desk. Rachel went in and took the screen off the window and it flew out.

Rachel's parents sent her a great pair of shoes, exactly like the pair she wore out. She was so happy to see such nice pretty shoes and she had no problem wearing them. Perfect fit. No more limping around with unhappy feet.

The girl in the room next door had a visit from her mother. She told her that the police were out to their house with a warrant for her arrest. Her mother said she told them, "She's not here," and slammed the door. This girl expected to leave here in two months and felt that these apparent new charges jeopardize that. Maybe they won't find her. Oh, well.

Rachel hadn't heard anything about if the time she spent in City had caught up with the time she did in County. That added to the time she's done here will determine when she will be eligible to file for super shock probation from the judge and even her out date. She hasn't heard any more about the decision on the appeal. This was her attorney's responsibility and he had failed her. The legal system had failed her. Being able to go to school saved her sanity.

She did some intense studying for a really small test. Only four chapters. Several classmates that have never spoken to her before have asked to copy her "notes." She told them,

"I have no notes, just study your book." She didn't tell them she used her yellow highlighter, that the lectures followed the text and she followed her book as he talked. She highlighted what matched and assumed that was important. They were pissed, having expected her to come up with an "answer sheet."

She really surprised herself getting a 97 on the accounting test. Never thought she was that accurate. Bonnie got an 87 and had agreed to sit next to Emily who wasn't comprehending it at all—so she could get a respectable grade for the final. There's rumor of all kinds of cheating, swapping answers with the other class and one girl had a tape recorder with ear buds. Someone must have stolen it from an office because it certainly isn't on a list of approved items. Whatever these lazy girls are doing didn't impress anyone and they sure were taking a risk of spending more time here.

The fire alarms rang all day long in Pierce so those ladies came to Wilson to get away from it. One girl was in her pajamas and robe. She made a nuisance of herself and complained to us about the ants which she found crawling all over her Bible the other morning. Like so many of the women here, she expected to be taken care of and wasn't about to lift a finger to do something for herself—even for her own well-being.

There have been a series of real fires in various old structures. The gray stone entrance building had two of them from faulty electrical wiring and a couple of old buildings where girls lived caught fire. There's rumored to be the ghost of an ex-inmate that clatters about on the third floor in one of the older buildings.

The fire alarms in all the new buildings blare constantly and no one as yet knows why. They replaced all the alarms and can't figure out what triggered them, so more often than not they're just disconnected.

Fire trucks left P.F.S. earlier and all fantasized about how bad the damage was and if Pizza Hut would have to deliver lunch. Everyone yearned for the simple things back home.

Lots of excitement because our Governor was here to sign requisitions. It seemed the food allowed for the maximum people count allowed ran out. We're 215% over capacity so no wonder the food ran out. No conscience about it, though, because he isn't thinking of letting anyone out early.

The girl who raped the other girl with a broom handle last month was given a new case. The two girls who assisted her were sent to "max." So that's over, except for the victim. Hopefully some attempt would be made to keep them separated.

A former C.O. was given five years for harboring a fugitive (an escapee from here.) Everyone wondered when she would show up in admissions. Rachel also heard that the gun another C.O.'s escapee's husband used to shoot himself in a suburb of Riverview was registered to the former C.O. Three female guards lost their jobs after it was learned they were having relationships with him and they helped him with his escape. What a circus!

Rachel aced a recent test in Labor Relations Law and the teacher commented on the back, "Your tests are referred to as the 'answer key' by your colleagues." Cute! Didn't do so well on a Business and Government test—86% but had the best grade in the Micro class. She spent her weekends studying to the point of obsession, while most others played.

A fly flew up a girl's skirt during Micro. She screamed and caused quite a commotion. When things calmed down, Rachel told her "I used to be afraid of flies too—but then I opened one up." She didn't get it. Then a very strange thing happened during class. Someone passed a fly to her (dead, she thought) from across the room. It was wrapped in a paper towel. How much can one get away with here is a big part of the culture and Rachel has become part of it, so when she looked up and saw a staple gun within easy reach, she carefully positioned the fly so she could staple the wings to the towel. Mission completed, she passed it back and watched who it went back to. She should have known. Bonnie had killed it, or so she thought. By the time it got back to her, the critter had regained consciousness and was pawing the air.

She tried to study but it was a waste of effort. People would not leave her alone and the noise level on the TV was outrageous. The flies were a nuisance too. Can't imagine how bad they were in P.F.S. as she lost her appetite thinking of it.

Ellie had a birthday and Bonnie made her a pie to be shared by many. Graham cracker crust, tapioca pudding, Oreo cookies, and Rachel donated an O'Henry candy bar cut into crumbles for the topping. Bonnie can sure put together a good-looking pie. It was way too sweet for Rachel to enjoy, but many of these ex-alky's can eat the sugar straight.

Rachel had hoped to stay over at the school after class to do some studying in the air-conditioned room the computers needed and even had a good start on it, but aids were putting tests together for next week. Because mass cheating is suspected, and rightfully so, she left because she didn't want to be anywhere around them.

Back at Wilson, a TV, a large fan, a hair dryer and two smaller fans all being used on the same line blew the breaker. Rachel was grateful for the quiet, but the girls all started to scream and complain they had to see the movie. Half a dozen white shirts came by with their walkie-talkies to look over the situation but couldn't figure it out. They moved the fan to the other side of the room and the TV to another socket, but didn't have a clue as to where the breaker box was.

Rumor was that something big is happening here on Monday. The overcrowding was presenting a problem with the Environmental Protection Agency who said we had to cut way back on water usage, that it had more than doubled over the last couple of years. Supposedly, they had been reviewing the records of first timers and old timers for early release and hoped to let go 500 women. A guy named Johnson was supposed to be in charge of it. Don't know the criteria.

This quarter of school was coming to a close and Rachel has done quite well so far. Her roommate, Molly, is forever asking her if she ever got tired of the books. She tells her "I don't have choices." One more quarter, then graduation.

The cows were gone. The drought has left nothing for them to graze on and bringing in feed was expensive. They must have taken them to slaughter. Hopefully, the meat would be distributed to all the penitentiaries.

Meanwhile, Bonnie and Rachel kill flies—lots of them every day. They were everywhere and on everything. Sometimes they piled up the little black bodies on the floor and other times they just scattered them around. At the present time there's enough of them scattered about to make a good-sized carpet. The survivors came by and landed on the fly swatter (well stained with fly juice) to pay last respects to their buddies. Whapp! Just caught a double header. Two copulating on the table. More fly meat, more carpet. A huge horsefly buzzed around but landed higher than their reach.

The ants disappeared, or at least no one is complaining about them and the gnats aren't back yet. She remembered how disgusting they were last fall, sticking all over the food like pepper and catching in our noses when we breathed. Well, this place is out in the country.

Some of our teachers were really good and made their points in a way we could grasp. Others just didn't seem comfortable here, and rushed through the material. We had to spend days trying to translate what it was all about.

A dietician came from Central Office to spot check how we were fed. Her visit was expected and we were served a banana for breakfast and two ears of sweet corn for dinner—in addition to the standard fare of slop. Rachel hadn't had seen a single ear of corn since she checked in here two years ago and bananas were rare. Whenever a visitor came they served us a pretty decent meal. There's a printed menu they were supposed to follow, but adhered to that loosely.

According to the records Rachel requested here, she had been given no credit for the days she spent in City or the weeks in County. The attorney was supposed to handle that and doesn't seem to be able to, even though friends and family had been on his back. She needed to find the date after which she can file for Super Shock. She's served nearly 2/3 of the actual drug time which is all she's required to do, she thinks, before filing for shock with the judge, but she can only file for it once so the timing had to be right. Things like this really got her riled up and she found it hard to focus on the things she does have control over.

Fire alarms went off in the middle of the night for no apparent reason. We had to get up sleepy-eyed and sat in the day room. All of us except for Ellie who gracefully descended the staircase with all her make-up on and every hair in place. They used to let us sleep through the noise if we could, but due to all the recent real fires in the old buildings, we had to get up and out. It turned out to be nothing but an inconvenience.

The drinking water developed a bad taste and color. Can't blame it on the livestock because they're gone. It could be that they switched the water source again, but it could be anything.

Rachel had finals in all her classes and felt she did okay. She sort of short-circuited and got kind of flip in Labor Relations. One of the questions was "Why did the then governor of NY, Nelson Rockefeller, refuse to send in the National Guard to pick up the slack when the N.Y.C. sanitation workers went on strike and the garbage piled up 15-20 feet before it was finally cleaned up." She thought about how photogenic Mayor Lindsay was and about him being a Democrat and Rockefeller being a Republican. She figured she'd give her instructor, who she knew would be bored grading the papers, a chuckle and wrote "Rockefeller thought Lindsay looked good in all that garbage." She also noted the quotes from Rockefeller when he gave his reason, but really felt her first answer was more on track.

In accounting she really lost it. Brain lock. Bonnie told her that her last answer was wrong and she answered, "I don't care," and turned in her paper. Why was she looking at her paper anyway. Maybe the 97 she got on the first test will be strong enough to let her keep the "A."

Bonnie finally got called to the dentist. She's been on "the list" for months. One tooth was taken care of earlier, but now another tooth was falling apart in her mouth and she had been trying to pull it herself. It came out a piece at a time, a lot of blood and pus and pain. Of course, her face is badly swollen. She finally got what was left of her tooth pulled. Isn't there a law against cruel and unusual punishment?

Rachel's teeth needed attention too. They made her whole head hurt all the time and the broken tooth was still cutting the inside of her mouth. She tried to spend time walking every day that weather permitted. When she saw a white shirt walking across the compound that she felt comfortable talking with, she told her about waiting months and sending as many kites requesting dental care and all they did was to tell her to stop sending kites. She asked if she could help? She said she'd see what she could do.

Rachel's name was finally on the Shock Parole Board list and there was a chance they would release her. The thought made her both giddy and apprehensive. The board date isn't for a few months, but her name is on there. If she doesn't get it, she'll just have to get the judge and prosecutor to give her Super Shock Probation—somehow.

The girl who was raped in Pierce had been moved to Wilson. They put her in a room with the same crazy woman Rachel shared a room with briefly. Clearly a dirty trick. She wondered if they fixed the weld on the bed.

The flies were horny, mating and pregnant. They were all over the place and everybody. When they got swatted, they exploded and squirted blood. No lightening bugs, no mosquitoes, just flies in all sizes.

There was a problem keeping the washing machine going. It didn't work with the lid up because there's a tiny button, a safety feature, on the back of the machine between the lid and machine that signaled the lid position. These cows sat on the washer lid for various reasons and bent the lid so it wouldn't make contact with the button. Rachel wedged in some pieces of cardboard which got it going until the steam softened the cardboard but she got her laundry done while the others assumed the machine broken and stayed away. Necessity is the mother of invention. Rachel was just so disturbed, distracted and upset about being here she had trouble being around these sleazy women. The entertainment value ended months ago.

The stress of school is over for now, but she was still charged up about it. Break was only one week this time not a whole lot of time to wind down from studying for and taking the finals. She decided to take in a softball game between the inmates and staff.

Ellie had been involved somewhat seriously with one of the long-time inmates. Everyone would see them holding hands walking together and feeling each other all the time. That was until the softball game. The teacher she liked and lost his job here returned to play in the game. We were all glad to see him, but Ellie flirted with him outrageously and her "girlfriend," who was also at the game, became intensely jealous. After the game she let Ellie know how she felt and everyone knew she was red hot about it. She told Ellie that she was making a fool out of her. Ellie felt bad and wrote letters to her defending herself, but the girl didn't buy any of it, avoided her and retuned the letters unopened. It was a very sad few weeks for Ellie.

They served us a banana for lunch today—only because there were visitors. Rachel ate hers quickly, then got someone else's.

A couple weeks ago when she first learned she would see the parole board within the next few months, she really did not have that much confidence she would get anything from it—or maybe she just couldn't imagine being out, so there was no real excitement about it. Now, since everyone had been telling her (fellow inmates) she is as good as gone, there seemed to be a bit more reality to the possibility. It felt good to have someone cheering for her, but she wasn't ready to face the possibility of denial. She was afraid to hope and her sanity was on a fragile tether.

Rachel wrote the judge a letter asking for a date he might consider her for super shock probation. She doesn't expect any response, but one never knows. The more lines she has in the water, the more chance of getting lucky.

New books should be here soon. One of the classes was Computer Management Decisions. That could be fun. Natural Science, whatever that was, may be a refreshing change of pace. Psychology could be interesting—but it might be a drag. Small Business Systems would be a good one.

There were some problems with the water pumps and the pressure was down to practically nothing. Got in the shower and had difficulty getting wet. The E.P.A. shut down the power plant so the "scrubbers" could be replaced. The air rained soot. They burned coal, so just imagine.

Rachel was attacked by a family of spiders while she slept. She woke up with a couple dozen bites on a swollen neck. She scratched gingerly at herself all day. If she could catch the critters, she'd pull their faces off. They'd have a hard time biting anyone else.

Grades came out and once again Rachel was able to pull off all "A's." She amazed herself. The only "B's" she's had since the beginning were the two when she missed a month of class while in County waiting for the property hearing. Only one more quarter of school and then graduation. When she'd signed up for school it was only to do something positive with her time and she'd never thought that she'd still be here to finish.

Rumors were rampant about moving all the blue shirts out of here and to Springfield in the next few days, but there were also rumors about it all being a lie. They did open a new pre-release in Springfield.

There was talk of a small war at the Riverview pre-release. There was a big lummox working there that used to be a C.O. at Lotusville. He was a totally disrespectful fool with a big mouth. After beating up a drunk in a weekend bar fight in a nearby town, he was transferred to the Riverview pre-release. The girls all knew of his penchant for violence and to avoid him at the pre-release, but he goaded a girl into getting smart with him and he belted her in the face. Six of her friends then pulled him away and beat him pretty bad. He was hospitalized there. They brought back the "Riverview 7" and locked them all down. One of the girls has had several broken bones set and a visit to the dentist getting broken and loosened teeth pulled. Those that have seen her say her face is a mess.

A girl in Wilson had a hysterectomy last winter and has been really sick from it ever since. Finally after several months of complaining about pain, fever and cramps they stopped giving her Tylenol and sent her back to I.S.U where she had the original surgery. They opened her up again and discovered they had not completed the operation, and parts were disconnected but left in.

Hadn't seen Mattie around since the ball game and discovered she'd had hernia surgery and Rachel was concerned about her.

School was back in session and had hit full force. New books to read, and lots of homework.

Went to a movie with Bonnie and Emily. Ellie, who was now back with her girlfriend were necking in front of us and their hands were busy under a yellow sweater that covered them both.

School has Rachel's concentration, but she heard there was a marijuana bust in Pierce. Reports are they took three girls into town for new charges. Two of the three had visit's the previous Saturday.

Already have a test to study for in psych and just sat down with a book when suddenly there was a commotion in one corner of the room. Rachel watched the C.O. press her "panic button" then went to investigate the situation. The former mayor of Chicago's inmate cousin was in her 70's and was somewhat tolerant of her young bull-dyking roommate who was using their room for their monkey business. When the roommate and her friend came out, she asked them if they had cleaned up the room and was told she "would get to it" and tried to push past her. The elderly woman shoved her back and demanded she do it now because it never got done in the past and the girl repeated that she'd "do it later." Lots of push and shove and yelling. Witnesses who were drawn to the noise. Then the frail 70 year-old-fist wound up and neatly cold cocked her roommate with a mighty uppercut. A flourish of cussing issued forth from a bleeding mouth. The elderly woman grabbed a nearby broom to finish the job, but the C.O. snatched it away just as white shirts burst through the door like storm troopers. They were both cuffed and hauled away, the elderly lady still crowing.

Charla had a crush on Bonnie and has been following her everywhere. Bonnie likes the attention but her Christian roommate is giving her a lot of guff about it.

Bonnie, and Rachel were out on the walk/jog with a new girl in the building when they were approached by a full-grown grey and white cat. It is rare to see a cat around here anymore. The girl gushes, "Oh look, that's the cat that was hanging around the door of P.F.S. this morning.

Rachel reached down and snatched up the friendly thing. It didn't resist and even cuddled a little.

"It likes you," Bonnie commented.

Then Ellie walked over with a panicked expression on her face. Now Ellie likes cats and even has two of her own at home, so Rachel didn't know what the problem was. "You're holding it," she observed with a strained look on her face as she halted her approach. The kitty started to purr as Bonnie stroked it's head. Ellie looked at her uneasily.

"I should, like, tell you," Ellie stammered. "But, like, did you hear what happened at Jefferson Cottage? I wanted to pet it too, but like, I can't do it. Two girls took that cat in their room and had it lick them. Then they both, like," she paused. "Like they caught something. I'm afraid of it."

Well, the poor thing realized it was being talked about in a negative way and wiggled to get down. We'd heard similar stories before, yet we laughed all day about the "supposedly" true tale. It was a diversion from studying.

*        *        *

In Computer Analysis everyone was paired up to make decisions about sales, inventory, product improvement, issuing stock, bonds, investing and the like and had to keep accurate records as accountants. It was neat to use the computer. The Case Analysis class was boring. The teacher in the Psychology class talked too fast and doesn't enunciate and she seemed to ramble. Science was an interesting class. The instructor had a Ph.D and seemed afraid of us, but Rachel did enjoy having a science class.

Bonnie went through a lot of roommates. Now she had Jean who is doing a year. She's apprehensive about her because she said she talked a lot and wasn't too clean. Bonnie cleaned all the time and one doubts anyone could meet her standards.

Rachel went to Science class to take a test but had no sooner sat down when she was summoned to the Parole Board. Then she had to go back in the afternoon to take the test. She drew some blanks but felt confident she did well.

The board was another issue. It had no intention of letting her go. They had her down as a serious drug addict who had made no move to help herself and participate in drug programs. She talked to them for about fifteen minutes, pleading her case, explaining she'd never taken drugs in her life, that her case was possession, not using or selling They said they'd continue her for two months, investigate what she told them and request a community report. That usually consists of an opinion from the prosecutor's office and probably verification of her claim. She hoped they would come up with something positive for her. Either that or offer her a blindfold and cigarette. What a mess of errors and incompetence this whole thing has become.

Whether or not all the stress that's smothered her like an evil cloud was the result of dealing with the daily issues of living here or that she was pressuring herself to do well in academia, she doesn't know, but the forces were immense.

Rachel heard that along about November there were going to be a big exodus from this place to the Springfield pre-release. All minimums with less that 18 months to their next board and no recent tickets were supposed to go—but as with everything else, there were exceptions and to this point, it was only a rumor. They were not taking people on serious medications and had agreed to let students finish.

The showers were crowded. They were turning off the water for two days. Don't know why.

Rachel got a 98 on the psych test and aced the science test. All's well at the school, but came back to Wilson and found the place torn up. Big time search! Rumor was we're moving out of Wilson Cottage and into Jefferson sometime in the next couple of days. Those in Jefferson are moving to Pierce Cottage and Pierce people moving to Wilson. Then a selected 200 will go to Springfield. Again, rumors. She did hear they received a lot of bright orange jumpsuits for traveling a couple of days ago.

Bonnie and Rachel tried to sneak into the computer room to study but were caught. No one was supposed to use them unsupervised. Oh, well, then supervise. They were only trying to get a leg-up on their studies.

A girl on "honor status" in another building that was here for arson, hid an iron in the linen closet and left it plugged in all night. During the night flames ate all the sheets and towels and created confusion and a mess. On another occasion, big fire trucks had to come again because a girl in "disciplinary control" deliberately caught her room on fire. The hundred or so girls confined in the new DC-4 building were released to a large adjacent room while they fought the fire. Then they started a brawl and reinforcements had to be brought in to quell that. Those girls here for arson and sex crimes are a strange bunch. Can't relate to them.

Got up early and spent the whole day in the books. No tests this week, but Rachel wanted to have everything under control. Everyone was asked to make plans for graduation and were measured for cap & gown. They said pick two from the visiting list to attend. Rachel asked, "How about three?" She couldn't see asking her parents to come when they would have to drive here alone. They needed a driver. Rachel explained this but they did not seem to listen or care. Little did they know that she didn't care about attending either—in fact she thought it would be better if they just sent the diploma to her parents home through the mail.

She tried to spend as much time with Mattie as she could but it was usually limited to trafficking in popcorn. The building she lived in had a lot of restrictions and those in Jefferson, for the most part, were not allowed to mingle with the rest, work being an exception.

A mouse that had been terrorizing Wilson for about a week trotted into Vi's room this morning with a cookie in its mouth. She screamed and scared it so much it dropped the cookie and ran. Then everyone who saw it started screaming and all those that thought they were going to sleep in, gave up. It was 7am. Rachel had a science class, then will stay after school to work on a project for Management Decisions. Emily and Rachel were partnered in that and work well together.

The second night in a row this whole place was locked down. They couldn't get the count straight and school was cancelled. Rachel was all prepared for the test, too. It seemed the count was off and they suspected there was an escape in progress. A girl was moved from the hospital to the "hole" and there was a laundry basket with black plastic garbage bags nearby that wasn't supposed to be there, and that was a clue. It turned out it was a foiled escape attempt. It seems that as the Holidays approach these girls think, "I'm not going to spend another year here, this is the time of the year to be with loved ones," and that seemed to precipitate the escape attempts.

A putrid stink filled the air while everyone was locked in their rooms and unable to escape it. After unlock, Rachel went to the day room window, opened it hoping for fresh air and was watching the lights in the darkness and the bugs flying around them. Half a dozen people got real curious as to what she was seeing. She told them, "I'm watching the world rot." The stink turned out to be the backed up septic system.

Bonnie and Rachel were out on the walk/jog in the afternoon and saw a friend walking with a new duck. They wondered if the old duck was aware of the new one. They stopped us and asked for a light, but as non-smokers we couldn't accommodate them. They were probably finalizing plans because later that night they tunneled under one fence and were trying to scale the other when caught.

Rachel studied science for a couple hours then Bonnie found a canasta game. After dinner Bonnie found a pinochle game. She does not have any interest in studying science, so Rachel decided to make up a "Trivia Pursuit" game for the science test. Bonnie won't like it but will study if she can make the studying fun. They both learned from it. They were both doing really well this quarter but both were also running on nerves.

The superintendent of programs was making her own job easier by shutting down all the programs (kind of short-sighted as far as her job security goes,) which not only included toastmasters and J.C.s but also popcorn sales. She said she wanted to get rid of the schools, as the girls are here to be punished, not to be educated. Also kind of short-sighted. She expressed her humanitarianism by noting she wants us locked up, down, and in, as often as possible.

The air in the day area filled up again with the smell of someone getting a perm in their hair. The C.O. investigated and found a big-time beauty shop operating in the laundry room. Busted! Someone got a "contraband perm" every week (by the smell of things) but this is the first bust. They must have given the C.O. a good lie because Rachel was eavesdropping on the C.O.'s telephone conversation and heard her tell someone, "I really don't know what they are allowed to have and what they aren't." Actually there is a "beauty shop" on the premises, but you get on a list for it and if you're lucky you can get an appointment once a year. Nevertheless, we are not permitted to trim our own hair. They do mostly haircuts and perms, but there are a very few that can get their hair colored. Sometimes a girl with gum disease was given peroxide to rinse her mouth. She would use it, but instead of spitting it in the sink would save it in a cup. It was a popular item to trade or the girl would use it in her own hair. The girls that work at GBS (that's what they call the beauty parlor) are in school, training to take the state test so they could do hair once they are released.

One of the girls who worked on the Lima Rehab. Project brought a dead mouse to her duck. It was posed real cute, sitting up with a curly upturned tail. They had it perched on their table all evening. What makes more sense? Girls trying to improve their appearance or staring at a dead mouse. The scary thing is that the girls on this job are searched when they return because they have access to the public and drugs, guns, etc. Where did she tuck that mouse to smuggle it in?

The Science test was postponed so Rachel had more opportunity to badger Bonnie with the Trivia Pursuit cards she made. She slipped them into her pocket and forced her to get familiar with the material while they walked on the track.

A girl outside Rachel's door was making toasted cheese sandwiches with the flat iron. Stolen bread, stolen cheese, and using the iron to make toast. Talk about creativity. One wonders how much grease stain will be on the next ironed shirt.

Rachel only scored 94 on the Science test. She wasn't happy with it but was satisfied. She came back, went for a walk, cleaned her room, read a chapter in psych, then ate a bag of popcorn. Charla and her friend challenged Bonnie and her to a game of pinochle.

The newest fad here is blue nail polish. Rachel doesn't indulge, any more than making it. Just add ink from a ball-point pen cartridge—a couple drops into white pearly polish and stir. It looks great with the bright blue shirts, but isn't easy to get off.

For the third time in less than six months, the same filling fell out of Rachel's tooth and she only has glue from the school to put it back. She hated the thought of having to go to that dentist because he was such a poor excuse for one. He did buzz the sharp edges off her broken tooth when the white shirt got her an appointment. She wished she knew when she would be leaving here so she could make an appointment with a real dentist. This imposter was a joke who probably did more damage than good, but the joke was on the inmates.

Bonnie lost another roommate. All her roommates go home. The December board list came out in October and Rachel's name wasn't on it. She checked with the social worker. Seems the Community report isn't in yet. If it comes in shortly, they said they'd add her name. Everyone wants out of here. Two more girls had their escape attempt foiled. They were casing the fenced area behind the school after dinner. A C.O. spotted them and snuck up behind. "Escaping are we?" she asked.

Fall came and went and Rachel didn't notice the leaves turning color and falling off.

Two girls were caught in the bathroom at school, two more were caught in a room together in Wilson and a girl from admissions ran for the fence. Busy day.

All day Rachel reviewed income statements, balance sheets, made comparisons and graphs and started a written analysis for Small Business Development. Psych final is tomorrow and science final the next day, along with Speech. Time flies in school but not outside of it.

She went over to the school to type her science notes and was asked to tutor someone in accounting. Rachel spent some time with her, but her mind wasn't on it. The girl said she thought she understood but it was obvious she wasn't that interested. She traded Rachel a brand new pair of jeans for three candy bars.

She studied hard for all the finals and they were over. Everyone was sure they did really well. Rachel missed three out of 200 on one test. School was over and she spent her time working on her graduation speech. She decided to do it in rhyme because she would be less intimidated doing it that way. What really surprised her was that no one asked to "help" or "guide" her in the writing. No one was checking on her or censoring her effort. She had a good time writing it and got a lot of input from Bonnie. She thanked all the teachers that helped them through the classes and was careful not to miss any of them. She encouraged everyone to go to school and take advantage of every educational experience available to them.

Went to dinner with Bonnie and as the C.O. handed them silverware at the door, Bonnie says to her, "Governor Essex, party of four." Everyone laughed. Then Rachel was totally surprised when a big black face looked wide-eyed at Rachel and called her by name. Lots of girls have come and gone and come back since she's been here, but she was puzzled for an instant. She knows that this prison experience has scrambled her brain and has adjusted to accepting it. "I've been watching for you," the girl said. Then she gets a clue as who the girl is. It dawns on her that she worked with her back home. This place has a way of eating away at your brain and so much you know you put in there is gone when you try to call it back up. She explained she was here for killing a dope dealer who threatened to shoot up her house and she got him first. Vigilante justice! She'll do three years for the gun, then start her 5-25 sentence.

The noise was outrageous as Rachel sat down and tried to eat. You'd swear that their mother's had abortions and somehow the afterbirth lived—real sub-humans. The sound of their laughing alone could be a sound track from a science-fiction movie. Some days were like this. Something must be in the food.

The January board list was posted again, and Rachel was still not on it. If they'd accept collect calls, she'd call them and find out what is wrong. Why was she being ignored? Kited the social worker and told her that she'd met the board three months ago and they said they'd reschedule her for December. Now the January list was out and she's still not on it. What's going on? She said she'd check into it. How easy it would be to get lost in the system and she wondered how many are.

The girl who got raped by the broomstick in Pierce last summer was attacked again at her job. She was in the hospital in protective custody. They took pictures at the time of the attack, her bruises and scratches, building a case against her aggressor. There's probably a grisly story that precipitated this, but Rachel doesn't have any interest in finding out.

Big Bessie got into a fight with a guy in the visiting hall and they won't let him visit any more. It doesn't take much to get her riled. Don't know any details and really don't care.

There was a very sad girl in Wilson. She wanted to hook up with another girl—who seemed game until she saw the sores her clothes covered. "I'm not going to catch that," she said as she backed away. A year and a half ago the sores were really out of control and she almost had a leg amputated. Don't know what the sores were, but they oozed constantly and the garbage was always full of used stinking dressings. Sometimes she was in such pain she couldn't walk. Don't know what she had, but it wasn't curable—at least not here. They just took her back to the hospital, and someone said she had syphillis.

Meanwhile the school experience was winding down and Rachel's class was ready to graduate with an Associates Degree in business from a college in Springfield that teaches off-campus courses in the prison. From the get-go, Rachel never imagined being there long enough to get a degree, but she really enjoyed the classes and felt she'd accomplished something positive, which included keeping her sanity, and she'd met some nice people. She planned to stay in touch with some of them once she was released—but first she has to get on that board list.

Bonnie, Emily, and Rachel were invited to interview for the job of warden's secretary. The girl who did the interviewing was an ignorant lifer inmate. She never told them her name, but announced she was in charge of hiring and if hired not to ask any favors of her because she wasn't giving any. Immediately, Rachel thought, "bad work environment" and lost interest. She just wanted to go home. Bonnie and Emily were very interested. Lots of prestige in that title while here, but put that on your resume once released—secretary to the warden at a women's prison. Salary, $22 a month. Emily was best suited to the job and a week later was informed she had it.

Graduation Day: Everything went off really nice and in many ways not unlike any other college graduation. There were many speeches and caps and gowns and the usual accolades in the gymnasium. Rachel's speech, which none of those running the show had yet read or censored, was perfect and some said it was the best one. She was somewhat nervous when she walked to the podium, but that turned to edginess, and after she started to speak, she felt she owned it.

Good afternoon, Chaplain Sothersby,
        Mr. Chorris, and staff
Illinois State administrators,
        Faculty, family, friends, members of the class.

In June we started one by one
        to become somewhat acquainted
Like portraits at the master's hand
        Each detail gently painted.

We laughed, we cried, we just reflected
        Our thoughts grew even deeper
As furloughs, boards, and cottage changes
        added tensions from our keeper.

Fall quarter brought such great advances
        as enrollment surged and boomed
Remodeling classrooms for our sessions,
        we put up walls and painted rooms.

Speeches, projects, and props well crafted
        each mind its own creation
Happy campers, preference, songs were drafted,
        Fantasy dance and dream vacations.

The breezeless air—the summer heat
    flies on the window sill
Thursday night in finance class
    at Stancil's Bar and Grill

Thinking caps flashed on for tests
    as papers filled our basket.
Sniffling, sneezing: we'd cough and choke
    and swear we'd never make it.

In the darkness of this prison
    we have studied day and night
seeking wisdom from the lectures
    reaping food for wings of flight.

When our paths traversed the rough spots
    Terry Bibbles and Lisa Rose
Were there to process grants and grades
    placate, pacify, keep peace

They coached our students softball team
    giving time beyond the clock
and cushion to our woeful plight
    between the hard place and the rock

In every quarter we've been blessed
    with a man of caring heart
Our mentor, Mr. Weiertag
    We'll miss you when we part

Dr.'s Frazel, Mittlefield, and Brandis
        kept us on our toes
While we studied hard and enjoyed the humor
        of Mr.'s Read and Bose.

Rick Young and Susan Birkendall
        gave confidence—awakened thirst
As did Morrie Edwards
        and the colorful, Jim Hurst.

Pumpkinseed, Welkett, Stewart and Hooper
        shared their minds with us
The wisdom of Weatherton, Lanion, and Hardin
        will be an eternal plus.

We'll face more lumps—our challenges
        the milk of life is full of curds
We'll bear the brunt of our mistakes'
        in the sound of swallowed words.

We're given now, a seed of light
        it's up to us to make it grow
To find again the human race
        and respect within its glow.

To all the inmates sitting there
        watching us graduate
Take advantage of the good things here
        go to school—it's on the state.

Get your GED's, don't waste your time
    Get your beauty license
Or hone your computer skills
    Be ready for your release

Learn to grind eyeglasses, that's a useful skill
    or take college courses
and get yourself a degree.
    Be ready for life's forces.

For each of us the call is different
    but listen for the voices
We can make our life a better one
    smarter, we make better choices.

They did allow a family member to attend with Rachel's parents, so they had a driver and that put her at ease. She thought they might be proud of her for giving the graduation speech, but since they were both hard of hearing, she doesn't think they heard much of it. At least they had her diploma that said Magna Cum Laude in gold letters at the bottom.

She was sad for Emily, whose dad passed away a few months before and her mom was in the hospital so no family was there for her. Immediately after the ceremony, Emily was called back to work.

It was exciting to finally meet Bonnie's mom and son. She was glad that her family got to meet her friends so they could see that not everyone here was bad.

But then, Emily's cute little roommate got all excited about the kid that drove Rachel's parents and was very bold in making out with him. The girl explained to him that she's doing 8-25 for stabbing her boyfriend's wife—like he would be impressed. Then she justified it by saying that her intent was to stab the guy, but the wife interfered and tried to grab the knife and got a cut requiring three stitches on her hand. The kid just stared at her, not knowing what to say. That's assault with a deadly weapon. She's just a kid, but definitely someone to avoid. Even at graduation, you can't get away from it.

Almost immediately, Emily was complaining about her job. She said she hated it. The person that was supposed to train her spent her time drawing greeting cards. When Emily didn't understand what to do, the girl didn't help. "You got the job, bitch, do it."

Neither Bonnie or Rachel had been assigned any kind of job. The girl that runs the school said she'd try to get us over there, but there was little chance of it. They will both miss that place.

Bonnie hung her coat on a big rack in the day room. That's the purpose of the rack. But this place was crawling with thieves. Rachel always took hers to her room and tucked it in a box under the bottom bunk. It was a rare clean one. Well, someone helped themselves to Bonnie's coat and the state wants her to pay $75 for it. She's hoping someone took it by mistake and it will turn up

The next month when the board list was posted and again, Rachel's noted her name was not on the list. She's completed two years of school. Shouldn't she have two months extra "good time" for that? Besides, the board was going to reschedule her in two months and it has been five. She panicked and she kited everyone, even the social worker who has made false promises to look into it for two consecutive months. She sent a letter to the Parole Board in Springfield asking them why she's forgotten. Then the social worker summoned her to say that she's not on the board list because she was arrested again last October. She told her that must be in someone else's file, or there was a mistake, that she went to Riverview for a property hearing in October, not to catch another case. Said she'd recheck tomorrow. She did not need that kind of crap on her paperwork. Two weeks later her name appeared on the "add-on board list."

Her window to freedom! She was asked again to fill out her parole plans. Stuff like what do you plan to do if you are released, where will you live, etc.

Rachel heard somewhere that the more mail an inmate receives, the better the score on re-class. They also rate on number of visits. She doesn't get that many visits but they are every month, and she doubts anyone here gets the volume of mail she did. Most everyone writes at least once a week and she gets a letter from Eric every day. They also scored us on job performance. She's averaged 69 of 70, and number of tickets. Never! Her G.P.A. was just shy of 4 and no one was even close. That should speak for itself when she faces the board—in a perfect world.

A few weeks later Rachel met that board of three. They wanted to know why she wasn't going to drug meetings and trying to rehabilitate herself. She reiterated that she had never in her life taken drugs so was never an addict. She reminded them that they went over all this at the last meeting nearly six months ago when they continued her for two months. They were as unfamiliar with her case as her attorney—even after the four months hiatus they needed to investigate her case. She tried to tell them about the case, but they didn't want to hear it. After all the delay, she found they'd never requested a "community report." Told them she spent her time in school to avoid the troublemakers—got a diploma and never got a ticket. They had hard ugly faces, but that was God's fault, not hers. She felt so much negativity. Why?

They told Rachel to leave the room and sit in the hallway while they made their decision. There were two lights above the door. Red light meant stay out, great thinkers at work. Green meant come in and meet your fate. She stared at the lights. Fear! Did they know she was the one who had the inspectors called about the asbestos and the cost of renovations wreaked havoc with their budget? She had to do it. It was the right thing to do. Apprehension! Other things she did? No tickets, but only because the dice rolled good for her. Did any of them care that she did well in school? For ten, maybe fifteen minutes that seemed like hours she stared at that red light. Then it flashed green and summoned her back in. They told her that two of the three said "no" and there was a long pause. They watched her face. They taunt. She just looked at them, one face at a time. Then one of them capitulated and said "yes." The spokesman said, "I know you were lying all along, but now that you have your shock, just tell me the truth. Where did you really get all that cocaine?"

She looked at him square in the face and said "I've told you the truth, over and over again, and I'm glad that two of the three of you had the sense to see that." She thanked the other two and excused herself. Relief! Get out of there quickly before they changed their minds again. The sweat that her body had been held in abeyance broke through her skin. Her stomach started cramping as she walked through long corridors to get outside the building. Washrooms everywhere, but not for inmates. Have to reach Wilson and don't want an embarrassing accident. Yes, it would take a few more weeks, but she was on her way out of there. So much for depending on the attorney for the appeal or the judge for shock.

Autumn met the board too. They told her to come back next year. Her eyes were pink from tears. She was a total basket case.

Everywhere Rachel goes, people stop her and say what a great speech she made last week. One girl she didn't know stopped her on the walk/jog and asked her if she was the one who gave the speech. She told her she was and she said, "I thought I recognized those shoes under your gown. Where did you get them?" They even stopped my roommate to tell her about the speech. That was really nice.

She was delivered a stolen chicken today. We all had contraband chicken chunks and stolen cheese in our soup. Tonight we'll have a hard-boiled egg that Molly snatched for her. It beat the slum gully they served the population. A girl just walked by and whispered, "I have a couple pieces of baked fish upstairs." Bonnie told her to bring it down.

Bonnie's new roommate reprimanded her for spitting in the sink while brushing her teeth, telling her it made the sink unsanitary. Nothing around Bonnie is unsanitary. Then Bonnie looked over and saw her washing her crotch in the sink. Her coat still hasn't turned up. Two weeks later, they gave her another roommate.

She heard that another girl just fell into the man-hole that the other one did and they took her to I.S.U. in an ambulance. Rachel was amazed that no one had thought to put another lip on it or something to keep it from flipping.

Haven't a clue what was down there, but one would think it could be a security risk.

Most of the County lost power before daybreak. Schools and plants were closed. The facility was on auxiliary power and locked in. Everything was shut down and that included the kitchen. It took a couple of hours to feed everyone so although the day got an early start, it would be late before anyone got started.

Guards drive around the perimeter in a little truck. They haven't dismissed the night shift, so there's a lot of guards on duty. Daybreak and we're still locked in. After they figured the power outage wasn't an inmate plot, they let the girls working the Rehab Project go to work.

The day was still young when Bonnie and Rachel were called over to the school on the pretense of working there, but to watch Rudolph the Red Nosed Reindeer. No word yet about what the institution wants to do with us so we just stay out of sight. They took a bus load of minimums to Springfield. Can't figure a pattern as to why or who was selected. One girl was pulled from school to go.

Clouds covered the sky today like a cataract over a giant eye. Only occasionally does the sunshine blink through. The cold wind was tossing around the last of the leaves and a hint of snow was drifting through the air. Winter's coming. Went over to the school and watched "Wall Street." Rachel had to leave in the middle to go to the vault to pick up her food box. Her parents do their best, but the rules are so stringent, most of it had to be sent back.

Rachel came back to Wilson, took a shower and washed her hair. Just as she was drying off, the fire alarm started blaring. She wrapped her towel around her head, put on her robe, pulled the blanket off her bed and wrapped it around her "Indian style" and had went outside for half an hour. Then at 2:30 am it jolted everyone out of bed. Morning started at its usual time and we all looked at each other's sleepy faces all day.

Bonnie got her food box and planned a major diet to start in January. Meanwhile, she loaded up for her "fast."

Vi was having a difficult time. Her sister was shot in the head a couple days ago and killed. Her mother sent money for her to come to the funeral, but this place won't let her go. They feared for the safety of both her and the guards that had to accompany her because Vi's victim's family vowed revenge. She was devastated by the decision.

Emily was losing serious weight. Her pants won't stay up when she walked. Because she lived in a different building Rachel doesn't see her very much. Says she hated her job at the warden's office because they "treated her like a slave" and she's worried because her mother was back in the hospital again. The ever smiling Emily, who always had a dancing step while in school was now walking around like a stoned-faced zombie. Bonnie and Rachel feel lucky they haven't been assigned a job.

The boilers went "down" in all the new buildings. The maintenance men were working so everyone hoped to have heat and water soon. Whatever the problem was may well be the reason the fire alarms went off twice last night.

One of Bonnie's former roommates wrote Rachel a nice letter. She's home and seemed happy but described her mental state as "like coming home from a war and having no one to talk to about it."

Another week went by and still no job assignment. Went over to the school and watched a comedy on their VCR All those from the class that were working jobs were miserable. One of the girls that worked in the business office came in from lunch and said she overheard conversations about Bonnie and Rachel "slipping through the system." They were just jealous about them getting so much time off. Rachel told her they did not slip though the system—but into it. She said there was a job opening in her office and Bonnie immediately started pushing for it. (Earlier, she said she was getting a complex because Rachel was always outshining her.) Rachel told her she could have the job, that she only wanted a ticket out. The girl looked at her strangely and Bonnie breathed easily. She hoped Bonnie got whatever job assignment she wanted and was happy in it.

Yesterday Rachel was requested for a job by Mr. Evergreen over at the school where the girls can go to classes and get a GED. He was a very good natured, but a dirty old man. He and Bonnie shared dirty jokes, but when they start Rachel walks out of earshot. She doesn't think there would be any job pressures from him. His boss, however, is rumored to be an ignorant hot-headed prick. From what she understood, though, he centers his anger at noisy people and bull-dykers. She has yet to be interviewed for the job and if they want her, she has no choice but to take it. She heard there's a job opening in payroll where they make flags, but that one hasn't been posted yet. Molly put in a good word for her there, but Bonnie would be better suited to it. Let a long-timer have the jobs and get her out of here.

Bonnie and Rachel went over to the school to watch a movie, but they were having plumbing problems over there and those running the school don't want those in command at the front office to know about the movies. Everyone is supposed to be working. The inmate plumbers smoke their cigarettes, drink the coffee and wander around. They don't want to work either, or maybe they were spies. The drinking fountain was leaking sludge onto the floor and the spigots in another room were leaking. There's three of them sent here to work, but after three hours they are still scratching their heads and nothing was accomplished. Bonnie left for church, came back an hour later all bubbly and happy, then started telling those plumbers how to do what they were supposed to do.

Later that afternoon they were called back to the school for some kind of "scared straight" program. They had troubled kids visit the school and wanted inmates to talk with them. They let a couple inmates talk about what a nice place this was and how comfortable they have made themselves. Then Rachel tore them a new backside, only because she saw that those kids could not relate to them. "We were the outcasts" they would never be. She zeroed in on the tall one with a big mouth and asked her if she were a young mother and if she saw her kids, who were playing in their own yard, being attacked by a big man, and she knew she was no physical match for him, let alone her children, would she consider it a crime to run into her house grab a gun and fire one shot in the air if she thought the noise would intimidate the man into running away? "No" she answered, "I'd have just been protecting myself and my kids." The smug look left her face when Rachel reminded her this state had no self-defense laws. It is also illegal to fire a gun in the city. She assured her she would be arrested, come here, spend her first day naked in a room full of other naked ladies, being tormented by the intense burning of their scalp and crotch, the result of being sprayed head to toe with RAID insect repellant, of being poked inside and out for "contraband" and humiliated in unimaginable ways. She told of girls getting their throats cut by fellow inmates, beat by C.O.s and raped in the shower. She reminded her that because she chose to save her kids from the man, she would now be part of this and worse—be separated from her family and loved ones for at least six years probably more. She explained the "gun law" which required one to do three years for firing the gun—even though no one was hurt—before starting her sentence.

Rachel touched on some other things, too, but the whistle blew and she had to go and they had to leave. The school administrator thanked Rachel for coming and said she added to his education as well as the kids'. The teacher who had escorted the kids also said he appreciated her being there and gave her a piece of candy.

Rachel just learned that one of Cowboy's ducks, who left here a year ago, was now in a live-in relationship with a female C.O. here—the one Bessie referred to as a "big teeth dog." Other inmates called her "the last man." She's also the one that allowed Rachel to walk past her station with the large plastic garbage bags of fragrant popcorn.

About a week ago, Molly was told to go to a furlough screening. She thought of spending time with her daughter and grandchildren. Emily was invited too. She had been fantasizing for the last week, hoping to spend a few hours with her ailing mother. Both were denied. This was a program offered to one in a thousand inmates with exceptional behavior records. They are permitted to go home for a few days at their own expense to be with their families. If all goes well, it can happen again.

Some auditors were touring various buildings and one of them stopped to talk with Emily about the "quality of life" in her building. They talked for a while and she mentioned she was turned down for a furlough and he responded, "that must be your own fault because furloughs are granted solely on behavior." Her unit manager, who happened to be lurking and heard, spoke up and said, "that's not true, Emily is one of the nicest people you'll ever meet. There's never been any behavior issues with her." The people on the outside have no clue that behavior has absolutely nothing to do with furloughs or getting out and the key was kept secret.

Several students were invited over to the school and had a little Christmas party. A movie, which was really great and a Pizza Hut pizza. What a day! Then Bonnie requested the next movie be Fatal Attraction. The next morning they were called back to the school and saw that movie.

The Salvation Army donated a bunch of Christmas cards for us to send out—complete with envelopes, which this place won't let us use because they don't have the embossed stamp.

Rachel learned officially that she will be working as a clerk at Clearview school. Could be worse. Ginger, one of the retarded girls that works as a porter promised she'd "watch over her." Rachel was really touched and got a kick out of that. Every day the blue shirts are leaving by the bus load for one pre-release or another.

Christmas eve and no one could shower—no water. The upstairs toilets don't have water to flush and so it was only a matter of time before the first floor loses its water power.

Most of the girls felt really bad because they're away from their families. Others complained how much money they're losing not being able to work the streets. No passing, trading, touching, and Christmas gifts are illegal. Vi gave Rachel four packs of "grits" and Molly a half pound of cooked bacon and an orange. Everyone gobbled all of it quickly. Gun grabbed Rachel for a quick hug, calling her by her pet name for her, "Brocco" and wished her a Merry Christmas. Then a chicken breast appeared, then a bag of walnuts.

Ellie was in her glory. Her girlfriend knit her a white sweater and scarf, then ordered her a pair of matching boots through someone's box. She's hugged everyone.

Rachel got the job at the school, working under Mr. Evergreen.

First impression? It was a dumb job—at least so far. Type, file, and answer the phone. No challenges. The people she's working with were nice and she knew several of them. Regardless of how bored she was with it, she was still tired at the end of the day and ready to go to bed early. Can't walk during the day anymore because she was assigned to a job. She just ate two hard-boiled eggs someone stole for her.

Rachel had Christmas brunch with Molly, Vi, and Mattie. All good company. Turkey dressing, cranberries, and sweet potatoes. The girls who worked in the kitchen said there was so much left over that it would be served again tonight along with the scrambled eggs that were on the menu.

Molly was up prowling all night—sick. She had a gall-bladder problem and maybe a kidney infection too. She tried to be quiet, but Rachel woke up several times to her moans and each time she heard rain dripping down the downspout outside her window. Molly's health has been precarious since she got here and she does worry about her.

When day light broke, the rain turned to light snow and by noon there was a couple inches on the grass. The sidewalks were mini canals and for some reason the administration put out a "riot alert."

They tore up the room of a known thief then zeroed in on the room of a girl who works as a dental assistant and was able to supply many girls with peroxide for their hair. Her room was really trashed, supposedly looking for marijuana. They confiscated lots of stuff, but no dope.

# BACK TO BRUCE

Child Protective Services visited Lola regularly, making sure Bruce wasn't living at the house with the kids. He's home from prison but on parole and living in a half-way house. C.P.S. was making her life miserable, she having to pick up signs of him most every day, always worrying she'd missed something and not knowing when someone would show up. He'd have to come and go by night and not be seen at all by day, as once they asked the neighbors if they'd seen him hanging around. Good thing most of their neighbors mind their own business. Lola worked nights for the money to pay the bills, buy food and clothes. Bruce had to sneak into his own house. It just wasn't right. They had to get out of this place.

*       *       *

A year ago, someone sent Rachel a subscription to People Magazine and it came every week. She got a little behind in her reading for awhile, but was catching up. Then after Molly read them, she smuggles them to Mattie who sees to it we keep supplied with popcorn.

Mr. Evergreen finally put in an appearance at the job, hanging over her shoulder as she worked and asking about Bonnie, but he was so close his body heat was getting to her and making her nervous. Then he asked if there was anything she wanted to talk about, he'd be available. Thanks, but no thanks. Too many people get into serious trouble like that, and she only wanted to get out and go home.

The girl with all the oozing sores was still looking for a duck. She's a very attractive girl but those here know of her problem and avoid her. Several new girls came over to make her acquaintance and had their tongues dripping for her. They don't know. One of these new girls was also checking out Riverview's most famous "madam," Jackie Blue, who was in the process of sizing her up for the commissary and clothes she could play her for. Then she noticed the girl was also giving the eye to a girl who put her stinking gauze pads in the garbage the eye. She cut her off real fast with no explanation.

Vi was trying to grieve for her sister but had a hard time coming to grips with the fact she was dead. Her family came to visit and told her that family took photos at the wake— of all those that came, and of the body. So far they haven't sent them but wrote how nice they tuned out. The sister was in a coma for 2 ½ hours before she died and Vi kept asking Rachel if she could still think during that time. It is important to Vi that her sister had time to make peace with the Lord before checking out. She assured her that people in coma's can hear and think and she seemed relieved to hear that.

Molly just laid in her bed wrapped in blankets, trembling and muttering she was freezing to death. She's really sick but doesn't want to go back to the hospital. Fortunately she wasn't scheduled to work for five days because there's an inventory going on at her job.

Three days on the job and Rachel had things well under control and everyone was pleasant. The C.O. that has a reputation for being a prick was so far an agreeable pussy cat. His reputation also extended to stupid, but she hadn't noticed him doing dumb shit. She kept her head down and quietly did her work. She trusts no one and doesn't want to be in a position she may have to.

Bonnie asked Rachel if she was growing fingernails to make tracks on one of their backs. When she told her there weren't any backs in Lotusville worthy of her nails, Bonnie almost choked as she sat back wide-eyed and as she held her breath, her face turned pink. Bonnie thought she was being funny, and she was dead serious. Rachel wouldn't be surprised if Mr. Evergreen put her up to asking about his chances.

The commissary ran out of brand name cigarettes and that left the generics. A couple people expressed their opinion loudly, and once again we're on "riot alert."

Molly slept all day—too weak to stay awake and she's breathing heavily. She indicated her depressed state this morning when comparing herself to an old car headed for the junkyard. She says all her parts are wearing out. Finally they took her to I.S.U. for a week of tests and haven't given her a diagnosis. She wanted to have her daughter try to find out the results of those tests. Don't they understand that she needs to get out of here? She's certainly no hazard to society.

Rachel heard a rumor that the people Bonnie worked for are not happy with her. They said she's too nosey and doesn't stick to her job. She doesn't want her to get into trouble so they discussed it. Bonnie told her the porter does not clean well enough and she always had to redo it. Then she brought back to her room copies of confidential material and helped herself to pre-stamped state envelopes.

Bonnie's friend, Mr. Evergreen stopped by the job to ask Rachel what was new. Rachel, not wanting to encourage him, had nothing to say, so replied, "One day closer to getting out." He walked away.

At 9:30 last night, the white shirts gathered in the Captain's office with their binoculars trained through the windows and on the C.O. on duty in Adams Cottage. They saw him unlock the C.O.'s bathroom and minutes later an inmate slipped in. Everyone else went to their room to be counted. The C.O. made his count and turned it in, then went to the bathroom. Those at the Captain's office called him on the phone, but no answer. They put down their binoculars and walked over to investigate. Quickly opening the bathroom door, they, and some inmates who could see from their rooms, got a clear shot of the C.O.'s bare butt, with his pants wrinkled around his ankles. The inmate was sitting on the sink, her bare legs wrapped around his waist. He was surprised when the Captain put him in handcuffs. They all waited for the highway patrol to take him away, and the inmate was taken to the hospital where they gathered evidence.

Bonnie's mother received some information from the parole board that her daughter isn't eligible for a damn thing for another three years. Meanwhile, an attorney took what was left of her pension fund from her mother, saying he'll get her out. No one seems to know the law or can keep records but their hands are out for the last dollar.

Rachel got up early this morning and washed her sheets and Molly's. That is illegal because they are supposed to be washed in the State laundry and Rachel risked getting a ticket but when you send them to the laundry you always get back someone's ripped and bloody castoffs.

Fifty minimums are supposed to leave for Springfield this week and fifty next week, but the overcrowding here was intense. Heard a rumor that they are going to close the gym to put new admissions in there.

Meanwhile, someone in authority decided to shift everyone around and those in Wilson had to move to Jefferson where the lifers previously resided, and those in Jefferson were coming to live in Wilson. The rumor mill had part of it right. It wasn't done all at once, however. Sixty five pink shirts moved in as sixty five blue and green shirts moved out. Pink shirts don't have the privileges blue shirts have, so at first there was war over the phones. Then the pink shirts, who have to be locked down at 9:30 pm didn't like that blue shirts could stay up until midnight. So, during the switch, the blue shirts had to conform to pink shirt rules. Who was driving the bus?

A couple days later, the remaining minumums in Wilson packed up their stuff and moved over to Jefferson. Change was rarely good. The rooms were smaller—if that was possible—barely room to be double bunked, filthy and no toilet seats. The shower across the hall from Rachel's room trailed water across the floor and into her room. The building was really torn up. Toilet paper holders clothes hooks and towel bars had been torn from the walls and not replaced. There were asphalt tiles on the floor, as many loose as glued down. The walls and ceilings were coated with years of accumulated cigarette smoke. She and Molly cleaned their little area, shifting the bunk to get the ceiling. There was no hot water or washing machines. No one was permitted a phone call. Others seemed to adjust to living in this cave. Rachel was so anxious to leave this garbage can. She awaited her name on the bus list to Springfield. Rumor was it was pretty nice there. Waiting . . . . She has become jumpy, and didn't think she had the strength to deal with another day. Rachel worried about Rachel. She couldn't sleep. Stick a fork in her before she exploded!

Now, she put all her energy and thoughts into her job. She couldn't wait to get there each day and thought of nothing else until she had to trudge back to the "unlife" at Jefferson. Her blood pressure must have risen thirty points each time she had to return, signified by a constant roar in her head. Hate exploded!

The girls that previously occupied Jefferson were very possessive about their chairs in the rec. room—so much so they painted their names on them with nail polish. The chair Rachel sat down on to play cards read "Butch." She couldn't focus on the card game. She couldn't stay put. She couldn't live in this crowded filthy disarray and no one seemed to care enough to clean it up.

Because of shifting everyone around, all the mail was on hold. That doesn't help morale. Living in Jefferson was a nightmare. At least she went to work every day and was away from it. That was now her savior.

She wasn't on the posted list for the bus to Springfield Tuesday, but learned from Bonnie that she was on for Wednesday. She looked forward to being out of here and a hot shower.

Support systems were essential to get one through each day. They all needed their friendships which were a lifeline. Families on the outside were essential, and Rachel could now understand why those here for the long haul, without those families, formed new ones here for emotional support. Positive mental stimulation was a necessity to escape the environment one had to live in, whether it is school, a job, reading, or writing letters. It usually takes a combination and one must pick and choose wisely. Many find spiritual comfort in attending church, singing in the choir, Bible study, or just talking with someone willing to listen. So many girls don't have the strength to fight this system and fail to grab onto one or two of these and then become bogged down in the muck of life and let the poisons that permeate this place eat at their sanity.

It was hard for Rachel's friends to see her leave, but she knew they were happy for her. They don't know how close to sinking into the abyss Rachel was. Bonnie had tears in her eyes as she made her promise to write. She wasn't nearly as strong as she came across. Molly said she was the best roommate she ever expected to have. Danita kept grabbing her and kissing her cheek. Vi is retreating away and says she was losing her Rachel. What can she do but promise them all she'll write. They've heard the same promises before, though, and never heard anything, so they're used to disappointment.

The girl who ran the college summoned Rachel over so she could say good bye to a lot of the people she knew from school. Some of their good-bye's were phony but most were sincere. It was really nice of her to do this. She wouldn't have had the chance to see Emily again and she happened to catch one of the teachers between classes. He asked her to stop in at the school in Springfield when she hits the streets and he'd give her a tour. She thanked him for the offer but reminded him she was from Riverview and was anxious to get home. Another girl said there was going to be a class reunion for our class. Rachel thanked her for telling her, but knows it will never happen because very few of them have anything in common with each other. She was proud of what she accomplished there but the school was just a tool she used to keep her sanity.

She may see Ellie again fairly soon at least she hoped so, Bonnie and Emily for sure, but they'll be there awhile yet. She'd stayed in touch with those who got out ahead of her even though they lived out of town and Mattie and Vi who may be locked up for another decade or more. She'll write to those friends she'd made there.

*Mama stood there looking and screaming as she held my baby sister close. The sound of the hostile onslaught drew her from her chores to the back porch. Neighbors poked their heads from windows, a reaction to the piercing screech of the malicious attack.*

*A few minutes earlier, this curious three-year-old was attracted to the friendly chirping of baby robins, nestled safely, high above in the branches of an old lilac. Their greedy little beaks opened to accept their loving and dutiful parents' donations of worms which they seemed to chuck all the way inside them. She could only see their furry, hungry heads and wanted to see more.*

*The bush had many branches coming up from the bottom and she must have made an attempt to climb, for the next thing she remembered was cowering in the grass, the robins descending in a terrorizing attack. They were swooping down to what must have been inches of her head, their beating wings creating a hideous sound and a wind she could smell.*

Her own scream woke her and she jolted the cot. Molly woke up commenting, "wow, that was some climax. You sure you're alone up there?" She had to leave this place behind—soon.

Wednesday came and Rachel was called to gather her things and get on the bus, headed for the Springfield Pre-Release, just two hours from home. The pre-release in Chicago would have been 20 minutes, but she was relieved to be going anywhere. When that bus drove out, she didn't look back. Never wanted to see that ghoulish place again. The ride out was short but it took half a day to get processed in—mostly line up, stand around, and wait. They asked her if she was a smoker. No? Okay we'll put you in a non-smoking room. Good! Can't believe anyone cared.

First thing she did was write a letter to her parents, told them that she had a release date. They wanted to pick her up, but the last thing she needed was for them to make another long drive. She told them that she had already checked a Greyhound schedule and would be able to get on a bus that stopped very close to their home so they wouldn't have to even drive downtown. She also told them that bad things could happen that could delay her coming home, so would keep in touch by letter and call them from a pay phone in the bus station in Springfield once dropped off. Then they would know she was on her way and what bus to meet.

First thing they did was call D.D. Knight, her attorney, who assured them that there was no possible way Rachel would be getting out, that she had to do a couple more years unless he was able to get her out on appeal or shock. They didn't know what to think. Wouldn't the attorney know more about it than Rachel.

At the Pre-Release Center, Rachel had a huge/normal sized room to herself and she really needed that. The space to walk. The privacy. Yes, there were three other beds there, but they were empty. She put her things in a footlocker next to her cot. She felt "freedom" spun around and giggled. The cafeteria had lots of good food and a separate salad bar, and she could serve herself. There were girls she knew there, but her only friend was the door marked EXIT.

This new pre-release center was originally built for men, had big single rooms separated by a bathroom that was shared. There was a big exercise room too. When they decided to house women there, they put three additional beds in each of the rooms, took out the exercise equipment and added beds there too.

There was a pre-release in Chicago now, and she wonders why she wasn't taken to that one. It would be closer to Riverview. No complaints, though. She was away from Lotusville.

The atmosphere was refreshing. The administration treated everyone with respect instead of suspicion which was something Rachel was not used to. The first day was long and tiring. Waiting in lines for things, for people and just waiting for no reason. The air was smoggy and caused headaches. Then the day was over and she slept like a dead cat from 8:30 pm until 7:30 am. Most likely stress. She missed a good breakfast, but had pork chops for lunch—real pork chops with a bone. There was some fresh fruit but all the cooked vegetables were reduced to mush. There's still plenty of starch.

Rumor that we're not allowed outside is false. They have both basketball and tennis courts—around which Rachel had already done many laps. No balls or rackets and no one was ever using them for anything else. She went right up to the fence and touched the razor wire. The hooped part is no sharper than a table knife, but the little attachments on the arc are sharp and prickly. She wondered if someone was watching her as she checked it out. Probably!

Went back to bed for a nap. Yesterday really knocked the shit out of her. The C.O. needed her zip code at home and woke her up to get it. Her commissary money didn't travel with her so she couldn't shop for a while.

They issued her TV back to her today with the face plate over the controls missing. They claim to be looking for it. Can't get any UHF either. The antenna got screwed up on the bus trip out here.

Almost immediately, she got sick. Probably brought it from Lotusville. Totally miserable, nose and eyes itched and ran, head, ears, and teeth ached, skin burned and even her hair hurt, so she stopped by the nurse's station (Yes, easy as that. Didn't have to get on a list and wait.) and she gave her some kind of pills, probably an antihistamine which really helped. Whenever she put something in her stomach it got confused about what to do with it. She knows her body will adjust soon. Luckily she had this nice big room to herself for awhile so she had plenty of time to rest.

So far she'd much rather be here than at Lotusville—not solely because of the atmosphere, but she also had the freedom to walk around the inside of the building. That was something she needed to get used to. Time would probably go faster here with a job and people she knows—but she is here and feels less locked up. Some people count down the days, but at this point she just kissed each one off as it passed and just kept in mind that each one is one day she won't have to see again—flushed.

There was juice in Rachel's right ear. It crackled whenever she tipped her head and it blocked her hearing somewhat. The sinuses were still dripping at a good rate down the back of her throat and gagged her. The food had little taste because of it. She kept telling herself, "nothing lasts forever."

Bonnie wrote that they moved Emily into Molly's room at Jefferson. Molly told her she'd give her a chance because Rachel liked her. Then Emily wrote that it just wasn't working out.

A week later they moved two more girls into the room. Didn't know them and didn't want to. Rachel was so thankful that she had the room for one week alone. These girls were pigs. They both smoked. One snored and snorted really loud and kept her up. Sometimes she rolled over and it stopped. When it started up again she hoped her breathing just stopped—permanently. This morning when Rachel went to shower, she noted the drain looked like someone's pitiful attempt at gardening. Until she cleared the clog, the water flowed into the hall. She went to brush her teeth and found the sink drain was blocked by what appeared to be the result of two Brillo pads who'd fought to the death topped by colorful globs of toothpaste as tombstones.

Rachel didn't realize how tight she was wound and the space and quiet helped her decompress. She spent less time in her room and she could walk outside when she wanted and often did. She watched the cars drive by. She saw a dog. Her first sighting in nearly three years.

The girls in the room on the other side of the shared bathroom stayed up all night long. They talked loudly and Rachel spent the night trying to figure out how they can use the word "motherfucker" at least twice in every sentence. They usually slept through breakfast and lunch. Should she leave her TV on all night long and maybe she won't hear any of it. No, she'll adjust. Again, nothing lasts forever.

Mail call came and it had finally caught up from Lotusville, about a dozen letters waiting for her. Things were probably held up because of the move to Jefferson then they arrived by the pack. Some of them from people she'd never heard of—men on the outside seeking to pen-pal with women locked up. Where have they heard of her? Of course they were sending stamps which she couldn't have so she had to mail them back, with a note explaining she didn't want any pen-pals, that she wasn't going to be there long. Rachel thought back to an envelope Bonnie received from an inmate pen-pal she'd been writing. He had hand-drawn and duplicated the embossed stamp required to send mail from the penitentiary. He had the color perfect. The only difference was that his wasn't embossed. Some people were ingenious.

One of the letters was from Vi, a good friend back at Lotusville, who did a very bad thing. She's probably been locked up for more years than any other woman in the state. Her boyfriend, who was supposed to be babysitting her two pre-school kids, decided instead to test out new hookers for his stable—in her bed in front of her kids. When she found out and he was fast asleep, she took lighter fluid, wet down his dick and lit it. He woke suddenly, tried to bat down the flames but only spread them to the rest of the bed. It took him two weeks to die. Anyway, Vi's letter explained that she wrote to a magazine personals, and put in an ad for her to meet men. She thought she was doing her a favor finding all these men to write her.

Well, in a way she did. With Rachel's name being called so often for mail the next few days, it caught a social worker's attention. Rachel hadn't had anything to do with the social worker and didn't know who she was. After mail call, the social worker approached her and told Rachel that she had arrived there at Springfield without any paperwork and they were trying to figure out why she was even there. Apprehension slammed at her like a punch in the gut. She explained to her that she met the board and was given her release date. Told her the board was five months late scheduling her and she was anxious to get home. Rachel's chest tightened until she could hardly breathe, but no point in venting to the social worker. She told Rachel she'd check into it and see what she could do to expedite things but didn't think there was time enough now to do it. Rachel looked into her eyes and said, "Yes there is."

Rachel had been thinking of what she will do when she left here. Yes, she'll get on the bus and go to Riverview, but what would she do? She'll have to earn a living and support herself. What kind job? She'd never had a problem finding work, but would there be a problem getting hired?

A girl she rode from Lotusville with but didn't know her there, offered her a lock for her footlocker for three packs of generic cigarettes. She really didn't have that much to lock up, but she'd be less concerned if her box was locked. The three in her room ignored her and the four next door we share a bathroom with steal from each other but she's sure they're too lazy to come across the way to steal.

Rachel got up early this morning, she always did so she could have the bathroom to herself, and camped out on the case manager's/social worker's doorstep. After over an hour she showed up and they talked, making sure all the necessary paperwork for her to leave this place was filled out. Now she had to wait and see how long it takes to process.

The C.O. asked Rachel to go upstairs and get someone for her. When she went into the room she found this person still in bed and sleepy-eyed. She gave her the message that the C.O. wanted to speak with her. There was another girl sitting on the toilet with the door wide open. At Lotusville, there wasn't a door to shut. Here they have one and it doesn't make any difference.

After Rachel left Lotusville, Emily started pen-paling with a guy in another prison who claimed to be a member of the Weathermen Underground and told her of some of his capers. He told her there was still a murder charge hanging over him, but he, acting as his own lawyer, was going to beat it. She went on to say she knew she should probably avoid this guy, but added, "What do you expect in a world of women kissing women and men are a fairytale."

Another rough night! The girl who slept above Rachel talked in her sleep—incoherent babble that had her convinced she was in a jungle and had an owl as a protector. As the night progressed she drifted in and out of realism, the darkness and the slurping, sucking and snorting coming from several feet away warned her she had stumbled into a den of bears having oral sex. The owl was still with her.

Morning came slowly and after Rachel showered and started a load of clothes, she grabbed her jacket and started toward the basketball and tennis courts, the perimeter of which served as a "walk/jog." She saw the yellow dog again running along the side of the road. Not so rare to most, but she so enjoyed the sight. "Stay out of the street, Fido."

Then it hit her! Suddenly a sickening sweet stench permeated her senses. She checked around by her feet, knowing that a smell so disgusting could only exist below the level of slime. She walked fast to get away from it, but it was everywhere. Trapped, she retreated back to her unit where she questioned the C.O. "Oh," she answers matter-of-factly. "There's a plant over there," she pointed a finger toward a wall, "where they grind up dead animals." The stink was fierce. They must wait until Sunday morning to clean out their squishers.

She remember as a kid, she had overheard a friend of her parents say he had just purchased stock in a rendering factory. Later she asked her dad what that was. It took till now to smell one. "The final resting place," he told her "of racehorses who could no longer attract para-mutual ticket sales." Maybe that's the ground meat (they never promised beef) served us at Lotusville.

For the last couple of weeks, the girl on the bunk above Rachel had been telling her how badly she missed the Bible study at Lotusville, that she just lived to understand it. When Rachel noticed on the bulletin board that one was scheduled for that morning she woke the girl up and let her know. She thanked her for the information then rolled over and pulled the blanket over her head.

The concrete walkways at the entrance to the building have raised because of the frost and the doors scrape. She's sure it wasn't doing the doors any good. If they have a really cold winter, there will be a problem opening and shutting the doors.

One thing that is nice about the cafeteria here is a salad bar from which one can help themselves in addition to the entrée. That became Rachel's first stop after leaving her room. Then she walked in circles around the perimeter of the building, then back to her room to fall asleep. Two of her roommates insisted on polluting the air with their smoke so she went to early dinner for double helpings of corned beef and cabbage to get even.

Afterwards, she went back out and walked again and met a girl with really short hair that was a little younger than herself who was an "old-timer" in the system. Cora Ann did a life sentence at Lotusville, then was released on parole. She reported to her parole officer in a pair of tight pants and he saw something in the outline of her pocket that made him curious. She had a small pocket knife and he violated her parole for carrying a concealed weapon. All those years of being locked up, she was sure she was a boy—and boys carry pocket knives.

Not many girls were caught together here because their minds are more centered on getting out and leaving that life behind. The talk was more realistic like what they're going to steal or who they plan to rob and finding a man—not necessarily in that order. They discussed the new drugs on the street and their desire to get buzzed.

Rachel's money finally came from Lotusville so she went to the commissary and bought all kinds of soap. Then she cleaned the shower and bathroom and ran the mop (after she washed it) over the room floor. These women just don't care. Yesterday she went to use the toilet and found that one of the five shit bags she shared it with had exploded all over the seat and walked away.

Rachel sat down and wrote Alice about her impending release and her concerns about adjusting to real life. Alice wrote back and warned her that adjusting will be a slow process. She'd given thought to her past, and remembered hearing that her mother-in-law encouraged her boys to marry women with jobs but to go on disability themselves. Talk about encouraging the welfare mentality!

She mentioned she'd received a promotion at work and was now making nearly twice her starting pay. She's proud of her self-confidence. Things were looking good for her. She also wrote that her "bad boy" ex's only hope for a better life was to win a lottery or sell more dope that he can use himself. She's sad for him but is no longer interested in being a part of that life.

Rachel did a lot of thinking/worrying and didn't know if she could handle every day things like shopping, driving, or even answering a phone. She was scared of facing life and people. Yet she's driven to get out—visiting the social worker every other day to find out about her paperwork.

Her ex roommate, Molly, had a birthday coming up so she folded a piece of notebook paper into an air plane, wrote birthday wishes and told her it was "air mail" then made an emblem of a birthday cake on the side. Someone at the mailroom probably unfolded it looking for contraband and didn't know how to fold it back.

Huge amounts of mail continue to come in from Vi's letter inviting men to write a lonely female inmate. A C.O. made a comment about all the mail she got and she assured her it was just bills. She just tossed them all in the rubbish, but the girl on the bunk above her fished them out to answer them.

Ellie went to the board today and one hoped she made it out okay. Someone will write Rachel, let her know and hopefully she will show up here in a few days.

Somebody with a clipboard came by and told the girls on the other side of the bathroom to clean up their room. They probably had dust bunnies and more sticking in spilled Kool Aid on the floor. They're called each other "sorry hoes," but did nothing to change that status.

They connected up the ice machine as spring hinted it's presence. It's been just sitting since before she got here. Almost every day a pair of mechanics come out, move it away from the wall, rattle some tools, smoke a cigarette, tell a couple of jokes, push the thing back to the wall and call it a day. It's been a real tease—and when you get teased by an ice machine—things are bad.

About 9:30 am a team of inmate workers came through the building turning on all the showers full blast and hot, claiming it was to keep pipes from freezing. As soon as they left, and with steam clouding the windows, Rachel shut it off before the room became a sauna. The girls on the other side, turned it back on—even when she told them it would probably activate the fire alarm. It took about fifteen minutes, but sure enough the fire alarm shrieked it's high pitched whistle. The C.O. came running and opened the door on an unbelievable cloud of steam condensing on the walls and running down onto the floor. She shut off the water and opened the windows. Rachel had her door closed off to the mess. Yard patrol stormed in followed by maintenance. The alarm was quickly shut off, but they had some difficulty removing the battery that fueled the high-pitched whistle. Eventually the excitement was over and the area filled with over-zealous moppers.

A couple of hours later, the C.O. came to the door hollering "Rachel Williams! "Go see Dr. Warrington." He's the psych doctor at Lotusville and must have an office here. She had no idea what he wanted from her. She'd never had a conversation with him and only heard his name through others. Was this some ploy to keep her here longer? The C.O. ran off, clearly harried and overworked. The morning has taken a toll on her. Rachel donned her coat over her sweatshirt, over her shirt and off she went. Bad News! Nothing ever goes smoothly! What's the hang up now? Will it hold up her release from here? Oh well, if we didn't put wrenches in the hands of monkeys, they wouldn't have anything to throw.

She charge into his office ready to attack whatever the situation was. Then she saw him! There sitting in a chair is the smiling face of the good looking handsome man she and Bonnie met on the walk/jog so many months ago. They talked for a while and he really lifted her spirits. He asked her how she felt about going home. How did he know?

"Afraid," she told him.

"Of what? Coming back?" he asked

"Why would I be afraid of coming back?" She asked. "I know everybody." He laughed, but she continued. "I'm just not sure of myself anymore. I'm so internally restless and externally confined."

He said that after he left Lotusville he went back to school to get his doctorate but stayed in touch with Bonnie by mail. That's how he knew she was here. He said it is easier to get in here to visit than at Lotusville. He suggested she write him when she got home with her P.O.'s address he will write him a letter and also any prospective employers who might hesitate to hire her because of being here. The guy is all right. She thanked him and left. No, she never wrote him and never expected to hear from him again. But she did.

It's almost mail call. She hoped to find out if Ellie got her shock parole, but it's too soon for that news to get back. Maybe she'll hear tomorrow but probably Saturday. Someone wrote that she's making a real fool of herself chasing after her "duck." She needs to be here and away from the craziness that is that place. The duck has someone else and has rejected her in public, but Ellie has been following her around like a pet. So degrading! Ellie is going home. Her friend will be left behind—again. The women here seem to get much more emotional/possessive about their attachments here than she's ever known a man to be.

It's very boring here. Can't go outside because of the storms. Not much to do but watch TV and the construction project across the street—but even that is shut down because of the rain. Strong winds blew down one of their new unsupported green walls overnight and nothing was happening over there today. Her roommates spend their days watching the daytime "soaps" and everything else that comes on. She told them they're watching musical dicks.

Ellie came Wednesday after getting her freedom at the board and is very disappointed they don't have an exercise room or any place she can "work out." She says they have been promoting the availability of exercise equipment in this place on TV and in the newspapers. There wasn't any room for any of that now that they've filled all the rooms with beds. Rachel told her to be patient, that a month ago when she came, there were no clocks, no ironing board or iron, no ice machine, and they just brought in a pool table. "But I can't wait" insists Ellie, who usually got whatever she wanted. "I want it while I'm here."

She said it was not a "good" board but they had some tough characters to deal with. She felt lucky to get out and anxious to return to real life. The girl who micro-waved her baby got another five years. Rachel isn't sure if she ever met her.

Rachel's family went to see D.D. Knight to find out the resolution of the property hearing and verification of her out date. He told him flat out that "she isn't getting out any time soon" and "I don't know anything about any hearing." It was obvious he wasn't thinking of her, but only of himself when he said he was "really peeved that she put him in a position he had to defend himself in front of his peers." Hearing that made Rachel feel good. When he was asked to return her possessions, receipts and insurance paperwork, he told them that he had relegated her files to the "dead file." When asked to retrieve them, he had the nerve to tell them, as he shook his head sadly, that, "I was going to do so much for her." We all know now that her files were relegated to the "dead" the day she was found guilty.

Got a letter from Emily today. She says, "They finally got hot water in Jefferson, but it is only temporarily. This place is a still a real dump." She went on to explain that a cold water line broke underground and formed a huge pool of water. The hot water pipes traveled through this cold lake so cooled the hot water. In trying to fix it, they damaged something else and that led to there being no hot or cold water in the building. She thinks it is back on track now. A huge group of girls signed up for the Rehab Project so they can move to another building.

If stuff like this and all the earlier building code problems happened in the Real World, the property would be condemned and the owner would have to fix it before it was habitable again. All the slum lords aren't in the ghetto!

Rachel gets letters from her friends that tell her that things were getting real tough back at Lotusville for both inmates and staff. There were supposed to be lawsuits over the lack of medical care, they have dogs searching the rooms regularly for drugs and that was totally new. The C.O.s were on edge about everything and no one was relaxing. There was an investigation of criminal activity within the staff, and the usual rumors of divorces and hook-ups among them.

Ellie spoke with her attorney who told her he would have her record expunged. Rachel was looking forward to that too—to flush this life away. She wondered how long one has to wait. Ellie didn't know.

There was a sanitation inspection and her unit came in dead last—again. Her room was clean, and she heard them yelling at the girls on the other side of the bathroom, but don't know the problem. Went to use the bathroom. It stunk. A wastebasket full of bloody Kotex, the sink full of kinky broken pieces of hair and toothpaste globs. The floor was full of fuzz and hair which stuck to dried blood spots. Rachel cleaned the bathroom after she used it every morning, top to bottom, toilet, sink, and even the window, but does not clean it up again after those that sleep in till noon. She doesn't do it for inspections, but just to have it clean. Her roommates laugh at her, referring to her as their white maid, but she has to live here too and can't be content in their filth—and there's eight that use it now.

Rachel had to do something entertaining to break the monotony. Bonnie mailed her a very official looking memo all about peckers. There was a bulletin board by the door so she hung it there, and it attracted a lot of attention. It's after "office hours" and coming up on a weekend, so the C.O.'s on duty (two men) don't have anyone to call to see if they have the authority to take it down. That done, she got a picture of a man holding a gun to another man's head and the caption read "Is that all you have to say?" She wrote R.I.B on the top of it. R.I.B is the court system within the penitentiaries and inmates are nearly always found guilty. Rachel posted that one too.

Ellie came right over to Rachel when she saw it, rightly suspecting it was her handiwork. It was only a diversion from this place. Personal entertainment. The other day Ellie asked why she was reading so much. She told her, "to keep my sanity." She laughed.

Rachel was told that they want her to attend classes for an hour each day. She was anxious for the change of pace and curious about what they offer. Whoever is conducting these classes was about to be put to a test. Don't know when they start.

Those papers she put on the bulletin board caused quite a stir. She's glad that someone was getting a laugh over them.

Cora Ann made a rare appearance in the hallway. She's really depressed. Her out date was three months ago and she's still he here waiting for her paperwork to come in. She's from Riverview but says the screw up is in Springfield. Her attorney is working on it and tells her to "be patient." Scary words. Where has she heard that one before.

Bonnie wrote saying that a C.O. there is in trouble. Seems that one of the girls he was seeing kept a detailed journal and it turned up in a search. He's married with two kids.

Bonnie's mom and son have been to talk with two judges about getting her released. So far it doesn't seem they are making any progress, so her attorney is going to file her super shock with the judge next week. She says she expects her judge to bring her back immediately. One hopes she gets it, but also wonders if this attorney is just taking more money for nothing. One hears on the news of scammers taking advantage of seniors. How about lawyers taking advantage of the desperate.

Ellie's name was called a couple dozen times at mail call today but she wasn't there to pick it up. Then later, she appeared, took away a handful of letters, saying nothing to anyone, and went back to her room. People were curious about whether or not she's still corresponding with her duck.

Family has sent job applications to Rachel. Where it asked "Have you ever been convicted of a felony," she answered yes. The next question is "if yes, explain." She writes, "Will explain at interview. She used her home mailing address. So far, no responses. She didn't expect any.

She knows that she will have to find some way to get a job that would please the P.O. and start some cash flow. She also knew she'd have to spend a lot of time getting her house and yard together—and get reacquainted with life. Foreign territory that must be explored.

They brought in a girl from another unit and locked her in the "solitary" cell this afternoon. It was like a closet. The units each have one cell for "solitary" and the unit she was in must have been busy.

Rachel's roommate in the bunk above suggested she go to aerobics with her. She wasn't interested and wasn't going to do it until Ellie suggested it too.

Rachel had been busy rattling a lot of cages making sure her paperwork was showing up where it was supposed to and it was being handled in a timely fashion. The social worker just rolled her eyes every time she saw her at her door and assured her she was working on it. At least she didn't tell her to "be patient."

They snatched a young girl, a Cuban National, from here first thing in the morning and took her back to admissions in Lotusville to await "deportation hearings." She's not a citizen and has drug charges. They couldn't deport her to Cuba because there weren't any diplomatic relations with them and the consensus here was they won't drop back there with a parachute. She says her father was a general in Castro's army and she escaped (a Mariolito) Her family has disowned her and she claims she will probably be killed if returned. They're serious communists! They have established several jails in the south, specifically for the undesirable Cuban castoffs. Bonnie wrote she thinks they are going to put her in a boat, aim it toward Cuba and put it on automatic pilot.

Rachel was disappointed that she never heard any more about the class she was supposed to take.

The library deposited a couple dozen books on a table about a month ago and Rachel had been reading through them one at a time. She didn't care what the topic was. She just needed something to do, to read. For some reason, all the books were suddenly confiscated. They just disappeared.

There's a really big girl here, easily over six feet and really built. Don't know how long she's been here as she is working cadre. She's an inmate whose job happens to be here, not someone awaiting release. She's shapely, but in huge proportions. Her breasts were so big they couldn't get proper circulation and became discolored. They took her to I.S.U. hospital for breast reduction surgery. Rachel hasn't seen the results, but understood from someone that has that she is in intense pain and has little more than a nipple. One thing she noticed about the medical facilities there was when they operate, and it doesn't seem to matter on what, they find a way to turn the inmate patient into a freak. They took the sweat glands from the armpits of one girl and she lost some use of her arms. They operated on another girl's legs and now she's bow-legged. They do countless hysterectomy's and botch most so they have to be redone and they always left horribly conspicuous scars.

Rachel's family made a doctor and dentist appointment for her when she gets home, and for that she was grateful.

Rachel's unit as once again the filthiest unit inspected. There were three constantly really dirty rooms and one of them was Ellie's. Her roommate was sleeping in and when the inspectors were on their way, Ellie woke her roommate up and told her to get dressed and make her bed. The girl brushed her teeth and got toothpaste all over the sink and wall and when she combed her hair, that was everywhere too. Ellie was furious.

Rachel was desperate to get home and kept on that social worker and she did her job. Within minutes of being told that she would be on the bus the next day, Rachel excitedly got on the phone with her parents. They hesitatingly told her they'd called the lawyer earlier that day and he told them there was no chance she could be released so soon. She assured them again that she was coming home the next day, and please pick her up at the bus station. They were really worried. "You aren't going to get into more trouble coming home, are you?" The thought of all the heartache she's caused them by being locked up brought tears. She told her mother, "I am so bad they don't want me here anymore. They are throwing me out." Will the nightmare ever end? She told them she was to be released in the morning and she would call them from the bus station in Springfield with the bus schedule and would let them know what time she would be in Riverview.

Rachel was among 57 girls who were scheduled to leave here on the next bus to Springfield, but no one knew for sure whose paperwork was in order and whose wasn't. Rachel packed up her box and left it with the others. It would be searched.

Early the next morning, Rachel was issued a new purple jacket and the money from her commissary which afforded her the bus ticket home to Riverview. It took close to an hour to get each person processed, packaged up, searched for contraband and dressed into their street clothes. It took twice that long to get checked in here. Then they did not release on weekends even if the paperwork was complete so she had to leave today—or wait.

It was wonderful to get on that bus with her box of possessions and a lot of good memories. She watched the miles fly by the window during the two-hour ride home and it should have made her feel free, but she felt conspicuous with her cardboard box of belongings on her lap. Living out of a box was normal back there, but now she was in the real world. Was everyone looking at her? Did they know she was just released from prison? She didn't look around.

Seeing her parents in their car at the bus stop waiting for her gave off mixed feelings from everyone. They seemed glad to see her, but were very quiet. Rachel was quiet. She was scared but wasn't sure why. They offered to take her to lunch. She didn't think she was hungry but went to please them and she ate. It help her to settle some.

They stopped at a grocery store to put some food in the house and after a few minutes the store seemed to close up around her and she couldn't stay. There was just so much to see, layers of food on shelves and people filling carts. He chest became heavy and her breathing became short and shallow. Too much stimulation. She had to get out of the store. Had to leave. She was all tight and panicky. Her parents said, "all you need is a good night's sleep, but she knew it was more than that.

Her kids would be home shortly and she'd have to fix them something to eat. What? She hadn't cooked in nearly three years. She had to be a mommy again. Would they accept her? Her parents had been taking care of the kids, but now they were hers to be responsible for. Could she handle it?

She was scared as she saw her daughter getting off the school bus. All this time and she was so anxious for this moment but now she feared it. "Mommie!" her daughter yelled when she saw her and raced across the lawn for a hug that nearly threw her off balance. Wow, that was a homecoming. Rachel squatted down and looked at her girl. She was so beautiful and happy. "Grandma always makes me soup and a sandwich when I come home."

Rachel was so glad that her parents had done some shopping for her earlier and had also taken her to the store. Now, her daughter was leading her back into mommyhoood.

"Well, let's do that together." Rachel set out the makings for a sandwich and heated the soup.

Half an hour later she saw her son come walking down the street. He wasn't as easy, but they muddled through. Not saying much, he downed a snack and headed for his room to study. She baked a chicken she found in the fridge and put on a nice meal. Her daughter bounced around setting the table and babbled about school. She was a happy kid.

When she called her son down to dinner, she grabbed him for a quick hug. He was bigger than she now. Her eyes met his and she said, "I'm so happy to be home with you kids."

"Yeah, mom. Me too." and he sat down to eat.

For days she didn't want to go outside. She just stared out the window, mentally floundering. She wasn't interested in anything or seeing anyone. She felt like an intruder in her own house. She didn't want to answer the phone. Friends stopped by to visit. They commented that she "looked much better than they expected, considering all she'd been through." They couldn't see all the confusion and agony inside. They wanted to take her shopping so she went. She had kids to feed. It was always the same. In the store, she'd get all tense, get the jitters and tear up. Couldn't stay. Gray pants meant C.O.'s. Khakki pants meant inmates. Repeated trips eventually became longer but it was months before she could function.

She didn't think she could ever be part of the world again. She just didn't fit anymore. No one wanted to hear the prison stories. She didn't know anything else. She felt socially retarded. Getting behind the wheel of a car was scary. Paying bills, writing checks, responsibilities. She could handle that because it reminded her of school. She could do it without interacting with others. Life became overwhelming and there were times she thought she'd rather go back, but those times were fleeting. She did miss her friends from there and wrote to one person or another weekly. That place stripped her of pride, dignity, initiative, and human-hood. Will she ever adjust to normalcy? Was this a form of post-traumatic stress?

Within a few days of being released, Rachel had to report to a parole officer. Eric drove her but waited in the parking lot. Their relationship was strained. It was a very uncomfortable place to be in an unfamiliar part of town. She was kind of scared, but her head was still in a fog. The parole officer sat at a desk in a small cubicle that was overflowing with paperwork and asked her how she was doing. She told him she didn't know, that she was trying to get used to being home, felt as though she was a compressed spring just released and still zinging. He said he expected her to find a job or return to school, and she told him she was looking into both options but wasn't sure she was ready for either. He was very nice and told her he'd see her in another month. On the drive home she saw so much that had changed. The world had continued to spin while her life was on hold. She needed to jump back on, but how? Life was a blur, and she had to grasp a handle—somewhere.

She constantly wrote letters to several friends back there that were important to her. There was a strong need to stay in touch with them. Part of her was still there, she guessed. She also wrote letters to those from there that were recently out. Things were becoming a little more relaxed with her son. He was looking into colleges and wanted her opinion. There wasn't money to work with but he assured her he'd manage somehow. It was what he wanted.

The phone rang one warm afternoon. The voice was warm and friendly and it turned out to be the psych guy. He had time to talk and asked how she was doing. Then he got into the reason for the call. His family had given him all kinds of grief after the fiasco in the prison. It was a bad time for him, but they held everything together. He'd gone back to school and earned his PhD. He said that he wanted her to know that all those girls came on to him and their bold behavior took him by surprise. He said he wasn't guilty of participating in their game or encouraging it. He said it was important to him that she understood and would tell others that knew him. Yes, it was good that he continued his education and got away from that awful place.

Ellie was released a couple months after Rachel returned home. She went to live with her parents, a suburb away. They got together one evening to garbage pick, hoping to recycle some things (to make a better world) and make a little money, but that evening was cut short when flashing red, white, and blue lights pulled up behind us and we were told to stop. The officer took our ID's back to his car and we wondered if he would see we were both on parole for drug violations. He just told us to cease the garbage picking and go home.

She got a job waitressing at the Waterview, a high-class restaurant on the river and was making great tips—especially on the weekends, sometimes $1,000. Management discovered that a lot of steaks were missing from the kitchen so started "strip-searching" the help before they went home. That was just too much for Ellie. She wasn't going to subject herself to that any more. It just reminded her too much like being locked up and quit. Still living with her parents, she wasn't strapped for money.

Ellie was interested in furthering her education. After all, she'd already completed two years and had her associate's. She was half way to her bachelor's. She applied at a good school that happened to be geographically convenient for her. At interview, she told them where she got her two-year degree, presented her transcripts and detailed why she was there. They as much as told her that they didn't want "her kind" to be around the kids going to school there and dismissed her. She was really hurt.

She devoted herself to going to meetings, N.A, AA, wherever she could go and she told her story over and over. She traveled to different cities and became quite a sought-after speaker. She was dynamic in her presentation, detailing how she sunk so low as to take on whole local professional basketball and football teams at parties for drugs. Then she told her audience how her life was restricted through prison, yet earned her associates' there, that when she tried to finish her education once out, she was denied acceptance at a college because of her past.

After that meeting, one of her audience told her that he was on the board of a college outside Riverview that would be proud to accept her as a student. They talked for awhile and when he told her the name of the school he worked for, she told him that was the one that had bounced her. He told her to apply again and she would be accepted. She did and was.

Her parents were proud of her. She drove their second car and for her birthday present they asked her what she wanted expecting her to ask for a car. She shocked them by asking for new boobies and though surprised, they accommodated her. Ellie was so proud, that meeting a friend coming out of the school administration building, she raised her shirt to show them off.

Ellie attended college for about a year, then dropped out. She'd met her perfect man and planned to marry. He was a cop and convinced her he would take care of her, she didn't need any education or any of her friends from that past life. She dropped out of sight.

A year later and about the time Rachel started adjusting to being human again, she heard on the TV and read in the newspaper that the Governor was releasing several women from Lotusville that had crimes relating to battered women's syndrome, and Mattie was on the list. Here she was, doing a life sentence and now she was coming home. Rachel was so excited for her. We had a single desire and that was to make sure Bruce Muley got his due, and with both of us working on it, we might just make it happen. She had to admit that she had been too messed up emotionally to focus on Muley and until that time she'd given little thought to him. Didn't know where he was, but knew if he wasn't in prison, he was out doing bad things.

Bonnie was told she could come home to Riverview and stay at a half-way house to finish her sentence. That seemed to be a good idea and she was told to go find a job. She was given lots of coupons for clothes. Then she interviewed a lot, but the last question on all the applications was "were you ever convicted of a felony" and when she answered "yes" they lost interest fast. She did work briefly at Wendys, then toyed with the idea of a job at another chain, where they did hire convicted felons. What she really thought she wanted to do was get back into school and put in applications for nearby schools and for grants. She had trouble getting her transcripts and financial aid paperwork. She was frustrated. Bonnie did not handle frustration well.

She was assigned a room with two other girls at the half-way house. Mae, an older woman smoked two cartons of Bensen & Hedges a week! Needless to say, living in that amount of smoke was a killer. Plus, she snored like a wild boar caught in a snare. She'd wake up struggling for air, run to the bathroom and hacked up her polluted mucus that will undoubtedly kill her in the near future. Bonnie frequently woke up disoriented thinking she was in a war zone but didn't know who was attacking.

The other roommate watched TV way into the night and snacked constantly. In the 45 days this roommate was there, she showered twice but never had body odor, which the older lady definitely had. Both were there awaiting a bed in a nearby in-patient drug treatment hospital.

Bonnie had been warned not to have expensive jewelry and to closely guard any possessions she brought there. Against everyone's advice, she chose to wear a butterfly charm on a gold chain. It was a gift from a long ago friend and had great sentimental value to her. One day she found that it pulled on the hairs on the back of her neck and made her uncomfortable so asked one of her roommates to unhook it. She plucked out the hairs caught in the clasp and put it in cotton in a box in her dresser drawer. That's the last she saw of it. Distrust of all those unknowns around her began to fester.

Thoughts of Easter, family, home, and reminiscing of what was and what is no more. An infected tooth, nausea, vomiting, the sweats the chills caused Bonnie to lose all focus. She started crying and sobbing as she sat on the edge of her bed at the furlough house after she found her way back from breakfast. The rest was a blur. Flashes of being at the furlough officers office, booking at County Jail, and an early morning ride back to Lotusville. But it is supposed to be home they're taking her. Yep, it's May 1st and time to go home. Not so, for again the joke was on her. Once again, she felt the pain of being life's fool, for home was still out of reach. Her mind was working but not thinking. Wait . . . your weight . . . . Kuwait. Where's the peace she's longed for, for so many years. Freedom of our boys returning from the war, and of me finally going home.

Bonnie spent the next night alone in a room in a big wooden old-fashioned crank up hospital bed trying to pull body and soul together. Then she gets a 70 year old roommate from Riverview who accidentally shot and killed her 68 year-old-boyfriend who beat her on top of her head. Ginger is down the hall, also returned on medicals.

Then she saw Dr. Ovens, who gave her the Heimlich Maneuver on the examining table while talking into his tape recorder. "There seems to be something lodged in the upper digestive tract" then ordered an upper GI at I.S.U. That's it—she's in a movie, no, she's being experimented on—in a mad house. She's put in a room with three other women, jammed together on cots.

The upstairs shower is flooding and dripping through the ceiling. They're told to use the kitchen sink to wash up. Cockroaches are everywhere. Her cot is next to the radiator and she gets burns when trying to roll over. They run a battery of tests on her, psyche, blood, urine, chest X-Ray and all is normal. Still no upper GI, but, Dr. Ovens tells her it all takes a while. The social worker tells her that they plan to release her on Wednesday and she wants to believe—has to believe, but can't trust. She'll have to wait to sign her release papers, then maybe it will become a reality. Fear is the most awesome of enemies. When will it end?

Rachel received a letter from Emily. She asked her if she would help her mother put a food box together. She gave her mother's address and phone number and she called her, then visited. Emily had a nice mom and she showed her pictures of her family, and Emily's boys. We put the food box together and mailed it off. Remembering her parents effort putting together one for her and the frustration of most of it having to go back, she was glad she could help. She visited with her several more times before Emily was released. Her mom was interested in how she was faring there and said she was proud of her going to school.

Rachel had heard rumors of Emily taking up with a "girlfriend" after she'd last seen her. Letters about this affair drifted in from a couple of people and letters from Emily became further apart. Emily and her "friend" made arrangements to live together once both were out.

Visiting the parole officer every month became a chore. He was pleased she had a clerk job in an insurance office and she was elated when he told her he didn't think she was going to have a problem in society and released her from that duty two months early. On the last visit, she asked him about getting her record expunged. He said he didn't know anything about that and she'd have to have a lawyer do that for her.

Rachel called an attorney that handled an auto accident for her shortly after her arrest and he said that he needed $1,500 up front before he could start the paperwork to expunge her record, but didn't see any reason it couldn't be accomplished once her term of parole was completed. There just wasn't any "lawyer money" in the coffers, so she visited Legal Aid. They told her that with the drug charge she wasn't eligible to have her record expunged—ever. It was like an elephant stomping on her. Ellie's lawyer told her some time ago he'd get hers expunged for her and her case pretty much matched hers. Do the Legal Aid lawyers know more about the law than paid attorneys?

Rachel got a nice letter from Alice, the first one since she came home. Things were looking up for her. She'd found a little house to rent that was sort of out in the country and wasn't far from her new job. She had to disappear from that other life. She was finally holding to the promise she made to herself that she'd not let "trouble" come into her life again. She was now working in the field she was trained to do and at a huge medical facility. The better pay afforded her decent clothes and a new car. She was happy.

Her husband called her occasionally on her cell. He didn't have her address and she had to keep it that way. But his time in captivity was ending and the facility wanted to know where he would be going. He told them, "to my wife." They wanted the details and address but he told them that she moved around so much he couldn't keep track of her, that the post office forwarded his mail. The person taking the information assumed that was true and went out of her way to help him. With the aid of her sources she tracked down Alice and gave him the information. They called Alice and told her that he would be coming home to her.

"Oh no, he can't come here," she pleaded. She explained that he made her life a nightmare and she was afraid of him. Nevertheless, two months later he was on her doorstep with his smile and box of possessions. And she felt back to square one. He was still her husband and he had no other place to go. He needed her. But it wasn't long before he became restless and asked her to drop him off in the City because he had business. He was gone for two months, during which time she filed for divorce, rented a condo and moved out.

# BRUCE

Bruce, being on parole, was required to get a job. He washed and moved cars around at an auto auction. He would never prostitute himself for money. That was women's work. To him everything had to be an adventure. He took the bus to work and was there on time every day, shining up those cars on the outside, making the interiors like new, steam cleaning the engines and doing whatever was asked of him. His employers liked him and found additional work inside for him, mostly janitorial, like polishing the floors. The babe in the office was a flashy bitch, all tits and no brains and totally ignored him. She was the wife of Andy, one of the owners, and he had suspicions she was sneaking around with his partner, James. It didn't take him long to sense that.

Bruce always had a knack for getting to know people, getting into their confidence and having them like him, and it wasn't long before he and Andy were sharing lunch as well as "war stories." Andy told him he did time when he was in his twenties for hot-wiring and stealing a car. Bruce told him he was barely out of his teens when he caught a murder wrap.

"It was just something that had to be done, you know," he justified. "He wasn't the first or last, either. Some people have it coming." He just shrugged.

Bruce worked hard every day. He loved the physical things that kept him in good shape. He occasionally had lunch with Andy. A month or more went by and he quietly observed the babe and Jim, their secret smiles and touching and kissing when they figured no one was looking. Well, he was just the hired help and didn't exist.

Andy knew, or at least suspected. He was frequently short with Jim. His wife would go "out with the girls" and not come in until late or not at all, saying she had more to drink than she should have and spent the night with one of her girlfriends. He never checked on her. When you love, he reasoned, there's a difference between "knowing" and "knowing for sure." Andy figured it was something that would pass. But the weeks went by and they became less discrete. Now, that was an insult!

He didn't like looking at Jim—didn't want him around. Jim was good in the field. He had a knack for buying from estates, private sellers in the newspaper or police auctions around the state at a price they could turn a good profit. Sometimes he'd be gone a couple of days at a time, visiting southern states and come back with a handful of titles and cars with no salt damage on the chassis. Business was good, but it would burn him to see his wife's face light up when he'd return.

Bruce was readying a car for auction when he watched a troubled Andy walking over to him, carrying a sack of food and drink. They usually ate inside. His heart started racing. Maybe this stupid work wouldn't be for nothing. He'd planted the seeds but hadn't seen them growing.

"Hey Bruce, ready for something to eat? You sure put in a good day's work. We have another six coming in tomorrow on the truck. Do you mind eating here in the car. He'd indicated the car Bruce was working on, a Ford Taurus. He paused and looked him in the face. I want to talk to you about something that's really getting to me, and it has to just be between us."

Bruce nodded. "No problem, Andy." Bruce got into the back seat, Andy in the front, sandwiches and coffee were distributed. They ate in semi silence, Bruce being quiet by nature didn't want to push, but was anxious to know what was up.

Andy was agitated and had downed his chicken salad and opened his coffee before he asked. "Bruce, you remember we talked about our past, shortly after you stated working here? You were serious? You weren't putting me on."

"Yeah, that parole officer still coming around to check on me?"

"No, twice, then figured he had better things to do." He opened up another sandwich. Bruce was only half way through his. "No, we're okay there. You're a good employee. When you're ready to move on, I'll give you a good recommendation. I've got another problem and can't deal with it myself. Thought it might be up your alley, but if you don't want any part of it, just say so."

"I'm a big boy, Andy, and you're my friend. What can I help you with." Yes! This lousy job is finally going to pay off.

He'd had to come and go by night and both he and Lola were tired of that

"Well, first of all, let me tell you I appreciate all your hard work around here and I know you get here faithfully on the bus every day. I want you to take a car home each night—kind of test-drive it for us. You do have a license?"

"Yeah, sure, it didn't expire while I was locked up." There'd better be more than this, Bruce grumbled to himself.

"But that isn't the reason I wanted to meet you out here, Bruce. Don't know if you've picked up on it, but my partner, Jim, and my wife are, you know, getting a little too close. I love my wife and he needs to back off. Can't talk to him about it and I'm kind of embarrassed this is happening. Don't know what to say to either of them. I just want it to stop.

What a fucking candy-ass, Bruce thought. "So you want me to talk to him? Rough him up? Make him go away—permanently? Whatever you want is a go with me as long as it is between you and me. Don't want to go back to the joint or nothing."

"What will $5,000 buy me?

Whoa! This guy is serious. "The money is good, and I guarantee the problem will be solved. You'll be paying for the risk. $3 G's up front and the balance when you're satisfied."

Andy breathed relieved. He'd been thinking of talking with Bruce for a while, but didn't know how to approach him. Friends? No way. More of a tool. "Stop by the office after work and pick up a set of car keys. Just return them with the car in the morning and take a different car each day. I'll give you a piece of paper with Jim's address and the cash. Then, we'll never discuss this again."

Bruce nodded and they shook hands. "Deal."

That night when Bruce drove his new car into their driveway, Lola was surprised and anxious to go shopping in it—especially when he held out a big roll of $100 bills. "We need to get us some cell phones, I need a piece, and we can get some stuff down the street. Don't want to return this car tomorrow with bullet holes in it," he chuckled from deep inside his chest.

They were lucky to find a 44 mag. at the local drug house. It was big and black and made to impress and he was sure it would. The cells took a bit longer. Then together they drove by Jim's place, twice around the block. He lived alone and a plan was forming with Bruce, one that amused him to no end. There was always a plan in the making.

"Do you need me for this?" Lola asked.

"No, I'm on my own with this one."

"Once you're off parole, Bruce, I want to move away from here. Get out from under C.P.S. so we can be a real family again. Get out of the county, start new.

"We get a lot of protection here. The cops are our friends. You have a lot of regular customers. You'd be giving up all that."

"But C.P.S. really bothers me, Bruce, I need to get away from them. They'll never leave us alone. They even asked the kids if you've been around. I don't want to lose them and I don't want to lose you. We can make it work somewhere else."

The bitch is always nagging about something, thought Bruce. The timing could be right, though. He could see his job coming to an end really fast and his parole was nearly up.

Next morning he returned the car keys and went to work with a hose and bucket. Some job for such a brilliant person! No one said anything to him all day. He picked up another set of keys at the end of the day and headed home. He liked the freedom of driving back and forth to work, like some executive. They had a beater at the house that he thought of as Lola's.

"Where you want to move, Lola?" He asked over dinner, their shades drawn so no one would see him from the outside. Sometimes he felt like a snake hiding under a rock. Lola was right. It was time to move.

"I'd like to look around south of here or maybe west. I've heard it doesn't cost that much and our mixed race family would fit in. Maybe we could drive out there when you're not at your job and rent a nice house. We have all that money now.

"Sounds good to me. We find a place, rent a truck and be gone. Don't tell nobody nothing. We'll deal with the schools when we settle in."

Bruce dropped the car keys off and put in another day's work. Andy casually asked him, "How's it going."

Bruce smiled, knowing Andy was getting anxious and didn't want him having second thoughts and canceling his operation, so confidentially responded, "Plans complete." and started to walk away.

Andy spoke up quickly. "He'll be out of town tonight and maybe tomorrow, so . . . . just so you know."

"Thanks for the heads up. Don't need a dry run."

They parted, Bruce relieved because he wanted the move to a new place to be in progress first. Then everything would happen quickly—but not the way Andy thought. He smiled later that day as he scrubbed a stain off a carpet.

The babe in the office—he didn't think of her as Andy's wife—walked around swinging those hips side to side and at the same time her tits bounded up and down. How did she do that? No one else was around. Was she doing it for him? Just then she looked up and smiled. Keep your mind on the plan, Bruce, he told himself. He knew she'd caught him watching her so asked, "Do you think it would be okay if I took off a couple hours early today? My wife wants to check out a new place to live. Things are pretty well caught up."

"Sure, go now if you like. I was thinking of closing up for the day anyway. Here's your keys. It's the blue one over there."

"Thanks, Just some equipment to put away, then I'm out of here."

Lola was excited to be looking for a new home, so picked up the twins from pre-school early and told the neighbors to watch for the boys coming home from school They'd be okay by themselves. She'd leave them a snack and please keep an eye on them."

When they reached a town she had in mind, they bought a newspaper, then stopped at a real estate office and found an agent to show them houses for rent. The first one was too expensive, the second was a dump, the third seem perfect, 3 bedrooms, close to schools and shopping and on a bus line. She didn't think they'd find anything so soon and was delighted.

They went back to the real estate office to sign the paperwork and laid out in cash the first and last month's rent and security deposit. The agent gave them a surprised look. It wasn't often someone had the cash. She was happy about it, not only not having to wait for a check to clear but she'd get her commission right away. Because the house was vacant, she handed them the keys and told them the rent started on the first, so they had some time to move in before the meter started running.

They went home, fed the boys, then boxed and bagged their belongings. The next morning while Bruce was at work Lola rented a truck and two men and in a couple of hours they were out of there. She picked up the boys from school and headed west, hoping to have the boys beds set up before Bruce called.

Bruce went into work, apologized for being late, turned in his keys as usual, but instead of starting work, headed down the street to a diner. He called Lola on his new cell to have her pick him up. He'd help with the moving. Nearly an hour later she was there.

Lola was content as she put things in order at their new place. All things were perfect with a man at the helm and he was her man.

# BRUCE AND JIM

I t was dark when Bruce knocked on Jim's door. He could see him through the window, sitting watching TV, eating something.

Jim got up at the sound of the knock and was surprised to see Bruce. He was about to invite him in when Bruce kicked the door open with a bang, knocking the bowl from Jim's hand, it's contents spilling across the room. He strode in pulling his 44 from inside his blue vest. Jim went pale and fell back a couple of steps. He started to stutter something, but little came out.

Bruce wanted to laugh at this weasel, but kept a penetrating stare as he shoved Jim into a chair and stood over him. He knew how to intimidate. "take your pants off, bitch. Now!" he barked. "I have to see what Andy's wife likes. He's paid me to shoot you dead, cut you up and put your pieces out with the trash," He lied.

Jim just stared, shocked. Bruce leaned over inches from his face, spittle flying and repeated his demand. Jim slowly reached for his belt, then stopped, getting back some of his bravery. "What's going on, Bruce, what the hell do you want?"

"Andy isn't tolerating you messing with his wife. It's over! Drop those drawers now. If I have to do it for you I'm going to have a little fun. He paused as he flipped open a switchblade with his other hand.

Jim slowly eased down his pants. Bruce laughed. "That's all you got? Why she waste her time for that? Wish I had a camera—send it to Ripley's. Well, back to business. Andy paid me 10 G's to get rid of you, make you disappear", he lied again. "Bang. Bang."

Jim started to whimper, said something intelligible, probably begging him not to shoot. The more he begged, the bigger the hard-on Bruce was getting. He loved the process.

"Have any last words, Bruce barked.

Jim cried, tears running down his face. Yes, he was trembling, begging for his life, pleading. Bruce was enjoying it all, sometimes asking him to repeat. He loved watching people who thought they were better than him grovel.

Finally, Jim stammered out his plea. "Andy gave you ten. I'll give you 12 to let me go and I'll never look at the broad again."

"You have that kind of money here at the house?"

"No, I'll get it from the bank first thing in the morning. I'll bring it to work with me."

"Bullshit! You'll call the cops soon as I go out the door." Bruce bellowed. Everything was going as he'd planned. Jim just wanted him to be gone so he could get to the phone, but he'd seen though it. He looked over at Jim and imagined his frantic fingers were already dialing 911 even though the phone was across the room.

Bruce pulled a length of rope from a pocket and tied Jim securely to his chair, pants still down. "I'm letting you live for the moment," he granted. First thing in the morning we visit the bank. If all goes well, we'll never see each other again."

Bruce went over to the chair he'd first seen Jim in and finished his beer. He shut off the TV then spread out on the couch for the night. Several times he heard Jim squirming to get loose, but unless his name was Houdini, he'd be there in the morning.

Morning came and Bruce was awakened by Jim's need to pee. Bruce laughed as he brought over the food bowl he'd been feasting from the night before, the contents now on the floor. He set the bowl down about four feet away from Jim. "See how good your aim is with that little pea shooter," He chuckled.

"Damn it Bruce, I'm ready to go to the bank to get you the money. At least untie my hands so I can hold the bowl."

"Don't think so, Shorty. Shoot for the bowl," he laughed. The bank doesn't open for another three hours. Can you wait that long?

Bruce stood with Jim at the teller so he wouldn't pass any messages to her. He'd instructed Jim to smile. He joked to Jim about the car better worth twelve thousand. Andy and Jim had their business account there and the teller knew they dealt in cars. She asked how they wanted the money and was told big bills. The money was turned over to Bruce and in front of the surveillance cameras, they shook hands.

Jim drove them back to his house and was relieved Bruce went to his car and drove away. He went inside, locked the door, and called 911.

# RACHEL AND MATTIE

Mattie called Rachel when she got home and back with her family. They met for lunch and Rachel was surprised to learn that she's already landed a job at a battered women's shelter. They hadn't a clue as to how they were going to deal with Bruce Muley, but knowing what a bad person he was, knew it was only a matter of time the opportunity would come. And it wasn't too long before there was an article in the paper about him, and what really bothered them was that the police and FBI were making a joke about it, and they knew it was anything but.

The article said that Bruce was working washing cars at an auto auction and learned that one of the owners was fooling with the wife of the other and mentioned to the husband that he'd be glad to take care of the problem if the price was right. A short while later, the husband came up with a bundle of money—half now and half when the job was done. Bruce took the money. Later that day he went to the partner's house. He pulled a gun on him and told him that he was being paid to get rid of him for having an affair with the wife.

The partner begged for his life and agreed to pay more than the husband did, just to save his life. Bruce went to the bank with him, collected the money and let the guy live. As soon as he was free of Bruce, the partner went directly to the police and told them what happened. The Riverview Police had a good laugh over it, saying they knew the guy. The FBI got involved for some reason (maybe a possible kidnapping to the bank,) but they thought it was funny too. The newspaper made a joke out of it.

So, Rachel and Mattie knew he was out and still doing his thing.

Rachel and Alice stayed in touch, mostly by email. Alice found some information about Bruce on line. It seems Lola was interviewed by a detective regarding the murder of two males. Could they be the two he said he abducted from the American Steel parking lot and told them he was taking them to Connecticut?

Emily came home and moved in with her mom. She knew it was temporary because she had other plans that had yet to mature. She got a telemarketing job selling vacuum cleaners. She called Rachel and told her she met a nice guy on the phone who lived on her street and was going to go on a date with him. Rachel advised her against it because she knew him and he had a drinking problem, but she went and found out for herself. The "date" was a pub crawl, not her idea of going out.

It really knocked her mom for a loop when she came home after work and introduced her to her friend that she'd met at Lotusville. Her mom thought she was done with Lotusville, and now she brought home this "woman" from there. The whole thing made her uncomfortable. She couldn't believe it. But it wasn't long before they rented a big house and her mom and sons all moved in together. Rachel never learned the dynamics of the household, only that Emily's mom passed away and the boys were soon out on their own. Bonnie and Ellie contacted them and they all met for dinner at a steakhouse, but things didn't click and they all closed the book on that.

Months went by. Rachel found work. Where the question on the application asked, "Have you ever been convicted of a felony?" She answered "no." and got the job. Bonnie was still incarcerated. Six years now, and she never hurt anyone. Yes, she did shoot up her boyfriend's car, parked at a girlfriend's house but no one was in it. We write regularly. She's anxious to come home, real home, not the half-way house, and her board is coming up soon.

They finally decided to release Bonnie and sent to the new Riverview pre-release, which was built just south of the city amid a tangle of highways and exits and entrances to them. In a few weeks she'd be home.

Ellie called and said she was going to give an AA lead there and would Rachel like to come with her and spend some time with Bonnie. She jumped at the chance. Then entering the building, old apprehensions returned and her legs didn't want to go through those doors. Bonnie knew in advance they were coming so signed up for the meeting. Several of the girls attending recognized her and soon she was able to relax and take in Ellie's lead. She is a wonderful speaker, her voice low and clear, and talking with such confidence. Bonnie appeared healthy, and now had her out date and was excited about soon being able to sleep in her own bed. Her nightmare was coming to a close.

# MATTIE AND RACHEL

It was a slow night at the shelter and Mattie was perusing some intake files when a familiar name jumped out at her. She read details as to why this wife and kids needed shelter. As she read she was horrified but not truly surprised to read the details in black and white. Bruce and Lola Muley, then living in Riverview together, picked up a "john" and took him home. He tied him up in their basement. She took his wallet, credit cards and keys while Bruce kicked and punched the life out of him breaking every bone in his body. He tortured the man to death. Lola detailed how they folded him into a black trash bag with a brown lining and secured it with the man's belt. Then they loaded him into the trunk of the man's car and drove him somewhere north into Michigan, she thinks, and Bruce carried him into the woods and dumped him. If the story was true, Lola needed to be away from him. She and her kids were accepted for temporary shelter until she could find a place of her own. She didn't stay at the shelter long, and it was assumed she went back to Bruce. So many abused women return to their abuser.

Mattie called Rachel and she told her about this amazing find and asked her opinion about what she should do with it. She reminded her that we didn't know how true it is so just hold on to it. Make a copy and return the file.

# BRUCE AND LOLA

Lola liked her new home. She was comfortable with the neighbors, even though she was never one to mingle socially with them. The boys were happy in school and didn't seem to miss the old neighborhood.

For Bruce, it was a different story. He was restless and had trouble finding his footing. He didn't have friends there and didn't seem interested in being there. He went out with Lola to work the streets a couple of times a week, but business was slow and the "johns" wanted to bargain with her for her services. One evening a half dozen teenagers approached her for a "group rate." He couldn't understand that and it infuriated him. The world was going crazy. She'd wave down a car and try to do business. In the old neighborhood, it was pretty much a sure thing, but these guys all wanted to negotiate. As the weeks went by Bruce started spending more of his time back at the old neighborhood. When he did show up, he was usually wasted and wanting.

Lola had her government checks and food stamps. She made a little money working the streets, but didn't have any regular customers yet and she didn't have the protection of the police. She picked up two soliciting tickets and paid a fine. The neighborhood was just different—more sidewalk sleepers and street rats, and there's no money in that. She hoped if once customers got used to seeing her out there things would change, but mostly wondered if she'd ever get her family back for her four kids. Bruce no longer contributed, more often than not took money from them and leaving for days at a time. Things were tight. She liked being there and didn't want to go back to the neighborhood.

She discussed her plight with a neighbor, and worried about putting a Christmas together for the boys. They came up with a plan. The neighbor lady successfully pulled it off the year before and it worked perfectly for her, but knew she couldn't do it two years in a row.

Lola and her friend set up a decorated tree then bashed in the front door and called the police. Within hours, the TV cameras showed up. She psyched herself to frantic and told them the kid's gifts had been stolen while they were out. The TV and newspapers told of the robbery and the four little boys that would have nothing for Christmas. The kids cried for the camera and there was a lot of sympathy for the family. She had an agreement to share the donations with her neighbor who had been so helpful. Well, the donations came in like she couldn't believe from people they didn't even know. Bikes, scooters, puzzles, games and hundreds of dollars in checks and cash. Someone even donated a computer none of them knew how to even turn on. TV cameras were set up in the home on Christmas morning and captured the surprise and delight of the kids. Lola graciously and from her heart thanked all those who gave her boys a wonderful Christmas. Her smile glowed as she talked to the cameras.

That afternoon, they watched themselves on the news. They enjoyed watching themselves ripping open prettily wrapped gifts, playing and they begged to go outside with the bikes.

Several hours later, in the dead of night, there was a horrendous noise and crash of broken glass. Lola stumbled cautiously from her room to see Bruce brushing himself off. She was relieved to see it was Bruce, not a stranger, but she was very apprehensive about his method of arrival. The room that was cluttered with toys was now littered with glass. What a mess to clean up!

"Bruce, what's wrong? Why didn't you use the door?" She waved her arm to bring his attention to the destruction. She hadn't seen him for a couple of weeks, and his time with the family had become less and less frequent.

"Saw you on TV. Great con. You're a real movie star. Came for my share." He was breathing heavily and his sweat smelled funny. That look on his face frightened her. Lately, she wasn't sure who he was. She had to reason with him.

"Bruce, this stuff is for the kids."

"I'm not after the junk. I want the money—the cash.

Lola gasped and shook her head. "No, Bruce, it isn't yours."

Without warning, he punched her in the stomach. When she doubled up. An uppercut broke her jaw. A twist of her arm dislocated her shoulder and one kick and a crack of bone took her down where she drifted into unconsciousness. "Where's the money, bitch?"

She might have tried to answer, he wasn't looking for a response. Furious, he kicked her still form, then stalked to the bedroom and began rifling through and dumping the drawers, looking for what was his. He found her stash, some bills but mostly checks, and tucked them into his pockets with a grin and a chuckle. Neighbors must have called the police because he heard sirens in the distance. He stepped over the greedy bitch and left. She had it coming.

The boys woke at the ruckus but kept quiet until they heard their dad leave. When they came out and found their mom bleeding on the floor. They called 911 but the police were already pounding on the door. Scared, they didn't answer it but huddled next to their mom and cried. A policeman cleared the window frame of glass and came in. Neighbors came over and gawked through the window.

The sirens came and stopped. Paramedics came inside. Then the ambulance took their mom. The boys were crying and said it was their dad, they hadn't seen him, but they knew his voice. One of the neighbors volunteered to keep the kids, but Children's Services took them. At the hospital, Lola's condition was regarded as extremely critical. Later, a doctor commented to a TV newsperson that he'd never seen anyone take such a beating and survive. She had a concussion, internal bleeding, her jaw was broken and she'd lost teeth, shattered ribs punctured her lungs and her arms and legs were in traction.

Two days later the police were able to talk to Lola in the hospital. After surgery and broken bones now set, still in pain muted by drugs, her jaw wired shut she indicated to them she didn't know who did it. She told them she was sleepy and it was dark. If it was Bruce, he had a key and wouldn't have come through the window. They told her they needed to talk to him. Did she know where he was? No, but she'd let them know if he contacted her. They didn't tell her hospital security was on alert if he showed up and her phone calls were being monitored.

But Bruce was back in the neighborhood he knew. He'd scored nearly $500 at the house that night even after losing money on the checks. Lola thought she could hold out on him. "She had to understand her place in his family. She'd needed the beat down. She'd get over it. Don't know why she wanted to move to the sticks anyway.

# MATTIE AND RACHEL

Mattie was watching the news on TV and saw the story about a young mother of many who had just purchased her kid's Christmas gifts and an intruder stole them from the house. Mattie recognized the "young mother" as Bruce Muley's wife, Lola. Later she read the story in the paper. She called Rachel who had also heard the story on TV about the kids having their Christmas stolen, but didn't know it was Lola. They'd never met. Then she'd read the story in the newspaper. She also saw the story of the assault on TV a few days later. They were still looking for Bruce as a person of interest.

Mattie and Rachel keep in touch regularly. Maybe another year went by, then we see an article in the newspaper about some hikers in Michigan who had come upon a body half in and half out of a black-lined brown plastic bag, bones scattered by animals. The police and coroner's office were called to come and collect it. They hadn't a clue as to who it might be. Artists were assigned to do reconstructive drawings of the skull to determine what the person may have looked like. No one around there had reported anyone missing but the body had been in the woods for an estimated five years now. No one claimed him. The story in newspaper detailed how badly the bones were broken, the way the man's belt was tied around the bag, and how nearly identical it was in description to Lola's intake paper from the shelter. According to the estimated date from the medical examiner, Mattie and Rachel were just going to trial when the murder occurred.

Mattie and Rachel decided they finally had a chance to give him his due. Rachel told her she'd call the Riverview Police, and did. She asked to speak to someone in homicide. A detective answered and she told him all the information that she had and how the information on the shelter intake several years ago corresponded with recent news clippings. He laughed and said, "I've known both Bruce and Lola for years and they're the biggest liars I've ever met. I wouldn't believe a thing either of them told me. You're wasting your time on this and I'm wasting my time on the phone talking about it." He hung up. Lola was probably doing the whole police force and they were all in Bruce Muley's pocket. She was mad. She was hurt. She still didn't have any control. Rachel didn't know if this person had anything to do with her case or Mattie's, but birds of a feather . . . .

Frustrated, she called Mattie right away and told her the police weren't interested and repeated the conversation back to her. They decided to go down to the prosecutor's office with their information. Rachel called and made an appointment for the next day. Jack Rivers came out and introduced himself. They went back into his office where Rachel told him about being turned away by the police department when offering their evidence. Then they showed him the newspaper clipping about the body being found in a

Michigan woods and he was aware of it. Then they showed him the intake file dated five years before with the detailed description of the murder. He asked where it came from. They couldn't tell him for fear that Mattie would lose her job. He made a phone call and said that Bruce Muley was incarcerated at the present time and he had the address of Lola. He said he wanted to talk with Lola and do some work with what he had and they should come back downtown and see him in a couple of days.

Mattie and Rachel had no idea that the police already talked with both Bruce and Lola about this murder, but nothing came of it except paperwork.

Jack Rivers took a policeman and an investigator with him when he went to talk with Lola. He found her at home recovering from the beating she'd taken over the holidays. The front window was still boarded up. The kids were in school. She told them she was scared of Bruce, that when he was high she didn't know who he was going to be, that she was done with him. Lola repeatedly said she knew he was bad, but never thought he'd turn on her. No, she wasn't about to admit it might have been Bruce who had attacked her.

She was interviewed at length about the evening the man was murdered in her basement back in Riverview. She talked openly, only too happy that the conversation got away from her recent beating. She told them that while working as a prostitute, with Bruce as her pimp, a man approached her for "unusual sex." He had no cash, but showed her his credit card. She told him to go to an ATM, that she wasn't interested in his credit card and to come back when he had some money. Then she said Bruce and the man left in his car. She was thinking it didn't seem right because he didn't have any money so why would Bruce rob him, further explaining that sometimes he did that, if they weren't regulars.

After work she walked home and found him in her house having a beer with her husband and watching TV. They seemed kind of friendly. She took a bath then came downstairs to find the TV still on and odd muffled noises were coming from the basement. She opened the door saw the guy tied to a pole and there was Bruce, tearing him apart. Most of the noises were from Bruce now, as he kicked and punched. The man was beyond making any noises of his own. She talked without emotion as though watching a movie. Then Bruce untied him and he asked her to bring down some trash bags and help him bag-up the guy. Then he bear-hugged him up the basement steps and out the door. She saw him gripping the belt around the bag as he dumped him into the trunk of his car. A cold wind came rushing down the steps as Bruce came back inside. After she'd cleaned up the basement and they got a little sleep they drove the guy's car several hours to Michigan or Pennsylvania, or some place, she wasn't sure. Lola said she thinks she fell asleep from smoking and drinking and suspected Bruce dumped him into a woods.

Two days later, Rachel and Mattie went back down to the prosecutor's office and Jack Rivers told them that he went with a police detective to see Lola. He told us he offered her immunity from prosecution if she told the truth in court and said he was surprised that she spoke without hesitation to him about the murder and pretty much described how it happened—the cries and sound of breaking bones, the dying noises and the silence of death. She detailed all the questions he asked and seemed very honest with him, if a bit "floaty."

He was amazed, and said he really couldn't believe it. She told him that at one time she was married to Bruce for a while, but was divorced a few years later. Now that he had all the facts first hand, Rivers didn't need Mattie's intake papers any longer as he had the facts. He returned them to her. He had enough to build a case but had to insure that Bruce remained incarcerated. He was only being held on a minor violation.

He asked if there was anything he could do for us. Rachel told him of Bruce's involvement and what happened in her case and asked that her record be expunged. Mattie told Mr. Rivers about Bruce Muley lying on the stand in her case and about his eye-witnessing her brother and another guy shoot her husband in the head, that they were all three given life sentences. She was out only because the Governor recognized "battered women's syndrome." He said he'd check into it.

Immediately, Jack Rivers and an investigator went to the jail and talked with Bruce Muley about Mattie's family's case. And after he was promised he would not to do additional time for perjury, he admitted he lied to get even about something. He didn't admit to her husband's murder, though, only that he witnessed someone doing it and it wasn't her brother.

Nothing happened quickly and the legal system cranked slowly. Mattie's brother, locked was locked up for twelve years before he attained his freedom. The judge, after hearing this new evidence, declared their whole case a mistrial. It was too late for the other man convicted with them at the same time. He died in prison. Did Bruce have any idea what he did to this man and his family?

Mattie's brother had to sign all kinds of papers that he wouldn't sue the state for his being locked up. He was so grateful to be home, he would have signed anything. His family was thrilled that he was home.

Rivers told Rachel to file for her expungement, that the prosecutor's office would not object to it. She was finally free of that ugly past.

Alice wrote a wonderfully happy letter. She still had occasional contact with her ex and those times were less and less frequent. She learned how to keep him on the fringes of her life. She detailed how happy she was sharing in her children's and grandchildren's lives, that she knew now that that is what life should be. Rachel had a lot to share with Alice too. She was very involved in her kids' lives and appreciated each giggle and hug. Her job was going well, her parents had survived her incarceration and her son passed his driver's test. Life was good!

The investigators got busy and learned that Bruce and Lola were stopped in Riverview for a traffic violation driving the victim's car a few weeks after the murder. The ticket was unpaid. They checked ownership of the car license on the ticket. They interviewed an elderly couple at that address who said they had reported their son missing over a decade ago, the first night he didn't come home. They learned he was separated from his wife. The body was soon officially identified by dental records.

Bruce Muley was ready to be released on a lesser charge when they slapped this new case on him. He denied everything even when told that Lola had said differently. His lawyer found Lola and called her requesting her to come down to the jail for a visit. She obeyed as Bruce had trained her to do.

Bruce ranted at her at length, demanding she had to recant everything she told the prosecutor, claim she was on drugs, that he wasn't doing time for another murder. She was mesmerized by him and agreed. But when she tried she was told that she would be subpoenaed and would have to tell the truth. He reminded her of her immunity deal and was told she would do the time as accessory to the murder, that her kids would go to foster care and she'd probably never see them again. She told Bruce she was stuck. But Bruce always had a plan, always thinking steps ahead of others. On a subsequent visit Bruce arranged for a fellow inmate, who claimed to be a Muslim cleric, perform a marriage in the visiting hall. They arranged to all have their visits at the same time. The marriage was performed so she couldn't be forced to testify against her spouse.

The prosecutor tried to throw out this marriage claim, but the Judge, who was a Muslim said it was valid, regardless of the "ruse performed to hobble the States case." The prosecutors told her if she didn't testify, she would be probably be charged with the murder that she had already admitted partaking in. She made several more visits to Bruce in the visiting hall and they invented a different round of stories.

Lots of contradictions. She told the prosecutor's office that she knew who the victim was because she had and used his credit cards. Then she said she never saw the guy in her life and was pressured by prosecutors to turn against her husband. Then she said she was high and under the influence and didn't remember. At first she said the man he beat was a light-skinned black man, then said he was white. Eggo didn't waffle as well as Lola. She told her attorney that the prosecutor threatened her with the electric chair and the loss of her four children if she didn't testify against her husband. Eventually she agreed to tell the truth if they gave her immunity and took the death penalty off the table for Bruce. Her idea of the truth didn't actually coincide with what actually happened.

# BONNIE AND RACHEL

Bonnie was released and came home during the investigation and was glad to hear that things might be working out for Mattie and Rachel. What Rachel found amazing was the fact that the once frail Bonnie easily bounced right into life, taking her driver's test and getting her license. One day she asked Rachel if she would drive to Pittsburgh with her. She had to visit the cemetery to say her good-byes to the love of her life. They made the drive and spent the day. She needed that trip and they both enjoyed spending the time together—outside the bars.

She found a good job shortly after coming home. When it came to "that question" at the end of the application, she answered "yes," and explained it was a domestic dispute. No one ever checked it out and she was hired and worked there for ten years. Then she opened up an ice-cream/candy store for a couple years. When she retired from that, it was to take care of her ailing mother. She told Rachel that she still thinks she made a mistake by not taking off in the middle of the night all those years ago so she could have more time with her boyfriend. He would have become her husband. She

411

explained that she'd only have lost the $500 bail money, and she would have turned herself in later. Romantic thinking does not a good fugitive make, but maybe she was right. Interesting that she didn't make any more visits into mental illness during this time. Much later, when she took on a part-time job and tried to sell her childhood home, she had a short lapse from reality.

# VI

Long after everyone Rachel knew left Lotusville, Vi stayed behind and Rachel tried to stay in touch by letter. She sent her money she requested for a food box but never received a response. Vi met the board several times after that and was always continued for another couple of years. She was not a trouble maker and accomplished her beautician license. Rachel sent her letters and cards but never heard from Vi again. She does follow her in the internet, though, and thinks of her often. She read her Bible looking for answers and thinking of her family (her two children were babies when she was arrested and now she is a grandmother.) They've stayed close and they all prayed. Rachel learned on the internet that she was transferred to work cadre in a pre-release for a couple of years, then was taken to a rehabilitation facility where one hoped she could prepare for life and an occupation on the outside. She's been locked up thirty years. Adjustments for her will be enormous but she has her family.

# RACHEL AND MATTIE

It was another two years before this prostitute/john murder mess came to trial—and nearly two decades since Bruce dumped the body in the woods.

Rachel and Mattie met outside the courthouse and found their way to the courtroom. Years before they'd ridden those elevators and walked those same cold and unfriendly halls connecting the courtrooms. Their own cases had been tried here. They were told which room and entered quietly and sat in the back row.

Bruce Muley was charged with aggravated murder, robbery and kidnapping. Jack Rivers retired. The prosecuting attorney depended on Lola's testimony being the foundation of his case. He explained in his opening statement to the jury that the drama began when the victim solicited Lola for unusual sex acts but he didn't have any money—only credit cards to pay. She refused. Bruce, listening nearby became angry and walked to his car and he had him drive him to their house. They talked for a while on the couch while Lola took a bath. She said she found them in the basement. Bruce, a karate expert had the man tied to a pole and she watched him chop him to death with his hands.

Bruce Muley sat smug with his attorney, the two of them talking in hushed tones. Someone pointed out to Mattie the victims parents, sitting quietly like statues, worn and battered, a few seats away in the same back row as Mattie and Rachel.

They listened to the prosecutors case, detailing the battering tortuous death. The County coroner describing the way the broken body appeared to him on examination. The defense attorneys tried to discount what the coroner testified to, claiming he was an elected official and wasn't a medical doctor so wasn't qualified to testify.

Rachel looked over at the elderly couple that were the victim's parents, his arm tightly around his wife, her head resting on his shoulder, the drained look on their faces. They looked well into their sixties but were probably much younger and just as much a victim as their son. During a break in the proceedings, they left the courtroom. Their clothes were as worn and old as the couple looked. When they returned, they took their same seats and were now holding hands. They just stared ahead, their faces blank, hoping to find justice. How painful this had to be for them, yet they sat there unmoving, totally focused, taking it all in. They were learning the details of the last few hours of their son's life. People talk of finding "closure" but for this couple, how could there ever be?

Bruce listened too, with the expression of a sainted soul. During a recess, he stretched and looked around. His eyes briefly locked on Mattie and Rachel, but otherwise didn't acknowledge them. They only saw evil at its deepest level.

When on the stand Lola's testimony was a cascade of lies, contradictions and shifting implications. She testified that she stopped working for an outreach program for prostitutes because of her indictment in this case, but a supervisor who came to court testified she was fired for theft. When asked to retell the events on that fateful night, she couldn't remember. The prosecutor commented to the jury, "One wonders how one who witnesses such a gruesome murder could possibly forget any of it."

Three days of testimony and Mattie looked over at Rachel. "I think they're going to get him this time." Mattie hadn't said much during the testimony, but appeared to make quite a study of it, leaning forward and absorbing every word.

Rachel responded, "I think he's going to get away with another one. I thought Lola's testimony would nail him, but she rolled all over herself and didn't say much. She was the whole case against him. They gave her immunity and took the death penalty off the table for him—for her testimony, that didn't amount to anything. They sure got short-changed. Can't imagine what the jury will make of her. He has so many connections and he's always on the street. I sure hope you're right, Mattie, I've lost faith in the system. If he gets back on the street, I'll be afraid to sleep at night."

They spent the days spellbound, listening to the grisly details of the testimony. Mattie was able to arrange her work schedule to make every day of the trial. Rachel went when she could. She didn't want anyone she worked with to know of her connection with the killer on trial. But she worried she'd have to move.

When the jury went into deliberations they twice asked the Judge questions relating to Lola's credibility. The judge asked them to stay to discuss the case with attorneys if they chose, that he couldn't answer their questions. They weren't interested. Every man and woman on the panel left immediately, some visibly upset with what they had to deal with. They knew the defendant was bad and felt he was guilty, but the only evidence against him was delivered by a witless witness with a scrambled brain—or was she being wiley?

After three days of deliberation they came back with their verdict. Bruce Muley was convicted of murder, aggravated robbery and kidnapping.

Mattie was in the courtroom to hear the verdict. Rachel was just home from work when Mattie called her with the news. "The jury saw through all their lie's."

"Thank the Lord that the jury saw that he shouldn't be turned loose on the streets again."

"Yeah, he sure did mess up a lot of lives."

They never thought they'd see the day. Rachel was totally convinced that somehow he'd weasel out of this. But they got him. They really got him. It wasn't payback, but justice. He was done. Rachel thought she would have liked to see him get the death penalty to be sure he doesn't put more lives in jeopardy when he gets out. He screws with people's lives for his own entertainment and doesn't know anything else.

The next phase was the sentencing. Because the death penalty was taken off the table in exchange for Lola's testimony, the judge levied on Bruce Muley, a sentence of 40 to life.

Both Rachel and Mattie spent time away from their families because of him. Both their families suffered. Mattie's brother was locked up for over 10 years, sentenced to life for something he had no part in. The other man's family never saw him again.

More than twenty five years after the murder and ten years after the sentencing, Bruce Muley had enough of being locked up and filed for an appeal, claiming newly discovered evidence. When Lola "lost her memory" of the event when it became time to testify in court, the police and prosecution suggested that they hypnotize her to give her a clearer memory of what happened. The prosecutor did not notify the defense so this was entered as "new evidence."

The detective that witnessed the hypnosis said they no sooner got started and Lola said she didn't feel well and the session ended. The detective was asked if this hypnosis was an important step in the investigation and he testified at the hearing: "This was a total waste of time and I found out nothing." Had they gained information from Lola, it might have been a different story.

Rachel was relieved to learn he was turned down on the appeal. What she found really sad was that Lola was still supporting Bruce, emotionally, and probably financially. Another example of battered women's syndrome.

# ERIC AND RACHEL

Eric never stopped his pursuit of Rachel, but for Rachel something just wasn't right. On the surface he was the perfect boyfriend, maybe too perfect. With the stress of Bruce and Lola in the past, she convinced herself that maybe she could start her life again and stop worrying about what might happen in the future. Eric promised her the world, a new place where he could never find her in the unlikely event he survived prison.

She considered going back to school and getting her BA but then figured that it wouldn't make any difference in the long run. She'd put more effort into her present job at the insurance company. She liked it well enough.

Eric asked her out to a first class restaurant to celebrate the start of a new life for them, soft music and candlelight. He was such a romantic, and sometimes it made her uncomfortable. The waiter delivered their drink orders. Eric must have been to a travel agent because he spread out three vacations he thought she'd like to go with him, an island hopping trip to Hawaii, a cruise in the Bahamas, and a trip to Paris. The waiter watched from a discrete distance and stayed away.

"Let's get away for a couple of weeks, make a clean break from the past. We can go wherever you want, these are just ideas. I want a life with you." He reached over held her hand and looked into her eyes.

Yes, a trip would be wonderful. She looked into his eyes that became so soft. What implications would there be agreeing to the trip. She couldn't make any promises. She was afraid to commit. "I'm still too close to the past, Eric, and maybe you're right, getting away would pull me away from it. I don't know.

"I don't mean to rush you, Rach, but I think we're supposed to look at the menu." He laughed easily. "I do love you, Rach, but for now, let's love the food and pick a trip."

The waiter took their order and as promised and they loved the food and relaxed in the ambiance of each other's company. Maybe . . . . just maybe.

He held her hand as they ordered a dessert to share. As the waiter walked away, her fingers dug into his. He looked up as her eyes got wide with a strange stare. Her mouth opened as if to yell or even breathe, but nothing happened. She collapsed at the table. Eric yelled for someone to call 911 and life went into slow motion. Someone carried her to the restaurant lobby. Someone else started compressions. No pulse. They tried to start her heart. Now she was bleeding from her mouth. Technicians arrived and took her to the hospital. He followed in his car to the hospital and learned she had probably died in the restaurant. Her parents . . . . her kids. No he wouldn't call. He went to Rachel's house where her parents had just put the kids to bed. He was devastated and her parents saw it at once. The three hugged and cried as he told them what happened. Her dad called the hospital. The kids. They'd know in the morning. An autopsy identified the problem as an aneurism.

The funeral was a nightmare for Rachel's parents. They had just gotten their daughter back and now she was gone. The kids were just getting to know their mom, and it was over. They were moving back in with the kids now to finish raising them. Social Security would send each child a monthly check. The little insurance job Rachel had turned out to be a windfall as now there would be money for both kids to get an education.

It's never the end.